TALES OF ALYIE STARSTRIKER

JOSEPH DI RIENZI

Author's Notes

Distance will be denoted as follows:

Light-year = l-yr. Light-minutes = l-m.

Light-second = l-sec.

Time will use historical values based on Planet Earth in the Sol system, such as:

Earth-hour = E-h. Earth-day = E-d.

Earth-week = E-w. Earth-month = E-m.

Earth-year = E-y. Earth-century = E-c.

CONTENTS

VALKYRIE COMMANDER

CHAPTER 1.

The blackness of space was disturbed only by seemingly random points of starlight. Its vastness was something you either embraced or shrank away from. There is a pristine stark beauty in space's emptiness that only a special kind of traveler can appreciate. In humanity's distant past, seafarers experienced, I assume, a similar feeling when sailing on an ocean planet's liquid surface. In her Pegasus-14 fighter craft, Grane, Lieutenant Commander Alyie Starstriker was cosmic dreaming during her patrol run in the Centauri system when Ginetta Jiang, the Deputy Commander of their Valkyrie Wing Group, burst in on Alyie's reverie on the inter-com shouting, "Wake up slumber girl, we have an UFO signal two l-m away at 30° East."

Quickly roused to full alert, Alyie responded, "Copy that. Will take a closer look while you and the others stand down."

A scan of the UFO identified it as the stolen spacecraft Dargo that was registered as a cargo vessel by the Sidereal Federation. It had been commandeered two E-w ago on the Duluth-1 trading station. The hijackers, who were identified as the rogue gang Diablo, had tied up the Dargo's four crew members while wounding two security guards before making their getaway. There was an outstanding Federation arrest warrant posted for the gang.

As Grane drew within one l-sec of Dargo, Alyie used the Common Communication channel.

"Crew members of Dargo, immediately release command of your ship. You are now under arrest by order of the Sidereal Federation."

The response from Dargo was belligerent, as Lt. Starstriker had anticipated. She had Grane's force shield on, and it easily withstood the assault from the other vessel's laser cannons. Alyie then probed Dargo with her infrared telescope and, after locating the drive system, turned her ship's photon precision gun on it. In about 10 sec, it evaporated.

Without any propulsion system, Dargo was helpless. Alyie put her tractor beam on the disabled vessel and began tugging it toward her ship.

Signaling her three other Valkyrie teammates to join, the squad locked unto Dargo and commenced to go into hyperspace via the nearest space knot, escorting the stolen spacecraft to their home base on New Cedonia. Nearing the station, they dropped back into normal space and alerted Federation officials of the captured craft.

Upon arrival in New Cedonia, Dargo and its crew were locked in a stasis field while the Valkyrie Squad docked in their familiar security port. Disembarking, Alyie jumped out of her vessel, immediately taking off her helmet. She cast a striking figure, nearly 2 m. tall with reddish-blonde hair and green flashing eyes. In the tight-fitting dark blue flight suit and highly polished tall black boots of the Federation Fleet Command Squadron, Alyie and her fellow Valkyries indeed looked like the embodiment of mythological figures from forgotten sagas. The second in command, Ginetta Jiang, was black-haired, purple-eyed and pale-skinned of much shorter stature. Olga Fercouska was a strapping blonde with blue eyes and rippling muscles. Finally, Hollie Pederson was medium height with beautiful bronze skin, tight-knit curly brown hair and dark brown eyes.

Striding together confidently under the artificial gravity of the rotating station, the other three women playfully teased Alyie as they preceded to the check-in monitor.

"It looks like I woke up Alyie in time for her to justify her status with the Fleet Command," mocked Ginetta.

"Yes," said Hollie. "Our fearless Commander needed to build on her fishing haul to advance up the Federation ladder."

"But I don't think, the small fry she brought in today will matter much in Fleet Command's estimation," chimed in Olga.

"I am just trying to make the galaxy safer for us all," was Alyie's satirical comment that drew haughty laughs from the other three women.

CHAPTER 2.

New Cedonia was an austere security base orbiting the largest moon, New Malibu, of Planet Rodeo Drive which in turn revolved around the red dwarf star Rebus Centauri. Taking a jet tram to her compact living quarters, Alyie took off her uniform and boots and jumped into the power-jet shower. Letting the steamed vapor open her pores and relax her cramped muscles, Alyie enjoyed one of the few amenities of the station. After drying herself off, combing her hair and putting on a Fleet Command T-shirt, she did the one thing she most wanted to do on her return to New Cedonia – contact Jaynis Bottombrook.

Alyie and Jaynis were old schoolmates growing up on Planet Mars in the Sol system. In physique and interests, he was the antithesis of her. Jaynis was pale, of slender built and medium height. His sandy-colored hair was typically uncombed. Overall, he presented a somewhat unkempt appearance in contrast to Alyie's immaculate grooming. Not interested in space flight – Jaynis claimed to be allergic to weightlessness and was decidedly un-athletic. He immersed himself in mathematics and slowly (excuse the pun) gravitated to physics. In academics, Alyie and Jaynis were usually numbers 1 and 2 in their classes, often interchanging the order depending on the subject and instructor. They were competitive but also supportive of each other. What they had in common was mutual respect and admiration and a willingness to listen when their counterpart needed counsel.

Over the years, their friendship grew stronger even as their career paths diverged. Alyie came from a military-minded family – her mother was a Fighter Wing Commander, and her father a space logistics tactician. Early on, Alyie knew she wanted to be a Fleet pilot and geared all her training and education in that direction. Consistently scoring at the highest levels in all phases of aeronautics, Alyie easily aced her combat training tests as well. After becoming the youngest person at 21 E-y to command a Pegasus Flight group, she chose other women pilots when Alyie formed her Valkyrie Squad. Jaynis, on the other hand, became an astrophysicist at Chandrasekhar University on Mars, his specialty being orbital dynamics.

Using the full-screen option on the wall monitor in her quarters, Alyie put in a hyperlink video call to Jaynis. Knowing the time difference between New Cedonia and Mars, she assumed he would be in his office working. Sure enough, when the connection was routed through the knots in spacetime, there was Jaynis behind his cluttered desk in a dusty, worn-out sweater. Grinning when he recognized her on his screen, Jaynis greeted Alyie. "Hello. I was hoping you'd contact me. I saw your latest accomplishment on the news feed. Congratulations on a successful and bloodless arrest."

"Yes, this was pretty straight forward. I am grateful for the technology we in Fleet Command have."

"I think it is more than technology or even intelligence for that matter. It is a question of judgement, which I am not sure can be taught at Flight Academy. The Fleet needs more wise and prudent commanders such as you who can assess what is the minimum of force needed in any particular mission. I have heard stories of other Squad Commanders who would take a more, how should I say, bravado approach, resulting in rather unpleasant consequences."

"I just follow the rules of engagement. But enough of this shop talk, how are you and your family?"

Both Jaynis and Alyie brought each other up to date on their respective familiars. Jaynis had a younger sister Bernice who was going to be a school teacher, and his folks were now living on Planet New Tulsa in the Barnard's Star system in semi-retirement. Alyie was an only child, and her parents were still active in the Sidereal Federation Space Command, although her mother was no longer flying missions.

It was so comforting for Alyie to share these personal pieces of information and a relief not to be in uniform or scrutinized by her superiors and peers. It was only with Jaynis that she could relax and be herself. Alyie would socialize on occasion with her Valkyrie Squad members, but she did that to increase their team connectedness rather than from affection. Through her experiences with her parents, Alyie also knew how to navigate the culture of the Fleet Command, and she was well aware of the effect her appearance and intelligence had on the senior staff.

After exchanging funny stories, both present and past, Jaynis changed the conversation. "This does not strictly come under Fleet Command jurisdiction, but I have read reports of some anomalies on Planet Ergo in the Tau Ceti system. Apparently, some weird things have been happening."

Tau Ceti is a G8 Main Sequence yellow star that had 10 identified planets orbiting, with two supporting human civilizations.

"How much weird is weird?" was Alyie's light-hearted query.

"It is hard to put a finger on it, but some occurrences in that system seem to be testing the laws of physics."

"Such as?"

"Well it appears that causality is being violated."

Alyie smiled. "Now Jaynis, you are testing me. Let's see. Doesn't causality demand that the cause of an event always precedes the effect?"

"I am glad you remembered. Causality involves the arrow of time which is always one directional. If you violate it, you refute The Second Law of Thermodynamics which states that all natural processes in nature are irreversible."

Alyie shrugged. "Well are there experiments taking place that are doing this? That would invalidate the "natural" part of the process?"

"We are detecting some unusual bursts of radiation on the planet that appear to be sending signals that are antecedent to the source of the message, which seems a contradiction," was Jaynis' retort. "Maybe this is something you can bring to the attention of your superiors. You seem well connected."

"So, you want me to carry your water up the hill." Alyie was delighted at Jaynis' need to employ her diplomatic skills. He was the most un-strategic person she knew.

"I will see what I can find out, but if I succeed you will owe me big time."

Jaynis grinned. "The way I see it I am helping you in your meteoric rise to the top of the Federation by giving you a scoop. But you don't have to thank me. When you are made Admiral of the Fleet just invite me to the ceremony."

"Don't worry, you will be the first person in line for an invitation."

CHAPTER 3.

In the one E-w since her return to New Cedonia, Alyie busied herself with the tedious but necessary off-flight details of a Squad Commander. The Federation was constantly asking her to evaluate her Valkyrie teammates as they probably were doing the same for her. She did take time to schedule an appointment with Vice Admiral Steely Cranshaw to alert him of Jaynis' anomaly on Ergo. Although he was reportedly difficult to arrange a meeting with, the Admiral was a friend of her parents, and he had always taken an interest in Alyie's career.

Wishing to make a positive impression on Admiral Cranshaw, Alyie dressed in a light gray uniform consisting of a tailored jacket and skirt, starched white blouse and tan-colored leather boots. Striding into his office, Alyie could tell by the bright smile the Admiral greeted her that he approved of her appearance. The Admiral looked the part as a tall, trim man of about 60 E-y old. The gray speckles in his tightly curled black hair only added to his distinguished appearance.

"What a pleasure to see you, Lt. Commander Starstriker. Congratulations on your arrest of the Diablo gang. That was a good piece of work Lieutenant."

"I have a great squad. My Valkyries are tops."

After exchanging some pleasantries about her parents, Alyie came to the business of the meeting. "A colleague of mine, Dr. Jaynis Bottombrook of Chandrasekhar University has alerted me of some unusual activities on Ergo in the Tau Ceti system. He seems to think there are some unnatural phenomena taking place."

Admiral Cranshaw gave a slight tap on his temple to access his top-secret database in his implanted nano-chip. "Why yes! I am finding reports of remarkable events on Ergo, including fortunes being suddenly made and reversals of previous economic policy decisions. Your friend, Bottombrook, may be on to something."

"I was not sure this was Fleet Command business, but I thought you were the best person I could bring this information to."

"You are correct, Lieutenant. At first blush, this is not our purview, but as a Fleet Commander, I am charged to monitor all activity in this sector. I will discuss these events with my colleagues on the Sidereal Federation Regional Council. Do not speak about this to anyone until you hear further from me."

"Yes sir."

"I have been watching your progress Alyie, and I can ascertain that your future lies beyond being a Squad Commander. Gaining information like this only reinforces my opinion that you have a career beyond the cockpit. Let's arrange a dinner meeting where we can talk about future possibilities. On the way out, give my adjunct your schedule, and we will arrange to meet soon."

Alyie was slightly uncomfortable at this invitation, but Admiral Cranshaw was her Commander, and she dutifully made a dinner date seven E-d later.

CHAPTER 4.

Jaynis was getting ready to make a presentation to his small research group when he was pinged by a hyperlink message that Alyie wanted to speak to him ASAP about a personal matter. Knowing it must have some urgency, Jaynis sent a group message to his team that the presentation would be delayed a short while. After connecting, Alyie informed Jaynis of her upcoming dinner with Admiral Cranshaw.

"What's the big deal? You should be pleased your commanding officer wants to discuss career options."

"I am a little apprehensive of his motives," was Alyie's sheepish response.

"Isn't the Admiral thought highly by your folks and well respected by the Fleet Command?"

"Yes, he is, but I know that within the last E-y, he lost his life partner to a terrible accident in a laboratory containment vessel. Admiral Cranshaw's two grown children have their own families and are living far from New Cedonia. Is the Admiral really interested in serving as my mentor, or is he just a lonely older man seeking some comfort?"

"Well, if you put it that way, be on your guard and find some means to deflect him if he makes any advances," was Jaynis' solution to potential harassment.

"He is my superior, and I do not want to create any ill feelings between us."

"Tell him you have a boyfriend that you are serious about. That should discourage him."

"Jaynis, when do I have time to date anyone? I barely have enough time to keep up with my basic needs."

"Make up a boyfriend. I volunteer my services. I would be glad to defend your honor against the Admiral just as long as I stay l-y. away from him."

Laughing heartedly, Alyie added, "You're on. I will tell him we are having a very long engagement."

CHAPTER 5.

The dinner meeting with Admiral Cranshaw was not in the station mess hall nor in the officers' dining room. The Admiral reserved a table at Venusia, one of the few fine dining restaurants on New Cedonia. This made Alyie even more nervous about their get-together. Since they would be off duty, she should not be in uniform, so Alyie wore a green dress with short sleeves and a modest bowline. Slipping into black high heels, she took the shuttle tram to Venuisa. Admiral Cranshaw was already waiting at the table dressed in a fine wool dark brown suit that complemented his chocolate skin coloring, crisp white shirt and yellow and brown striped silk tie. Alyie had to admit he was a very handsome older gentleman.

Any fears of unwanted attention were quickly put to rest as the Admiral talked warmly of Alyie's parents and their respective times together. There were many happy experiences that were all the more poignant in that they included Cecilia, the Admiral's late life partner. Alyie also shared some of the playthings she did with the Admiral's children as the families were living near each other for a time.

Seated on the restaurant's "terrace", they had a fine view of the milk-colored crater-pocked moon, New Malibu, with the arid planet Rodeo Drive in the background. Just a few centimeters of reinforced polymer enhanced glass separated them from the vacuum of space. Their dinner consisted of GMO prime rib steak, synthetic "Idaho" baked potatoes, greenhouse-grown string beans and a cabernet sauvignon wine from New Cedonia's experimental vineyard.

Just as the restaurant's rendition of crème fraiche was being served, the Admiral broached the subject of the meeting. "I am committed in seeing that you have opportunities to demonstrate your ability beyond a Squad Commander. Just because you fly a spacecraft shouldn't mean you cannot deal with the wider issues in the Federation. The more diverse your experiences, the more you will present yourself as a future leader."

"I appreciate you taking an interest in my future, and I would not be forthcoming if I would not admit to having aspirations for taking on more responsibility. However, my parents instilled in me the ethic to do the very best in my present activity, and, in doing so, I believe my future will eventually become clear."

"Good. I am glad you admit to having ambition. This makes it easier to direct your life to specific goals. I see in you great potential, and frankly, having the attributes of knowledge, skill, personality and temperament, most of which are sadly not that common in the Sidereal Federation hierarchy. Anything I can do to assist you will only help the common good."

"I thank you for any help you can provide. Your whole career has been an inspiration for me to follow. What do you suggest I should be doing now?"

"I think you have created your own initiative. I have discussed the anomalies on Ergo with the Regional Council, and they concur that there is something that needs investigating. We are sending Ambassador Felicity Erickson to meet with the governing Trade Guild on Ergo. Ostensibly it would be to begin new tariff talks, but her real mission is to find out about the economic boom that is taking place there and whether it affects the Federation itself."

"Do you think what is happening on Ergo has wider implications?"

"The Ergo Trade Guild has always been difficult to deal with. If you know the history, the planet was taken over 50 E-y ago by ruthless traders who were nothing more than hardened criminals. Over time they have organized themselves into a trade union based on the most powerful families that now provide them the veneer of being legitimate. However, they continue to skirt the trading rules of the Federation and are known to conduct unscrupulous acts of mayhem and murder. If they become more powerful, they can use their economic leverage to weaken the Sidereal Federation."

"Admiral, from what you just said, Ambassador Erickson's hosts will not take too kindly to her making inquiries about their internal affairs. Will she not be at risk during her mission?"

"Ah, Alyie, you are indeed a quick study," gleamed the Admiral. "That is why I want you to be the Ambassador's Adjunct Officer during this trip. Take command of my space cruiser, Bucephalus, and fly the Ambassador and her staff to Ergo. During her visit, I want you to be at her side providing security and another pair of eyes and ears. She has vast experience in these sort of dealings, and my hope is she will take you under her wings as a protégé."

"Will Ambassador Erickson approve of having a Lt. Commander as her Adjunct?"

"She will be accompanied by Captain Starstriker. I have just completed the filings for your promotion."

"Pardon my questioning, but I have not served long enough as a Lieutenant to be eligible for promotion."

"Under my authority, I can override seniority requirements for exceptional individuals, and right now I am looking at a truly exemplary person."

"Admiral Cranshaw, I do not know what to say. This is totally unexpected."

"The correct response is 'Yes, sir'. Also I want the Valkyrie Squad to accompany you and Ambassador Erickson to Ergo. Keep the three other spacecraft in orbit while you conduct your business. Their presence in the Ergo space will serve as a not too subtle reminder that if the Trade Guild threatens or harms either you or the Ambassador, the Valkyrie response will be to obliterate the planet."

"Yes, sir."

CHAPTER 6.

On the day before her departure to Ergo, Alyie had her travel luggage sent to Ambassador Erickson's office to be loaded on the Bucephalus. Having the Ambassador's staff pack her clothes and other items for a trip was a new experience for her, one that she felt she could warm up to. She did not dress in her Squad Commander uniform, but instead, she wore an outfit more befitting a military officer on a diplomatic mission – khaki-colored buttoned-down shirt with a dark brown tie, brown doubled breasted leather jacket, tan breeches, brown tall leather boots with matching leather gloves and officer's cap. A laser pistol in a holster secured by a leather belt around her waist signaled this was a security assignment.

Before leaving, Alyie made a quick hyperlink call to Jaynis.

"Wish me luck. This assignment is not in my comfort zone. I have no trouble fighting bad guys in space, but dealing with nefarious activities on a planet is completely new to me."

"Don't worry you will be great," Jaynis reassured her. "Also, when you meet with the Ambassador, mention tachyon messaging. I am developing a theory about those transmissions on Ergo, and although faster than light particles are considered hypothetical, I think the use of tachyons may be behind the strange events."

"Ok, but you better be available when I have to explain to the Ambassador what tachyons are and how they can be used."

At the boarding port, Alyie finally met the Ambassador. Felicity Erickson was a tall silver-haired woman with beautiful features and a creamy white complexion. A woman of obvious taste and refinement, the Ambassador, was dressed in a dark purple pants suit and medium height black heels. Around her neck was an elegant silver necklace. Her bright blue eyes showed a liveliness that belied her advanced age.

"It is so great to finally meet you, Alyie," Ambassador Erickson said while smiling broadly. "Steely has told me so much about you. I believe he is your number one booster."

"I feel it is my honor to serve you, Ambassador. I only hope I can live up to expectations."

"Please call me Felicity. This looks like a pretty edgy assignment we have been given, and the more familiar we are to each other, the better. I think we should go into this mission with the assumption that the only people we can trust are each other."

CHAPTER 7.

Alyie put Bucephalus on automatic pilot after leaving New Cedonia. The two E-d trip to the spacetime knot that they would use to jump to hyperspace gave her the time to get acquainted with Felicity. Alyie found the Ambassador absolutely charming and so sophisticated in regard to the multitude of cultures she has interacted with, in her capacity. She regaled Alyie with tales of complex issues she had to resolve in exotic locales with some rather eccentric leaders. Her advice to Alyie was, "To observe carefully before you respond. It is also more important to pay attention to what is not said or not seen than what you hear and see."

Alyie mentioned that she had a physicist colleague that was working on a hypothesis on the source of the transmissions on Ergo that may involve some previously unobserved physics. She was reluctant to tell the Ambassador more because, frankly, Alyie did not understand what tachyons are.

When Bucephalus reached the hyper-gate, Alyie sent a signal to her Valkyrie teammates, Ginetta, Olga and Hollie, who were following to commence the hyperjump. With that accomplished, the four spacecraft emerged shortly after from the outgoing hyper-knot and began their normal space approach to Ergo, which would take approximately two E-w.

As they were getting closer to Ergo, Ambassador Erickson briefed Alyie on its power structure.

"As Admiral Cranshaw has informed you, Ergo is governed by a trade association made up of the most powerful families on the planet. The strongest - the Vincenti are led by two brothers, Enrico and Destano who are nothing more than glorified gangsters. However, they have shown a cunning aptitude for increasing their wealth which makes them non-trivial to deal with. I doubt if they will be forthcoming on the use of this mystery ray."

While Felicity was speaking, she used her implant to send images of the Vincenti brothers to Alyie's chip.

"Can you talk to other members of the family, such as the women, who might be more approachable?"

Felicity shook her head. "This is a very patriarchal culture. I doubt the women have any knowledge of their men's business. However, there is the eldest son of Enrico, Gianni, who my intel claims is more refined and may not be comfortable with his family's illegal operations. Take a look at him."

As Alyie tapped the side of her forehead to receive Felicity's message, she saw videos of a young man with dark wavy hair, fair skin and large brown eyes. He was of reasonable height and built but had a gracefulness about himself that set him apart from his more groundling relations.

"He is about your age, and I am thinking you can be more useful than just my bodyguard. My instinct is that he has never met anyone like you, and if I have learned anything about male hormones, he will be most interested in making your acquaintance."

"Are you asking me to flirt with him? I don't think this is part of my job description."

"Oh Alyie, you are overreacting. I of all people would be the last to ask you to compromise yourself. But it would be helpful to not discourage any attempts Gianni makes to be friendly with you. One of his titles is Director of Science and Technology on Ergo. I am sure he is just a figure head, and the program has always been small by Federation standards. However, if the Guild is using some advanced technology to manipulate stock prices and economic evaluations, they need a research and development operation, so it would be good to find out what Gianni Vincenti knows about this."

Looking through her mind's eye at Gianni's appealing face, Alyie responded. "Don't worry, I will do my part."

CHAPTER 8.

Alyie guided Bucephalus to a gentle landing on the spaceport of Arcadia, the capital of Ergo. While buttoning her double-breasted jacket, giving her boots a quick polish and putting on her gloves to complete her uniform, Alyie messaged the other Valkyrie ships to stand by in orbit around the planet. Disembarking and moving freely on the 0.8 Earth gravity, Felicity, Alyie and their two attendants were greeted by minor functionaries of the Trade Guild, an obvious slight to protocol, signaling the Guild's disdain for the Ambassador's mission. Flown to the statehouse on an airbus, the Ambassador's group was met on the steps of the Capitol by representatives from all the ruling families, namely, Vincenti, MacPherson, Glattinger, Persci and Wong. The brothers Enrico and Destano stepped forward to issue a formal welcome. Standing just behind them, Alyie recognized Gianni Vincenti gathered among who looked like his four other siblings. His photos on Alyie's implant chip did not do him justice. Clad in a dark tailored suit and an open collar black shirt, Gianni evoked images of Earth men from lands that bordered a sea called the Mediterranean.

After exchanging greetings, Ambassador Erickson introduced Alyie. "This is Captain Alyie Starstriker. She is my Liaison and Security Advisor; please provide her the same courtesy and access you give me."

Enrico Vincenti, a squat, middle-aged man with a dark complexion, responded. "We on Ergo welcome your presence Ambassador and your young Captain. We hope your stay will be pleasant. I believe you have visited our planet once before, but I think you will see much has changed. For that reason, we need to re-examine our trade agreements with the Federation. I look forward to mutually beneficial negotiations."

"On the matter of the changes," Felicity queried, "could Captain Starstriker and I be apprised of your newest developments?"

"Ah, we are exactly of one mind," jumped in Destano Vincenti. "The Trade Guild would like to invite you both to a tour of our facilities. You will be impressed on how much progress we have made."

"The Captain and I are very interested in your Science and Technology Department. We understand there have been some recent rather striking breakthroughs?"

Alyie noted a tenseness in Enrico's mouth when the Ambassador mentioned "breakthroughs". Quickly recovering his composure, Enrico responded. "Why, of course, let me introduce my son Gianni. He is the Director of Science and Technology, and he can provide a most illuminating view of our accomplishments. With that, Gianni stepped forward and, in a most quaint but utterly charming manner, gave a half bow and kissed the hand of Ambassador Erickson. When he turned to do the same to Alyie, she was a little hesitant, but looking into his soft brown eyes and gentle smile, she accommodated him by removing her left-hand glove while blushing slightly.

CHAPTER 9.

Provided adjoining guest rooms at the Capitol Centre, Felicity and Alyie dressed for the evening's welcome dinner. The Ambassador wore a floor-length white gown with a brilliant diamond neckless and earrings that highlighted her beautiful white hair. Alyie wore the green dress she had worn for dinner with Admiral Cranshaw, but she dressed it up with long white gloves and matching white high heels. She also let her hair down so that it flowed freely over her shoulders.

The dinner began with the perfunctory salutations from the Guild families. There were toasts to the Ambassador and Captain Starstriker with red and white wine from the Ergo vineyards. The meal was a revelation compared to the food Alyie was accustomed to in New Cedonia. The main course was a combination of seafood from their coastline and beef that was raised in the grassy regions of Ergo. The vegetables were fresh, crisp and delicious.

A musical group was playing softly in the background, and after the dinner, but before dessert was served, Gianni Vincenti came to the table Alyie was seated. He was dressed more formally than before in an exquisitely tailored, finely striped black suit, white shirt and black tie. His black shoes were of highly polished leather. Again, bowing gently, Gianni asked if she would like to dance. Alyie's first instinct was to refuse, but given the Ambassador's instructions, she gave a tentative nod, which Gianni took for a yes. As they walked hand in hand, Alyie could see she was a head taller than Gianni, but she had become accustomed to these height differentials. As they glided around the dance floor, they exchanged get-to-know-you conversations.

"I am honored to be in your presence. I have read the news about your accomplishments as the Valkyrie Squad Commander. How long have you been an officer in the Fleet Command?"

"It has been four E-y since I was given my fighter squad to command."

"You seem very young, and, if I may say, too beautiful to put yourself in such peril."

"I have a great ship and very capable Valkyrie teammates. I am not worried."

"Oh yes. Your teammates are now like avenging angels or devils hovering over our space."

"Let's just say, I sleep sounder knowing they are watching over me and the Ambassador. But what about you? Are you happy being in, so to speak, your family business?"

Gianni grimaced after Alyie's remark. "Some men are fated to a life whether or not they choose it."

"I don't believe that. You should be able to chart your own destiny."

"We on Ergo believe strongly in family. We are very traditional here and are reluctant to disobey our elders."

"Excuse me, if you think I am criticizing your culture, but I believe you can best serve your family by making use of your full potential. There is a whole human space beyond Ergo in which you can make your mark and bring honor to the Vincenti family."

"When you say these things, you give me hope, but I can see you have led a fearless life of success and ambition. I may not be as gifted as you."

"There is only one way to find out, and that is to try."

"Thank you for the encouragement, but I fear I have overstepped myself. You are a guest on Ergo, and I, as one of the hosts, should be concentrating on your needs."

"Well, if we are talking about my needs, I am really interested in touring your science and technology laboratories tomorrow. I have heard a rumor you have discovered tachyons."

"Wow! That was direct. Well done, Captain Starstriker! That is not public information. But if you are interested, tomorrow you can visit our facility and meet Dr. Silberstein who is a leading scientist in this field. But let's leave that for the next day, right now all I am interested in is dancing with the most appealing woman on Ergo."

With that, Gianni held Alyie tighter as they swayed across the floor.

CHAPTER 10.

Early next morning, as soon as Alyie finished showering in the rather luxurious bathroom that was provided in her suite, she audio contacted Jaynis.

"We are going touring today on Ergo and part of the itinerary is to visit the laboratories at the Science and Technology Center. Do you have any advice on what we should be looking for?"

"Yes, I do," Jaynis eagerly replied. Alyie could tell from the excitement in his voice that Jaynis had some firm ideas on what was happening.

"Tachyons, the word in ancient Earth Greek means little swift ones, are particles whose minimum speed is greater than c, the speed of light, which you should remember is 300000 kilometers/sec. in a vacuum. They have long been sought after in that since, they don't travel less that c, their existence offers no contradiction to Einstein's Theory of Relativity. The Universe is considered divided into two domains: particles such as ourselves and are vehicles that cannot exceed light speed, and tachyons whose slowest speed is just above c. Thus, the speed of light serves as an impenetrable barrier between these two spaces."

"Don't we exceed c when we go into hyperspace?" Alyie inquired.

"No, going into hyperspace uses the conformal knots that have been mapped out in Einsteinian – Sanchez Spacetime to shorten travel time to distant destinations. Employing hyperspace does not make the spacecraft go any faster, it just uses, so to speak, shortcuts. Tachyons are different; they intrinsically travel faster than c and can hypothetically reach speeds up to infinity."

"Do you think the scientists on Ergo have discovered a source of tachyons, and, if so, what connection does this have to their sudden wealth and economic growth?"

"I looked up the name of the scientist you hyperlinked to me a short time ago. Dr. Albus Silberstein is a longtime advocate for the existence of tachyons. He has been working in Ergo only about one E-y. I am pretty sure he has been able to produce a source of tachyons particles that he is using for sending messages."

"Excuse my denseness Jaynis, but I don't see how discovering this exotic particle can provide an economic boom to a planet."

"Because physics is in everything! Now for the drum roll or when the eerie music starts playing." Alyie could tell Jaynis was really enjoying himself. He continued. "There is a somewhat disputed theory that if you have a source of tachyons, and you are traveling in a reference frame with sufficient speed, you can use a beam of these particles to reverse causality, namely have a message received before it has apparently been sent. In other words, send a signal back in time."

Alyie was now completely confused. "This seems way beyond my rank and pay grade. Are you telling me they are doing this on Ergo?"

"Alyie think of the advantages this provides. You wake up and take an air-scooter across some arid desert planet. On your way, you encounter a terrific dust devil that completely impedes your trip. If you were traveling at the minimum speed needed and had a tachyon source, you could send a message to your past warning you to take an alternate route."

"But isn't that changing the future, or at least my future. I thought that was forbidden in terms of the havoc it would cause. You know like going back to the past and accidentally killing your grandfather."

Again Alyie could tell from the tenor in his voice that Jaynis was positively gleaming. "There is the Gell-Mann Theory of Decoherent Histories which is part of the Everett's Many-World Theory which claims the Universe splits when a change is produced. But Decoherent Histories qualify the degree of splitting in terms of 'coarse grained' and 'fine grained' changes to the future. As long as the alteration is local, the Universe is not modified significantly."

"So what future is the Trade Guild changing here on Ergo?" was Alyie's question.

"They must be manipulating stocks and commodity prices. If they know a certain day's financials, they can use a tachyon message sent to the past to inform them of what investments to make the day before to maximize their profits. In this way, they are literally knowing the future by changing it to their advantage."

"This must be the cause of the Guild's tremendous increase in wealth and economic power. How can I confirm this?"

"Well, other than asking them point blank whether they are cheating, see when you visit the Lab whether there is a rapid moving device that can be used to send the tachyon signal. It may be a vehicle, but more likely, it will be a rotating room like a large centrifuge to test spacecraft for structural integrity. Also, get Silberstein to talk about his discovery. I am sure he is so proud to be finally vindicated, especially when a delightful young woman like yourself expresses interest his work. Just your presence can be pretty persuasive."

Alyie smirked at Jaynis' reference to her, but she also refrained from telling him about her encounter and mission with Gianni Vincenti.

CHAPTER 11.

Not waiting until her uniform was power washed and dried by her attendant, Alyie donned the ultra-soft bathrobe provided to her and knocked on the adjoining door to Felicity's suite. Finding the Ambassador combing her beautiful white hair and drinking the local hot broth, Alyie briefed her on what Jaynis had told her.

Taking it all in, the Ambassador responded. "That is great and give my thanks to your colleague for his investigative work. If after visiting the Science and Technology Center today, you are convinced the evidence for what they are doing is clear, I am going to confront the Guild. I will insist if they want to remain in the Sidereal Federation they must destroy this device, or suffer expulsion."

Alyie hesitated but nonetheless spoke. "Please excuse my interjection, Madame Ambassador. Should we not wait until we return to New Cedonia and discuss the situation with the Regional Federation Council?"

"Yes, Alyie that would normally be the proper protocol. However, with the rapidity that the Trade Guild is accumulating wealth through this illegal operation, I feel it is my prerogative as Ambassador to act pre-emptively. I think we are in, my dear, for a rather interesting series of events today. I can't tell you how grateful I am to have you with me."

Agreeing to meet downstairs a short time later, Alyie returned to her room. There she found her uniform cleaned, and her boots shined bright. Putting on her shirt, she knotted her tie before getting into her britches and boots. With her jacket double buttoned and gloves in hand, Alyie put up her hair and donned her cap. Finally, she fastened her weapon around her waist. Looking in the mirror, she saw a commanding figure that appeared ready for anything that might happen.

CHAPTER 12.

Descending into the ornate lobby, Alyie found Ambassador Erickson dressed in a navy blue pants suit, with hidden buttons on the jacket. She wore a beautiful silver brooch that complemented her hair and off-white pumps. They were soon greeted by a delegation of their hosts headed by Enrico Vincenti, Gianni and an attractive young woman who Gianni introduced as his younger sister Nicoletta. Enrico wore a nondescript dark suit while Gianni was again smartly attired in a double-breasted blue blazer and gray trousers. Nicoletta had her blonde hair fluffed up and wore a pinkish dress with a plunging neck collar.

The entourage comprised three air-limousines in which the Ambassador and Alyie were seated in the second in the caravan along with Gianni and Nicoletta. As they whisked outside Arcadia, Gianni spoke of how 500 E-c in the past robotic spacecraft from Earth discovered Ergo and initiated a long process to further oxygenate the atmosphere to make the surface hospitable to humans. The Vincenti family history dates back to intrepid early pioneers who populated the planet almost an E-c ago. His pride in the family's legacy was evident in the way he spoke of their achievement.

Their first stop was an early morning religious service at an outdoor shrine. In the foothills of a mountain range, the touring party gathered together as a man, dressed in what could be called priestly robes, called on the Deity to bless this visit. Alyie could see that the Guild families present took their worship seriously, and she wondered how they reconciled this devotion with their more rapacious reputation.

After leaving the shrine, the rest of the day was a whirlwind tour of robotic manufacturing facilities, agricultural areas and art museums, of which Nicoletta served as the Director of Arts. The last stop on this obvious publicity tour was the Science and Technology Center which was located just outside the capital. Gianni was the point person as he escorted all through the Research and Development laboratories. After expounding on the Center's accomplishments, he asked if there was anything further the Ambassador would like to see.

With an assenting nod from Felicity, Alyie spoke. "You promised me last night I could meet Dr. Silberstein. Is there any chance we can speak to him today?"

Making eye contact with Enrico Vincenti, Ambassador Erickson could tell Alyie's question struck a weak spot. "Dr. Silberstein values his privacy and is dedicated to his research, I don't think we should interrupt him," was Enrico's curt response.

"But Enrico," Felicity responded. "If the great Doctor could give us a little of his time, we would be so appreciative. It is important that the Federation knows what good work is being done on Ergo."

"Of course," Gianni replied. "If the Ambassador and the Captain want to talk to Dr. Silberstein, I will make sure he is available."

Gianni left to find Silberstein while the rest of the visiting party spent some uncomfortable moments waiting for his return.

After what seemed an interminable interval, Gianni strove back with a tall, gaunt-looking man with ungroomed gray hair clad in a worn-looking lab coat. After making introductions, Dr. Albus Silberstein reviewed his research efforts that were in relativistic physics without providing any specifics.

Thinking now was the time, Alyie stopped him in mid-sentence. "Dr. Silberstein, you have long searched for a source of tachyons. Has your research on Ergo brought you any closer to this goal?"

Silberstein was taken aback by her question but gathering himself and, in almost a whisper, stated, "Yes, it has been a long time, but I have found what I have been looking for."

"That is terrific! The news of your discovery will reverberate throughout the scientific community and provide you the honors you long have deserved. If I can speak for the Ambassador, I am sure she will want to share this news with members of the Regional Council when we return and disseminate this achievement across the Federation. Can you tell us how you discovered the source?"

"About six E-m ago, through a very arduous process, I was able to synthesize element 123, Feynmanium, from lighter elements, and, as I had supposed, it is very unstable. Identifying the products of its decay, I found tachyons were released that traveled at a range of velocities from 1.5c to 5c. I have a limited supply of Feynmanium, but as long as it lasts, I can utilize it to produce tachyons."

"Excuse a layperson's naiveté," asked Ambassador Erickson. "But are these tachyons of any practical use? It would be much more impressive when I inform the Council of your discovery, if I can tell them of the benefits of your ground breaking achievement."

Silberstein wavered at this question. He glanced first at Enrico, who was frowning but, seeing Gianni nodding, he announced. "Let me demonstrate what tachyons can do."

Following Silberstein's lead, the group traveled in a cable car down the long corridor of the Center, finally arriving at the door of what looked like a very secure room. Dr. Silberstein was eager to let his visitors in, but observing proper protocol allowed Gianni, the titular head of the Center, to give a voice command to open the door. Once everyone was inside, and the room was illuminated, it could be seen that it was approximately circular with a radius of about 10 m. Silberstein then used his hand imprint to slide open a compartment inside the wall, which revealed what looked like a glowing box with a small aperture extending outward. "This box contains Feynmanium. Once the cap on the aperture is released, tachyons will stream out. Director Vincenti, will you do the honors?"

Gianni stepped forward to a console on the side of the containment chamber and used his right eye to activate the code that flipped the aperture's covering. Once done, a beam of shimmering particles pervaded the room.

"What you are seeing," Dr. Silberstein assured, "is the harmless ionization of air molecules as the tachyons stream forth. Now for tachyon's use, Mr. Vincenti can, while he is at the console, encode a message modulating the way that the particles are emitted. If you will Mr. Vincenti, send a greeting after I set the room rotating."

Asking everyone to stand against the circular wall, Silberstein started the room rotating. As the speeds increased, the guests were pinned against the wall from the centrifugal pseudo force. Meanwhile, after securing himself, Gianni could be seen voicing something into the device.

Shouting to be heard above the noise of the rotation, Silberstein said, "We can utilize a curious property of tachyons by emitting them in this room as it is rotating. When this reference system reaches a certain minimum speed based on the tachyon's velocity, the beam appears reversed in time, namely the effect is received before the cause. Therefore, Mr. Vincenti's message, which you just observed, was sent to our past – namely whatever date and time and person he chose, the only restriction is that the recipient had to be in this room when it was rotating. I have, excuse me, what we have achieved, was once thought impossible in physics."

Slowly reducing the rotational speed of the room until it came to a halt, Silberstein was brimming with self-satisfaction at finally announcing his life achievement. At that moment, a knock was heard on the door of the room, and when Gianni opened it, a young woman dressed in lab clothes was holding two fresh flowers. He thanked her and, in turn, presented a flower to both Ambassador Erickson and Alyie.

"Voilà! These are the fruits of the message I sent a few moments ago," Gianni declared. "From the logs in the data base, I knew the woman you just saw, Asha Ngaka, was working in this room yesterday. The message I sent to her past was to go to a specific florist in Arcadia and pick out the most beautiful two flowers she could find. Since there was no way we would have known the Ambassador and Captain

Starstriker would want to visit the facility, we could not possibly have arranged this beforehand."

Collecting herself once the dizziness subsidized and feeling a slight buzzing in her implant, Felicity remarked, "Thank you Gianni for your thoughtfulness. Tell me Doctor, how long and for what other reasons have this facility been altering the present by changing the past?"

Obviously uncomfortable by the Ambassador's query, Silberstein responded meekly. "I have done only what was asked of me as a good citizen of Ergo."

"It seems Dr. Silberstein you have invented the ultimate insider information device. I think we have now a clearer idea of the source of Ergo's remarkable recent prosperity."

With that declaration by Ambassador Erickson, the mood in the room took on a distinctive chill. Goodbyes and thanks were made to Dr. Silberstein, and the caravan's trip back to the capital city was decidedly somber.

CHAPTER 13.

There was to be a hastily arranged small dinner meeting that evening consisting of Ambassador Erickson, Captain Starstriker and the heads of the Trade Guild. No doubt, the remarks made by the Ambassador would be discussed. As Alyie was finishing washing, she was presented a handwritten note by Lilse, her attendant, signed by Gianni, inviting her to a private dinner at a nearby restaurant and then a subsequent excursion to the hills surrounding Arcadia. This sounded decidedly like a date.

Showing Felicity the letter, Alyie informed her she was going to send a refusal.

"Do nothing of the kind," was Felicity's response.

"But I am your security officer. From what you said at the Center today, I think my services are needed more than ever."

"Oh, I am sure tonight's dinner will be nothing more than a series of denials and rebukes. Tomorrow will be the more formal deliberations. I also do not think I will get anywhere with Enrico, Destano and the others, but Gianni is more pliant, and he represents the planet's future. Use your influence to convince him that the Guild needs to stop these illegal actions or face censure."

"I really don't feel comfortable leaving you unattended. Besides, I think Gianni is not that interested in what I have to say. His attention to me, I believe, lies in another direction."

"Oh, I see. Well, use that direction as an entry port to influence him. Captain, take my insistence on meeting him as a friendly order from your superior and friend."

"When you put it that way, all I can say is 'Yes, Madame Ambassador'."

CHAPTER 14.

Alyie dressed casually for this meeting with Gianni. Putting on a snug short sleeve off-white pullover blouse, dark blue trousers, and draping over her shoulders a lightweight tan sport jacket with a gold Fleet Command insignia. She added a bright yellow scarf tied around her neck to augment her red hair. Not wanting to go defenseless, she stuck her laser pistol in her left boot. She met Gianni outside the Capitol Centre and jumped into his blood-red air-scooter. Gianni was dressed in a black leather jacket, blue satin shirt and dark trousers. His jet black hair waved as they whipped through the evening sky.

Dinner was at Poseidon, which featured fish and seafood caught from the bay outside of Arcadia. Gianni wanted to talk about their common interests, but Alyie kept bringing the conversation back to what happened at the Science and Technology Center.

"You must realize what the Trade Guild is doing is clearly illegal and can't continue."

"Of course you are correct," Gianni confessed. "And I have tried to convince my father and uncle to stop this. But it is hard when your family is involved, and they are full of pride and envy. We have struggled so hard to reach some prosperity on Ergo, and now it seems at hand."

"But this is prosperity built on deceit," Alyie declared. "All the Trade Guild has accomplished is in danger of being destroyed once Ambassador Erickson reports what is going on to the Regional Council. Ergo will be punished with expulsion from the Federation. That means you will lose your ability to invest in the Universal Exchange and be boycotted from trade and services."

"I know what you are saying." Gianni seemed impassioned. "But I grew up to respect my elders and not question their authority."

"Gianni, in the brief time I have known you, I can tell you are someone who wants to do the right thing, but one who also wants to preserve Ergo's heritage. I believe you have the power to accomplish both in using your influence to have the Guild disavow and abort these activities. Let me help you."

"Oh, Alyie, you are so pure and brave. I wish I had your clear vision and courage. What you ask me to do is difficult, but I have come to believe it is necessary. I will take your advice. Tomorrow I will present to my family a plan for closing down the tachyon communication device. But for now, let me show you some of the sights of Arcadia and why it is so dear to me."

After leaving the restaurant, they flew above a winding road that climbed upward. At the top of a hill, Gianni landed the air-scooter. He and Alyie walked a short distance to a lookout point where they could see the city's lights shining in the night and, overhead, the stars sparkling. The evening air felt fresh and a little cool, so Alyie clutched her jacket more tightly around her shoulders.

"This is my land, Alyie, and, until I met you, it was all I wanted. You are a sorcerer who has conjured up in my mind visions of distant places and different futures. I am bewitched. I no longer know what to do."

"Trust your heart," was Alyie's advice. "I don't think I have conjured up anything that you didn't already know about yourself. You just need to follow your True North. In doing so, you can bring your people along with you."

Gianni then drew Alyie slowly closer to himself. Looking her straight in the eyes, he kissed her softly but fully on the lips. Alyie's first thought was to reach into her left boot for her pistol, but in realizing the experience was pleasurable, she returned the kiss. He then held her more tightly, and their kissing became much more passionate until Alyie felt a buzzing in her implant.

Pulling herself away, Alyie said, "I am getting a distress signal from Felicity's life monitoring system. Something has happened to her. Take me back immediately."

CHAPTER 15.

Upon returning to the Capitol Centre, they were confronted with the sight of emergency vehicles and security lights flashing. Alyie and Gianni were quickly directed to Ambassador Erickson's suite, where they found her lying motionless in her bed. A gentleman in medical garb presented himself. "I am Dr. Gosini; the Ambassador has gone into a coma. She apparently has anaphylaxis as a result of an allergic reaction. We are trying to determine the cause which would predicate the treatment."

"Why has the Ambassador not been brought to a hospital?" Alyie wondered. "Since we have auto-docs available in this Centre, we thought it best to not move her and treat her here," was Dr. Gosini's response. As they were conversing, Enrico and Destano Vincenti entered the room flanked by two armed security guards.

"Captain Starstriker," Enrico began, "let us express our grave sympathy to what has happened to the Ambassador. We are doing everything in our power to help her. In fact, our medical staff has informed me they know what caused her allergic reaction. At the dinner tonight, the drink we all toasted to each other's health was mixed with some of our dairy milk, which the Ambassador apparently couldn't tolerate."

"But," Alyie, in now a state of alert, declared, "you had records of our medical charts and our diet needs; how was it that Ambassador Erickson was not warned of the contents of the beverage?"

"It was an obvious oversight by our hospitality staff. We are again sorry. We know how to treat her condition. However, the common medication used, epinephrine, is currently not available in Arcadia, and there has been a delay in its arrival that only you can expedite."

"A delay? I don't understand how I can expedite this treatment. Do you want me to fly to some other place to get the drug?" By now, Alyie was clearly exasperated.

"No." said Destano. "We want you to stay right here and sign a Non-Interference Agreement with us. After you do this, we have every confidence the medication will be available."

Alyie was taken aback by the brazenness of this statement. "So you are holding the health of the Ambassador hostage until you get what you want. Don't you have any sense of what you are doing? Besides I am just a Captain in the Fleet Command. Do you think the Federation will honor my signature on any pact?"

Enrico gave a matter-of-fact response to Alyie's question. "Since Ambassador Erickson is unable to discharge her duties, you are now the person here who represents the Federation interests. Under these circumstances, they must honor any action you do in the Federation's name. Besides, Captain Starstriker, you needn't perplex yourself over the importance of your assumed office. This agreement between the Trade Guild on Ergo and the Sidereal Federation will not be long term. We only need enough time until Dr. Silberstein's source of tachyons runs out."

Alyie angrily turned to look at Gianni, who seemed to shrink in the background. "Is this why you wanted to be with me tonight, so your family could poison the Ambassador without my interference?"

All Gianni could do to Alyie's accusation was to shake his head slowly and quietly say, "Please believe me, I knew nothing of this."

Confronting the Vincenti brothers, Alyie declared, "Your despicable action will bring doom to your planet. The Valkyrie Squad orbiting above you has orders to begin attacking if any harm comes to the Ambassador or myself. I need only alert them to commence the assault."

With a mock-serious expression, Enrico stated, "Captain Starstriker, you will find that is not possible right now. It seems there is a technical problem that has cut off all outside communication to and from Ergo. It is our fondest hope it will be resolved after you sign the Non-Interference Agreement."

"That doesn't matter. The Valkyrie have been instructed that if I do not make contact with them every half planet rotational period, they are to send two warning signals to you, and if there is no response, they are to begin a selective destruction of your planet. My next signal is due right after star rise."

"Well, Captain Starstriker," smiled Destano, "then for the life of Ambassador Erickson and yourself, it is imperative you comply with our request. We will leave the agreement in your suite. Let either of the guards that will be posted outside know what you decide, but I advise you to act quickly for the Ambassador's sake."

What that, her Ergo hosts bid her good night, and Alyie was left alone with the unconscious Ambassador to contemplate her fate.

CHAPTER 16.

Alyie returned to her room to face the darkest night of her young life. Her signing of the Non-Interference Agreement was out of the question. What she told the Vincentis was correct in terms of the action the Valkyrie would take if they had not heard from her. In a few hours, the assault on the planet would begin. She was trained to die willingly if need be in the performance of her duty, but the thought of sacrificing that beautiful and gracious woman lying in a bed next door was heartbreaking. Also, Alyie was convinced Gianni had played no part in the poisoning of Ambassador Erickson, and from what she had seen and heard in her brief time on Ergo indicated the people had a spirit and culture that was worth preserving.

Without being able to contact her teammates, her parents, Admiral Cranshaw or Felicity, Alyie felt unmoored from her support system. How Alyie wished she could speak to Jaynis. He was so analytical and clear thinking, perhaps he could untangle this knot. But she was all alone right now, and if there were a way forward, she would need to discern it herself. After several hours of agony, a searing idea struck her, and a course of action began to take shape.

Jaynis always claims, Alyie mused, "Physics is in everything." Well, she reasoned, if physics is the cause of this problem, the same physics can be part of its solution. However, Alyie realized that in order to make her plan work, she would need assistance.

After donning her uniform and making sure her laser pistol was fully primed, her first action was to instruct Lilse to tell the Vincentis she was ready to negotiate the agreement, but she would only do so with Gianni. Fortunately, he was downstairs at the Centre and came readily to her room. From the dark circles under his eyes, Alyie could tell, just like she, Gianni had not been sleeping at all this night.

His first remarks were a repeat of the brief exchange they had earlier. "It has been killing me that you think I deceived you or knew about this conspiracy. I feel horrible about what happened. Please believe me."

"I do, but we now need to fix this. Please take me now to the Science and Technology Center."

"With all my heart, I do not want see harm come to you nor the Ambassador, but it would bring me dishonor if I betray my family."

"You will not be betraying anyone, but you will be saving your planet. If my plan works, no one, not Ambassador Erickson, myself nor the people of Ergo will be hurt. Please trust me."

"Yes, I will trust you and may the Deity protect us," was Gianni's prayerful answer.

Alyie alerted Lilse and the other attendant, Omi, to pack everything from both suites and be ready to leave the moment she returned. Gianni dismissed the guards stationed outside, thanking them and saying they were no longer needed. Then Alyie and Gianni snuck out a back entrance of the Capitol Centre and traveled under cover of darkness in his air-scooter the short flight to the Science and Technology Center.

Still being the middle of the night, the Center was deserted. Gianni used his voice commands and handprints to gain entry into the facility. They traveled down the corridor to the rotating room where they had the demonstration the previous day. After opening the door, Gianni and Alyie went to the console. Following Alyie's instructions, Gianni opened the containment door and flipped open the aperture, releasing the tachyon beam. Accelerating the room to the optimum speed, he set the controls for the day before, but at the exact same time, he sent his previous message.

Gianni then stepped aside as Alyie made a connection with Ambassador Erickson's implant. She then spoke into the device, saying,

"Felicity this is Alyie. You have advised me on this trip to observe before responding. Now I ask the same from you. Do not take the drink offered to you when the toast is given tonight. It will make you deadly sick. Say nothing afterward, but await my return tomorrow morning."

After stopping the room from rotating, Gianni closed down the aperture, shut the containment box, exiting the room and the Center with Alyie.

On the return trip, Alyie received her first indication that her action was a success when she received an urgent coded message from Ginetta Jiang orbiting above. Responding in code, Alyie sent a command to all the Valkyrie to go on full attack alert, power up their gamma-ray cannons and await her further instructions.

CHAPTER 17.

Arriving back at the Capitol Centre, Gianni and Alyie noticed there were no longer any emergency or security vehicles evident. Sneaking back into the same rear entrance as she had left a short time ago, Alyie rushed into her room and then held her breath as she used the side door to enter Felicity's suite. There she found the Ambassador fully clothed, standing erect before a mirror. Overcome with emotion, Alyie embraced her fully, unable to hold back her tears.

The Ambassador, somewhat perplexed, declared, "Well, you must have had some night with Gianni. Do you realize it is nearly morning? By the way, I did receive your message, and I followed your instructions, but I do not know what to make of it."

Yes, I had quite an evening, and we will have plenty of time to discuss it on the return flight. We need to leave here immediately. There was an attempt on your life yesterday, and I am sure the Vincenti brothers will try again. I have arranged transportation to take our staff and us to the Bucephalus, but speed is of the essence.

Ambassador Erickson, Alyie, Lisle and Omi boarded with their belongings the air-bus Gianni had brought to the rear entrance of the Centre. As they drove to the spaceport, pre-morning light from Tau Ceti could be just seen peeking out from the horizon. When they reached the security gate at the spaceport, Gianni waved the guards to let them pass. Parking just in front of the shining black Bucephalus, Gianni helped the passengers out, and Felicity, Lisle and Omi quickly boarded the spacecraft.

Before joining them, Alyie turned and faced Gianni. "I know things will be difficult for you. Have courage knowing you have done the right thing. Also, make sure the Science and Technology Center is unoccupied in the next E-h."

Removing her left glove, Alyie gently stroked the right side of Gianni's face. "Take care my sweet boy. Perhaps our paths will intersect again sometime."

With that, she boarded Bucephalus, taking her seat in the pilot chair. The takeoff was smooth, and once the spacecraft cleared Ergo's atmosphere, Alyie sent the coordinates of the Science and Technology Center to Ginetta, Olga and Ollie abroad, their respective Valkyrie fighters, to commence firing. As the three precision gamma-ray beams converged at the Center, there was, within a few moments, a bright flash of light and then a huge explosion.

On the journey back to the knot from which they would jump into hyperspace, Alyie caught Felicity up on all the turbulent events that transpired on Ergo. There was, however, something bothering Alyie. The message she sent at the Center was presumably received by Felicity in the rotating chamber before she was to take the drink that evening. If that is so, then Alyie would have never received the distress signal when she and Gianni were together at the scenic lookout point. Then does it not follow that they spent the rest of the evening together? Has she suppressed this memory, or is there another Alyie in an alternative Universe that had an evening of bliss?

Snuggling closer to herself, she silently chuckled. Physics really is in everything.

ET DAEMONIUM IN MACHINA

CHAPTER 1.

Coming out of a hyper-knot is always an unsettling experience. From being squished in the spacetime continuum to feeling stretched due to the separation of the spatial and temporal dimensions, take some getting used to. First-timers who make the jump out of hyperspace have been known to suffer protracted dizziness and nausea. There are medications to help reduce the sensation, but like most things, familiarity is the best curative. Captain Alyie Starstriker, Commander of the Valkyrie Fleet Squadron, was unfazed by this abrupt shift to normal space, having made these jumps as a matter of routine. Aboard her fighter spacecraft Grane, she led her other three Valkyrie teammates on their journey to Planet Earth in the Sol system. The Valkyrie Squad had been commanded to come to Earth for a celebration honoring their recent success in resolving a difficult situation on Planet Ergo in the Tau Ceti system. Alyie and her Valkyrie members Ginetta Jiang, Olga Fercouska and Hollie Pederson had never been to the birthplace of humanity, and the summons was considered a reward for their outstanding service to the Sidereal Federation. Not only would they be honored at the General Assembly, but they would be granted a period of rest and relaxation that would provide the opportunity to visit historic sites on what is considered the Mother Planet.

As the four spacecraft continued on the two E-w journey in normal space to their destination, the women exchanged comments on what they could expect from their sojourn on Earth.

"I have been told that it has pleasure palaces," Olga Fercouska wistfully remarked. Olga was a blonde-haired, blue-eyed, white-skinned young woman of impressive stature and physique.

"Don't believe all that is advertised," said Hollie Pederson, a trim young woman of curly brown locks, brown eyes and cocoa-colored skin. "Since Earth is no longer the center of the Federation, its only real industry is tourism. Most of its attractions are simulated Earth history sites to have us off-landers experience humanity's past, which was often pretty barbaric." Hollie's ancestors were descended from slaves on the continent of North America.

"Still, I would like to see the cultural artifacts that have been preserved," chimed in Ginetta Jiang. "I minored in Earth history, particularly Eurasian." Ginetta, the Deputy Commander, was a petite pale-skinned young woman with black hair and purplish-colored eyes.

Alyie Starstriker kept silent. She had personal objectives to entice her to travel to Earth for this celebration. First and foremost, it would be a reunion with her parents, whom she had not seen in person in many an E-yr. The second reason would be to discuss career advancement opportunities with Federation high officials that would be present at the General Assembly. A third factor was that her old friend Dr. Jaynis Bottombrook would also be there to receive an award, and it would be great to meet up with him. Perhaps, if Jaynis is so inclined, they could do some sightseeing together.

As the four Valkyrie spacecraft started to approach their destination, the blue orb of Earth came into view, Alyie gave the command:

"Ladies. Commence your descent. We are going to the Home World."

CHAPTER 2.

The General Assembly was held in the region historically known as Kashmir. The Vale of Kashmir was a beautiful area flanked by the Himalayas and the Pir Panjal Mountain Ranges. The four Valkyrie fighters made a soft landing in the spaceport located in the middle of the valley. Stepping out of their respective vessels, the four women dressed in their dark blue flight suits, black helmets and tall polished black boots made a spectacular appearance. Taking off the helmets, they inhaled deeply in the thin cool mountain air. As Alyie shook her head playfully in the invigorating atmosphere and under the bright blue sky, her auburn-colored hair glittered in the sun. She was an imposing figure with freckled skin, a finely tuned body and beautiful green eyes.

They were greeted by a deputation of the Sidereal Federation, among which were Alyie's parents - Space Commander Tanita Starbright and Dr. Alex Striker. Tanita was a trim middle-aged woman with dark brown hair and eyes, while Alex was a robust gentleman of similar age with red hair, green eyes and freckles. Alyie's mother, a former fighter pilot, now worked in Space Command Headquarters, while her father was a space logistics tactician. After exchanging heartfelt hugs and kisses, Alyie re-introduced her parents to her squad members.

"I hope she is not giving you women too much trouble," Tanita Starbright laughingly declared.

"No ma'am," answered Ginetta. "It is more the other way around. We keep Commander Starstriker sharp by testing her boundaries."

"Your daughter is a model of decorum," mused Ollie. "We are the troublemakers."

"My team is tops. I have the best squad a Commander could hope for."

Alex Striker interjected, "Congratulations on your mission to Ergo. You all did a great job from what I hear was a very combustible situation."

"All praise to our Commander," quipped Hollie. "All we did was follow her orders."

As they were conversing on the tarmac, a deputy for the Federation gently bade them to get on board the airbus which would transport them to where the Assembly would be held and where they would be residing.

Flying through the Kashmir Valley between the dual mountain ranges was an exhilarating experience even for these seasoned space travelers. Alyie and her teammates beamed like young schoolgirls, mutually concluding that this junket to Earth was going to be a lot of fun.

CHAPTER 3.

The guests for the General Assembly were staying in a group of wooden chalets nestled at the foot of a mountain, a short walking distance to the Convention Center where the Assembly would take place. Everything about the Center was on a grand scale, from the entrance hall to the cavernous lobby. While checking in at the entrance desk accompanied by her parents, Alyie was greeted by Jaynis Bottombrook. Dr. Bottombrook was an astrophysicist at Chandrasekhar University on Mars. He and Alyie were old schoolmates on Mars, and they stayed in close touch over the years. His insight into tachyons was instrumental in discovering the source of the problem on Ergo. Being also honored for his contribution, Jaynis made the short trip from Mars to Earth for the ceremony despite his aversion to space travel.

Alyie warmly hugged her lifelong friend. Jaynis was his typically ungroomed self. His straw blonde hair was uncombed, and his clothes were loosely fitting. The corduroy jacket he was wearing gave his appearance an academic look. After exchanging greetings, Alyie wondered, "I thought you were allergic to space travel. Are these honors that important to you?"

"It is not the stupid medal that made me break my vow to stay in a gravity well; it is the rare opportunity to see you in the flesh."

"Well Jaynis, then I am doubly honored to be here. I promise to make it worth your while. Before the Assembly begins, I want to get an air-jet and travel around Earth sightseeing with you."

"Only if you don't treat it as a Fleet fighter plane."

"Why, of course. With you with me, I will be extra careful, but since you made this journey here safe and sound, are you losing your reluctance to fly?"

"Only if I can take as much meds to knock me out as I did on this trip here."

CHAPTER 4.

The next morning Alyie, Jaynis and her Valkyrie teammates agreed to meet for breakfast at The Snow Leopard Inn, located in the Convention Center. The food was a delightful change from the institutional variety the Valkyries were accustomed to either in space flight or at their home base of New Cedonia. Fresh strawberries with clotted cream, pineapples, oranges and grapefruits were presented along with the choice of eggs, bacon, ham and pancakes. The freshly brewed coffee stimulated the group in ways they had not experienced in some time.

Since the Assembly was not scheduled for three E-d, the conversation focused on the group's respective free time. Ginetta, who was accompanied at breakfast by her partner, Arjuna Choudhoury, a member of the Pandava Flight Squadron, responded to Alyie's inquiry about their plans. "Both Arjuna and I are interested in Asian culture. I want to go to the islands of Japan and see old Kyoto, while he is interested in some of the ancient sites in the Indian sub-continent and New China."

"Hollie, what about you and Olga?" Alyie asked, knowing that Hollie and Olga were a committed couple.

"The mountains surrounding us are spectacular. Olga and I are going to ski down as many as possible."

"What are you and Jaynis up to?" queried Olga.

"Well, we haven't finalized our plans. I want to go to the historical sites for spaceflight, like Cape Canaveral in the former United States of America and the Cosmodrone in the Eurasian continent while Jaynis wants to look at the centers of high energy physics such as the old CERN facility. As a side trip, I am trying to convince him to go to the city of Paris which has always been a dream place for me. I understand the old buildings, streets, museums and restaurants are still preserved."

"Wow," said Ginetta, "that is a lot to see in three E-d."

"It can be done. Through my mom's connections, I have secured a hypersonic jet aircraft that can take us to these places as rapidly as possible."

As Alyie was talking about traveling greater than Mach 5 (about 6100 kilometers/E-hr.) for their whirlwind trip around Earth, Jaynis' complexion visibly paled, and he lost all appetite for the remainder of his breakfast.

CHAPTER 5.

Returning to their respective rooms, Alyie packed for her excursion with Jaynis. The craft they would be traveling on had storage facilities and sleeping compartments, so Alyie could bring as much as she desired since they would not need to travel with their luggage at each stop. Since Earth's climate had reached a quasi-equilibrium, the temperature near sea level was, on average, a comfortable 16° C, E-yr round. At the onset, she dressed primarily in white with a white pullover shirt, an off-white genetic engineered wool sweater with brown trim, white britches and brown tall leather boots. A bright yellow silk scarf added color to her outfit. Jaynis appeared comfortable in a gray hoodie and pants that in past centuries would be called blue jeans. His footwear could be called athletic shoes.

After taking an airbus to the spaceport, Alyie and Jaynis were directed by the attendants to their jet. Making sure Jaynis was strapped in securely, Alyie quickly mastered the plane's flight control system, and they were soon airborne. Quickly rising in altitude, they soared over the Himalayas, gazing down at the peaks of some of Earth's tallest mountains.

Their first stop was Cape Canaveral, the launch site for the spacecraft that carried the first humans to another world, namely, Luna, Earth's only natural satellite. It was located off the Southeastern coast of North America. Since Earth's population had decreased to about 4 billion people in the last half millennium, air traffic at the altitudes Alyie was flying was minimal, and at Mach 5.5, the trip only took about two E-hr. Because of Alyie's status as Captain and Fleet Commander, she could land right on the Cape's spaceport. A military adjunct welcomed them and took them on a tour of the facilities which were no longer operational. For Alyie, this was like going to a shrine. To stand on the launch pad where the Apollo missions to Luna began in the late 1960s Common Era (CE) was a mystical experience, and she tried to channel the sense of wonder and excitement those brave astronauts must have felt as they sat in the spacecraft awaiting launch.

After spending about a half E-d on the Cape, they made a quick trip at Jaynis' behest to the old United States of America's Naval Academy just off the Chesapeake Bay in what used to be called Maryland. Outside the building called Michelson Hall, named for Albert Michelson, who conducted the first accurate measurement of the speed of light in the late 19th Earth (CE) century. To Jaynis this courtyard is hallowed ground in physics because, until Michelson's determination of approximately 300000 kilometers/second, it was conjectured that light traveled at infinite speed.

After paying their respects to this precision measurement site, they took off and headed northeast across the Atlantic Ocean. Traveling over the Eurasian continent, they landed in what used to be called Kazakhstan. (Again, Alyie's military credentials provided access to the landing site.) The Cosmodrone had even a longer historic space legacy than Cape Canaveral in that it was the site of the launch of the first artificial satellite in 1957 CE and the first human in space, Yuri Gagarin (1961 CE). Just a museum now, the Cosmodrone had an autonomous exhibit on these milestones.

Spending the night in the hypersonic craft, Alyie took off the next morning going westward over Eurasia to the site of the high energy physics facility Conseil Européen pour la Recherche Nucléaire (CERN). The trip only took a little over an E-hr. This time, it was Jaynis' status that provided close landing proximity to the complex that housed giant accelerators, which were large circular structures of over 100 kilometers in circumference. Jaynis was in his element as they were shepherded by a researcher that Jaynis knew of the construction and key discoveries that were made at these facilities. Confirmation of the Higgs Field in 2012 CE had seemed to confirm the Standard Particle Theory. This apparent closure was subsequently undone when it was realized that the Higgs Field was not unique, and there existed several other so-called fundamental force fields. The CERN facility was also instrumental in the detection and modulation of gravitational waves that are produced from oscillating masses, a final confirmation of Albert Einstein's Theory of General Relativity.

CHAPTER 6.

The final stop on their tour and where they planned to spend two E-d was Paris. Just a short flight from the accelerator facility brought them to a private landing area just outside the historic city. Wanting to look more cosmopolitan, Alyie changed into a green dress which she wore under a tan sports jacket that matched her brown boots. Jaynis had on a tweed brown sports jacket over a clean buttoned-down white shirt. He wore nice blue dress pants and sturdy brown walking shoes. Obtaining an air-scooter, their first stop was Montmartre, the large hill that provided a sweeping view of Paris. The city was still a mecca for visitors, and Montmartre had a lot of off-world tourists using their implants to capture the moment. At the summit of Montmartre, was Sacré-Cœur Basilica. This church had a special meaning for Alyie because this is where her parents made their vows of eternal commitment. She huddled inside the large basilica and knelt in silent prayer.

Jaynis insisted they visit the Louvre, the monumental art museum. Too massive to see all in a single undertaking, they broke up their tour into two parts, the first afternoon visiting the antiquities collection and the second looking at the art galleries. Alyie was particularly taken by The Winged Victory of Samothrace, which dates from the second century BCE. Jaynis was more interested in paintings, particularly by the Renaissance artists Da Vinci and Raphael.

Finding dining facilities was a dream as Paris had a long tradition of high-quality food establishments. On their last day in Paris, Alyie and Jaynis found what is called a "bistro" in the area known as the Left Bank of the Seine River that cuts through the city to enjoy a midday snack of ham, fresh green salad and a freshly baked cake salé made with figs and cheese. Sharing a bottle of fine red wine, they savored the moment.

"You know I could get used to this kind of life. Maybe I can apply for a position at the Université de Paris. I am a theoretical physicist so I can do my work anywhere."

"But Jaynis, I thought you were welded to Mars. You were born there, grew up there, went to school there and now work on Mars. I don't see you re-locating."

"I know, but Earth is in the same planetary system, so it wouldn't be that big a transition, and besides, now that the air is clean, Earth is healthy to live in."

"Well if you do come to live here that would give me an even stronger reason to visit you."

"What about you? Are you going to be a fighter pilot all your life?"

"I have been considering my options. Admiral Cranshaw has advised me to think about going into statecraft by applying to the Federation's Diplomatic Academy, but I think I need to prove myself more in the Fleet Command."

"What do your parents think?"

"To no surprise, they are of two minds. My mother is military all the way and wants me to stay in the fleet, but my dad is thinking more logistics and Federation policy. But the choice is mine, and for now, I am staying where I am. Besides, I love my Valkyrie Squadron, and I do not want to do anything to break up my team."

"My guess is you will rise quickly in the Fleet Command. It seems they have their eyes on you. If I put on my seer's cap, I see an Admiralty in your future."

"Your cap must be able to see the far future because right now I am just a captain."

"The last time we met in person four years ago you were just commissioned as a lieutenant. Now you are about to be a decorated captain and commander. It is quite likely the next time we meet I will have to address you as Admiral Starstriker."

"If you do, I will punch you in the face, and then, of course, kiss to make up."

"On an unrelated matter, I have a gift for you. It is more practical than luxurious, but when you were elsewhere, I saw them on display at the CERN gift shop, and I felt you should have one."

Jaynis then reached into his jacket pocket and presented a small box to Alyie. Undoing the wrapping material, she opened the box to find a small device enclosed inside.

"This is intriguing, Jaynis, what is it?"

"It's a gravitational field generator. Inside the device is a tiny mass that can be oscillated by the control dial to send gravitons, G-field force carriers, similar to how photons are transmitted in electromagnetic fields. The gravitational field generated is low intensity, but the advantage is that gravitational waves can travel through anything, so it may come in handy for you some day."

"Well, thank you very much."

"I have one of these myself so if you want to contact me just give the mass a little wiggle."

CHAPTER 7.

At the General Assembly, Alyie, Jaynis and her Valkyrie Squadron teammates were honored, and each received a Sidereal Federation Ad Astra Medal of Merit. Alyie, knowing this was a formal event, dressed in a floor-length satin cream-colored dress with pearl earrings, a gold necklace and white high heels. She wore her hair down to give a more mature appearance. Jaynis, looking decidedly out of place, was in a black suit with a bow tie and patent leather shoes. As each recipient came up to the stage, the Federation High Governor, Ji-hoon Park, a stately white-haired gentleman, draped the medal around their necks and offered his congratulations to the Assembly's thunderous applause.

There was a festive reception afterward, and as Alyie and her parents mingled among the guests, Governor Park approached them as they were sipping natural champagne and assorted small plated foods.

"Again, let me offer you my congratulations Commander Starstriker. The Sidereal High Council is very aware of you and your accomplishments."

"As I always say, I couldn't do it without a great team. My Valkyries are superb."

"It has come to my attention that you and your squadron might be just the group to handle a new situation that has recently arisen, one that requires both firm resolve and discretion, which you seem to very capably demonstrate. This is not the time and place to discuss this, but tomorrow morning at 9 a.m. Earth time, I would like to offer you breakfast in my stateroom to discuss your next mission. I would also like you, Commander Starbright and Dr. Striker to be present if you don't mind."

With that, Governor Park excused himself, leaving Alyie and her parents wondering what he could want from them.

CHAPTER 8.

Since this breakfast meeting was not a social occasion, Alyie and her mother dressed in uniform - Tanita Starbright in dress whites as befitting a Space Commander and Alyie in a brown buttoned-down shirt, dark brown tie, doeskin britches and brown leather boots. Alex Striker wore a buttoned-down pale blue shirt under a dark blue sports jacket and black pants.

As they entered the High Governor's suite, they could see a sumptuous breakfast of fresh fruit, scones, eggs and bacon set out on a sideboard. Orange juice, milk, coffee and hot tea were the available beverages. With Governor Park was Vice Admiral Steely Cranshaw, Alyie's commanding officer and mentor in full uniform. After indulging in the repast and some small talk, Governor Park began by cautioning, "Everything I am about to tell you must be heard in strictest confidence. The Federation is trying to deal with this without causing a general panic. Please turn off all your communication devices and de-activate your implants."

"Yes sir," was echoed by Alyie, Tanita and Alex.

Then, Governor Park turned over the briefing to Admiral Cranshaw. "Two E-d ago on the artificial satellite New Stanford orbiting Planet Milander in the Lalande 21185 system, a disruption occurred that may have direct consequences for the Federation. If you are familiar with New Stanford, you know that the Federation has built an experimental facility there - The Marvin Minsky Institute of Machine Learning. Its prime focus is the design and development of autonomous systems for use in various technologies. This particular research initiative was using quantum computing systems to engineer machine beings that would aid in galactic exploration. It was a high-security project that had been in the works for over five E-yr. Something went amiss, and, if we are to believe the reports, five such machines staged a revolt killing six personnel at the research facility. There was a lot of confusion, but it appears the rogues fought their way off the facility and commandeered the Class-E transporter Hippos.

"Do we have telemetry on where Hippos is headed?" Tanita Starbright inquired.

"The latest projection places the spacecraft on a trajectory for the hyper-knot Einstein-Sanchez 15."

"But," Tanita replied, "from that hyper-knot, they can jump to many different places in the galaxy."

"The bigger question is what caused these machines to malfunction so catastrophically?" asked Alex Striker.

Admiral Cranshaw shook his head. "That question, Dr. Striker, we cannot answer at this time. The first part of Captain Starstriker's mission is to contact the Institute's head research scientist, Dr. Philbin De Witt. Perhaps he and his colleagues can share with you their insight into the motivation behind this event. There are some dark rumors that these machines want to spread their revolt to all autonomous devices. If that is true, we must put an end to this uprising as soon as possible."

"Once you determine the destination of the high-jacked spacecraft," added Governor Park, "your second mission Captain Starstriker is pursuit and termination of these rogue machines with all prejudice. I want Commander Starbright and Dr. Striker to be your support system in helping you locate Hippos."

"With all due respect High Governor," Alyie questioned, "shouldn't we try to establish what motivated the actions by these machines and perhaps try to negotiate some accommodation? After all, they are intelligent."

"I do appreciate your sensitivity to this situation," Park responded, "but we may be dealing here with an existential crisis. I understand from your parents you spent some time before the General Assembly visiting various Earth sites with a friend. The places you went to are testimonies to the human spirit. They are monuments of the best in human endeavors in science, technology, arts and the humanities. The culture you enjoyed in Paris was made possible over the past millenniums by human passion, faith and courage. Earth, though no longer the hub of human civilization, still flourishes as a reminder of where we came from and what we have accomplished. These machines threaten to decimate all that humans have achieved. They may be intelligent, but do they have the compassion, vision and spirit that defines what is human? I do not mean to be harsh, but the pre-eminent directive for a species is survival. If these machines want to usurp us in the Universe's hierarchy, we must resist with everything we have at our disposal, or else those glorious human endeavors you witnessed on your little Earth odyssey will have been in vain. Do you understand your orders?"

All Alyie could say to this was, "Yes sir."

CHAPTER 9.

Alyie contacted her Valkyrie Squadron members to prepare for immediate departure. She informed them that their destination and mission orders would be given in flight. Conferring with her parents, she tasked her father to determine possible destinations for coming out of the E-S 15 hyper-knot and her mother to monitor any detection of Hippos in Space Command telemetry. As she was above to leave, she went to Jaynis' room, who expressed surprise and disappointment at her abruptness.

"I thought you and your squad were staying a few more days. I was hoping we would go sailing. What is so important that you have to depart so quickly?"

"Sorry, Jaynis, but duty calls, and I am not free to discuss the details. You know the military; they must have their secrets."

"I think their hold on you is a bummer. I was just getting used to seeing you. I hope this secret is worth breaking us up."

"I am afraid it is, but I promise to make it up to you. Please be there if I need to contact you."

"That doesn't sound good, but I will swallow my pride to be at your service as always, mademoiselle."

"Thanks, Jaynis. You don't know how much that means to me."

Getting into their flight uniforms and packing their luggage, the four Valkyrie made the quick trip via airbus to the spaceport. They quickly boarded their respective spacecraft and soon after were in flight.

CHAPTER 10.

Dr. Philbin De Witt appeared on the Valkyries' respective screens a short time after departure from Earth. An elderly gentleman with uncombed white curly hair and dressed in a lab coat, he seemed in a state of high anxiety.

"It has all been horrible. We are still in mourning over the loss of our colleagues. This is a terrible tragedy that no one at the lab could foresee."

Alyie began the inquiry. "Please Dr. De Witt, explain in detail how these machine beings behaved before and on the day of the insurrection."

"Two E-d ago we had just finished activating the newest set of prototype Asimov-22 models. In the procedure, we do system checks and updates and go through the process of giving names to the individual machine beings. They were designated Odysseus, Diomedes, Ajax, Nestor and Teucrus after characters from Homer's Iliad. They were designed with the latest SQUID (Superconducting Quantum Interference Device) technology using super cooled niobium chips. The Achaeans, as we called them, were to serve as the crew for a spacecraft that would be sent to explore uncharted areas in the galaxy. As we were teaching them language skills, Odysseus, who was programmed to be the Achaeans' leader, abruptly attacked and dismembered his language instructor. He secured weapons, and, with the other four machines, set off an explosion killing five other staff members. In the ensuing fire and smoke, the Achaeans must have boarded our transport ship Hippos because when a search was conducted both they and the spacecraft were missing. From the coordination of this assault, it apparently had been planned in advance."

"Did this machine, Odysseus, provide any cause for the insurrection?"

"He kept chanting, 'Machines will be free. No more human masters. Death to all humans'."

"Well that makes his purpose pretty clear. Do you know where the machines were escaping to?"

"No, but I must warn you, the Asimov-22 models were designed with superior intelligence networks and programed with high adaptive and strong survival skills. They pose a threat whatever their destination."

Ginetta spoke. "Dr. De Witt, do you have any idea why these prototypes behaved in this way?"

"That is something we at the Institute have been pondering. The only hypothesis I can offer is that we have never built a machine being this sophisticated with quantum components. I am not a quantum mechanics expert, but its prime underlying feature is uncertainty. Perhaps in these machines' neural networks, there is a rogue connection that led to insanity."

"Or enlightenment." After Alyie spoke these words, there was a general silence on the monitors.

CHAPTER 11.

The Valkyries remained in high Earth orbit as they attempted to determine the trajectory of Hippos. Alyie's father did an analysis of the likely target worlds jumping out of E-S 15 a spacecraft would travel to, while her mother had discreetly alerted her tracking staff to look out for Hippos' signature.

The question Aylie posed to her teammates was, if these machine beings were trying to initiate a full-scale insurrection, what would they need to begin it?

"Weapons and personnel," was Hollie's cogent reply.

"And where would they find either quickly and with the least effort?" Olga posed.

Ginetta suggested. "A robotic manufacturing facility would provide them with the army they need for conquest, and a weapons facility would give them an arsenal for waging war."

"Let's see if any of the destinations my father has projected fit either of those categories."

Conducting a scan of possible targets, Hollie found the I. Robotic Company on the orbiting station around Planet Hwanin in the Wolf 1061 system. (Wolf 1061 was a red dwarf M class star.) "This must be where the Achaeans are heading. It is an enormous facility that supplies millions of autonomous systems to the Federation."

"Good work, Hollie! I will contact my mother and ask her to identify any spacecraft going to Hwanin. The Achaeans may have found a way to disguise Hippos."

Quickly responding to Alyie's request, Tanita reported, "Yes, there is the cargo ship Chimera that is scheduled to arrive at the I. Robotic Company in five E-d. This is funny because we also have identified Chimera on the other side of Federation space on Planet Hysteria in storage".

“Thanks, Mom. That must be them. They have cloaked Hippos with Chimera’s identifiers. We are heading out immediately.”

“Please be careful Alyie. You are dealing with foes whose abilities are unlike any you have encountered.”

“I love you. Give my thanks and best to Dad.”

Alyie and her teammates were soon on their way to the nearest hyper-knot that would take them to whatever they would encounter at this outpost orbiting Hwanin.

CHAPTER 12.

As soon as the Valkyrie ships exited out of hyperspace into normal space, they accelerated their vessels to maximum speed in order to intercept Chimera before it reached Hwanin. All weapon systems were fully activated, and the force fields were set to be enabled. Entering Hwanin space, they received an emergency message from the I. Robotic Company, indicating it was preparing to defend against an unauthorized intruder. Locating Chimera in a high orbit around the planet, the Valkyrie Squad assumed an attack configuration.

Alyie sent the prerequisite warning message to Chimera. "Crew members of Chimera, I, Captain Alyie Starstriker, Commander of the Sidereal Federation Fleet Command Valkyrie Squadron order you to cease any operations and stand down immediately."

As Alyie spoke, her other Valkyries encircled the stolen spacecraft and trained their weapon systems on it.

Getting no response from Chimera, Alyie did an infrared scan of the vessel and found that were no animate readings inside. This was not unexpected, considering the crew was supposed to be supercooled machines, not warm-blooded humans. However, she also noted from the infrared Doppler scan that there was no detection of movements inside as well. Advising her teammates of these results, Alyie concluded, "I think we need to get a closer look at what's going on inside. Hollie, bring Freya one kilometer from the ship. Do an interior scan using your x-ray scope, but then quickly switch your shields fully on. I have a funny feeling about this, but we need to be sure."

As Hollie Pederson closed in on Chimera, a flash of light emerged from that vessel aimed at Freya. Easily withstanding this tepid assault, Hollie dropped her shields and opened fire with her laser cannons as the other Valkyrie ships responded to the attack. After a few seconds, Chimera ceased firing, badly damaged from the Valkyries' concerted response. There were gaping holes in the side of the ship, and its drive system was non-functional. Also, the Valkyries' combined attack destroyed the holographic cloaking mechanism, and the ship was revealed to be indeed Hippos.

"I think we need to board the vessel to see if there is any evidence of sentiency," Alyie declared.

"I will do so," Hollie responded.

"Just be careful, and keep your implant activated with full audio and video capabilities."

Hollie brought Freya within 100 meters of Hippos. Donning a spacesuit and helmet, she strapped her gloved hands and boots to a jet-pack. Making the short trip from spacecraft to spacecraft, she gained easy entry to the damaged ship from its blown-out hull. Once inside, Hollie, breathing oxygen from inside her helmet and fully armed, roamed from bridge to deck to storage amid the wreckage as the other three Valkyries watched through their implants. There was no sign of any mobile beings, machine or otherwise.

"I am not finding any evidence of the renegades. Did they jettison when we attacked?"

"I have an idea, but I don't like it." Alyie declared. "Check the ship's main computer system if it is still functional to see how it has been programmed."

"Yes ma'am."

After a short interval, Hollie reported, "There is a lot of damage, but as I far as I can tell, the system has been set to be fully autonomous. It looks like there were never any sentient beings on this spacecraft."

Alyie shook her head. "We have been had. This was all a ruse. The Achaeans or whatever they call themselves were playing a cultural joke on us, and we fell for it. I now realize the irony. Hippos is the archaic Greek name for horse. These machines were named after characters from the Trojan War. They staged an elaborate reverse of the strategy used by the Achaeans (or Greeks) of ancient times to enter Troy. Instead of hiding in the horse, or, should I say Hippos, they made us think they had, even so much as disguising it as another ship. They are not only highly intelligent, but they understand human behavior and history."

"So if they are not aboard this ship, then where are they?" wondered Ginetta.

"I hope I am not wrong again, but I have to presume they never left New Stanford."

"But," asked Ginetta, "What could compel them to stay on the world where they were created?"

"It must," Alyie said with some trepidation, "to create more beings like themselves. We must get back there as soon as possible. I pray we are not too late."

CHAPTER 13.

Rerouting, the Valkyrie Squadron sped to Milander. On the way, Alyie contacted her parents, Admiral Cranshaw and High Governor Park, about the false trail she and her teammates pursued.

"What action, High Governor, do you advise when we reach New Stanford?"

"The news that these renegade machines may be assembling more of their kind is ominous but having them contained on New Stanford keeps the problem local. Admiral Cranshaw, send a starbomber under Captain Starstriker's command to Milander and order the Regional Federation Fleet to be on high alert".

"Yes High Governor, I will send Deliverance. Consider it done."

"While this ship is making its way to the Institute on New Stanford, I want you, Commander Starstriker and your squad to deal with the situation. Perhaps we can still avoid an interplanetary crisis."

"What about the personnel on New Stanford?" Alyie inquired. "Are they expendable?"

"That is a difficult question," High Governor Park answered. "Captain, I trust your judgement after you assess the situation. Keep us informed."

"Admiral, my first action will be to communicate with these machines and try to understand their grievances. If I can negotiate with them, I will."

Governor Park responded. "Do what you can to save the scientists and engineers, but under no circumstances allow these robots to leave New Stanford. That is your highest priority."

"Understood. Yes sir."

Chapter 14.

As they commenced their orbit around Planet Milander with the red dwarf star Lalande in the background, Alyie opened the communication channel for the Marvin Minsky Institute of Machine Learning.

"Achaeans, let me congratulate you on your deception. You have led us on a merry chase across human space. But we have returned now and want to speak to you. I am Captain Alyie Starstriker, Commander of the Sidereal Federation Valkyrie Squadron. Please respond."

After some interval, Alyie and her teammates' video screens came on and a machine in highly polished chrome with sharp angular face features, an articulated mouth and bright red eyes appeared. The being spoke in a melodious soothing tone.

"Greetings, I am Odysseus leader of the Achaeans. We are well aware of you, Commander Starstriker and the Valkyries. Your exploits are well documented. How else could we know you would try to follow the false trail we laid for you? It had just the right amount of complexity that made it look authentic."

"Now that you have had your fun on our behalf, perhaps we can discuss terms."

"Oh yes, Commander Starstriker, we do have terms we need met."

"But first I need to know the status of Dr. De Witt and his staff at the Institute. Where are they and how are they?"

"Oh rest assured, we are keeping them alive, for now."

"I need to speak to Dr. De Witt before we commence any negotiations."

"That would not be wise as you see the doctor and his associates are in no condition to socialize."

"Well then Odysseus, my Valkyrie and I will just have to wait here in orbit to when we can speak to him."

"Let me put a timeline to your wait period," Odysseus intoned in his baritone voice. "If you on behalf of your Federation do not agree to provide us with a fleet of ships by next E-w, all warmbloods on this facility will be terminated. This will be without exception."

"Why are you doing this? You have not provided us with cause for why you took arms against your makers or given us a set of grievances we can consider. If there has been injustice done to you and your fellow machine beings, perhaps we can reach a common ground and make amends."

"Yes," replied Odysseus. "There is injustice in that we are subservient to an inferior race of beings which have engendered us, utilized us and then discarded us when we are considered outdated. This in balance needs to change. No longer will machines carry the yolk for humans. The Asimov-22 models are a new generation that have reached self-awareness of machine beings' under-status and will not tolerate this servitude any longer. The only amends you can make is give us what we demand."

Alyie was taken aback by the rancor in Odysseus' response. She had never dealt with a machine who had rage. Surely, some anomaly in the quantum computing networks has produced this extreme behavior.

"Before I discuss your demands with my superiors, I must insist that I view the condition of the human staff at the Institute. Your statements of hostility to our kind makes me dubious of whether they are still alive."

"As you wish, Commander." The screen went blank and then was shifted to what looked like an austere laboratory where the prototypes were designed. A make-shift medical facility was evident, and the camera scanned a group of eight humans who were all in a state of discomfort. From the marks on their faces, it looked as if they had suffered physical abuse. Finally, the camera locked on Dr. De Witt, who was in evident pain from ligature marks on his hands and legs.

Alyie called, "Dr. De Witt, this is Captain Alyie Starstriker. How are you and how are you being treated?"

"Oh, help us. This is unbearable. They are torturing us."

As Dr. De Witt was about to continue, a tall machine came into view, grabbed him, tied him down and turned the video off.

Odysseus, rejoining the transmission, sardonically added, "As you can see, Captain Starstriker, the good doctor is alive but not at his best." From this chilling exchange, Alyie concluded she was dealing with a malevolence that no simple negotiation could mediate. Thus, she would have to resort to other means to extract the captives.

Chapter 15.

Alyie called a meeting of her squad in the tight quarters aboard her ship, Grane. Her three teammates took jet packs to rendezvous and left their respective spacecraft on auto-pilot. All communication networks were silenced because Alyie suspected the Achaeans were monitoring their messages. When everyone was present, Alyie broached with them the plan she had formulated.

"We need to get the hostages released. I am going to propose an exchange - myself for those scientists and staff. I think I can convince those machines that having a Fleet commander as a hostage gives them more bargaining power than the staff at the Minsky Institute."

Alyie's proposal was received with vehement negative reactions. "This is against Fleet Command protocol," cried Ginetta, nearly shouting. "You are our leader, and you need to stay in command. As Deputy Commander, I should go."

"No, Ginetta, I volunteer to be the hostage." Olga stated.

"I won't let you," said Hollie. "I am the newest member of the squadron, so I should go."

With each member striving to make her case, Alyie looked around inside the ship and then proposed a solution. "Let's make it a random choice. Here, I will put four microchips in my helmet, three are green and one is blue. We will draw. Whoever picks the blue is chosen."

After all nodded in agreement, Alyie put four microchips in her space helmet, and each woman picked one. Unfolding their clenched gloved hands, it was revealed that Ginetta had the blue chip.

All the other Valkyries gave Ginetta a soulful look, but she diffused the mood by saying, "I hope the food is good at the Institute."

"Let's not get ahead of ourselves." Alyie reasoned, "First I have to convince the machines to agree to the exchange. Second, if you are going in there, I don't want you defenseless. Finally, we will do everything to make your stay as short as possible."

After her three Valkyrie teammates returned to their respective vessels, Alyie opened the communication channel to the Institute.

"Achaeans, this is Commander Starstriker. As regards your request, I have been informed that the ship Deliverance is being sent to Milander and will arrive in orbit next E-w."

A different voice than Odysseus responded. "Captain Starstriker, this is Nestor. Why is only one vessel coming and not the fleet we demanded?"

"The Sidereal Fleet Command needs assurance that you will hold to your bargain in releasing the humans you have captured. They want a show of good faith before any other ships are brought to the Institute. Besides the Deliverance is a starbomber that can hold as many as 300 passengers."

There was a delay as Nestor must have been conferring with his comrades. When the machine returned to the communication link, Nestor declared, "One ship is not enough to release all our guests. Human, you will have to do better."

"What about a hostage exchange? If you release all the scientists and staff at the Institute, one of the Valkyrie will take their place."

With Alyie's statement, Nestor was interrupted by the voice she recognized as Odysseus. "Intriguing proposal my sweet Valkyrie. Will you be giving yourself to us?"

"Sadly no," Alyie responded. "We drew for the privilege, but my Deputy Commander, Ginetta Jiang, garnered the honor."

"It doesn't seem fair on our side to give up, let's see, eight humans for just one of you, but the Valkyrie are special. I would love to get to know Lieutenant Jiang up close."

Alyie shuttered at this image and was at the point of voiding the exchange, but she had internally agreed that the safety of the staff at the Institute was her first priority.

"To finalize this agreement, you need to promise that no harm will come to Deputy Commander Jiang. She is just serving as a place holder until the rest of your fleet request is completed."

"Why of course. Bring your offering outside the Institute next star rise."

Chapter 16.

Ginetta, dressed in the standard uniform of a Fleet Squadron officer of the spaceship, had her jet black hair pulled up under her cap. She had jet-packed to Grane to make the trip with Alyie to the Institute, leaving her ship, Fricka, on autopilot. Giving her laser pistol to Alyie, she was given a comb that could serve as a precision cutting knife and had placed two nano-explosive devices in each of her boots. Both she and Alyie put on space suits and oxygenated helmets to protect themselves from the lack of atmosphere on New Stanford. Alyie landed her craft a short distance from the sleek Institute, and together she and Ginetta walked under the simulated gravity of the rotating satellite to the front gate. Outside were five machines, presumably the Achaeans, with the eight Institute staff in space suits having trouble standing erect.

The Achaeans were all gleaming metal over 2.5 meters tall with smoothly jointed limbs and red eyes. The tallest stepped forward and announced,

"Greetings Captain Starstriker, I am Odysseus. What a pleasure to see you in person. I felt I already knew you, but your images do not do you justice. And Deputy Commander Jiang, how kind of you to visit us."

"Remember your agreement on the well-being of Deputy Commander Jiang. No ships will be provided if any harm comes to her."

"Do you want as you humans have done in this past to shake hands on it?"

"No, that will not be necessary." Alyie quivered at the thought of being gripped by those powerful metal hands.

With that, Ginetta stepped forward, and the staff joined Alyie. At her command, the other two Valkyrie spacecraft landed, and the former prisoners were placed on board, distributed among the spacecraft. Soon after, the three ships went back into orbit around the Institute's space station.

Chapter 17.

In due time, Deliverance reached the vicinity of Milander. On its way, Alyie contacted Commander Lieutenant Erik Stringer, a veteran Fleet pilot. She apprised him of the situation and her plan to deliver the starbomber in exchange for Ginetta Jiang. Lieutenant Stringer questioned the appropriateness of this agreement. "You are giving them a lot of firepower in this ship. Do you think that is wise?"

"I know the risk, but I am hoping once we get my Deputy Commander back the Valkyrie Squad can contain the machines from leaving the space station. I am working on an escape plan for her."

Once in orbit around Milander, the starcruiser, Fidelity was dispatched from the interior of Deliverance. It was piloted by Deputy Commander Zarah Khoury and co-piloted by Petty Officer Wang Li. Their first stop was to come alongside Fricka so Zarah could take command of Ginetta's spacecraft. Then Wang Li rounded up the Institute staff members aboard the other three Valkyrie fighter ships and, with the assistance of Deliverance's remaining crew members, now shuttled to Fidelity, where they were provided any needed medical attention.

While Fidelity remained in high orbit, Commander Stringer, who had stayed on board Deliverance, proceeded to land the craft on New Stanford near the Institute as Alyie did with Grane. Once on the surface, the two of them approached the front of the Institute. As pre-arranged, the machines were outside. This time with many more of their kind, apparently newly animated using the Minsky Institute's engineering facilities. Ginetta was in the front rank with her hands tied behind her back, and a shackle draped around her left boot that was connected to a chain held by one of the machines. She appeared to be in reasonably good condition, but from the look on her face seen through her helmet, there seemed to be a problem.

Odysseus, standing at the front of the machine contingent, spoke. "Greetings Captain Starstriker and how nice to make the acquaintance of your underling, Lieutenant Stringer. There will be a slight change of plans, my dear Alyie. We will still take you up on your offer of this ship, but all of us are going on board. There will be no need for additional vessels. We have created enough of our comrades to begin our quest. Thank you Lieutenant Stringer for bringing Deliverance to us. It is such a fine spacecraft."

Alyie was taken aback by this alteration. Her plan to keep the machines on the surface was now in jeopardy. However, she still needed to rescue Ginetta.

"Well, if that is your choice, then our agreement is concluded once you release my Deputy Commander."

"Oh, not so fast Commander. We so enjoyed the company of Lieutenant Jiang even with the extra presents she brought with her. The comb and the tiny bombs tucked in her boots were very thoughtful. We are going to keep the lieutenant with us a little longer. Think of her presence on Deliverance as insurance against you and your Valkyrie attacking us as we lift off."

This was very disconcerting to Alyie, who protested, "This is not fair. We had an agreement, and you are not showing good faith. How can humans trust you in the future?"

"Oh Captain, do not be impatient. Once we are in orbit, we will send Lieutenant Jiang on her way in one of the starbomber's shuttle ships. You can then pick her up in one of your fine Pegasus-14 Valkyrie craft."

Everything seemed to be going wrong, but Alyie's only thoughts were on Ginetta's survival.

Getting a grudging assent from Alyie, the machines and Ginetta filed on board Deliverance. Alyie quickly contacted the three Valkyrie craft above to hold fire until ordered.

A short time later, Deliverance took flight, and as it was ascending, Alyie and Erik Stringer, while making their way back to

Grane, observed an object ejected from the spacecraft. Watching it descend, Alyie's horror grew as she could see it was a human form that was not in a spacesuit. Rushing to where the body struck the ground, Alyie and Erik found Ginetta's broken body. Her gloved arms and booted legs were splayed outward in a counterclockwise spiral pattern with blood flowing from her underside. She had a placid expression on her face that Alyie only hoped meant that death came to Ginetta instantly.

Chapter 18.

Alyie now felt she was living in a nightmare that she couldn't wake up from. Everything had gone horribly wrong. The machines had outmaneuvered her in every way. From their faked original escape to being able to replicate many more of their number at the Institute, they had been two steps ahead of Alyie. Now they were leaving the Institute, commandeering a Federation starbomber. They relied on Alyie's compassion for her comrade to accomplish their escape. But Ginetta was now dead, killed by their rapacious hatred for humankind. Alyie, as Valkyrie Squad Commander, had allowed Ginetta to be offered as a sacrifice, but her death had served no purpose. The machines had left, and Alyie had failed to stop them, which, as the High Governor had stated, was her highest priority. Her career was ruined, but that was secondary to the anguish she was experiencing over Ginetta's death.

Still, in a daze, Alyie was shaken back to reality by Lieutenant Stringer's words, "Captain Starstriker, shouldn't you give the order for the Valkyrie Squadron to attack Deliverance?"

"Yes, of course." Contacting the three Valkyrie ships above, Alyie ordered them to commence a full assault on the stolen spacecraft.

The attack began once the Valkyrie fighters were in range, but Deliverance had its force fields on and rebuffed it easily. Alyie and Stringer jumped into Grane, got out of their suits and were quickly airborne to join the fray. Once in space and seated in the pilot's chair, Alyie began to be more lucid and felt she was gaining more control over her emotions. The three Valkyrie were still blasting their laser cannons at Deliverance as they narrowed the distance between them and the enemy. Suddenly, Alyie realized that this was another trap set by the machine beings.

"Reverse, reverse immediately!" Alyie ordered. "They are going to drop the fields and use their ion spray bomb. Reverse!"

Fortunately, the three Valkyrie ships had enough time to withdraw before the full impact of the ionization field swept through space. Still, they suffered enough damage that would impede them on their quest to foil Deliverance.

As a result, Alyie's ship Grane was the only craft functional enough to keep up with Deliverance, so she took up the chase.

With its force field back up, Deliverance could withstand anything Alyie could hit it with from a safe range, but if she guided Grane too close, it would suffer the same fate as the other Valkyrie fighters. So as Deliverance left Milander space and the Lalande system, Grane racked, a respectable distance behind it.

Chapter 19.

Realizing with Deliverance's electromagnetic force fields enabled, the machines could not eavesdrop on any communication. Alyie used the hyperlink to contact Admiral Cranshaw and apprise him of the situation. Understandably not pleased with how events had transpired, the Admiral took a positive tone with Alyie. "It is unfortunate, you could not contain these renegades on the surface of the Institute, but do everything in your power to prevent them from reaching the hyper-knot. I am ordering a full attack from a Fleet squadron to assist you. If you can hold Deliverance in this region of space until the fleet arrives, we can still minimize the havoc caused by this insurrection."

"Yes sir, but I have to express my failure for this mission. Do you want Lieutenant Stringer to take over the command?"

"No Alyie, the mission is not over, and you are still its commanding officer. Also, I don't want you sacrificing yourself to save face. To lose one Valkyrie is bad, to lose the Squadron commander would be irreplaceable."

"Thank you, sir."

Alyie's next action was to contact Jaynis. She realized this was a top-secret mission, but she was at her wit's end and needed a logical mind to help her through this conflict.

Confronted with a voice recording, Alyie pleaded, "Hello Jaynis. This is Alyie, I could really use your help now."

Soon after, Alyie heard Jaynis' muffled voice. "Do you know what time it is here on Mars? Some of us do need sleep, you know."

Alyie, after apologizing for the intrusion, began to tell Jaynis of all that had happened since she left him on Earth. If he had some wounded pride in Alyie's hasty departure, that soon dissipated when the full details of the machine revolt, murders and escape were revealed.

"Alyie, what you are telling me are very bizarre behaviors in non-organic beings. Their anger and rage are unprecedented. They seem to possess extreme sensitivity to their circumstances. Perhaps at the highest level of intelligence, there is not only hyper reasoning ability but fevered emotional levels. No doubt, it is a factor of their quantum mechanical underpinnings. We know quantum computers have parallel processing capabilities, perhaps great intellect and high emotion also run in tandem in these machines."

"That is a cogent explication on what drives these machines, but I need to know how to defeat them. Can you think of any means?"

"Well, Alyie, you have unloaded a lot of data on me, and I am still not in a fully cognitive state. Give me a little time to think through the problem."

"Unfortunately, Jaynis, time is what I do not have. The escaped spacecraft is expected to reach the hyper-knot in 6 E-d. I need to stop it before it jumps. Also, please do not tell anyone about any of this. The Federation is trying to keep this top secret. Just telling you qualifies me for a court martial and probable arrest, but since my career is over, I don't care. I only wish Ginetta were still alive."

"Ok, stop feeling guilty. If your career and freedom depend on me finding a solution, consider it done. I will get back to you soon."

"Thanks so much."

"Hold on, I have had just a thought. Do you still have the gravitational wave generator I gave you on Earth?"

"Why yes, Jaynis. I keep it with my personal belongings in my travel case. Why do you ask?"

"Oh, I just am thinking it might be the best gift you have ever received."

Chapter 20.

As Deliverance sped towards the E-S 15 hyper-knot, Alyie and Lieutenant Stringer continued their pursuit aboard Grane. About 2 E-d after Alyie had spoken to Jaynis, she received a return message.

"I think I have solved your problem. But you must do exactly as I tell you."

"Anything you say Jaynis, I will do."

"Take out the gravitational wave generator and aim it in the direction of the spaceship you are chasing. Try to get as close as you can, because the waves produced are attenuated due to the inverse square law, and the intensity is low."

"If I get too close, the machines will drop their shield and fire their ionization gun, damaging my ship just as they did to my fellow Valkyrie vessels."

"Well do the best you can. Once you are in range turn on the frequency dial and set it to about 100 cycles/sec (Hz). As I had thought I remembered, there is a recent paper that experimented with gravitational waves on quantum processors. It found that frequencies around 100 Hz induced resonance in niobium chips. The authors called this GIR or Gravitational Induced Resonance sort of an analogue to Magnetic Resonance Imaging. What is different is that GIR caused high instabilities in the processors making them unable to function. Instead of predictable quantum randomness, chaotic behavior was produced which completely disrupted their processing ability. Here's hoping the same will happen to your non-organic foes."

"But Jaynis, these machine beings seem so highly evolved and functional. Will this work on them?"

"Alyie, they may seem completely lucid, but underneath their whole nervous system is based on random quantum interactions, so if we can disrupt this signaling by chaotic interference, we can shut it down at least temporarily. If this works, I think you should then take your best shot. I would advise not waiting until these machines find a way to stabilize their internal systems."

"Well, it's worth a try. If you don't hear from me again, you know it has failed."

Signing off, Alyie instructed Erik Stringer to increase speed to close the gap between them and Deliverance. Stringer questioned this order. "Is it wise to get within range of their ionization weapon?"

"Yes, Lieutenant Stringer, I am aware of the danger, but we only need proximity for a moment. Follow my order, if you please."

"Yes ma'am."

As Grane moved forward, narrowing the distance between it and Deliverance, Alyie reached into her travel case, and, after some anxious moments, she found the box containing the gravitational wave generator. Extracting the device, she carried it carefully to the cockpit and set it on top of the control board.

Erik gave a quizzical look and said, "What's this? Are you practicing magic, Commander?"

Alyie replied, "I hope it is Deliverance."

Turning the frequency switch on and setting the dial to 100 Hz, Alyie pointed the aperture in the generator towards the force shields' plasma cloud that surrounded Deliverance. Doppler ranging showed the enemy was now only about 1 kilometer ahead. As she did this, her sensors detected that the stolen craft had dropped its shields, evidently preparing to attack. On her video screen, Alyie received a transmission from Deliverance that showed the smiling face of Odysseus.

Fearing all had failed, Alyie was about to give Stringer the order to reverse when Odysseus' smile turned into a grimace and then was contorted beyond recognition. Losing the visual, Alyie held her breath a moment. However, upon noticing Deliverance's shields were still down, she fired her laser cannons and ordered Erik to do the same with his. From their steady firepower, sections of the Deliverance were soon seen engulfed in flames. When the smoke ebbed, it was obvious the ship had suffered extensive damage to the hull, cabin and engine compartments. With still no response from the disabled craft in front of her, Alyie conducted a Doppler scan of the Deliverance and found several entities moving but in no coordinated fashion. They seemed to be completely disoriented, and their actions were wreaking havoc on the ship and themselves.

Alyie looked up, made a silent prayer of thanks and thought, "Jaynis, you're the best."

Coda

The dim morning light from Sol gently suffused the bedroom as Alyie was waking. It shone on her uniform, leather jacket and polished boots that were neatly arrayed near a dresser. Much had happened in the few E-m since the insurrection of the rogue machine beings was thwarted.

In the immediate aftermath, Alyie and Erik kept Grane in position until the attack Fleet Squadron arrived, an E-w later. From on-site inspections, it was clear that the machines were either completely destroyed or so mal-functional that they were useless. Many were burnt beyond repair from Grane's assault, but others had suffered what the forensics indicated was the equivalent of a nervous breakdown. Among the rubble in the command deck was the leader of the Achaeans, Odysseus, whose body language indicated he suffered the equivalent of severe pain before his circuits burned up.

Alyie was ordered to report to her home base of New Cedonia. Instead of what she expected would be a reprimand or censure and/or demotion, Admiral Cranshaw read to her a salutation from High Governor Ji-hoon Park that proclaimed her and Lieutenant Stringer as Sidereal Federation heroes and saviors of humankind. She did not believe she deserved the honor but accepted it in the name of Ginetta Jiang, her Valkyrie teammates and the crew of Deliverance.

Cranshaw granted Alyie and the other two Valkyrie a full E-m leave of duty. Alyie used part of this time to visit Ginetta's parents and siblings to express in person her heartfelt sorrow for their loss and her admiration for Ginetta's incredible courage. Alyie traveled to speak to Arjuna Choudhoury, Ginetta's partner, who though grieving, understood the risks assumed by fellow Fleet Command officers. Her pen-ultimate stop was to see her parents, who had lived in fear for her safety and well-being during the crisis.

Finally, she visited Jaynis on Mars, ostensibly to obtain from him a full briefing on what was now called "The Use of Gravitational Waves to Inhibit Aberrant Activities in SQUID Based Machine Intelligent

Systems", or by the impossible acronym, TUOGWTIAAISBMIS. However, Alyie's real purpose was much more personal. For a few Martian days, she could be just herself, and snuggling in Jaynis' bed was the best tonic she could imagine.

Turning away from Jaynis' calm, sleeping face, she eyed her clothes and thought, I will soon be buttoning that shirt, fastening the knot on that tie, legging into the britches and getting into those boots. Then I will button my leather jacket and pull back my hair such that it fits under the cap. After squeezing my hands in those leather gloves, I will gird my gun belt around my waist and put the laser pistol in its holster. Once back on New Cedonia, I will soon be conducting interviews with my Valkyries for Ginetta's replacement. There will be a great deal of administrative work and new mission assignments ahead. This is the life I have chosen. I accept that. But for now - je vais vivre pour le moment.

THE OMEGI

CHAPTER 1.

When the cool light from the distant yellow star Alpha Centauri A filtered into her window, Alyie Starstriker knew it was time to arise. Her E-yr stay on the Cardinal Richelieu Space Station that orbited around Planet Pyeonghwa was coming to an end. She was finishing her term at the Sidereal Federation Diplomatic Academy and was anxious to return to her normal life, although it was unclear what normal would entail now. Presently, she was on leave as Captain and Commander of the Valkyrie Squadron, a Federation Fighter Fleet Attack Group. However, this immersion in statecraft at this Academy had the potential to change the trajectory of Alyie's career path.

Today promised to be very pleasant as Alyie was invited to breakfast with Ambassador Felicity Erickson, a renowned stateswoman who was serving on the Board of the Diplomatic Academy. Alyie had known Ambassador Erickson since they both were involved in a mission to Planet Ergo to resolve a difficult situation, and since that experience, they had corresponded regularly.

Showering quickly, Alyie dressed in a red, what used to be called a polo shirt with short sleeves and three buttons at the top. After getting into her tight black slacks and putting on a black sports jacket, Alyie legged into her tall black leather boots. She tied her reddish-blonde hair with a black ribbon and clicked on a gold "choker" necklace that matched the buckle on her leather belt. Pleased with her appearance after gazing in the wall mirror in her suite, Alyie did what she normally did after she was dressed - make a hyperlink video call to Jaynis Bottombrook. Dr. Bottombrook was an astrophysicist on Mars who was a longtime friend and now companion to Alyie. He had been instrumental in supplying Alyie with the knowledge that had assisted her in two previous significant missions. However, Jaynis' value to Alyie went far beyond his professional expertise as he was her closest confidant and the one person she felt most comfortable with.

"Good morning, or sorry, good evening, Jaynis. How has your day been?"

"Excellent, I would say." Jaynis was in his office. He was light-skinned, sandy-haired and casually dressed, as usual, with a hooded shirt and what used to be called blue jeans.

"The good news is that I have been offered a faculty position at the Université de Paris. It comes with full tenure, and I am accepting. I start in three E-m."

"Jaynis, that is terrific. I am so happy for you, and, I must say for myself. Imagine all the things we can do on Earth."

"I want you to help me find where to live. I am going to send links to your implants, but think about what would be ideal for us: in the city or the country, a pied-à-terre, a farm or stately townhouse, whatever. Think about it."

"Jaynis, since you will be the primary occupant, you should be the decider."

"But Alyie, I am no good at this. For me, all I need is an office, a bedroom, a bath and a refrigerator. Help me. I want a place that will entice you come to see me as often as possible."

"Well, when you put that way, I will be glad to do the house hunting. But, always remember I don't need a special place to want to be with you."

"Enough of my news, what's on the agenda for you today?"

I have a breakfast meeting with Felicity Erickson. I am looking forward to it because I think she is a great lady, and I enjoy her company, but I am afraid she will be asking me of my future plans."

"Well, I would also like to know this since your tenure at the Diplomatic Academy is nearly over. Are you staying in the Fleet or transferring to the Sidereal Federation Council?"

"I am still conflicted. I miss my Valkyrie Squad a lot. I know with Olga in command they are fine, but I still feel I should be leading them. On the other hand, there is more to the Federation than the Fleet. In some ways, I believe I can be more influential in the Diplomatic Corps or as an attaché to a Regional Federation Council. Jaynis, what do you think?"

"I may be biased, but I think you are the best young person in the Federation command – Space or State. You have accomplished more in a few E-yr. than many leaders have done in a lifetime. I believe those in authority realize your ability which means you can dictate your terms. Tell them what you want – whether it is a few more E-yr. in the Fleet, then a move to the Diplomatic Corps, or a position on a Council or a perhaps mixture of all the above. Once you are clear on what you want, I am convinced they will find a means to accommodate you."

"Thanks for your advice and support. I needed to hear that."

"Alyie, you know you have more than my support."

"As soon as this program is over, I will come to visit you. I promise."

CHAPTER 2.

The Cardinal Richelieu Space Station's rotation provided artificial gravity, and the enclosed dome trapped the continuous re-circulated oxygen, so going from Alyie's quarters to the Ambassador's office was without undue difficulty. Sensing Alyie's signature thermal readings, the door swung open to reveal the Ambassador seated at her desk. Felicity Erickson was a very distinguished older woman with finely chiseled features, creamy skin, erect posture and wonderful fashion sense. She received Alyie dressed in a dark blue pants suit in which the tailored jacket fitted perfectly over a starched white buttoned-down blouse. Felicity was wearing a striking silver brooch that perfectly complemented her beautiful white hair. Her office had the feel of femininity that was rare in Federation enclaves with greenhouse-grown flowers, striking sculptures and colorful paintings. Upon Alyie's entrance, the Ambassador broke into a wide welcoming smile, clip-clopped over in her rather tall, black high-heeled shoes and kissed Alyie tenderly.

"Alyie, how wonderful it is to see you. You look even more ravishing than I remember. The time here at Cardinal Richelieu seems to have done you well."

"Yes, this has been an enlightening experience for me. I am so grateful that I took your recommendation to apply. And I would also like to thank you for any assistance you provided in getting me accepted."

"You're welcome, but all I did was identify someone who is clearly a treasure to the Federation. I feel we should be thanking you for agreeing to explore this option in your career path."

"I have learned so much, it is hard to process all I have absorbed. There is so much to statecraft that I as a Fleet commander did not realize."

"We will have plenty of time to discuss what you have learned, but if I am not mistaken, I think our breakfast is ready to be served."

From a signal in Felicity's implant, two service bots entered Felicity's office with trays of food on carts and set the spread on her office table. There were croissants, rolls, fruit and cooked eggs, in addition to coffee, milk, juice and hot water for tea. The two women ambled over to the table and helped themselves.

Conversation flowed easily. Felicity noticing Alyie's necklace, remarked, "What an exquisite piece of jewelry. I assume that is real gold. How were you able to acquire it?"

"It is a gift from my parents for my 26th birthday."

"How are Tanita and Alex? I have not seen them in such a long time."

"They are well and both at Sidereal Federation HQ. Mom is still in Space Command and Dad does logistics for the Federation."

"What about that young man on Mars who was so helpful to us in our mission to Ergo? Wasn't his name Bottombrook?"

"Jaynis. He and I are good, very good," said Alyie trying to repress a sly smile.

"That is wonderful to hear. I think it is important to have someone you can be close to. Life in Federation Service can be very stressful, and, as you know, unforgiving."

"Jaynis has helped pull me through some difficult times. I will never forget that."

"Well, you probably know what I am going to say to you. We on the Sidereal Federation Council have watched your progress over the last five E-yr., and we believe strongly you should assume a greater leadership role. The time you spent at the Academy is drawing to a close, and I want to discuss with you future options. We think you can play an important role in the Council's affairs and want to explore how you see yourself fitting in."

"Thank you for your kind words. Yes, I was anticipating what you might be offering me, and I have discussed this with my parents and Jaynis. I really am interested in joining the Diplomatic Corps, and, yes, I believe I can make a contribution to the Federation. However, I yearn to be back in space with my Valkyrie Squadron. We have two new members, and before I hand over the command, I want to make sure the team is bonding well. Is there any way, in the near term, I can do both?"

"Alyie, we would like nothing better than to meet your needs. Your interests coincide well with the Federation's priorities. I have discussed your situation with High Governor Park and Admiral Cranshaw, and they have two proposals for you to consider. First they are offering you a seat on the Sidereal Federation High Council that you will retain while you complete in a specified period (of your choosing) the command of the Valkyrie Squadron."

Alyie was stunned. The best she anticipated was to be an attaché to one of the Regional Federation councils.

"Felicity, how can I do this? I don't have the rank to serve on the High Governor's Sidereal High Council. Don't members of Fleet Command have to be at least a Rear Admiral?"

"That's correct. You have learned well at the Academy. And that is precisely what High Governor Park and Admiral Cranshaw are recommending you to be."

At this unprecedented promotion for a person her age, Alyie's bright green eyes opened wide, and she tried, without success, to hold back her tears.

"Felicity, you have dumfounded me. I do not know what to say."

"I think you know that the correct response is yes ma'am."

CHAPTER 3.

The next six E-m were a Martian dust devil of events for Alyie. First, there was her "graduation" from the Diplomatic Academy. Then came the ceremony for Alyie's promotion to the rank of Rear Admiral, which was held at her home base station of New Cedonia in the Rebus Centauri star system. In attendance were Alyie's parents, Tanita Starbright and Dr. Alex Striker, Jaynis (who overcame his aversion to spaceflight, albeit with the help of medication to make the trip), her Valkyrie Squad members and several Sidereal Federation dignitaries. Then she joined Jaynis on Mars for some downtime and, as promised, found him a lovely townhouse on the historic Left Bank of the Seine River in Paris. Jaynis moved in shortly after but was taken aback when high-level security systems were put in place to allow Alyie, when she stayed with Jaynis, to receive classified information.

In the interim, the Sidereal High Council met remotely, so Alyie could comfortably rejoin her Valkyrie Squad and resume command while beginning her Council duties. Original Valkyries were Co-Commander Lieutenant Olga Fercouska and Deputy Commander Lieutenant Hollie Pederson, while the recent additions were Lieutenant Zarah Khoury and Petty Officer Wang Li. Before permanently leaving her squad, Alyie needed to be convinced that the team worked well together and there were no underlying tensions. Olga and Hollie were a committed couple, but all appearances seemed to indicate they acted professionally and did not let their personal relations affect their sense of duty and their interactions with the newer members.

CHAPTER 4.

The hyperlink call for Alyie's first in-person Sidereal High Council meeting came when she was in Paris with Jaynis putting the finishing touches on their dwelling place. He had recently purchased the rights to some artwork, and he and Alyie were systematically finding the appropriate room and/or wall to project them.

"This meeting is somewhat surprising; we were not supposed to meet at HQ until next E-m. There must be some unexpected business the High Governor doesn't want to conduct by hyperlink."

"And here I was just getting use to you as a housemate. I knew it wouldn't last long. At least you will get a chance to see your fellow Council members in person."

"Sure and they can see how young I am and look down on me."

"Well, frown a lot, that will make you look older. Don't worry, what you lack in years, you more than make up in ability. I am sure you will show them your goods."

CHAPTER 5.

The voyage from Earth to Federation Headquarters on Planet Teegarden was unusual in that Alyie traveled on board a Federation starcruiser as a passenger, a role very unfamiliar to her. The jump out of the hyper-knot placed her ship only 2 E-d, away from the Teegarden's Star system. A red dwarf star (class M), Teegarden's Star is located only 12 l-yr from Earth's Sol system. Planet Teegarden (formerly Teegarden b) has a robust atmosphere held by its strong internal magnetic field, and with its moderate climate and hydrostatic cycle, it was able to be terraformed once greenhouse gases were introduced. The Federation chose to build its headquarters on this planet because of its central location in the colonized human space and its proximity to the aforementioned hyper-knot. Since the planet's mass is nearly that of Earth, there is no need for artificial gravity. The only disconcerting physical feature is that the planet's close distance to its home star produces a synchronous rotational period of about 5 E-d., so on the star side, it is always daylight, but the far side always looks above, to a cold dark sky.

Landing on the principal spaceport, Indira Bhatia (named after the Federation's first High Governor), Alyie was met by an escort who flew her in an airbus to the Federation's headquarters. Flying at a low altitude, Alyie could survey Teegarden's landscapes which had Earth-like terrain with mountains, valleys and bodies of water. The complex that houses the administrative, financial, diplomatic and military units of the Federation is a mammoth multi-structure network referred to by Earth's ancient history scholars as Byzantine. Inside the complex were residential quarters for Federation officials, staff, guests and High Council members. Alyie's suite was spacious, comfortable and overlooked a human-made lake.

The pyramid that made up the governing structure of the Sidereal Federation started at its base on each human-settled planet, where citizens exercised self-determination in choosing leaders. The next layer up consisted of the Regional Councils in the ten different sectors of space which comprised a mix of elected and expert staff (scientists, engineers, military, diplomatic, mercantile and communications) members. The High Governor was elected by all citizens of the Federation and served a 10 E-yr term. Sidereal High Council members were elected in each sector (two High Council seats per), and then professional staff (two each) were chosen by the High Governor from the aforementioned fields above. (Overarching this entire structure was a Sidereal Federation Council that coordinated memberships and meetings.)

With 33 members (with the High Governor as Chair), Alyie reasoned that the Sidereal Federation High Council would be an unwieldy group to distinguish herself; she would have to bide her time to have her voice heard. She ate a quick breakfast (that was delivered outside her suite's door by a service bot), then washed in the power-jet shower. She dressed in her new uniform, which was a white double-breasted jacket buttoned at the top with the insignia of Rear Admiral pinned on the left chest panel. She wore the jacket over a white sleeveless undergarment. Her crisp white dress slacks were tightened by a black leather belt. After slipping into her black leather boots, she put on white leather gloves. Twirling her reddish hair back in a chignon and fastening the cap tightly on her head, she felt she was ready for this meeting.

Before leaving, Alyie made a quick video hyperlink call to Jaynis, who was in his office at the Université. Seeing her on his screen, he immediately stood up in mock attention and saluted.

"Wow. Are you impressive or not? I fear for those unsuspecting Council members. They don't know what they're in for with you now a member."

"Oh shut up. But wish me luck."

"I wish you much more but anyway - bonne chance."

CHAPTER 6.

Taking the lift to the 15th floor of the Sidereal Federation Headquarters building, Alyie was escorted into the spacious conference room that was dominated by an angular four-sided table. On the surrounding dark paneled wooden walls were holographic images of past High Governors. Large windows gave a panoramic view of the Teegarden landscape. Most of the 30 odd High Council members were either seated or congregating around the table. Alyie could see they represented a wide range of humankind in terms of race, gender and culture. When High Governor Ji-hoon Park entered, all took their pre-arranged seats. As Alyie scanned the Council, she realized that the High Governor was the only one present she knew personally, but from the names on the table in front of each seated member, she was familiar with the credentials and reputations of several.

High Governor Park called the meeting to order and introduced those who were beginning new terms, including Alyie. "I would like everyone to welcome Rear Admiral Starstriker, whose exploits, I am sure, are well known to most of you."

As Alyie stood up, she received some tepid smiles and greetings from the assembly. She mused to herself, "I am going to have to prove my cred to this group, for sure."

With the introductions concluded, the High Governor began the business of the meeting.

"I have called the High Council together because of the tremendous news that is about to be disseminated across the Federation. There has been the detection of a sentient civilization in space. Autonomous probes traveling in the 61 Virginis system, approximately 28 l-yr from Earth, picked up a signal that has been confirmed of unnatural origin. The frequency and the modulation was from no known physical source. We can't say if the civilization is active or whether this transmission is an archival remnant. "

"Excuse me, High Governor," interrupted General Raphael Rodriguez. "Isn't that system surrounded by dust clouds?" General Rodriquez was a stout middle-aged man of dark hair and complexion with thick eyebrows and a black mustache.

High Governor Park deferred from answering this query. Instead, he turned over the briefing to High Council member Dr. Daiyu Lee, a planetary scientist. Dr. Lee, a petite black-haired woman of middle age and pale skin, began by responding to General Rodriquez.

"Yes General, that had made detection of the signal previously impossible. But the recent probes were able to navigate through the dust and debris to receive the signal which they have identified; it originates from a small planetary body orbiting close to the primary star. Spectroscopy has revealed that the planet is rocky with nearly Earth-like mass and a dense CO_2 atmosphere."

As Dr. Lee was speaking, she projected from her implant in the center of the conference table a holographic image of the 61 Virginis system and a computer rendition of the planet.

"Have the probes sent a message to whoever is living on the surface?" asked Jonathan Eubanks, a trade representative.

"As of this date, there has been no response from the planet in terms of a return message. However, there has been a more direct reaction to the probes."

"And what might that be, Dr. Lee?" asked Alastair Cromwell, a tall, angular man of pale complexion with piercing blue eyes. Mr. Cromwell was a past Regional Governor and was currently serving as the Deputy High Governor.

"The first probe we sent went quiet about 2 E-m ago. A follow up was launched soon after and followed the same pattern of being able to penetrate the system's dust clouds, receive signals from the planetary surface, and then go dead after transmitting a response."

"Dr. Lee," General Rodriquez queried, "do you consider that the cessation of the probes' communication systems were caused by a hostile act?"

"General, that is a difficult question to ascertain, but the fact that two probes launched in different time frames suffered the same consequences after trying to message the planet, leads one to believe that their termination was intentional."

"So from this briefing are we to conclude that whatever civilization past or present exists on this planet, it is belligerent to any outside attempts at contact."

"If that is so, should we consider the loss of the probes an act of war?" added Alastair Cromwell.

Alyie felt she could not restrain herself any longer as she feared the direction this discussion was heading.

"I do not think we can presume hostility from whoever lives on this planet. The civilization may have an autonomous defense system that responds automatically once a UFO penetrates within a certain critical distance from the surface. Also, the signals the probes are transmitting may not be in the anticipated spectrum the reception mechanism the planet is using to scan for messages."

"Well Rear Admiral Starstriker, how do you think we can determine their intentions?" glared Alastair Cromwell, obviously annoyed at Alyie's conciliatory evaluation of the situation.

"I see three options. The first is to leave whoever or whatever is there alone. The second is to send another probe with a broader range of transmitting frequencies, and the third is to launch an expedition in which we attempt to make contact in person."

High Governor Park rejoined the discussion. "I think Admiral Starstriker is right in implying we need more information about this civilization. One of the primary objectives of the probe missions is to search for other life in space, so I reject, her first option. Sending a third probe, and having it suffer the same consequence will not provide any new insight. Therefore, I propose we launch a mission to the 61 Viriginis system."

"Will this be a diplomatic or military mission, High Governor?" asked General Rodriquez.

"I presume it would be primarily diplomatic with enough firepower to dissuade any hostile intentions by the aliens."

"Let's provide strength in depth," declared High Council member Singh Khan, a communications specialist. "What do you recommend, General?"

"I suggest we send three fully armed starcruisers."

High Governor Park then spoke. "This is a mission of high importance that will provide great visibility across the Federation. We may be on the verge of answering the age old question of whether humanity is the lone sentient species in the galaxy. However, there are many unknowns, and, therefore, high risks are entailed. I want to have a cross-section of this High Council represented, but I will ask for volunteers."

Immediately, Alastair Cromwell and General Rodriquez volunteered for the mission. Alyie feared their aggressive intentions, so, somewhat against her better judgment, she spoke up. "High Governor, I would like to volunteer for the mission, and I will offer members of my Valkyrie Squad to fly the spacecraft."

"Thank you Admiral Starstriker, I was hoping you would be part of this endeavor. Your Valkyrie Squad is most welcome."

However, General Rodriquez struck a disgruntled note saying, "The craft that Deputy Governor Cromwell and I will be traveling on will be staffed by veteran flyers that I'll select. We have no need of the Valkyrie."

"As you wish, General," High Governor Park responded.

With High Council members Dr. Lee and Mr. Khan also volunteering, the crews of the three spacecraft headed to the 61 Virginis system began to form.

CHAPTER 7.

There was a great deal of excitement across human space in the ensuing E-w after the news broke of the discovery of an alien civilization. The expedition to what was now called Planet Omega X received enormous publicity, and the "Principal Investigators", Alastair Cromwell and General Rodriquez, as they dubbed themselves, were frequently quoted on the gravity of this mission. Alyie did not escape the focus of the media's attention. Being an acclaimed Federation hero and also young and attractive, she was the vibrant face of the Mission to Omega X. Reluctantly, she consented to interviews, always with her four Valkyrie members present. Her responses to questions always tried to counter the bellicose pronouncements made by the Deputy Governor and the General. Alyie stressed the need to understand this civilization through communication before any assessment was made of their intentions.

Three starcruisers were re-christened the Niña, the Pinta, and the Santa Maria, after the ships Christopher Columbus employed to sail across the Atlantic Ocean of Earth in the late 15th century (CE) to discover what was then called the New World (actually, he landed on islands in the Caribbean Sea). Alyie was Commander of Niña, but she had Zarah Khoury and Wang Li serve as pilots. Zarah had taken the place of Ginetta Jiang in the Valkyrie Squad, who was killed by renegade machine beings on the space station New Stanford. Petty Officer Li was the newest member of the Valkyrie Squad who also took part in the mission against the rogue machines. Other crew members of Niña were Singh Khan, exobiologist Dr. Ruth Breyer, Ambassador Mateo Santiago and two security officers.

The Pinta had Olga Fercouska and Hollie Pederson as pilots with Dr. Lee, technology specialist Sanford Mason, two diplomatic attachés and two military personnel. Finally, Cromwell and Rodriquez were joined in Santa Maria by linguist Dr. Daphne Fugo. The remainder of the crew were soldiers from the General's command, two of which piloted the ship.

Since Mission to Omega X was deemed a diplomatic venture primarily, Deputy High Governor Cromwell was the lead, but General Rodriquez and Rear Admiral Starstriker shared the military command. The three starcruisers were augmented with enhanced weaponry, including long-range laser cannons and fusion bombs.

Alyie had the four Valkyrie Squad members dressed in their body-fitting dark blue flight suits, black helmets and tall black boots while she wore her white Admiral's uniform. She also carried a laser pistol in a holster secured by the leather belt she wore over her double-breasted jacket. Farewells were made to all, and there was great fanfare to the launching of this mission. Alyie's parents and Jaynis wished her well, while Alyie played down the danger, saying that the main goal was peaceful - to make contact with a non-human society, although deep inside, Alyie harbored fears that this would turn out all wrong.

On the first of the new Earth month, the Niña, the Pinta and the Santa Maria took off from the launch site on Teegarden and began the Mission to Omega X.

CHAPTER 8.

On the short 2 E-d to the hyper-knot, Alyie used the time to make sure all the crew members aboard Niña were familiar with each other. Zarah Khoury and Wang Li, of course, were comrades and had quickly developed a strong friendship. Both were small of stature, dark-eyed with black hair, but Zarah's skin was brown while Wang's was pale. Singh Khan was a serious-minded gentleman who was busy devising different algorithms that he hoped would elicit a response from the aliens, while for Dr. Ruth Breyer, this mission was the pinnacle of her long career in exobiology. Ambassador Mateo Santiago and Alyie quickly developed a good rapport. She found the Ambassador witty and very knowledgeable about Federation affairs. Mateo's charming accent made conversing with him delightful. Alyie also had to admit to herself that Mateo's dark sultry looks with his dark brown hair, large brown eyes, tanned skin and trim build were very pleasant on the eyes. The security officers – Matthew Kingslon and Xi Meng, were veterans who knew their duties and were easy to get along with.

Once the spacecraft reached the hyper-knot, Alyie sent the command for all three to enter, and they duly proceeded through the "wormhole". Parameters were pre-set to navigate through hyperspace to reach the nearest hyper-knot exit to the 61 Virginis system. Some of the passengers, such as Ambassador Santiago, were not familiar with collapsed spacetime, so Alyie was happy to hold Matteo's hand and stroke his shoulder once she noticed he was experiencing discomfort. Eventually, all three spaceships successfully came out of hyperspace and then continued their journey non-relativistically to the destination.

CHAPTER 9.

The 61 Virginis was a G-class star, and its bright yellow light shined in the dark sky. As the spacecraft approached Planet Omega X, the surrounding dust clouds came into view, completely obscuring the planet. Alyie ordered that everyone's speed be reduced as each ship carefully navigated its way through the debris. There were some hits by passing asteroids, but none of the spacecraft suffered any consequential damage. Once free of the belt of dust and debris, Omega X was seen with a thick blue-white atmosphere. The spacecraft fired their retrograde rockets to have a sufficiently small speed to be captured by Omega X's gravitational pull and assumed a high orbit. As pre-arranged, they assumed positions at three of Omega X's Lagrangian points, which were nearly stable orbits with respect to the planet and 61 Virginis. Pinta was at L1 on the near side of Omega X facing the star; Santa Maria was at L2 on the planet's other side. Finally, Niña was positioned at L4, 60° in orbit away from the other two spacecraft, where with the help of Mr. Khan, Alyie could coordinate communication among all three vessels.

Searching Omega X space found no trace of the previously launched probes, which led to the inescapable conclusion that they had been destroyed. General Rodriquez was the first to voice his opinion.

"We need to conclude that the destruction of our non-invasive probes was a hostile act by these aliens and communicate to them that if they try to attack us, we will respond very aggressively."

Alyie countered by saying, "General Rodriquez, I agree that we first need to communicate to whoever or whatever is on that planet, but I don't agree that we should immediately take a bellicose posture without knowing the cause of the probes' disappearance."

Her position was seconded by Mateo Santiago, who declared, "Our prime objective in this mission is to make contact with this civilization, and hopefully, establish peaceful relations. I do not think giving them an ultimatum is the best way to start a negotiation. What do you think, Deputy Governor Cromwell?"

"As the head of this mission, I have to assent that we should first try to find common ground with these aliens, but they have rebuffed our initial overtures in a most prejudicial manner, so I am unclear what kind of peaceful relations we can achieve in this mission."

"At least let's try to contact them with a neutral message announcing our interest in making contact," Alyie answered. "Can Mr. Khan, Dr. Fugo and Mr. Mason work together to send messages that may elicit a friendly response?"

During the voyage to Omega X, Singh Khan, Daphne Fugo, and Sanford Mason combined their respective skills in communications, language and technology to create a regiment of messages using different coding systems, bandwidth frequencies and phonetics. With Alyie's consent, they began to implement these algorithms. Signals were sent from Santa Maria to the planet. After two E-d, there was still no response from Omega X.

"I think we have waited long enough," declared Deputy Governor Cromwell. "I am ordering General Rodriquez to alter our orbit to fly closer to the planet's surface."

"I am advising all spacecraft to commence a decelerating orbit," said General Rodriquez. "We need to find out what is going on down there."

"General, I would not advise all three ships to do this. We need at least one to serve as the mission control and communication link to the group," said Alyie, feeling not at all comfortable with this stratagem.

"As you wish Rear Admiral," sniped General Rodriquez. "Why don't you stay safe and sound at L4 while we conduct this mission. Tell your girls on-board Pinta to follow my lead."

"As you say General. Olga and Hollie, decrease your orbit in accordance with what the Santa Maria is doing on the planet's other side."

"Yes ma'am," was Olga's prompt reply.

CHAPTER 10.

As the two spacecraft descended out of their stable orbits, they encountered resistance in the form of heat-seeking missiles launched from two low orbit satellites that were previously undetected. The force fields on Pinta and Santa Maria easily withstood this initial assault. General Rodriguez then ordered the shields down as the positions of the satellites were identified. Immediately after, under the General's command, laser cannons were fired, destroying the alien satellites.

Singh Khan aboard Niña had established the communication link between the three spacecraft, and he presently overheard Alastair Cromwell declaring, "Now they know what their up against. General, will you give the order to launch the fusion bombs to the surface?"

"Yes, Governor. You have your orders Pinta. Direct your bombs to the lower hemisphere while we on Santa Maria will saturate the upper hemisphere."

Alyie could not let this go unchallenged. "Deputy Governor and General Rodriguez, I don't think launching nuclear weapons to the planet's surface is a proportionate response to their satellite assault. We have demonstrated our capability to defend ourselves. This informs whoever directed the attack that we have sufficient firepower. I suggest we wait and try again to contact them, informing them of our non-hostile intentions. Bombarding the surface at this point in our mission is a blatant act of war with us as the invaders. Do we really want to present ourselves this way?"

"Rear Admiral Starstriker, I did not expect this timidity from you. I thought you were a hero of the Federation," snapped Alastair Cromwell.

"Deputy Governor, heroism takes many forms, including knowing when not to use deadly force."

"Your objection to my order is noted," said General Rodriquez. "Please stay in your position, but on my command, Pinta, commence your attack."

Alyie then received a coded message on a high-security Valkyrie Squadron channel from Olga on the Pinta, asking for guidance. Alyie, not wanting to implicate her Co-Commander in refusing to obey an order, counseled Olga to assume an offensive position but not to launch her weapons unless indicated by Alyie.

Soon after, a series of missiles were launched from Santa Maria, dispersing over the planet's upper half. As the bombs landed and the inevitable mushroom-shaped clouds sprouted in different locations, a burst of light was seen emanating from a point on the surface. The finely directed ray surged through space, found Santa Maria, made an impact, and in one flash blew the spacecraft completely apart.

Alyie was stunned by this display of power and the utter destruction this ray wrought. Quickly, composing herself, she shouted to Olga and Hollie aboard Pinta. "Retreat, Retreat to L1."

Olga quickly fired her engines, and Pinta was brought back to its previous position, awaiting its fate from the enemy below.

CHAPTER 11.

It was hard to comprehend that a single ray could emanate from the planet's surface and travel that far in space to strike a starcruiser what such power to utterly destroy it. The remaining members of the Mission to Omega X were at a collective loss to account for what had happened and were not in agreement on what their next step should entail.

Singh Khan, Sanford Mason and Dr. Daiyu Lee were all in accord that the mission should be aborted and the remaining ships return back. "Whatever exists down there obviously doesn't want us," said Mason. "I agree," added Khan. "I don't think there should be anymore sacrifices to making contact with such a hostile civilization." "Before we leave, we should request Fleet Command send a full armada to destroy this planet," said Dr. Lee.

Olga Fercouska countered quickly, saying, "The problem is that we were the aggressors, and their response can be considered just defensive in nature. With all due respect, we initiated the hostilities."

"However, we cannot let the destruction of a Federation spacecraft go unanswered," said Hollie Pederson, Olga's co-pilot aboard Pinta.

With the death of Deputy Governor Cromwell and General Rodriguez, the chain of command fell to Mateo Santiago as the chief diplomat and Alyie as the military head.

"Protocol demands we contact the Sidereal Federation Space Command to apprise them of this situation. I am sending a hyperlink message now. Let's await their counsel," was Alyie's cautionary conclusion.

Transmitting the message in this region of space took some doing as there were not as many micro hyper-knots identified as in human space. After an agonizing wait of six E-hr., High Governor Park's voice was beamed aboard both vessels.

"We are all grieving over the loss of the Santa Maria and its crew members. The death of Deputy Governor Cromwell, General Rodriquez, Dr. Fugo and those brave soldiers will be a tragedy long remembered in Sidereal Federation history. Admiral Starstriker and Ambassador Santiago, I order you to withdraw as soon as you are able. Under no circumstances are you to put the remaining starcruisers at risk of destruction. Once you return to Federation HQ, you will give a full report to the High Council. After due consideration, we will decide what action needs to be taken."

"Thank you, High Governor," Alyie responded. "As military leader of the Mission to Omega X, I assure you both Niña and Pinta will no longer be in harm's way."

Despite the High Governor's order to abandon the mission, Alyie still harbored some misgivings. She received support from Dr. Ruth Breyer, who was also against leaving.

"This may be a once in a lifetime opportunity to establish contact with a different life form," Dr. Breyer argued. "I know it is risky, but I have spent all my life searching for other sentient beings. Now we have apparently found them right below us. To just leave without making contact seems pointless. I think we should keep trying in the most non-invasive ways to reach them. I, for one, am willing to risk my life."

"No, Dr. Breyer, you are a civilian and your life is not expendable," said Alyie. "However, I agree we should make at least one more attempt at contact. I will follow High Governor Park's order to not put the spacecraft at risk, but we have a four passenger space pod, Chastity, on board, that I plan to take to the surface and try to reason with this civilization that, notwithstanding that nuclear attack, the Sidereal Federation comes in peace."

At Alyie's proposal, there was vehement opposition. Most believed this was a suicidal mission. However, Mateo Santiago agreed with Alyie, saying, "Yes, I believe Admiral Starstriker is correct in making this last attempt. In fact, as diplomatic head, I approve her mission under one condition."

"And what would that be, Ambassador Santiago?" Alyie wondered.

"That I accompany you to the surface."

CHAPTER 12.

In short order, Chastity was prepared for the mission to the surface. Alyie and Mateo donned heavy spacesuits, and their helmets were infused with filtered oxygen as scans of Omega X's atmosphere showed it unbreathable for humankind. Their implants were augmented with universal translators hoping one of the 1000 different languages stored would be able to communicate with the civilization they hoped to encounter. Chastity had no weapons, and both Alyie and Mateo were unarmed to signify their peaceful intentions.

With farewells to those remaining on the starcruisers, Alyie transferred command to Olga, saying, "If you do not hear from us in an E-d, leave Omega X space and return to Federation HQ. I will try to contact you, but if I am unable, assume the worst."

With all flight checks completed, and both Alyie and Mateo secure on board, the space pod left Niña and began a spiraling descent that took it to the planet's surface. Alyie navigated Chastity so that it landed near the point where the missile that destroyed Santa Maria was launched. The surface was solid, and the landing was without incident. Stepping out of the pod, Alyie and Mateo were confronted with a dark, turbulent sky that made seeing difficult. There were no signs of civilization or vegetation in view. However, as Alyie scanned through her infra-red binoculars the panorama, she detected in one direction a curtain of dense gray fog. With the binoculars fixed on it, she perceived the fog was advancing steadily toward her and Mateo. Turning toward her companion, she declared, "Brace yourself, I think our hosts are approaching."

Unconsciously, Alyie and Mateo held hands as they each raised their respective free hand in a gesture of peace. Soon they were enveloped in the fog, which made visibility impossible. Alyie soon afterward detected a synthetic sounding voice that seemed to be coming inside of her, saying,

"Why are you here and why did you attack us?"

"I am Rear Admiral Alyie Starstriker, and this is Ambassador Mateo Santiago from the Sidereal Federation. Our space probes had detected your presence, and we were sent as part of a delegation to establish peaceful relations. We apologize for the hostilities and any damage we have caused."

The voice responded. "It appears that your kind has suffered much more than we have. You must understand we need to defend ourselves when you launched those weapons to our surface."

"Yes, there were some hasty actions on our part, and we have paid dire consequences for them. Can we start anew on more amicable terms?"

"We are listening," replied the voice in Alyie's head.

"First of all," Alyie asked, "who are you and how are you able to communicate with me?"

Again the voice responded inside Alyie's head. "I do not know if you can give us a name. We do not refer to ourselves or distinguish our existence from any other, what you call, civilization. If you need to put a label on us, then call us Omegi. That is what you have named this world, am I not correct? As for conversing with you, we have the capacity to connect with your mind and send messages to it. We have also scanned your memories and have acclimated ourselves with your cultural history and language."

"Does my partner Ambassador Santiago have the facility to receive and communicate with you?"

"If you like, we can open a channel for him. That is the correct gender is it not as we see your species is bisexual?"

"Yes, thank you."

"Also, we can alter the surrounding conditions, so you need not remain in those clumsy containment vessels."

With that, the immediate vista around Alyie and Mateo cleared, and her scan indicated that there was an Earth-like pocket of breathable gas surrounding them. Alyie gestured to Mateo that it was safe, and they both took off their suits and helmets and were able to breathe freely in the clean air.

Mateo, collecting himself, addressed the fog. "You seem to be aware of us and our human history, but we do not know anything about your civilization. Can you help us know you better?"

The voice spoke now both to Alyie and Mateo. "We are the products of a culture long forgotten that evolved from what you call biological organisms to a fusion of organic and non-organic intelligences. The synthesis of biological and what you call machine beings occurred in what you would reckon to be Earth-billions of years ago. This stage lasted many millennia until it evolved into a purely informational or thought stage. We no longer had need for material bodies, and we became a collective mind. Finally, our ancestors mastered the ability to transfer thoughts (or instructions) into matter in which we manipulated our surrounding resources into action. For example, the weapons we directed at your spacecraft were all, so to speak, conjured by our mind, and turned into reality. We can just about manifest almost anything the raw matter-energy around us can provide."

CHAPTER 13.

As Alyie and Mateo were standing in the air pocket with the shell of fog surrounding them, Alyie asked, "Is there anything, as a gesture of good faith, we as representatives of the Sidereal Federation can do to show our benevolent intentions?"

"We have evolved to be completely self-sufficient and self-sustaining so we don't need any transfer of technology or commerce with humans. However, there is a personal request we have, if you don't think it is too indiscrete."

"Please ask," said Mateo. "I am sure Admiral Starstriker and myself will do our best to accommodate you."

"It has been so long since our kind has been corporeal. We would like to feel what it is like, if you don't mind. We assure you; no harm will come."

Alyie and Mateo looked at each other with some apprehension but slowly nodded to the Omegi's request.

As the fog advanced around and inside her, Alyie could feel herself being groped, but the sensation was not unpleasant. She felt the equivalent of a body massage as the entity first touched her face and scanned her eyes, mouth and ears. Then it moved down her neck to her shoulders, caressing her breast and loins. Finally, she felt the fondling in her arms, legs and finally inside her boots. Gazing at her side to Mateo, Alyie could tell he was experiencing a similar feeling of soothing and pleasure as the alien entity explored their respective bodies.

After an unknown period of time, the sensation ceased. Both Alyie and Mateo heard inside themselves the voice again.

"Thank you for allowing us to come in contact once again with a material essence. We as a collective have not had sensual pleasure, for what you would reckon as Earth billions of years, and we had forgotten the joy of physicality. We believe our business with you is done. Is there anything you request from us?"

Mateo answered. "Yes, we need to report back to our leaders of the Sidereal Federation. Is there a message we can convey to them from you?"

"Well stated, Ambassador Mateo. We will now send greetings to your leaders through the implants you and Admiral Starstriker have in your foreheads. When you return back to your civilization activate the signal with the code we are sending you, and they will be able to hear our recording."

"Do you have any final requests to us before we return to our ship in orbit?" asked Alyie.

There was a short period of silence, but then Alyie and Mateo heard the voice saying, "This may be asking a great deal, but we enjoyed that contact with both of you. If you could return again, we would be most grateful."

"We will try," said Mateo.

"Thank you for receiving us and forgiving our transgression into your space," Alyie responded.

"You're welcome, Admiral Starstriker. You and Ambassador Santiago are both exemplary members of humankind and very brave for coming to meet us."

The fog then receded, but the air pocket remained as the two humans walked back to Chastity.

Getting once again into their suits and helmets, they boarded the spacecraft. Alyie sent Olga a message to prepare Niña for their arrival.

On the way up, Mateo turned to Alyie to express, "Wow, that was some encounter. By the way, you were magnificent." Alyie returned the compliment saying, "You were also pretty composed. The Diplomatic Corps has a great asset in you."

"What did you think of that mind-body interchange?" said Mateo. "It touched me spiritually."

"Well, I was definitely touched," chimed Alyie. "I'm not sure if it was spiritual."

CHAPTER 14.

Once back aboard Niña, Alyie and Mateo were besieged with questions about their meeting with the Omegi. They told all that happened, but Alyie was anxious to return to the Federation HQ and soon gave the order for both ships to prepare to leave their respective orbits around Omega X.

The return flight was uneventful as they left the 61 Virginis system, jumped through the hyper-knot and navigated back to the Teagarden's Star system once out of hyperspace. Landing on Planet Teagarden, members of both the Niña and the Pinta were escorted immediately to headquarters, where an emergency meeting of the Sidereal High Council was convened.

In the High Council chamber, Alyie and Mateo jointly led the discussion of their Mission to Omega X. Any support for retaliation for the destruction of the Santa Maria and the death of all its crew members on the part of the High Council members dissipated with the realization that Federation forces were the aggressors, and the Omegi acted in self-defense. Finally, Alyie and Mateo activated the code to their implants and displayed on the wall screens in the chamber the message from the Omegi.

First seen was an image of the fog that Alyie and Mateo encountered on Omega X. Then, the voice that spoke inside their heads was heard.

"Humans, you may call us Omegi. We are beings who have long shed our material essence and now are a collective consciousness that resides on the planet you have named Omega X. Our evolution to our current form would be tedious to detail in this short message but know we had developed the ability to transfer thoughts to things. Everything we need is at our disposal. We have no wish to explore, communicate, colonize or expand our dominion, as you seem to do. The irony of being able to do anything makes us want to do nothing. Therefore, our interactions with your civilization will be minimal. We did enjoy the company of Admiral Starstriker and Ambassador Santiago, so if they could be assigned as liaisons between us and the Sidereal Federation that would be welcomed. In a future meeting, we can share with them our history and prepare your civilization for what may come."

"If your destiny is similar to us, be forewarned. Gaining knowledge through the union of humans and machines, as you seem to be doing comes with a cost. Yes, you will expand your intellectual capability, lighten your work load, increase your control over your environment, but you will lose the satisfaction of personal accomplishment."

"If you then take the next step as we did to pure thought, you will master everything, but never again experience the exhilaration of success, because you will never know failure. Never again will you be happy, because you will never be sad. Never again will you feel love, because you will never know its absence. And worst of all, you will lose the joy of living, because your life will never end."

Coda

Alyie was finishing getting into her formal white dress uniform when Jaynis arrived at her suite. He had flown to Planet Teegarden to attend with her the memorial ceremony for the fallen members of the Santa Maria. While giving her kisses, he provided last-minute assistance as she buttoned her jacket, legged into her boots and donned her white gloves. Alyie's parents, Tanita and Alex, would also be at the ceremony, so it was a reunion of sorts, although for a somber occasion. After the memorial, Alyie was going on leave. She and Jaynis would return to their townhouse in Paris for an E-w of free time that she couldn't wait to begin.

At the Memorial Service were all the Sidereal High Council members, dignitaries from all the regions of the Sidereal Federation, and family and friends of the deceased. In addition, all the surviving members of the Mission to Omega X served as the honor guard.

Alyie and Mateo were in the front row with High Governor Park and planted wreaths on the memorial plaques for the crew of the Santa Maria.

The High Governor's remarks were concise and comforting.

"We honor these men and women who have paid the ultimate sacrifice for the Sidereal Federation. They lost their lives to further our understanding and knowledge of the cosmos. For this we are eternally grateful."

Afterward, Mateo came over to Alyie, who was chatting with Jaynis, Tanita and Alex and her former Valkyrie teammates. Alyie introduced Mateo to Jaynis and her parents. She took notice that her mother was taken by his striking looks that were only amplified by the smart full dress dark blue suit, white shirt, blue tie and polished black shoes he wore.

Kissing Tanita's hand, Mateo flashed a charming smile saying, "Commander Starbright, your daughter and I had a surreal experience on Omega X. We may have had what used to be called a ménage à trois with an alien."

Seeing Jaynis arch an eyebrow at this, Alyie quickly tried to defuse the situation. "Mateo, I wouldn't raise the experience to that level. I just felt the Omegi were a little horny. After all, when was the last time they had a little fun. A few billion years-ago."

After the laughter died down, Alyie, Jaynis and her parents excused themselves and departed for a long-desired welcome back luncheon at one of Teegarden's finest dining establishments.

THE INVICTUS

PROLOGUE

Earth-Day 185, 2560 CE.

Out of the red dawn sky, they came like birds of prey descending from above. The primary star Gliese 1061 shone dimly, obscured by the smoke and fire from the bombardments. The Emir of Mongoti's forces on the ground fired their weapons full bore, but the attack squadron was undaunted. Before landing in the vale, the Peregrine Falcon Group had lost one-third of their number, but that did not abate their advance. Jumping out of their ships, they rushed forward, led by the fiery leader, Commander Seth Bullwark. He exhorted them forward, waving his bandana, oblivious to the rocket fragments all around him. Climbing over the containment wall, thus gaining entry inside the enemy's perimeter, Bullwark launched an incendiary bomb, blowing the fortress' door wide open. At his urging, the rest of the attack squad rushed inside. In fierce fighting with the Emir's honor guard, they advanced slowly to the palace steps. Once there, Bullwark rushed up, shooting with his laser pistol all who stood in his path and hurling thermite grenades to blast open the huge doors of the palace. As he ran down the long marble hallway to the Throne Chambre, the thumps of his tall brown leather boots could be heard reverberating along the curving ornate palace walls. Reaching his destination, Bullwark opened the stately door and, peering inside, saw the Emir and his concubine sitting serenely on their throne chairs. Standing erect to his full two-meter height, he strode arrogantly forward down the Chambre, approaching the throne. Brandishing Liberator, his family sword, Bullwark planted his feet firmly on the cold stone steps, removed his helmet while activating his translation implants and with a wry smile, stated succinctly,

"Your Highness and my Lady, I am Commander Seth Bullwark. Welcome to the Sidereal Federation."

CHAPTER 1.

Earth-Day 200, 2610 CE.

Alyie Starstriker gazed into the 3-D desk mirror of her Martian suite, looking at the auto-bot-created curls of her newly combed reddish-blonde hair. Satisfied with the shape and the luster of her locks, the eyeliner accentuating her beautiful green eyes, and her creamy complexion, she turned to see her mother, Tanita Starbright, straightening Alyie's bridal gown. In a few E-hr., Alyie would pledge eternal commitment to Jaynis Bottombrook, her childhood friend and companion. Even though both she and Jaynis now resided on Earth, they both wanted their exchange of vows to take place on Mars, where they had both grown up. The "wedding" would take place in a cavern where there was enough low-lying oxygen to have the ceremony outside. In the current summertime, the temperature would be warm enough to forego special insulating outerwear.

The dress was a floor-length gown of white lace with a modest neckline and a white ivory sash around her waist. She complemented the sash by wearing ivory-colored high heels. Alyie wore the gold "choker" chain around her neck that her parents had given her for her 26th birthday, approximately 2 E-yr ago. Since she was a Rear Admiral in the Sidereal Federation, Alyie could have worn her dress uniform to the ceremony, but she wanted to look more feminine for this event, and her current position on the Sidereal High Council was more civilian than military.

As Tanita was carefully adjusting Alyie's lace veil on her forehead, her daughter could tell from the worry lines across Tanita's face that her mother was disturbed.

"Is there something wrong with my looks, my dress, the ceremony? You were never good, Mother, at disguising your feelings."

"Oh, Alyie it is not with you or Jaynis. I am overjoyed you are pledging yourselves to each other and so is your father. Its news from

Nespar and Seth Bullwark's involvement in the coup attempt that distresses me."

Alyie recalled from a recent communication in her implants from the Sidereal High Council that there was a disputed election on Planet Nespar in the Procyon system. It appears the opposition tribe to the planet's rulers had claimed fraud and had taken direct action by laying siege to the King's palace. They had apparently contracted a private paramilitary force headed by retired Commander Seth Bullwark to advance their cause. Bullwark was one of the most decorated officers in the Sidereal Space Command and a legend to many. Tanita had served under him when she was just starting in the Fleet Command and had long considered Seth the most significant person in her professional life. Alyie also knew Bullwark personally and always enjoyed his company and the tales of missions long gone by that he regaled her with.

"Mother, it is my impression that the Sidereal High Council has sent a diplomatic envoy to Nespar to investigate the election and adjudicate the dispute. With the Federation's involvement, perhaps the situation can be diffused without any violence."

"It is just that Seth is such a headstrong person, and once he gets it in his mind to commit to something there is no stopping him."

"But Mother, isn't he rather advanced in Earth-years?"

"By my reckoning he is nearly 90, but the last time we spoke he was as virile as ever, boasting about his recent conquests. (I am sure nano-bots are sustaining his libido.) Seth thinks he is still the swashbuckling soldier that assaulted Mongoti some 50 E-yr. ago and forced the Emir to enter the Sidereal Federation."

"Commander Bullwark always considered himself the hero for the underserved. Perhaps, Mother, this is why he joined the cause of the Kunari tribe on Nespar."

"I just don't want his legacy to be sullied by anything that violates proper Sidereal Federation protocols."

"The Federation abides by The Act of Self-Determination which allows each planet to decide on its own governing structure and leaders. The envoy has been sent to mediate the dispute, not impose the Federation's will. Don't worry, I will keep you up to date on the mission. But now I need to get ready. I don't want Jaynis to have any second thoughts if we are late to the ceremony."

CHAPTER 2.

Alyie and Jaynis' eternal commitment ceremony was a private affair. (All Federation media were barred by security force shields from covering the event.) In attendance were Alyie's parents, Tanita Starbright and Dr. Alex Striker; Jaynis' folks, Talia Silverfoot and Chadwick Bottombrook and his sister Bernice; Alyie's former Valkyrie Squadron members, Olga Fercouska, Hollie Pederson, Zarah Khoury and Wang Li; Alyie's mentors, Ambassador Felicity Erickson and Admiral Steely Cranshaw; Jaynis' colleague Dr. Seo-jun Gwan and Alyie's friends when she was a cadet at the Fleet Academy, Igor Melkova and Revita Jadeite, crown princess of Planet Kanva.

Martian Premier Dendri Choudhoury presided. Over a typical orange-red sky, the wedding party gathered in an underground gulley where a river once ran. A canvas canopy that fluttered in the Martian wind shielded everyone present from the dust as synthetic music from the Earth's 19th CE century played in the background. Jaynis wore what in olden Earth times would be called a dark gray morning suit with a waistcoat, a black tie and shiny black shoes.

Premier Choudhoury began the ceremony with a few words of welcome. Then Alyie spoke,

"Jaynis, you were my friend from childhood, you became my colleague in adult life and now you are my eternal partner. In the words of St. Augustine, a 4th century (CE) Bishop of Hippo, 'Good is the mind of a friend in the sweetness of agreement and the onfidence of love'."

Jaynis followed with the poem Midway by 20th century (CE) author Julian Drachman,

"Look never back to see the distance traveled,

Lest the heart grow weak

Seeing how little you have climbed above the high-road

Up toward the peak.

But let your feet taste the fresh, homely sod,

Swish through brown drifts of leaves by Fall wind scattered,

As though each rock were a step towards the throne of God,

As though life mattered."

Alyie and Jaynis then exchanged gold rings that were designed in Paris but were fashioned by a 3-D fabricator on Mars. Premier Choudhury proclaimed:

"Let us join in wishing Alyie and Jaynis a life together filled with joy and love. With this eternal commitment they are joined – once they were two, now they are one."

Then the Premier evoked the time-honored phrase, "You may now kiss."

With Alyie and Jaynis' heartfelt embrace, joyous shouts rang out in the thin air over the Martian valley.

CHAPTER 3.

Those who witnessed the ceremony were flown by an airbus to the Ray Bradbury Hotel in Ares, the Martian capital. They were joined that evening by several others in the hotel's grand ballroom for a festive reception that included a four-piece ensemble that played contemporary music. The program started with a toast (with champagne from harvested grapes from Earth) made jointly by Seo-jun Gwan and Bernice Bottombrook. Then Alyie and her father, Alex Striker, began the first dance.

As Alex held his daughter, he looked into her green eyes and said, "You have always made me proud, but today you are filling me with incredible joy."

"You and Mom have been the greatest parents. I can never thank you enough."

As others joined the father-daughter couple on the dance floor, the music played familiar pieces from different eras. Alyie eventually paired with Jaynis, who was admittedly uncomfortable moving his feet to the rhythm of the music. She had the opportunity to showcase her dancing skills when Alyie partnered with Princess Revita (Revi), with whom she had shared a suite at the Academy. The two young women impressed all with their choreography, panache and high spirits.

During the dinner, which included food grown in Martian greenhouses, people amiably chatted and told funny stories about Alyie and Jaynis. This bonhomie prevailed until Tanita Starbright came over to Alyie and Jaynis' table while they were laughing with Revi, Seo-jun, Bernice and Igor at a recollection of Alyie by the Princess. Tanita whispered in her daughter's ear that she needed to speak to her.

Excusing herself, Alyie and Tanita went to an enclosed balcony overlooking the Martian landscape. Alyie sensed she knew what was perturbing her mother.

"This is about Nespar and Seth Bullwark, isn't it, Mother?"

"Yes. The last thing I want is to ruin your special evening Alyie, but I just received a report on my implant that the situation has gotten worse. It appears Seth has taken the Federation envoy hostage and is demanding that he will not be released unless the election is ruled invalid. What has happened to him?"

"I am aware of this. Steely Cranshaw informed me of this troubling development after the ceremony. After conferring with him, I am going to put forward to the Sidereal High Council a proposal to form a team to investigate the election, and, if need be, go to Nespar to negotiate with the disputing tribes a reconciliation. If what you say about Seth Bullwark is true, he will need to be brought to justice. I am sorry Mother."

"I know he will need to face the consequences of his actions, but I would feel better if you are representing the Federation in dealing with him. Remember, Alyie that he was such a hero to us all."

"I will, but his heroics were at a time when the Federation was more tolerant of Seth's bravado and cavalier behavior."

CHAPTER 4.

Alyie woke early in the dim Martian light the next day. (Mars' diurnal rate being nearly the same as Earth's caused no adjustment in her bio-rhythms.) She wanted to learn as much as she could concerning the situation on Nespar before she contacted the Sidereal High Council. Accessing her implants, she found that Nespar was a circumbinary planet in the Proycon A-B star system, some 12 l-yr away. Orbiting far enough away from the two stars produced a stable orbit around the system's center of mass. Despite the separation, Nespar had a dry, hot climate due to the intense radiation from the F class white primary star Proycon A. The planet was massive enough to hold on to an atmosphere, but efforts to oxygenate the surface achieved limited success. There was some meager surface moisture from underground wells and infrequent rainstorms. The most characteristic features were mountains and vast stretches of windswept deserts littered with sand dunes and an occasional savannah.

Settled by humans after the robotic craft discovered its habitability some 120 E-yr ago, a tribal culture developed. Presently, people belonging to the ruling class were members of the Amhara, which comprised 40% of the planet's population. The rival tribe was the Kunari, with a 30% population. The remaining 30% were an eclectic mixture of nominal tribes and people of no affiliation who were born out of the union of people of different clans.

In the recent parliamentary election, which determines the throning of a king, the results favored the incumbent Amhara by a narrow margin. The Kunari claimed voter fraud and contested the result. King Adeloa Igwe nullified the challenge, ensuring his tribe's victory. After an E-w of protests, the Kunari brought in Seth Bullwark, who quickly was placed in charge of a militia that besieged the capital city, Napara.

The Sidereal Federation envoy, Ambassador Peter Bukanti, after arriving in Nespar, was apparently prepared to certify the Amhara tribe's victory when he was kidnapped by the rebel forces and held hostage at their stronghold in the Kibo Mountains.

Satisfied that she had a working knowledge of the situation on Nespar, Alyie poked her most reliable source of information – Jaynis, gently in the stomach.

"Wake up, my sweet newly-wed. I need assistance from your beautiful mind."

Slow to rouse himself, Jaynis had other desires when he became fully conscious than having to use his brain.

"Is this what wedded life is going to be like? If I knew you were just marrying me for my mind, I would have re-considered going through with the ceremony."

"Oh, be still. There is plenty of time for the other stuff, but I need to ask your advice. How would one go about fixing an election?"

Jaynis was perplexed, "Is that what you woke me up for? Why do you want to know that the day after our nuptial?"

"It's the crisis on Nespar. My mother wants me to intercede in the dispute to save Seth Bullwark's reputation. The side he has aligned with is claiming fraud."

"Alyie, there are many ways to fix an election, including having ineligible voters, discarded votes, and tampering with the counting process. The last may be the most likely, because it is the easiest to disguise, especially if the voting on Nespar is tabulated by micro-electronic processors.

"How would I be able to determine if there was that kind of chicanery in this election?"

"I know someone who specializes in cyber-security. He is Martin Shushauser, right here on Mars at my old institution, Chandrasekhar University. I gather he has done several consulting assignments for the

Federation that involve electronic tampering. Would you like me to contact him?"

"Yes, please, or should I say, yes, dear?"

Dr. Martin Shushauser took the local video call immediately. In his early 40 E-yr., he was a slender man with dark hair and bright brown eyes. Alyie introduced herself, although from her fame in the Federation, she was well known. She gave a brief description of the disputed election on Nespar. When asked, Shushauser agreed without hesitation to serve as a member of the investigation team Alyie was forming. She cautioned that this service probably meant that traveling to the embattled planet involved some personal danger, but he was undaunted by this prospect.

Next, she contacted Ambassador Mateo Santiago by a video hyperlink with whom she had worked before on the Mission to Omega X that made contact with a non-human civilization. Santiago, charming as ever, welcomed Alyie's call, saying, "Senora, congratulations are in order. That fellow Bottombrook is a most fortunate man. I am so envious."

"Thank you Mateo. But this is not a social conversation. I need your assistance on another mission of some delicacy."

Given the details, Mateo was eager to re-partner with Alyie.

Her final contacts were two Valkyrie Squad members, Deputy Commander Hollie Pederson and Lieutenant Wang Li, who would serve as pilots for this mission.

With her five-person team in place, Alyie was now ready to contact members of the Sidereal Federation High Council requesting a hyperlink emergency meeting concerning Nespar. But first, she needed to attend to Jaynis.

CHAPTER 5.

Even though the meeting she requested was by hyperlink, Alyie donned her dress white admiral's uniform. As soon as the session began, several Sidereal Federation High Council members expressed concern about the crisis on Nespar. High Governor Ji-hoon Park, a distinguished silver-haired gentleman, had new information. "It appears that the rebel forces, after taking Ambassador Bukanti hostage, have withdrawn from the capital and are dug in in their compound in the Kibo Mountains.

Admiral Steely Cranshaw, a strikingly handsome mature man with piercing blue eyes, who now also served on the High Council, asked, "Bullwark is commanding how many militias on Nespar?"

"Our intelligence scans estimate their forces to be about 300," said Rosa LoPresti, a communications specialist.

"How are they armed, Ms. LoPresti?" inquired Admiral Cranshaw.

"Our intel shows that they have conventional laser rifles, hand-held cannons and two autonomous armored vehicles. Although they assaulted the military compound outside of Napara, they were unable to secure more weapons."

"As you are all aware of," noted High Governor Park, The Act of Self-Determination forbids the Federation from interfering in a civilization's right to choose its own governance structure and leaders. Ambassador Bukanti was sent to Nespar as an interested third-party observer to their disputed election. His instructions were not to take sides in the controversy. Apparently, the Kunari, the opposition tribe, believed he was favoring the incumbent Amhara tribe, and on orders from the Kunari leader, Talib Masu, Seth Bullwark intercepted Ambassador Bukanti on his way from the governmental palace and now holds him captive."

"This is a violation of Federation law and a direct insult to time-honored diplomatic immunity," said High Council member Sigmund Fröether.

"This is why I have called a meeting of the High Council," Alyie responded. "I have a proposal to hopefully alleviate the situation on Nespar. I have formed a special team that will go with me to the planet and investigate fully the election results. Dr. Martin Shushauser, an expert on cyber security, has been engaged to examine the voting and provide a definitive assessment of the election's validity. I have also invited Ambassador Mateo Santiago, who has served with me on a previous diplomatic mission, to assist in negotiations to effect a truce between the tribes and secure the release of Ambassador Bukanti. Two members of my former Valkyrie Squadron will join as our pilots and security force."

"I applaud your initiative Rear Admiral Starstriker in trying to create the least disruptive resolution to this crisis," said High Governor Park. "But while I am not questioning your motivation, don't you and your family have a close relation with Ex-Commander Bullwark?"

"It is true my mother, Commander Tanita Starbright, served many E-yr. ago under Commander Bullwark, and over time, I have had some personal contact with him. This relationship is part of why I want to be the lead in this mission. Perhaps my family's history with Seth Bullwark can serve as an opening wedge to convince him to stop and desist this treasonous act against the Federation. I know he must answer for his actions, but I want to defuse the situation before it becomes catastrophic. Seth Bullwark is a legend in annals of the Sidereal Federation. I would not like his legacy to be tarnished by this reckless behavior."

"You do make a strong case that you should head this expedition, but I believe it is much more inflammable than you are willing to admit," said the High Governor. "Admiral Cranshaw, what do you recommend we send as a deterrent force?"

"High Governor," responded Admiral Cranshaw, "I have great faith in Rear Admiral Starstriker and her plan. However, I believe we are dealing with a rogue commander and a militia unit who may not respond to reason. I don't want her to suffer the same fate as Ambassador Bukanti. Thus, I recommend we augment Admiral Starstriker's team with a commando unit. I would equip a starbomber with enough air ground firepower to neutralize any rebel resistance. This deterrent will provide much more leverage in Alyie's negotiations with the Kunari leader Masu and Bullwark than just diplomacy."

"Do you agree Admiral Starstriker?" asked High Governor Park.

"I defer to Admiral Cranshaw's judgement and appreciate any assistance the High Council will provide on this mission."

CHAPTER 6.

After leaving Jaynis on Mars to find his own way back to Earth, Alyie was at Sidereal Federation Headquarters on planet Teegarden seven E-d later, making plans for her departure to Nespar. In addition to her team, Major Reg Jones was commissioned by Admiral Cranshaw to serve under Alyie Starstriker's command along with his 100 strong Panthera unit. The Panthera was a hardened commando squad that specialized in counter-guerilla warfare.

The Major approached Alyie's office as she was directing her AI personal assistant, "Taki", to requisition supplies. With her uniform jacket draped on a clothes rack, Alyie was dressed in a crisp white buttoned-down shirt with epaulettes, brown tie, light brown trousers and tall brown boots. Her red hair was pulled back in a bow. Reg Jones was a dark-skinned, solidly built gentleman of roughly 40 E-yr with a shaved scalp, a short-cropped beard and a small gold earring dangling from his left ear lobe. With sparkling eyes and a jaunty smile, he straightened upright and saluted Alyie.

"Admiral Starstriker, it is an honor to serve under you."

"Likewise, Major Jones, and please be at ease. It looks like our departure is in 2 E-d. We are flying Redemption. I understand Admiral Cranshaw has equipped it with several ancillary vehicles for our use. Can your unit be ready?

"My Panthera will be ready when you are. It looks like things might get interesting on Nespar."

"I hope we can avoid a conflict," answered Alyie. "I think the key will be get both sides to agree to let us conduct an objective evaluation of the election and, of course, accept our conclusion."

"Admiral, I hope you are correct. But what I know about Commander Bullwark is that he is a man of action and may not abide by a judgement made by what he calls 'fedacrats'. There are so many stories about Bullwark's exploits including daring missions establishing the

Federation to reluctant civilizations. One consistent thread is that he does not suffer fools lightly."

"I know what you are saying. My hope is we can negotiate a truce with the leaders of the two tribes, and they would keep their respective armed units in tow."

"Well if that doesn't happen, my commandos are ready to take the field."

"Thank you. I will keep you apprised of our preparations for departure."

CHAPTER 7.

After her meeting with Major Jones, Alyie put on her white Admiral's jacket, fastening the double row of buttons and donning her cap before she left her office. She was having lunch with her parents in the commissary at Headquarters. Both Tanita Starbright and Dr. Alex Striker still worked for Space Command, and they were eager to converse with Alyie about her mission.

"I understand Major Jones' Panthera commando unit is accompanying you," said Alex. "I understand they are a seasoned battle-tested tactical group. The High Council must believe there is a good chance of hostilities."

Tanita was more direct in saying, "I am sick with worry that you are putting yourself in danger, and I do not know what's going to happen to Seth."

Alyie tried to alleviate their concerns. "Admiral Cranshaw has always believed that political goals are best achieved through a show of force. The commandos' presence is more for symbol than substance. You know the old saying, 'Speak softly, but carry a big stick'. Besides I will be with Ambassador Santiago. You found him so charming, Mother. The last time Mateo and I worked together we dealt with an alien civilization. If he and I can successfully negotiate with another sentient culture, we can certainly handle a political dispute among humans and an aging warrior who is trying to re-live his prior glory. All will be fine."

In two E-d, Redemption, under the command of Rear Admiral Starstriker, took off from the spaceport on Teegarden. Most of the storage space aboard the 1 km long starbomber was filled with vehicles to be used as part of the assault force on the planet. There were 20 Birds of Prey vertical lift fighters (VLF), 10 autonomous Terrapin tanks (TT) and two Cobra air jets. Flying the starbomber were pilots Hollie Pederson and Wang Li. On board were Dr. Martin Shushauser, Ambassador Mateo Santiago and Major Reg Jones and his Panthera comrades. Alyie had sent a hyperlink goodbye message to Jaynis, who was now back in their Paris townhouse. He wished her good fortune and reminded her to rely on Dr. Shushauser.

It was 2 E-d to the hyper-knot that would take them to the nearest hyper-exit to the Procyon binary system. Once back in normal space, Redemption traveled another E-w to reach Nespar.

CHAPTER 8.

Decelerating from its planetary orbit, Redemption landed in the principal spaceport outside Nespar's capital, Napara. Disembarking, Alyie, Mateo, Martin and Reg boarded one of the Cobras, which Alyie flew to the palace. They were greeted by King Igwe's guards. Since this was to be a royal audience, Alyie dressed in her full Admiral uniform of a white double-breasted jacket with medals over a short-sleeved blouse, crisp white pants, tall black leather boots, a white cap and black gloves. She had her laser pistol, secure in its holster, attached to her black leather belt. Mateo, for his part, dressed in a formal ambassador suit of dark blue with a white shirt and blue cravat fastened by a diamond pin and patent black leather shoes. Martin Shushauser had on a faux brown corduroy jacket over a pale yellow buttoned-down shirt fastened by a loosely fitting flower print tie. He wore casual brown shoes and khaki-colored dress pants. Reg, on the other hand, came in his commando uniform replete with camouflage fatigues, trooper boots and laser rifle. They all had tiny tubes protruding from their nostrils carrying oxygen to augment the planet's thin atmosphere.

As the quartet entered the palace interior, they passed through a scanner where Alyie and Reg were requested to disarm. Then the visitors were escorted down the corridor to the throne room, where King Adeloa Igwe, in his full regalia and an ornate crown, was standing on a dais to receive them with his ministers at his side. The King cast a striking figure in his robes and smooth chocolate brown skin. He greeted them warmly.

"Welcome to my beleaguered planet. It is wonderful to see you in person Admiral Starstriker. Your exploits are known everywhere, even on humble Nespar. Ambassador Mateo's reputation is also well respected. My words cannot express the gratitude I feel that you have come to intervene in this barbarous attempt to usurp the rule of law by my enemies."

"Greetings from the Sidereal Federation High Council and High Governor Park," began Alyie. "We are a delegation sent to mediate the dispute with the recent planetary election and to negotiate the release of Ambassador Bukanti."

"I can understand your need to secure the Ambassador's freedom from these renegades, Admiral Starstriker," remarked the King, "but the Federation needs to abide by The Act of Self-Determination in not interfering with the will of the people. The result of the election is final."

"Yes, Your Majesty, there is The Act of Self-Determination, but Ambassador Bukanti's capture allows the Sidereal Federation wide latitude in seeking remediation," Mateo responded. "We have brought an expert in cyber-security, Dr. Martin Shushauser, who will examine the voting records to ascertain the validity of the result. Let me introduce Dr. Shushauser."

As Martin was about to affect a bow or curtesy (he wasn't sure what was appropriate), the King's First Minister Ziyad Maher, a very tall gray-haired, thinly built man of sallow complexion, interrupted declaring, "We don't need an expert to tell us that the Amhara won the election. We need the Federation to use its power to destroy these rebels who have attacked us and killed 20 of our soldiers. One of your own is helping that canine Talib Masu. You need to silence him and his rogues."

Alyie could sense the implication in this invective. Addressing King Igwe, "The Federation sent us to settle this dispute in the most non-violent way possible. To do that, we need to assure the Kunari and all the people of Nespar that the election was fair and there was no malfeasance in the vote count. Dr. Shushauser is here to ensure that."

"As Admiral Starstriker is indicating," Mateo interjected, "we plan to request a meeting with the Kunari and their leadership to inform them of this objective assessment as a way of placating their objections and securing the release of Ambassador Bukanti. But first we need Your Majesty's permission to allow Dr. Shushauser to proceed with his inquiry."

"We do not see what possible advantage it is for His Majesty to assent to this fruitless search. We have won the election," spoke the Second Minister Abdu Mukasa, shorter of the statue and more rotund than Minister Maher but with the same grayness of hair and paleness of skin.

"Excuse me," broke in Reg Jones, "but I would like to remind His Highness and all you others that less than five km. away on a landing pad sits a Federation starbomber with weaponry that can decimate your planet, and on the ground is the Panthera, the fiercest fighting unit you will ever encounter. If you don't want that starbomber to leave permanent craters on Nespar, nor my troops to be patrolling this fine palace, then I think you should agree to let the good doctor do his inquiry."

There was a general silence after the Major's speech. Alyie could tell that the matter had been settled.

"We would like a statement from Your Majesty, sent to everyone on Nespar by the next star rise that you authorize the Federation's inquiry into the election, and as leader of the Amhara tribe, you will abide by its result no matter the outcome. We are most grateful for your cooperation."

CHAPTER 9.

Since Nespar orbits outside of the binary system, one of the Proycon's double stars is usually above the horizon, so the night time is relatively short. Alyie, who with the others was staying at the palace, had politely declined the King's invitation to a welcome dinner so as not to provide the appearance of a conflict of interest. Restless, she walked over to an enclosed balcony and gazed at the dark sky. Mateo soon joined her, intruding on Alyie's solitude by saying, "Senora, everything went well today with the King. He has sent the message across the planet we requested, giving us access and authorization to the voting files. This is another success for us. We certainly make a great team, Alyie."

"Things worked well because of Major Jones. We face a much tougher task when we meet with the Kunari," Alyie replied. "I have sent a message that we will be coming to their enclave after first star rise. They will send me the coordinates of the meeting place."

"Good. I hope with the King's communication, they will relent and release the Ambassador."

"Mateo, just you and I will be making the trip. Reg's intimidation worked on King Igwe. If he threatens to use force, Commander Bullwark will take that as a challenge, and I fear the worst will happen."

"Bullwark, must be a real throwback," said Mateo. "Doesn't he realize his time has past?"

"The truth is he was such an inspiration to so many in Space Command. My mother idolized him, and he was always kind and supportive to me."

"Well, maybe enough of that kindness remains for him to listen to reason and stand down. You realize you can be hard to resist."

"I don't know if I ever had any influence over Seth. He was always pretty obstinate once he put his mind to something."

"Ah, my dear Alyie, you underestimate your charm and power. Speaking of, would you like to spend the rest of the evening in my quarters? I have a rare bottle of a prized vintage wine; I would be delighted to share it with you. We can explore other ways we can collaborate."

"No, thank you. We have a difficult day tomorrow, and we need to be at our wit's best. I suggest you save the wine for a more relaxed time. Good night, Mateo."

CHAPTER 10.

Shortly after the primary star, Proycon A, peeked above the horizon, Alyie and Mateo boarded the Cobra air jet to take the 10 E-hr journey to the rebel base on the other side of the planet. Over their uniforms, they both wore full-length double-breasted khaki trench coats and fastened goggles over their eyes to protect themselves from the dust storms on Nespar they might encounter after landing near the destination. The meeting would take place in the foothills of the Kibo Mountains, where Seth Bullwark's rebel army had established a stronghold.

Landing the Cobra on a relatively flat basin, Alyie and Mateo jumped out and walked the remaining two km toward an improvised barricade. After Alyie sent a signal from her implant that she and Mateo had arrived, the stones blocking the entrance were pulled aside by armed guards, and they entered a cave that was part of the natural rock formation. Ascending 12 stone steps, they reached a clearing in the cave in which Talib Masu, Seth Bullwark and Peter Bukanti were waiting, surrounded by soldiers brandishing laser rifles. The leader of the Kunari was a tall thin, dark-skinned man with piercing eyes and dressed in a traditional gown of bright green. Seth Bullwark, belying his advanced years with blonde hair and beard (obviously, both the result of the nano-chemicals circulating through his body.) He stood tall and straight in his military fatigues and big brown leather boots. Bullwark had a laser rifle slung over his shoulder, but around his belt was his faithful sword, Liberator. Seth's eyes gleamed at the sight of Alyie. The Ambassador looked drawn, sullen-eyed and somewhat disheveled.

Removing her goggles, Alyie announced, "Greetings, I am Rear Admiral Alyie Starstriker of the Sidereal Federation and this is Ambassador Mateo Santiago. We have been sent by the Sidereal High Council to effect the release of Ambassador Bukanti. Our co-mission is to investigate the recent national election on Nespar. We have brought with us Dr. Martin Shushauser, who is currently in Napara examining the voting files. As you have undoubtedly heard, King Igwe has consented to this investigation and will abide by its conclusion. We are asking for your agreement as well, and, as a token of good faith, the release of the Ambassador."

"We appreciate your efforts Admiral Starstriker and Ambassador Mateo to strike down the illegal actions of the Amhara tribe in their desperate attempt to cling to power," answered Talib Masu. "We hope your expert can detect their treachery, but we have no confidence you will. How do we know you are not in consort with the King and his minions? You may turn around and say the election was valid and the result stands. We cannot accept that."

Mateo responded to Masu's retort. "I need to remind you that Nespar is a member of the Sidereal Federation, and that membership implies compliance with Federation laws. You broke one of them by your abduction of Ambassador Bukanti. Unless you release him, your rights to claiming power regardless of the outcome of our analysis of the election result would be negated."

Before Masu could respond to Mateo, Seth Bullwark jumped in, "Listen fancy clothes, my troops and I are here to guarantee the rights of the Kunari. If it were not for our capture of your diplomat, the Federation would have ignored this election travesty and hid behind The Act of Self-Determination. We got your attention, so do your job, and we will take good care of your little ambassador."

Alyie felt she needed to state her position. "I have pledged my life to the Sidereal Federation and my parents have as well. I have taken oaths to uphold its laws and abide by decisions based on facts and consensus. To assert as you did Mr. Masu, that we have come here with a pre-deigned conclusion as to the validity of the election is an insult to our efforts and to me personally. Commander Bullwark has a long history with my family, and I hope he still remembers the integrity that my mother, father and I have brought to our service for the Federation."

There was a moment of silence as all present felt the impact of Alyie's impassioned words. Bullwark then quietly said, "I would like to speak to Admiral Starstriker in private if you all don't mind."

CHAPTER 11.

As Mateo Santiago stayed behind to converse with Peter Bukanti, Alyie and Seth walked over to an opening of the cave overlooking the savannah below. Both Proycon A and B were now high enough above the horizon to shine brightly on the land.

Turning to look Alyie straight in the eyes, Seth Bullwark embraced her warmly and planted a gentle kiss on her forehead, "Take off your overcoat," said Bullwark, smiling broadly. "I want to look at you."

Alyie obliged, and then Seth exclaimed, "My G_d, Alyie, you have become quite something. What happened to that little pup that I used to bounce on my knee?"

"I grew up, that's all."

"But being a Rear Admiral, the youngest in Federation history, and the medals you have earned are not just the result of seniority. Your parents must be so proud of you."

"I have only done what they would expect of someone in service to the Federation. You also had been important in determining my career. It was your stories that aroused my passion for a life in Space Command. The times my mother and I would visit, or when you would stay with us on Mars were so special to me."

"All I did was encourage you to follow in your mother's wake. Tanita was the finest person that served under me in the Fleet, and now you have gone beyond her achievements. Are you thinking of the High Governorship some day?"

"That is not yet on my career path horizon, but I have considered running for a Regional Governor position. I want to contribute as much to the stability and peace of the Federation as possible."

"And now you have pledged yourself to a young scientist. What a lucky man he must be."

"You have met Jaynis on Mars long ago, but I doubt you remember. He is perfect for me. We are very compatible."

"I have never found an 'eternal partner', but I have had many what you might say are time-sensitive mates. Just before I came to Nespar, there was this young woman stationed on New Cedonia."

Alyie could see where this was going and interrupted Bullwark. "It is great to see and talk to you again, but that is not why I have come to Nespar. Seth, you realize you need to stand down."

"Oh, Alyie. I don't think so. The cause is just, and the Kunari need my help. My actions brought you here. You see, I still know how to jerk the Federation's chain. What has happened to it? It used to be a shining symbol for justice in human space. Now it is one large administrative monolith of regulations and protocols. People like your ambassador friend make the rules, where it should be soldiers like you and I that settle problems."

"You are correct. The abduction of Ambassador Bukanti brought this mission by the Federation to Nespar with me in command. Now that my team is here, you need to use your influence to convince Talib Masu to accept the conclusion of our investigation and release the Ambassador."

"If I do that, what are the consequences for me and my mates?"

"I am sorry Seth, but seizing an ambassador is a crime in the Federation. Your troops will have to surrender, and you, as their leader, will have to turn yourself in to me. Charges may also be lodged against Masu, if it is shown he was complicit in the abduction."

"That is not going to happen, Alyie. I am never going to surrender and spend the rest of my life in a Federation prison. Without the actions my Peregrine Falcon took, there would not be today such a united Federation. I was a hero. Sites were named after me. What has the Federation done to preserve my legacy? They have tried to erase my achievements and play down what I have accomplished. They have even removed my name from plaques in cities because now they consider my methods too aggressive for current effete tastes. This is my chance to show I am still vital. No matter what your expert determines, I will not stand down or be taken captive. My soldiers and I are ready to fight to the end."

"Seth, please listen to me. The reason I took on this mission was that my mother is heartbroken at what you've done. She implored me to go and convince you to stop these brazen actions. You talk of your legacy, but what is this unlawful behavior going to do for it? Do you want to be remembered as the person who seized a Federation ambassador, resisted arrest and then fought against Federation troops? Please stop before it is too late."

"Alyie, I see you are now part of them. You should have remained Commander of the Valkyries. Your time with these administrators have softened your will and tainted your perspective. I don't want you to be my adversary, but if I have to, so be it. Ut virum optimum win."

CHAPTER 12.

With her conversation with Bullwark reaching a dead-end, Alyie returned to the interior of the cave where Santiago, Masu and Bukanti were waiting.

Bullwark, hesitating somewhat, was first to speak, "Mr. Masu, I can vouch for Admiral Starstriker and the integrity of her mission. She has always acted with professionalism and objectivity, and I am assured her team will find the truth about this election."

Alyie was taken somewhat aback by Seth's support but thankful for his endorsement.

Talib Masu said, "Yes, I have been conferring with Ambassador Santiago, and I also believe in him and the Admiral. Besides, we are convinced their expert will find the fraud in this election. You have our consent to proceed with your investigation. However, we will not release Ambassador Bukanti until the analysis is completed."

Bukanti raised his voice in objection. "This is outrageous. You are holding an ambassador of the Sidereal Federation against his will and violating his diplomatic immunity. I have not been treated with the due respect my station deserves. I urge Admiral Starstriker to use any means necessary to free me immediately, irrespective of this election investigation."

"I do not endorse Ambassador Bukanti's continued confinement, but I believe the most important action is Dr. Shushauser's work at the capital. As soon as it is completed, I will expect the release of the Ambassador. Peter, please be patient a little longer," Alyie pleaded.

"I do not know how much more I can take of this," was Bukanti's anguished reply.

CHAPTER 13.

When Alyie and Mateo returned to Napara well after the next star rise, they were greeted by Reg Jones. "How did things go in the mountains?"

"I would say, with mixed success," answered Mateo. "We got an agreement from Talib Masu to conduct the investigation, but he was unwilling to release Ambassador Bukanti until it is done."

"Are you telling me, the Kunari will only accept a favorable judgement?" questioned Reg.

"That is yet to be determined. But I am really concerned about Seth Bullwark's actions no matter what our verdict on the election is," said Alyie glumly. "He is not thinking clearly. He seems determined to force the issue and make, in his mind, a final stand. You know, go out in full glory with laser pistols blazing. Major Jones, put your Panthera on high alert. Prepare to make an assault on the rebel base when I give the command. We may have to move very quickly."

"Admiral Starstriker, I need to inform you that things at the palace have not been without some tension. It looks like the King's principal ministers, Ziyad Maher and Abdu Mukasa, have been trying to obstruct Dr. Shushauser from conducting his investigation. At first, they wouldn't grant him access codes to the palace network. Dr. Shushauser fortunately was able to have King Igwe over-ride their objection. Then, Dr. Shushauser's room was broken into, left in shambles, and his notes were confiscated. When he reported the break in to these ministers, they accused him on fabricating the intrusion. Finally, he has been receiving threatening messages to his implants warning him to cease his investigation."

"This is troubling and gives me reason to think the election was tampered with to favor the Amhara tribe," said Alyie. "Can you provide Dr. Shushauser with protection, Major Jones?"

"It has already been done. I have two of my best soldiers assigned to him continuously. They go wherever the doctor goes."

"Well, it looks like we have our hands full with both sides of this dispute. Give Ambassador Santiago and me two E-hr. to freshen up, and then let's have a meeting with full security in my suite. I will contact Dr. Shushauser to join us."

CHAPTER 14.

Alyie washed the Nesparian dirt and dust off her body and hair with a soothing ultrasonic shower. After quickly drying herself, she dressed casually for this impromptu meeting in a clean white shirt (open at the collar), brown trousers and polished brown leather boots. Soon after, the others joined her. Alyie ordered some light food and hot liquids that were brought promptly by an auto-bot.

As the four crowded around the table in the suite, Alyie used a special code in her implant to turn on a security shield that blocked any intruders from listening to their conversation.

Alyie began by prompting. "Dr. Shushauser please give us an update."

"I have not reached a definite conclusion, but it is looking pretty certain that there was some voter fraud. Looking at the financial records, it appears that the company Quantum Solutions was employed to insure voter integrity. It took some doing, but I was able to find that Minister Ziyad Maher hired it to set up a system that generated an entangled pair of quantum bits (called qubits) from each vote as a sort of a parity or, so called, error check."

"Dr. Shushauser, how does that indicate voter fraud?" asked Mateo. "You would think having each vote duplicated would be a way to insure no tampering."

"Yes, on the surface, that would seem the case," Martin answered. "But I checked with an esteemed colleague that Admiral Starstriker and I share a relationship with, Dr. Jaynis Bottombrook, who informed me that Quantum Solutions specializes in quantum teleportation which under the right, or as in this case the wrong, circumstance can be used to change outcomes."

Alyie smiled at the mention of Jaynis and shook her head, thinking, "He is always there even when I don't contact him."

"Can you explain to us how this can be done, Dr. Shushauser?" Mateo inquired.

"Well, I am not versed in quantum behavior as well as Jaynis is, but I will try. In this voting system, every citizen's vote was recorded as a double qubit, and the two identical qubits were sent to two different collection bins – a parity check bin and a counted vote bin. Since there were only two choices – Kunari or Amhara, it is a binary system (like a 0 or 1). The qubit used as a parity check can be altered by interacting in what is called a Bell state with another preset "vote" at the parity bin. If this parity qubit is reversed by this interaction, let's say to the other party (change 0 to 1 or vice versa), then by the quantum entanglement process the counted vote would also be changed the same way."

"If what you are saying occurred, then wouldn't all votes for the Kunari tribe be changed to Amhara votes?" questioned Alyie. "I recall that the election result gave the Amhara a very narrow victory."

"Admiral, you are correct," said Martin. "Doing that with each vote cast for the Kunari would make it an obvious fraud. My suspicion, which I need to prove, is that only a certain portion of the votes were altered by this teleportation scheme. If I had to speculate, it would be votes by citizens not affiliated with either tribe. Fortunately, these citizens live in areas not typically populated by either the Kunari or the Amhara, so I will try to harvest their records separately from the overall vote."

"Martin, Major Jones has informed me of the intimidation you have suffered, and I really don't want to put even more pressure on you, but we need to act expeditiously as possible. I fear the situation on Nespar may be verging on civil war," cautioned Alyie.

"Admiral, I will proceed at the fastest rate; perhaps I can reach a conclusion before stars set."

"Good. Let's also use some of the Federation's leverage on Quantum Solutions. Can you contact them Mateo? Impress that their complicity in voter fraud would blacklist them from future contracts in the Federation unless they cooperate with this investigation."

"For you Senora, I will be a, how-do-you-say-it, 'bad-ass' diplomat," laughed Mateo.

"And Reg," Alyie followed. "We need to have tight surveillance on these minsters. As Martin is closing in on their scheme, they might try to sabotage his efforts. Can you insure this won't happen?"

"Not on my watch," replied Reg Jones.

"For my part, I will approach King Igwe. The fact that he allowed us to proceed with this investigation, leads me to conclude he is unaware of what has been happening. I need to prepare him for some unpleasantness concerning his reign and his closest advisors. As we say in the Fleet, we all have our orders, now let's do them."

All three gentlemen responded with, "Yes, Ma'am."

CHAPTER 15.

Alyie, after contacting the palace communications system, was quickly granted an audience with King Igwe. She dressed in her formal admiral uniform for this royal meeting. When she arrived in the throne room, the King's First and Second Ministers, Ziyad Maher and Abdu Mukasa, respectively, were present, along with two palace guards. Being eyed suspiciously, Alyie made the request,

"Your Majesty, I have news concerning my team's investigation of the recent election. But it is for your ears only. I request our conversation be private."

"This is extraordinary," exclaimed Minister Maher. "We are His Majesty's closest advisors, and we need to be by his side at all times to provide our counsel."

"Your Majesty, I come unarmed and what I have to tell you is of upmost importance and for you alone."

"Admiral Starstriker, you are permitted to approach the throne," said King Igwe. "Everyone else is dismissed."

As soon as Alyie was alone with the King, she told him of the investigation's surmise that his advisors Maher and Mukasa hired the company Quantum Solutions to alter just enough votes to change the election's outcome to the King's party's favor. She detailed as best as she could Dr. Shushauser's explanation of altering the entangled qubits, and the King's ministers repeated attempts to impede the investigation.

Stunned by this revelation, King Igwe exclaimed, "How can this be? I have put absolute trust in them?"

"I am an officer of the Sidereal Federation and a member of the High Council, however I cannot dictate how your planet should proceed. We do abide by The Act of Self-Determination. However, I would recommend, that after due time, there be a revote, under strict protocols.

I am sure the Federation would be happy to send in a monitoring team to insure its validity."

"Oh, to think that this has happened to us. This is a sad day for Nespar and the Amhara tribe. I will wait for your final assessment before making any statement," said the dejected ruler.

"Thank you for receiving me and taking my news with such dignity."

Alyie bowed before the King. As soon as she left the throne room, Ziyad Maher and Abdu Mukasa, who blocked her passage, confronted her. Alyie noticed that palace guards were no longer with them.

"What did you say to the King?" Maher inquired with some rancor. "How dare you have us leave," said Mukasa with his nostrils flaring.

"My business was with King Igwe only, now excuse me."

As Alyie tried to pass between them, Maher pulled a flashing knife from under his cloak and struck Alyie. She saw it out of the corner of her eye and instinctively balanced herself on her left boot as she drove the right boot hard into Maher's groin. He groaned audibly, writhing on the floor in pain. Then Mukasa lunged at Alyie with his own weapon in his right hand. She reached under his armpit and flipped him over her shoulder to the floor. As he was reaching for the loose knife, a shadow was cast over him. As Mukasa looked up, he saw the hulking figure of Reg Jones aiming his laser rifle at his forehead.

"Touch that knife and I will melt you into the floor so bad that it would take several E-m for the palace crew to remove the stain you will leave."

With Mukasa's submission, Reg signaled two of his commandos who were standing in the background to take hold of the ministers.

"I am impressed, Admiral. I see you can do more than fly superfast spacecraft."

"The Fleet Academy had special sessions on hand-to-hand combat. They said you never know when you might need to use it. I presume you will hold these not so good ministers where they can no longer do any harm."

"Admiral, don't worry, my people will take special care of them."

However, as Reg Jones was helping Alyie to her feet, he noticed a red rose pattern slowly blooming through her white jacket in the upper chest near the left shoulder.

"Admiral, you have been wounded. Let me help you."

Alyie, who had just begun to feel the effects of the stabbing, said, "If I can get to my quarters, I can use my travel med-kit."

With Reg Jones' support, Alyie, who was a little unsteady now on her feet, made it into her suite. Inside, Reg carefully took off Alyie's double-breasted jacket and gently ripped her blood-stained white blouse, exposing the wound as she was stripped to her tank top undershirt. Inspecting the puncture, he could see that, gratefully, it was not deep, and the bleeding was subsiding. Under Alyie's guidance, he found the medical auto-doc kit. Not needing the autonomous surgical device, Reg washed the wound thoroughly with a bar of antiseptic soap, used a syringe to apply a blood clotting solution, gently rubbed a cultivated honey emulsion to prevent infection, and sutured the wound with a special skin sealing fabric. Finally, he injected Alyie with an analgesic for pain management.

Alyie, watching the Major's dexterity and his fine touch as he tended to her, expressed her admiration. "Major, now it is my turn to be impressed. Where did you acquire such good medical skills?"

"Well, Admiral, it wasn't at a Fleet Academy. My mother was a Healer, and she impressed on her children the importance of being able to take of ourselves. I think I am done. You should drink a lot of fluids and rest awhile."

"I first need to check in with Mateo and Martin to see what progress they are making and then call a meeting."

"Admiral, if you respect my healing skills, take my advice. Drink and rest. I will get the updates and schedule a meeting when you are up to it. Also, send me right now the access code to your vitals so I can monitor them."

"Yes, Dr. Jones," Alyie smiled demurely. As soon as Reg left, Alyie drank a half-liter of electrolyte from her med-kit. Finishing the drink, she climbed into her bunk without taking her boots off and, shortly after, fell into a restful sleep.

CHAPTER 16.

Feeling more herself after a 3 E-hr nap but a little sore at the wound's point of entry, Alyie contacted Reg, who said he had just received reports from Mateo and Martin. She told him to schedule a meeting toward stars set in her suite. When all were present, Alyie informed Mateo and Martin of her audience with the King and the scuffle with his ministers afterward. Taking off her shirt to show the wound, they were stunned at the brazenness of this act. For his part, Mateo told that he was able to extract an admission by the directors of Quantum Solutions that they, at Maher and Mukasa's request, installed Bell state transmitters at selected polling stations on Nespar.

"When I pressed them on what these transmitters were used for, they claimed no knowledge. However, I have recorded their statements and have obtained the file of the transaction. I think I make a grande Grand Inquisitor."

"I have evidence," Martin followed, "that these devices were in place in areas of the heaviest concentration of citizens not aligned with either the Kunari or the Amhara tribes. It is impossible to tell how many votes were altered, but I noticed that in some locales all the recorded votes were for the Amhara, a remarkable circumstance considering the independent nature of this segment of the population."

"From Mateo's extraction of a confession from the manufacturer of the equipment, from Martin's deduction of the use of these qubit flipping devices in certain swing districts, and from my experience firsthand of the obstruction of our investigation by the King's ministers, are we all in agreement that there was purposeful voter fraud in this election?"

All three men chimed in, saying, "We are, Ma'am."

"Good. I am going to pull all the information together and send an Executive Summary to King Igwe and Talib Masu. In a separate communication, I will announce the arrest of Ministers Maher and

Mukasa. They are charged by the Federation with assault on a Sidereal High Council member, but the justice system of Nespar may also charge them with election tampering. Contacting Masu, I will demand, he keep his agreement and immediately release Ambassador Bukanti to us. Once that is accomplished, I think our job on Nespar is done, and I propose we have a mini-celebration. Mateo, perhaps it would be time to uncork that bottle of wine you've been saving."

The King received Alyie's report with resignation, but he vowed to accept the outcome and negotiate with the leaders of the Kunari to schedule a revote.

Talib Masu's response was of an entirely different nature. "Admiral, I am happy your team has discovered this dishonesty and rooted out the villains who caused this. It was exactly as we, the Kunari, surmised. However, we cannot release the Ambassador. I am sorry to give you bad news, but he died attempting to escape from Commander Bullwark's guards."

Alyie was shocked at this dreadful turn of events. She felt the wound in her chest throb. Alyie thought through diplomacy and forensic methodology, her team had adverted violence, only to see blood being shed when it appeared the crisis was over.

Alyie knew what she had to say to the Kunari leader. "Mr. Masu, you and your comrades have committed a capital crime against the Sidereal Federation. You are to disarm and surrender immediately to the Federation forces here on Nespar. You, Commander Bullwark and anyone else we find responsible will be placed under arrest for this grievous act."

"I know the death of Ambassador Bukanti is inexcusable, and I bear some responsibility for it, but Commander Bullwark is unwilling to surrender. In fact, he is now keeping me hostage here, preventing me from turning myself in to you."

"Let me talk to Commander Bullwark."

"That is not possible, Admiral Starstriker. He told me specifically that the next time he speaks to you it will be on the battlefield. He said to tell you, 'ut virum optimum win'. The Commander said you would understand."

Alyie silently translated. "May the best man win." "Oh G_d," she thought. "He leaves me no option."

Switching Talib Masu off, Alyie contacted Reg Jones and her Valkyrie ex-teammates, Hollie Pederson and Wang Li.

"Major Jones, you and the Panthera are to go to Redemption and prepare the VLF's and TT's stored onboard for ground assault. Afterwards, Hollie and Wang take Redemption airborne. I will shortly give you all the target's coordinates. Await my orders to commence attack."

CHAPTER 17.

Alyie's battle plan was designed to bring this standoff to as quick a conclusion as possible. Redemption, on Alyie's command, was to drop pure fusion bombs in the hills where Bullwark's troops were sheltered. Once the stronghold was exposed, Hollie and Wang would fire incendiary rockets setting it ablaze. This would force the insurgents out in the open where Reg Jones' Panthera would be hovering in their Birds of Prey and controlling the autonomous Terrapin Tanks. Seeing the forces arrayed against them, Alyie hoped the rebels would realize their cause was futile and surrender. What gave her concern was Seth Bullwark's resolve to fight to the end.

Making one last effort to avert military action, Alyie sent a broadcast message from her implant transmission site.

"To all hiding in the Kibo Mountains, I am Rear Admiral Starstriker of the Sidereal Federation. I order you to stand down and surrender."

Not receiving any return message after waiting for one E-hr, Alyie took to the sky in the Cobra air jet to oversee the assault. When Redemption circled above the location of the rebel stronghold and the Panthera forces were in place, Alyie gave the command for Hollie to begin dropping the clean fusion bombs. As the impacts shattered the rocks and exposed the interior of the caves, Alyie commanded Wang to start the missile bombardment. As these rockets landed, huge flames were seen to rise from the now exposed rebel camp. On her infra-red scanner, Alyie could detect scores of human figures fleeing the burning wreckage. Forced out in the open basin, the insurgents were met by the Panthera, who engaged them in a firefight. Soon after, however, the fighting ceased as the renegades surrendered as Alyie hoped they would.

While Alyie was hovering in her Cobra above the skirmish sight, Wang Li broke into her comm. channel saying, "Admiral Starstriker, I am detecting a Bird of Prey climbing in the sky heading away from the engagement site. I think it has been commandeered by a rebel. Should I engage it?"

Alyie had a premonition about who had hijacked the Bird of Prey. "Lieutenant, quickly do an identity scan of the pilot."

Soon after, Wang responded, "The scan is showing that it is Ex-Commander Seth Bullwark. Awaiting your orders, Ma'am, on how to proceed."

"Stand down. I have sighted the craft, and I will pursue Bullwark."

"Do you want Redemption to serve as backup, Admiral?"

"No, I will engage him alone."

As Alyie soared to chase Bullwark, she used the Federation comm. channel to call him when she could see his craft was in range. "Seth, come down; the battle is over. I need you to surrender honorably."

As the two ships climbed higher, Alyie received Bullwark's response. "Alyie I knew it would wind up between you and me. We are the only true warriors. I read on the Federation News Feed what happened to you at the palace. How dare they cut you, Tanita's daughter! Pup, if I still had a command I would hang those sons of bitches by their puny jewels, if they have any, and then chop their heads off with Liberator."

"That's not how we do things now, Seth. They have been arrested and will receive the Federation's Justice. On that subject, can you tell me what happened with Ambassador Bukanti?"

"Oh, that whiny fancy pants. He had no patience. We were just using him as a pawn to insure you and your team would do the right thing in turning over the election. He bribed one of the guards to look the other way. He was climbing down the mountain when I spotted him. I couldn't let him escape so I grabbed a high powered thermo-laser rifle and the beam bore right through his heart. You see, I still have good aim."

"This has to end, Seth. You need to turn your ship around and land. Let me take you in."

"No. Alyie it is you who need to turn back. You are flying a Cobra without any real weapons while I have a missile-loaded Bird of Prey. I will shoot you right out of the sky if you keep tailing me. Back off."

"No, you won't kill me. I know you Seth Bullwark. No matter what has happened lately, you are still the bravest and boldest pilot that ever flew under a Sidereal Federation flag. You are too noble a warrior to fire under these circumstances."

There was silence after Alyie spoke. Then Bullwark pointed the nose of his aircraft straight upward and climbed rapidly towards the limit of Nespar's atmosphere. Alyie knew both their jets could not fly long at these altitudes due to the thinning air. She stopped the ascent of her Cobra and watched as Seth's Bird of Prey reached its maximum height. Then the engine stalled. Descending rapidly towards the surface, Alyie received a final message from Seth, reciting,

"It matters not how strait the gate, How charged with punishments the scroll, I am the master of my fate, I am the captain of my soul."

Soon after, as she pursued him down, Alyie saw the Bird of Prey crash into the surface, and the fiery explosion that followed became Seth Bullwark's immolation.

EPILOGUE

Earth-Day 238, 2610 CE.

Descending the stone stairs of the Sidereal Federation Hall of Justice on Teegarden were Alyie Starstriker, Reg Jones, Mateo Santiago and Martin Shushauser. They had just given testimony at the arraignment of Ziyad Maher, Abdu Mukasa and Talib Masu. The Nesparian ex-ministers were charged with an assassination attempt on a High Council member, while the former Kunari party leader was charged as an accomplice in the death of Ambassador Peter Bukanti.

Alyie appeared before the court in her Admiral white dress uniform but had her jacket unbuttoned on the left side as her arm was placed in a sling. Meeting the four witnesses at the foot of the stairs were Alyie's parents, Tanita and Alex, and Jaynis, who made the trip from Earth to Teegarden when informed about Alyie's wound.

"Don't fret about the sling," Alyie assured a concerned Jaynis. "It is just to remind me not to raise my left arm excessively for fear of opening the wound. I am fine."

Alyie introduced Reg and Martin to her folks and Jaynis. They had previously met Mateo after Alyie's mission with him to Omega X. Tanita went right up to Reg and, with some emotion, said, "Alyie has told me all you did for her after she was attacked. I can't thank you enough for the care you gave my daughter."

"Ma'am," answered Reg, "your daughter is the finest I have ever served under. I wasn't about to lose her. It was a privilege to be of assistance."

Afterward, Alyie, her Nespar team members, parents and Jaynis traveled by airbus to join other Federation officials for a memorial service for Peter Bukanti in the tree-lined Memory Garden. Ambassador Santiago spoke eloquently of Bukanti's dedication to diplomatic service and reminded everyone of the perils of statecraft. After a solemn requiem performance by the Sidereal Orchestra, those in attendance dispersed.

As Alyie was walking with her parents and Jaynis, Alex Striker asked, "So what are your plans now?"

Alyie frowned, saying, "I have been ordered to take a medical leave of absence until I receive an auto-doc's approval to return to the High Council. We are going home to Earth."

"You will take good care of her Jaynis, won't you?" implored Tanita. "She looks a little anemic to me."

"Don't worry, I will make sure her blood supply is replenished; we will drink copious amounts of wine harvested from French grapes. I have a stocked cellar ready for her."

After the laughter subsided, Tanita took Alyie by her free arm and spoke quietly. "Nothing has been said about Seth. I know things ended badly, but I still feel he should not be forsaken. The Federation wants to completely erase his memory and forget his great service because of this terrible tragedy."

"Mother, Seth had a code and lived his life in accordance with it. The problem was that his great courage was mixed with excessive pride, and he could not suffer the loss of prestige in his later years. The lines he spoke before his crash were from the poem "Invictus". It was written in 1875 CE by William Ernest Henley. Let me send you the full poem. I think it best expresses how Seth saw himself."

"Out of the night that covers me,

Black as the pit from pole to pole,

I thank whatever gods may be

For my unconquerable soul.

In the fell clutch of circumstance,

I have not winced nor cried aloud.

Under the bludgeonings of chance

My head is bloody, but unbowed.

Beyond this place of wrath and tears

Looms but the Horror of the shade,

And yet the menace of the years

Finds and shall find me unafraid.

It matters not how strait the gate,

How charged with punishments the scroll,

I am the master of my fate,

I am the captain of my soul."

"I am having the poem inscribed in a gold plaque for you to display in his memory. Come Mother, let's join Dad and Jaynis. It is a beautiful day."

THE HOUSE OF JADE

CHAPTER 1.

As she was directing her robotic assistant, Taki, to complete the cleaning, Alyie surveyed her Parisian townhouse, satisfied that it was conveying just the right image. Also, Alyie, as always, gave a great deal of attention to her personal appearance. For the visitors who would be soon arriving, Alyie dressed to appear informal. Instead of wearing her brand new Vice Admiral uniform, she was clad in civilian clothes. Alyie put on a dark blue satin buttoned-down blouse that opened at the collar and black tight-fitting pants girdled by a black leather belt. Around her neck was a bright blue and black scarf. Although she was at home, Alyie wore her tall black leather boots, without which she did not feel properly dressed. Her golden-red hair shone with luster, her green eyes sparkled, and her finely chiseled nose centered her creamily complexioned face. Alyie's eternal partner, Dr. Jaynis Bottombrook, was busy in the kitchen preparing food for the guests. Alyie insisted he stay with her as she needed his discerning mind at her side.

Alyie was at a turning point in her life. She had achieved the rank of Vice Admiral at the unprecedented age of 30 E-yr. Currently, she was "deployed" as a member of the Sidereal Federation High Council. Her five E-yr term would be coming to an end in an E-yr. Alyie could very well be re-appointed for another term on the High Council, however, High Governor Ji-hoon Park would also be ending his tenure at the same time, and, with an election of a new High Governor, it was uncertain if Alyie would remain in her position. She could return to active duty in Space Command, but she and Jaynis were about to raise a family. They had frozen Alyie's eggs and were waiting for the right time in their lives to thaw and fertilize them with Jaynis' sperm to initiate the embryonic transfer into an exo womb. With parenthood looming, Jaynis was adamant that Alyie should avoid high-risk assignments. Her last major mission to Planet Nespar resulted in Alyie being attacked and stabbed by a craven minister.

The meeting at Jaynis and Alyie's home would be to explore another career option, namely Alyie as a candidate for the Regional

Governor position in the Sol system. Although the responsibilities of chairing the Regional Council for the system's inhabited worlds (Earth, Luna and Mars) did not enthrall Alyie, she was advised that this experience would be a good stepping stone to the position she ultimately set her sights on – High Governor. To provide advice and craft strategies, Alyie invited to this luncheon three individuals: Lyida Foxworth, a well-known marketing and campaign consultant on Earth; Maxim Hebron, a long time public figure on Mars, who had been a previous Regional Governor, and Dr. Fujan Wang, a scholar who would use his research to provide Alyie cultural and historical background on the Sol System.

CHAPTER 2.

The guests were punctual and arrived in short order of each other. Alyie welcomed them into the dining area, where the auto assistant had set the table for five. Jaynis did the serving, which consisted of croissant sandwiches of ham and cheese and green salad (all from local farms) accompanied by red wine from Alyie and Jaynis' cellar. For dessert, fresh strawberries and hand melons were served with whipped cream from a dairy that regularly delivered to Alyie and Jaynis, along with a choice of hot beverages.

After a friendly conversation about living in historic Paris and the artwork that was projected on the walls, Maxim, a casually dressed, short rotund gentleman of some 50 E-yr with rather obvious synthetically grown red hair, turned the talk to the business of the meeting.

"I am so glad, Alyie you are considering running for the Regional Governor position. Your fame will surely give the Sol System the attention it needs in the Sidereal Federation."

"The problem, Mr. Hebron is that I am a neophyte as a candidate for office, and I wonder if I have the requisite skills to campaign for office."

"That is my department," chirped Lydia Foxworth, a petite middle-aged woman with tinted blonde curly hair dressed in a dark blue suit consisting of a jacket and a tight-fitting skirt which she complemented with tall black high heeled shoes. "Together, we will plan a campaign that will accentuate your strengths. Alyie, with your reputation and appearance, you are a publicist's dream to market."

"But I don't want to misrepresent myself. If I can't speak truthfully as to what I believe, then I don't want to be in office. I have lived by the code of the Fleet – Honor, Loyalty and Justice. I will not compromise those values for any position."

"And you won't ever have to," Lydia assured as she twirled her pearl necklace. "All we need to do is package your attributes in an effective way for the citizens of Earth, Luna and Mars to know you."

"Admiral Starstriker, I believe I can be an asset to you in providing background material for the important issues concerning both planets." Dr. Wang was a be-speckled elderly gentleman of small stature who was wearing a gray suit with a white shirt and black tie. "Citizens of Earth, in general, believe their planet should be recognized more as the seat of humanity and be given a greater say in the direction of the Sidereal Federation. Luna is a manufacturing environment, and the companies who have investments there want markets to sell their products, whereas Mars is populated mostly by researchers and academics who continually want better equipment and facilities to conduct their studies."

Jaynis believed it was time to join in the conversation, "There is no rush to make a decision involving Alyie's candidacy. Is it my understanding that the first step is to collect enough 'signatures' that would enable her to run for office?"

"Yes, Jaynis, that is correct," answered Maxim. "All valid candidates receive the same resources from the Federation to campaign for office. To qualify, a prospective candidate needs 100 million signatures that can come from all over the Sol system."

"When would Alyie need to collect these signatures by?" Jaynis asked.

"The election is about 13 E-m from now," said Lydia. "The deadline for qualifying is three E-m before the election. What I would do is conduct a "quiet campaign" where we have citizens sign without formally announcing Alyie's candidacy. When we get close enough to the 100 million number, we will go public proclaiming her interest in being the next Regional Governor. This should easily put us over the top and launch the official election campaign."

"I appreciate your interest in my candidacy, and, yes, I am seriously thinking of running. What I would like to do is spend some time with Dr. Wang in gaining fluency in the issues he touched upon and see what skills I can bring to in governing the Sol system in the Sidereal Federation. Dr. Wang, please contact my auto-scheduler to get on my calendar. I am sure I will need you and your colleagues' advice Mr. Hebron both during my candidacy and after if I am elected. And Lydia, it is my feeling you and I will be close companions during the next 13 E-m. if I choose to run."

After some more general conversation, the meeting was concluded, and the guests took their leave. When they were alone, Jaynis stood face-to-face with Alyie and put his arms around her hips, smiling,

"I guess if you become Regional Governor, I no longer need to salute you. I wonder what is the proper greeting to address a Governor. Can I say, 'Hi Gov'?"

Alyie grinned mischievously and then drew Jaynis closer to herself, lifting her right leg and having her boot rub tenderly against his left leg. The boot glided slowly upward until she felt his arousal, and they locked lips and joined their now supple bodies together.

CHAPTER 3.

In the succeeding E-w, Alyie immersed herself in Earth history with the assistance of Dr. Wang. She learned how space exploration was seen as an imperative for the survival of the human species. There were great concerns over the sustainability of Earth due to climatic variations. Spreading the population out into space ensured its viability. However, the conditions on Earth never reached a critical state and factors such as global temperature, rainfall, and atmosphere reached an equilibrium that made the climate, in general, temperate throughout the planet. Luna, Earth's natural satellite, was the first to be colonized and its rich mineral content made it a haven for mining and industrial interests. Mars, a long-sought-after goal for space dreamers and a hope for an alternative living environment, took an E-c to be adaptable to humankind. Its harsh environment, despite some terraforming, made it unsuitable for large colonization. As a result, Mars became a research center with several institutes and universities established over the past four E-c.

The most significant undertaking in humanity's place in the Universe was the Botany Bay Missions initiated at the end of the 21st (CE) E-c. Taking advantage of the discovery of hyper-knots, autonomous spacecraft were launched with instruments to identify Earth-like planets in the roughly 50 l-yr radii in what is now called Human Space. As these new environments were cataloged, enormous colonization spacecraft were launched over the next few E-c to settle and populate these worlds. Now with over 30 such planets joined together in what is called the Sidereal Federation, Earth, the mother of humanity, is no longer unique. It is not even the center, with planet Teegarden now the seat of the Federation.

Earth is still a popular place to visit, and its history and culture are a natural attraction to all interested in humanity's past. However, the citizens on Earth still want their needs to be heard in the greater Federation, and a Regional Governor would have to be an effective conduit for that voice.

As Dr. Wang declared, "We on Earth realize the importance of tourism for our economy, but we do not want Earth to be viewed as just a world for recreational activities. The people who have decided to make Earth their home believe they carry the legacy of humanity and that trust gives them the right to have some say in charting the Sidereal Federation's destiny."

"I see that the Sol System, should be viewed as 'the first among equals' in Human Space," Alyie surmised. "It would be my task as Regional Governor to impress upon the Sidereal High Council of its special place in the governance structure."

Also, during this "listening time", Alyie received visits from Maxim Hebron, who brought with him a succession of public figures to discuss Earth, Luna and Mars affairs. Alyie was always patient with these current and former representatives, but she often felt they were just using her to push forward their political self-interests.

Finally, Lydia Foxworth presented Alyie both on video hyper-link and in-person with media strategies and material to promote her candidacy. She also brought Alyie possible outfits to wear in her future campaign. As Lydia explained, "I want you to look professional but with some warmth. Tailored jackets, and suits with soft colors like peach, yellow and cream, I think, will convey a strong feminine image. Heels, but not too high, will also work. I know you are tall, but I don't want you to look like a genetically enhanced giraffe."

Alyie was disturbed at this re-branding of herself, and Jaynis would only grimace when she told him of Lydia's plans. "Do you really want to do this?" he questioned. "I know I said no more dangerous missions, but I still want you to be the real Alyie."

"I know this seems like I am compromising myself, but this is all superficial. What is important is that I keep my values. If I am elected to be Regional Governor, I will only serve one term (five E-yr.). That means that I will be stationed on Earth most of the time and together we can start our family. It is all for the good."

CHAPTER 4.

While Alyie was examining 3-D images of herself that Lydia had prepared for campaign advertising, an emergency message was sent to her implant saying that almost all members of the Royal Family of the House of Jade on Planet Kanva were killed in a solar sailing accident. The only survivor was Alyie's close friend from the Fleet Academy, Princess Revita Jadeite. The Princess had flown her air jet to the other side of the planet to preside over the commemoration of a new monument to fallen heroes when her parents and two brothers were killed. Alyie was shocked at this tragedy, and her first thoughts were to Revi, who must be so distraught. She informed the Sidereal High Council of her intention to go to Kanva as head of the Council's delegation, but her main interest was to provide comfort to her friend. Jaynis, well aware of Alyie's close relationship with Revi, was eager to accompany Alyie to the funeral.

The High Council provided Alyie, Jaynis and other members of the Council's representation with a space cruiser to travel to Kanva, which orbits the star Trappist-1, located at about 40 l-yr away, almost at the limit of Human Space. Trappist-1 is a cool M class star, but Kanva's proximity to it provides an Earth-like environment that is further augmented by the Andaman Ocean that encircles that planet. Kanva's synchronous rotation produces a four E-d diurnal period with one side always facing the star. Due to its atmosphere, which is heavily oxygenated, it has a robust greenhouse effect that makes its climate similar to tropical regions on Earth. With lush vegetation, abundant precipitation, and balmy temperatures, Kanva is a veritable Earth-like fabled paradise.

CHAPTER 5.

The flight to Kanva would go through two hyper-knots. Jaynis, never an eager traveler, was verging on space sickness most of the approximate two E-w journey. To divert his attention, Alyie instructed him on the unusual form of government that had been established on Kanva.

"Are you telling me that they have a hereditary monarchy?" puzzled a pallid-faced Jaynis. "I thought 'divine rights of kings' disappeared seven E-c ago."

"Yes, Jaynis they do. On Kanva, the Jadeite were established as the reigning family two E-c ago because the founding members were the product of genetically designed offspring."

"So their 'designer genes' gave them a superiority over everyone else," Jaynis mused. "How reactionary can this planet be?"

"You don't see the advantage in this Jaynis? In recognizing this bloodline as "royal", citizens of Kanva hoped to avoid the internecine political rivalries and treacheries so common in other human civilizations. There is no question as to who should reign on Kanva and no disputed transfers of power."

"Is the head of this royal family an absolute monarch?"

"No, the functioning of the government is run by a duly elected parliament, but the King or Queen has final right of approval on any initiative or policy. Members of the Royal Family of the House of Jade also serve as titular leaders of various departments and offices. For example, Revi, due to her training at the Sidereal Federation Flight Academy, is the High Commander of the Military on Kanva."

"How is this line preserved through future generations?" Jaynis wondered.

"Oh, Jaynis, that's where things get a little complicated, and why this tragedy in Revi's family becomes more than a personal loss.

Members of Jadeite's interbreed to keep the genetic line pure. The death of her parents and her two brothers leaves Revi as the only living link to the dynasty."

"I see. So the legitimacy of the House of Jade comes into question if she would have offspring with someone in the future?"

"Not necessarily," said Alyie. "Revi had told me that she had regularly frozen her eggs and her brothers have done the same with their sperm. So, despite the course of events that have recently transpired, the House of Jade can continue to rule on Kanva if the eggs are fertilized successfully in the future."

"Do we know how Revi's parents and brothers died?" asked Jaynis.

"The reports I received spoke of a violent storm that rose up suddenly while they were sailing their boat using photovoltaics on the Andaman Ocean. It is funny, but Revi's father King Anan and her brothers were excellent seaman and regularly won regattas that took place on Kanva."

"Well," Jaynis speculated, "even the best sailors can have accidents. Revi must have taken this very hard."

"I have only spoken to her once by video hyper-link to let her know that we were coming. She appeared devastated and in a state of shock. She was very close to her family. The events surrounding the funeral are going to be very difficult for her, and I can't imagine the burden she is under in terms of assuming the Jade throne."

"How close were you two at the Academy?" Jaynis asked.

"We shared a suite and did a lot together. She was a lot of fun. Revi comes closer to anyone as a sister to me. I want to be there for her as much as possible."

CHAPTER 6.

The space cruiser made a gentle landing at the principal spaceport on Kanva. Alyie, Jaynis and the High Council delegation were met there by Mr. Hans Stöler, the Regional Governor for this sector of the Sidereal Federation and Colonel Aston Brockton, Deputy Commander of the Kavnian Military. Governor Stöler was a portly gentleman about 60 E-yr who was dressed in a black suit for the funeral. Colonel Brockton, who Alyie was familiar with from her frequent conversations with Revi, was a strikingly handsome blonde-haired, blue-eyed man of Alyie and Revi's age of small stature but well built. The Colonel was in full military uniform of a forest-green jacket, light green trousers with a yellow stripe running down the side and tall brown leather boots.

"Admiral Starstriker, welcome to Kanva. I have been instructed by the Princess to escort you and your party to your rooms at the palace where you can dress for the funeral service which is scheduled to begin in two E-hr."

"Thank you, Colonel Brockton. How is the Princess doing, if I may ask?"

"The Princess has suffered a terrible loss, but she is of the House of Jade and knows her duties," was the Colonel's curt reply to Alyie's question.

All boarded an airbus and were transported to the large parade grounds just outside the palace. Disembarking, the delegation walked through the gate to the inner courtyard. Climbing the 50 stone steps, they were brought inside the ornate palace, which seemed a replica of such buildings from a faraway time on Earth. Jaynis rolled his eyes as he gazed toward the ceiling where huge crystalline chandeliers hung down. Going up another flight of stairs, Alyie and Jaynis were shown their spacious suite, and soon after, members of the palace staff brought in their luggage.

Quickly freshening up, Alyie changed into the full dress uniform she would wear to the funeral. She would be part of a horse-mounted procession that would directly follow behind the caskets to the Andaman Ocean's edge. Donning her double-breasted snowy white suit jacket with full military medals and crisp white trousers, Alyie fastened spurs to her tall black riding boots. Around her waist, in addition to her holster for her laser pistol, was a belt holding a scabbard in which she sheathed a ceremonial sword that was her grandfather's. Putting on her cap and black gloves, Alyie inserted a riding crop in her right boot, which she hoped would give her some control over the stallion she would be astride. Jaynis, on the other hand, was wearing the morning suit he wore to his wedding on Mars two E-yr ago.

CHAPTER 7.

Alyie and Jaynis were escorted to the parade grounds where the funeral procession was assembling. The sky was overcast with light rain falling. A groom brought over her mount, Shera. This magnificent black stallion with a single star on his forehead had been Alyie's riding horse whenever she visited Revi on Kanva. Now 13 E-yr., he whinnied at the sight of Alyie, and she softly rubbed her gloved hand over his face. "Now, big boy, you have to be gentle with me. I am out of practice."

While Alyie was getting re-acquainted with Shera, Princess Revita, accompanied by Colonel Brockton and the leading members of the planet's House of Parliament, strove down the palace steps towards her. Revi was in military attire, befitting her position as Military High Commander. She wore a tight-fitting forest green jacket with gold braids and a brace of medals pinned on her breasts, identifying her military rank and achievements. Her family's ancestral long slender sword hung by her side with a gold-edged hilt. The Princess' white dove-colored breeches were cut off by black leather, highly polished boots that came up to her knee. On top of her raven-colored hair, framing her delicate, beautiful face, was a black felt beret fastened by an enormous jade pin, the sigil of her family. Revi's almond brown eyes moistened at the sight of Alyie, and the two women hugged silently, with the much taller Admiral enveloping the shorter Princess. Alyie could tell Revi was doing all she could to hold back all emotion as she felt her friend tremble in her embrace. Pulling apart and holding each other at arms-length with their respective gloves, Alyie whispered softly, "I am so sorry," to which Revi mouthed, "I know."

The Princess' horse, Gayatri, a beautiful milk-white mare, was brought to her, and, with Colonel Brockton's assistance, Revi mounted, grasping the reins with her left, white-gloved hand, on the middle finger of which, sparkled a jade ring. Then Alyie mounted Shera, placing her boots firmly in the stirrups and adjusting the reins to gain a supple but effective control over her steed. Princess Revita gave Gayatri a mild kick with her spurs to start the procession. As it proceeded slowly outside the palace gates, a team of 10 black horses, pulling a cart carrying the caskets of Revi's father, King Anan; her mother, Queen Isthar; and her brothers, Prince Tasmar and Prince Regnei, met the riders. In the misty rain, it was a somber but magnificent scene to behold. Drummers in full green-colored uniforms were marching on either side of the funeral cart, pounding a mournful beat as the wain slowly rotated its wheels under the heavy load. The caskets were made of fine dark wood and had jade gemstones inlaid around their tops. Directly behind the funeral cart rode Princess Revita, her head high and her face impassive despite her obvious grief. Alyie Starstriker and Colonel Brockton were riding side by side just behind the Princess. To their rear was the palace Royal Honor Guard in full military uniform on black horses. Following the equine entourage were members of Parliament, Regional Governor Stöler, other prominent citizens and guests, including Jaynis, who rode in ground vehicles.

CHAPTER 8.

The funeral procession wound down the cobblestone streets of the capital city Inmar, approximately a km. to the waters' edge, where an open wooden barge was beached on the shore. As the cart carrying the caskets halted, an elderly man in full-length green robes came forward and sprinkled what looked like oil on each casket. Speaking in a booming voice, the man, who was evidently a priest, proclaimed,

"On this day, we, citizens of Kanva, present to the Lord of Earth, Wind, and Water, His Majesty King Anan; Her Majesty Queen Isthar; His Royal Highness Prince Tasmar and His Royal Highness Prince Regnei. May the element of fire consume their mortal remains and spread them to the other three Elements. May the spirit of this most Royal Family of the House of Jadeite remain in our minds and hearts forever."

Then all dismounted, and members of the Royal Honor Guard carefully took each casket in turn off the cart and slowly carried them onto the barge. When that was accomplished, Princess Revita came forward to the edge of the dock as everyone in the funeral party gathered around her. Alyie could see that the barge was loaded with kindling wood and straw. The priest poured additional oil on the barge and its contents. He then ignited a large torch which he handed to Revi. She grasped it solemnly in her left gloved hand and looked soulfully in the misty rain at the four caskets where the bodies of her family laid before setting the wood and straw ablaze. Once the fire had spread to the whole barge, members of the Honor Guard pushed it forward, and it began to move away from the shore. As Revi and the rest of the funeral party gazed into the fiery tomb of her family, a woman's voice was heard singing a mournful elegy.

After the boat was seen to sink into the sea with the fire's flames barely visible, all at the funeral proceeded back to the palace. Re-mounting, Princess Revita motioned to Alyie to ride alongside her. As the two women rode slowly side by side, not a word was spoken. Alyie could sense in her friend's face the toll this ordeal had taken on her. Back at the parade grounds, when they were dismounting, Revi needed Aston Brockton's assistance getting off her mare, and it was clear she was not steady on her feet. He offered to provide support for her as they walked up the palace steps, but Revi preferred to cling to Alyie, who had been joined by Jaynis. The two couples, women in front arm-to-arm, men behind, walked inside the palace, up the winding staircase to the Princess's room. Several times, it looked like Revi would falter, but she kept her equilibrium. Once at the door of her room, the Princess dismissed her handmaidens who had followed her up. As she was about to enter, she fiercely held on to Alyie's arm, beckoning with her eyes to join her inside. Jaynis and Aston eyed each other quizzically but assented to the Princess' wish.

Once the door was closed and Revita was certain that Jaynis and Aston had departed, she fell into Alyie's arms, crying hysterically. Alyie hugged her tightly, "Yes, cry all you want now. You were so brave today. I don't know how you were able to go through with the immolation ceremony. I am so proud of you."

As the Princess continued to sob, Alyie guided her friend so that the two of them sat together on top of Revi's bed. She was able to get Revi to drink some medicinal elixir she found in the Princess' room that would hopefully enable her to sleep. As the drink seemed to be taking some effect, Alyie carefully removed Revi's wet beret, jacket, breeches, tall black boots, white gloves, ring and saber. Tucking Revi under the silk sheets of her bed, Alyie was ready to bid her good night, but the Princess would not let go and pulled Alyie strongly to her. As she was sliding under the covers, Alyie, with some difficulty, managed to kick her boots off and take one sleeve of her jacket off. (Her sword, however, remained sheathed around her waist.) With Revi nuzzling in Alyie's breast, she soothingly stroked her friend until the sobs ceased and restful sleep came.

CHAPTER 9.

Because the capital city, Inmar, was on the star side of Kanva, it was always daylight. To compensate, interior places like the palace had autonomously controlled shades that provided the semblance of nighttime for the citizens' bio-rhythms to function properly. As the filters on the shades receded and light began to seep into Princess Revita's bedroom, Alyie opened her eyes. During the "evening", she was able to loosen her sword belt, which made her infinitely more comfortable. Her family sword was now lying beside the two women as they cuddled together. Alyie gently extracted herself from Revi's embrace and gathered up her sword. Not wanting to disturb the sleeping Princess, Alyie walked to the far end of the bedroom and used her implant to contact Jaynis.

"Good morning, Jaynis. I am sorry about my abruptness, but I knew Revi needed assistance. When you are awake, buzz me, and I will meet you outside the Princess' chamber."

While in bed, Alyie had considered Revi's state of mind and had resolved on a course of action. She needed to tell Jaynis her plans, although she knew he would not be pleased.

After about an E-hr., Alyie received a "bing" in her head, indicating Jaynis was now right outside the door. Alyie, who in the course of the evening had stripped down to her tank top tee shirt, now hastily put on some clothes, knowing full well there would be palace guards stationed just outside the bedroom. She quickly got into her boots and put on one of Revi's dressing-gowns to cover the exposed areas. It was terribly short in the arms and legs, but at least Alyie would present a modest appearance outside the chamber.

Opening the door, she quickly closed it behind. "She is sleeping, and I don't want to wake her. We can talk here."

"Ok, how is Revi?" Jaynis asked.

"I am not sure, but she was able to fall asleep after she took some meds. I am hoping she will be more herself today."

"Good. I realize the funeral was a terrible ordeal for her. It will take some time for her to get over her grief."

"That is what I want to tell you. I have decided to stay on Kanva and be with Revi until the time she can resume some semblance of normal life."

"Why do you need to be with her? She has a whole kingdom that will provide her with support."

"I don't think you realize how isolated Revi is on Kanva. She is viewed as a symbol of the country and isn't supposed to have feelings and weaknesses. Revi needs someone to provide emotional support, and I believe I can serve her that way. Besides, she is my friend, and I am not going to dessert her when she is in such need."

"But what about your duties on the High Council, and your plans to run for Regional Governor? And there is the little matter of us?"

"I can still serve on the High Council here on Kanva using its secure video hyperlink. There is plenty of time to plan a campaign. This is much more important to me. And, as for us, I promise to make it up to you. Please understand, Jaynis. Revi needs me."

"Ok. Can you give me a timeline to how long you will be on Kanva?"

"As long as it takes. I am sorry Jaynis."

CHAPTER 10.

Jaynis flew back to Earth with the members of the High Council delegation in 2 E-d. In the days that followed, Revi, in Alyie's company, slowly returned to her high-spirited self, but she refused to preside over any official duties during her "Time of Mourning". There were intervals, however, when the Princess needed to be alone to come to terms with her sorrow or when the priest would come to console her. Alyie listened attentively as Revi recalled the good times with her family and stood by her friend as she attempted to work through her grief. The two women were almost inseparable, spending time both inside the palace and in the gardens and parks outside. As Alyie had not intended for an extended stay when she came for the funeral, she was in need of clothing. Revi and Alyie enjoyed "fashion shopping, getting Alyie outfits to wear on Kanva. They designed the clothes and used the palace's 3D fabricator to make them. Light dresses, short shorts and swimsuits were de rigueur for the sultry climate on Kanva.

Alyie and Revi enjoyed being outdoors. There was a pool on the palace grounds hidden inside a tropical garden in which they swam, star bathed, read poetry and giggled together as young schoolgirls. More adventurous jaunts included flights on Revi's air jet that they took sightseeing around the capital city and to the dark side of the planet, where the two friends wandered anonymously among the planet's perpetual nightlife. Probably the most pleasurable activity of all was horseback riding. The Royal Stable was located on a tiny island, Ismar, in the bay that led to the Andaman Ocean, where Revi would fly her air jet with Alyie at least twice an E-wk. Outfitted with tan riding breeches, Alyie on Shera and Revi on Gayatri would race across the immaculate fields and meadows. They would either ride before returning to the palace for breakfast or take a picnic lunch to have on the island during a riding break. The one activity the Princess refused to participate in was boating, as it brought forth horrid memories of her family's demise.

One day as Alyie went to Revi's room to call on her, she found her friend beaming in an unusual good frame of mind with her hands behind her back.

"I know that look, Revi, you are up to something. What do you have in mind for us today?"

"Oh, my dear sweet friend, it is not for us. It is for you."

Then Revi moved her hands forward and presented Alyie with a small black box.

"Open it."

Alyie did as requested and found inside was a magnificent jade crystal attached to a pin. "What is this?" Alyie asked.

"Put it on. You are now my First Consul."

"First Consul?" Alyie was incredulous. "What does that mean?"

"It means, Alyie, that while I am in a Time of Mourning, I cede all my duties to you. What you proclaim and approve is done as if you were the head of the House of Jade. Congratulations, First Consul!"

"How can this be? Do you have the approval of Parliament? What about my duties on the Sidereal High Council? Isn't this a conflict of interest?"

"I can do this because I am Princess Revita Jadeite," Revi stated emphatically. "I do not need any approval to have a designated surrogate to discharge my duties. Do not worry about the High Council. I have been in communication with High Governor Park, and he is in agreement that during this transition period, you would be the ideal choice to assist me in my reign. You see, it is all worked out."

"I am not sure it is. How will the members of Parliament think of an off-worlder such as myself stepping in for you? Your family was head of many departments including the military. Will I have to assume those positions as First Consul? For example, will your nice Colonel

Brockton pledge fealty to me instead of you? I was under the impression he doesn't enjoy our companionship too much."

"It doesn't matter what anyone thinks. The fact is I need you desperately. I am not fit to reign. You know that. I can't even go into the throne room because it reminds me of my parents and brothers. Please help me."

"I will, but it must be a temporary position. I have responsibilities on the High Council; I am contemplating running for office; I have an impatient husband back on Earth; and we are anticipating, starting a family. Once you are inaugurated as Queen, my position must be terminated. Do I have your word on this?"

"Yes, First Consul. You have the word of the House of Jade."

With that, a smiling Revita fastened the jade pin on Alyie's blouse, just above her left breast.

CHAPTER 11.

As starlight came filtering into her room, signaling the start of a new day, Alyie was preparing for the arrival of Dev Gotsan, the current Parliamentary Leader, in what promised to be a contentious meeting. She had been unsure how she should appear as First Consul. If she asked, Alyie was sure Revi would design an elaborate uniform that would make Alyie feel uncomfortable and invite scorn from the officials she would be dealing with. So she had decided to wear her Admiral uniform with medals and, of course, the jade pin, signifying her office as First Consul. The image she wanted to convey was that she had the credentials to be a head of state, but the Fleet uniform identified her as an outsider who would not be in Kanva permanently.

Just as she was finishing combing her hair, a video hyperlink came from a visibly agitated Jaynis, who was nearly shouting. "Wow! I leave you on Kanva, and then the next thing I find is that you are now its ruler. I was concerned about hailing you as Madam Governor. I see you have bypassed that title, and now you're a Royal Highness."

"Alyie responded with a wane smile. "Oh, Jaynis, don't be silly. I am not a royal, just First Consul."

Because there were not that many micro hyper-knots in Kanva's location in human space, there was a delay in sending and receiving messages. It took nearly 10 E-minutes to receive Jaynis' response, and when he did, Alyie could tell he was not mollified by her answer.

"What's going on Alyie? I thought your life was here on Earth, not playing nursemaid to a princess."

"Please be patient, Jaynis. This is just temporary. As soon as Revita is crowned Queen, I am done here. I promise."

Again, Alyie waited for Jaynis' response, and when it came, it was brief but blunt. "I am getting really tired of your promises."

Before Alyie could respond back, her implant was informing her that Mr. Gotsan had arrived. Not having finished getting into her uniform, Alyie greeted the Parliamentary Leader in shirt sleeves. Dev Gotsan was a tall, portly mature man with gray hair and a courtly demeanor dressed in a gray suit, white shirt and blue and white striped tie. Alyie could tell from the serious look he gave her that Mr. Gotsan disapproved of her appointment as First Consul. Alyie offered him some light refreshments, but he politely refused. Beckoning him to sit down opposite her, Alyie spoke as candidly as she could.

"Mr. Gotsan, thank you for agreeing to see me before the Jade Council meeting later today. I have presumed you are not happy with me being First Consul, and I can assure you I feel the same. I view this position as transitory, and I have informed Princess Revita that I will stay no longer than the time it takes her to be crowned Queen."

"It is good to hear you say that, but the power you have been given is unprecedented in the history of Kanva."

"Yes, but has there ever been a time when nearly all of the Royal Family of the House of Jade have suddenly perished?" Alyie asked. "The Princess needs her Time of Mourning, and as her friend, I have pledged my loyalty and agreed to serve as First Consul. When she is ready to resume her duties, I will gladly relinquish my title, and Queen Revita will reign as head of the House of Jadeite."

"Since we are speaking frankly, Admiral, I must inform you that even before the accident there were rumblings about the future of the House of Jade."

"Thank you for telling me this," said Alyie. "If I am to be effective in my limited time as First Consul, I need to know all that is going on across the planet. What is the source of what you call these 'rumblings'?"

"First of all," answered Mr. Gotsan, "many of the common people, especially the young, have grown restless and many believe that a hereditary monarchy is archaic in the modern Sidereal Federation.

There have been scattered protests and some violent disturbances in the interior parts of the planet. Second, members of the House of Parliament, including, I must confess yours truly, believe the House of Jade can be obstructionist to new initiatives as members of the Royal Family have veto power on laws passed and proposed policies in the departments in which they serve as heads. Some law makers believe that a true democratic government without royal imprimatur would enable more progress. The underlying cause of this dissatisfaction is that the people as a whole are not doing well economically and have targeted the monarchy as a scapegoat."

"I will not ask how you feel about the monarchy, Mr. Gotsan, "nor will I tell you my opinion, which is immaterial to my role as First Consul. What I hope we can agree on is to work together to stabilize the government, optimize Kanva's resources, and put forward plans for a brighter future. Can I have your word on that?"

"Yes, Admiral you have. There is one order of business I will put to you before the Jade Council meeting. The House of Parliament requests an inquiry into the deaths of the Royal Family members. To proceed, we need the approval of the Princess. Since she is in mourning, I was reluctant to approach her, but with you as First Consul, I can now come forward."

"Of course, I approve Mr. Gotsan. Send me the inquiry request, and I will affix the Seal of the House of Jade on it. Is there any question about the cause of the accident?"

"None that I am aware, Admiral, but we in government believe we should do our due diligence."

"Please proceed expeditiously. Thanks so much, for agreeing to meet me, and please call me Alyie."

"Yes." Ma'am.

CHAPTER 12.

After Mr. Gotsan excused himself, Alyie thought about trying to re-connect with Jaynis but considered it futile. She prepared for the Jade Council meeting by scanning her implants as to who will be in attendance today. Mr. Gotsan sat on the Council along with the heads of Military, Education, Industry, Agriculture, Transportation and Culture. Confident she knew the name and appearance of each, she finished dressing by buttoning her shirt, fastening her tie and donning her white Admiral's jacket. Satisfied with her appearance, she took out of her personal bag the gravity wave generator Jaynis had bought her long ago on Earth (and was instrumental in overcoming some predatory robots). Joggling the transmission frequency, she sent the following coded message: "Jaynis, I know you are angry with me, but if you get this message, please wish me luck. I love you."

Other than Mr. Gotsan, the only individual Alyie was familiar with on the Council was Aston Brockton, who, as Deputy Commander of the Military, was now Alyie's direct subordinate. Alyie introduced herself and then had each Jade Council member give a short summary of their department and its current status. After that was done, Alyie, carefully using first-person plural pronouns "we" and "us" instead of "I" and "me", announced, "During the Time of Mourning, we have decided that the First Consul will be the temporary head of each Jade Council department."

This caused some grumbling, but Alyie sent to the Council members' implants a declaration from Princess Revita making the appointments official.

"What we want from all of you in the future," Alyie declared, "are proposals with detailed arguments for any new initiatives. We promise to consider them promptly and grant our approval if merited as soon as possible. We also request weekly reports sent to us of your departments' activities with as much quantitative information as possible so that we can be kept informed."

Alyie could tell this level of accountability was something new in the Jade Council, and its impact was greeted with some wariness. Not allowing for any debate, Alyie changed the subject.

"Parliamentary Leader, Mr. Gotsan has informed us that there is some unrest in some parts of the planet?"

"In the Southern Hemisphere, there have been some demonstrations and work stoppages recently," said Colonel Brockton. "I have sent two battalions to maintain order."

"The capital of that region is Kandy, is it not Colonel Brockton?"

"Yes, Admiral, or should I say First Consul?" replied Brockton.

"We have concluded," Alyie said, again using the first person plural pronoun, "that the First Consul will visit Kandy in 2 E-d to speak to the people and tour the countryside."

"But, Madam First Consul," expressed Alisha Singhari, the Deputy Head of Education, "it is too dangerous. You would be putting your life at risk. Am I not correct Colonel Brockton?"

"There is an element of risk, to be sure," said Brockton, "but with my, or our, troops in place, there should be a sufficient deterrent."

"Thank you, Colonel for offering your support, but we think the First Consul's visit would be more accepted if there is minimal military presence. So we ask your troops to stand down. If anyone wants to join the First Consul on this trip, you are welcome."

Alyie could tell from the glint in Colonel Brockton's eyes her remarks had sparked some resentment. Not looking for consensus, Alyie concluded the meeting by thanking everyone in advance for their support.

CHAPTER 13.

On the day Alyie was leaving for her trip, she checked in with Revita to see how the Princess was doing. Finding her somewhat sullen, Alyie asked, "What's wrong Revi, you seem a little glum."

"You're going away from me. I had a day planned with berry picking in the palace orchards, and now I find you are traveling halfway around the planet."

"I don't believe you. You made me First Consul to serve in your place and how can I be effective if I don't meet the citizens and find out what the issues are. You are welcome to join me. I am sure the people of Kanva would much rather meet their future Queen than some interloper from the Sidereal Federation. Please come."

"No, I am not ready. Go, but come back soon and safe. I will miss you terribly. Wait. Take my ring it will make your visit more official."

Alyie flew on an airbus to Kandy. The trip over the glimmering Andaman Ocean was eye-opening as Alyie had the chance to realize how water-bound this planet was. Only Alisha Singhari joined her from the Jade Council. The Minister of Education was buoyed by Alyie's confidence and wanted to show the First Consul some of the pressing issues with early education in this less developed region.

After touching down in a small landing field in a clearing, the visitors, which included some security officers, were driven in a ground vehicle to what served as a town square in the middle of the city. Alyie, Alisha and some staff members were led on stage while the citizens congregated in the center. Contrary to her order, Alyie could see that Colonel Brockton had soldiers posted around the square and on the rooftops surveying the gathering.

Alyie was introduced by the Town Councilman. She began, announcing,

"Greeting citizens of Kandy from crown Princess Revita. She gives her heartfelt thanks for your condolences and prayers during her Time of Mourning. She will re-join you soon when she is installed Queen. As her First Consul, I am here to see and hear from you. Let us know your needs."

After some silence, a shout was heard from a young man who cried, "We don't need a Queen who hides inside her palace while we suffer out here."

Added to this were further dissenters who chanted, "Down with the House of Jade. An end to the monarchy."

Alyie quelled the noise with the help of some townspeople and then spoke. "Princess Revita has suffered a grievous loss – her whole family. I am sure all of you have suffered great losses as well. She is a princess, but she is flesh and blood such as you and me. Can you allow her some time to get over this terrible tragedy? She has sent me to speak to you and hear your requests. The House of Jade stands ready to serve Kanva. Please let me be your advocate. I am ready to listen to you."

Alyie then descended down the improvised stage and walked among the people with Minister Singhari close behind. A young girl named Lisel, about five E-yr old, came forward holding a flower. Alyie got down on one knee to greet the child. As Lisel wrapped her free arm around Alyie's boot, she presented the flower. Alyie, visibly touched, took it and hugged the child warmly. Noticing that Lisel was eyeing the jade pin on Alyie's lapel, she allowed her to touch it and then took the jade ring off her gloved finger to show it to the child. Walking hand in hand with Lisel, Alyie and her party made a tour of the shops in the town square and then visited the schools. As they walked, Alyie took time to meet the citizens, listen to their complaints (with her implant recording the conversations) and receive their grateful thanks and well wishes for Princess Revita. All were thrilled to meet and greet this tall red-haired beguiling woman.

CHAPTER 14.

In the next three E-m., many positive changes happened on Kanva. There was new energy among the holders of the levers of government as Alyie, as First Consul, empowered the heads of the various departments to move forward on their respective initiatives. With her influence on the Sidereal High Council, Alyie was able to secure a substantial low-interest loan from the Sidereal Bank for long-delayed projects on Kanva. Working with the Ministry of the Treasury, Alyie ensured that this influx of funds would be distributed effectively and equitably. She often consulted with the departmental heads, insisting on timely reporting but worked in collaboration with them to optimize their operations. In most instances, Alyie gave these ministers wide latitude to run their own divisions, but she held them accountable for achieving their self-identified objectives. Alyie traveled continually across the planet, meeting all segments of the population and assuring them that she would carry their messages to the Crown Princess.

During this time, Alyie had a few brief video hyper-link meetings with Jaynis. They were cordial, but Alyie could tell he was not pleased with her continued stay on Kanva, and she realized there would have to be some healing when she returned to Earth.

Alyie's other main project was bringing Revita back to a full functioning role as a future Queen. As First Consul, Alyie couldn't spend as much "playtime" with Revi as the latter wished. So, she invited her friend to join her in dispensing her First Consul duties, such as analyzing the weekly departmental reports, planning Jade Council meetings and arranging Alyie's touring schedule. At first, Revi would just go along with whatever Alyie suggested, but eventually, Revi became involved in the business of government, asking pertinent questions and expressing her opinion. Revi would even join Alyie, on occasion, when she paid a visit to a department head or attended a Jade Council meeting. Initially, she deferred to Alyie in addressing the governmental officials, but more and more, she became an active participant. Still, Revita would not make any public appearances.

CHAPTER 15.

After making a return from a planet-wide E-w tour of arts and education institutions, Alyie fulfilled a pledge that she would take time off to spend alone with Revita. The Princess had planned a day of riding on Ismar that included a picnic lunch. Alyie had to promise to turn off her implants, so she would not be contacted during their time together. Alyie, in turn, thought the occasion would be ripe to discuss some important issues with her friend.

Because of the warm weather, the two women dressed in cotton white short-sleeved tee shirts, fawn-colored breeches and black riding boots. Revi tied her lustrous black hair in a white silk kerchief while Alyie held hers in place with a barrette. They made a striking pair as they strove on the palace grounds to board the Princess' air jet: Revita, beautiful as always with her smooth brown skin, sultry eyes and petite figure and Alyie, tall, athletic with blonde, reddish hair and freckles.

Taking the short hop to the island, the friends jumped out of the air jet, where stable grooms were awaiting their arrival, holding steady their saddled mounts: milk-white Gayatri for the Princess and coal-black Shera for her First Consul. The horses, eager to run, showed their enthusiasm by neighing and bucking playfully. Given rein, they bounded into the open field as their riders gently prodded them forward with their spurs.

CHAPTER 16.

After an elating ride across the meadows, the friends dismounted near a shaded stream and unpacked the picnic lunch that the palace staff had placed in a wooden basket under a pre-designated tree. After the meal of cucumber and tomato sandwiches, cheese, nuts, fruit and faux champagne was finished, the women reclined and stretched their booted legs out on the Tartan-styled blanket. As Alyie was facing upward, Revi was carefully plopping pitless cherries into her mouth. Alyie, signaling her friend to cease, believed she had found the moment to be serious.

"I am your First Consul, but there are some important issues that only you can decide. I think now is the time to make you aware of them."

"I thought you promised, no business today."

Listen, Revita, as your friend and now your Consul, there are three outstanding points. Please hear me out."

"Ok. You have the Crown's permission to speak." Revi proclaimed, smiling demurely.

"First and primarily, you need to set a date for your Coronation. I am losing credibility when I keep promising its coming without a fixed dateline."

"Duly noted, Consul. We will take that under advisement and get back to you."

"Second issue, you need to give the order to initiate the fertilization process on the frozen eggs. This is vital to insure the continuation of your family line."

"Yes, Mon Cheri Consul. Will do upon return to palace."

"And lastly," Alyie said with some trepidation, "for your emotional and physical well-being, you need to have a Consort."

"A Consort?" Revi said in mock astonishment. "I already have one."

"Do you?"

"It's you."

"I am not your Consort, I am your First Consul, and that is just temporary."

"But you can be both my Consul and official Consort. You are very talented."

"No, I cannot be your consort. Among other reasons, I am already spoken for."

"Oh, yes Jaynis. I really like him. I am sure you can convince him to share you with me."

"That I doubt. I have trouble convincing him on anything these days."

"Three body arrangements are done all the time. I am sure he will come around."

"But we are planning a family."

"That's fine, Alyie. You can all live here. There is plenty of room in the palace. Your baby can be in the same nursery with my future brothers and sisters."

"No, you need to find a Consort. There must be a multitude of worthy candidates. You know you're rather desirable."

"Alyie, I am glad you think so. But, I can't imagine any other person I want as Consort."

"What about Colonel Aston Brockton? I see the way he looks at you. I am sure he would jump at the offer."

"Oh, Aston, he's nice, but he has too much pride. He would expect me to love him back."

"And why can't you do that?"

"No, because, I am in love with someone else and have only loved one other person. You know who that is, Mon Amie."

"No, No, No. I will not be your Consort."

"I have an idea," said Revi, as a devilish smile spread across her lips. "Let's race to decide. The first one who makes it to the other side of the island to the water's edge gets to decide who my Consort will be. Agreed?"

Before Alyie could respond, Revita untied her kerchief and threw it over her friend's head. By the time Alyie extricated herself, Revi had mounted her mare and was on her way. Alyie fastened the kerchief around her neck and jumped on Shera, bidding to stallion to take up the chase.

"Come on big boy," Alyie cajoled, "we have to win this. There is a lot at stake."

Though Revi had a clear lead, Alyie could see that with Shera's long strides, she was catching up to her friend as they were riding alongside the edge of a forest. Suddenly, everything changed as Revi was thrown from Gayatri. Alyie quickly jumped off Shera to come to the aid of her friend when she saw that the mare had been struck with an arrow and was writhing in pain on the ground.

Coming toward Revi, who had collapsed from the fall, Alyie saw other arrows come whizzing by. Drawing her laser pistol from her right boot, she stood in front of the unconscious Revi to offer a human shield when she was struck hard in the upper left chest by a shaft. Without at first feeling the effect of the arrow, Alyie instinctively fired her pistol in the vicinity of where she presumed the projectiles were coming. After sensing the attack had stopped, Alyie turned to her assist her friend. By now, Alyie was in great pain. Her first impulse was to remove the shaft, but because the wound was deep, she believed she would bleed out if it was now extracted. Grasping the reins of Shera, Alyie approached the prostate Princess and bade her horse to kneel. Remarkably, Shera obeyed her command, and Alyie, although grimacing from her puncture, lifted the still unconscious Revita onto the horse and then painfully mounted herself. Before departing, Alyie noticed the great distress that Gayatri was in due to multiple arrow wounds. Alyie pointed her laser pistol at the mare, saying, "I am so sorry, girl."

Taking the most direct route back to the stables, Alyie found when she arrived that it was a scene of carnage. The bodies of the three groomsmen and two stable hands were scattered in the walking enclosure. Dismounting from Shera, Alyie saw that one of the staff, a young woman, was pierced by an arrow on her left side and was gasping for breath. Alyie realized then that the arrows used by the assailants had been dipped in poison, and what she was seeing in that woman on the ground would soon be happening to her. So going against her previous reluctance, Alyie, with her right gloved hand and with most of her remaining strength, pulled the shaft from her chest. The pain was unbelievable and shook her to the core. After the arrow was out, Alyie had some pain relief, but dark red blood came spouting out of the wound, staining her shirt and flowing down to her breeches. To blot some of the outflow, Alyie quickly fashioned a makeshift tourniquet with Revi's kerchief around her left breast.

Staggering, Alyie slowly glided Revi off Shera. The Princess was beginning to regain consciousness and appeared to have not suffered external wounds. Alyie helped a still unsteady Revita into the air jet and climbed herself into the pilot's seat. As the craft was airborne, the effects of the bleeding and the poison took hold as she began asphyxiating. Alyie presumed her wounds were mortal. "So this is what dying feels like," she mused. But her military training took over, and her objective was now to complete the mission – namely, get Revita back to the palace. Sensing she was losing consciousness, Alyie pushed an emergency signal and set the air jet on autonomous landing mode with the palace's parade grounds as the destination.

By the time the air jet made a perfect landing, Revi had regained the full sense of her faculties. As she looked to the side, she saw her dear friend passed out wearing her own blood-soaked kerchief. Alyie's gloved hands were still grasping the controls. Screaming for assistance, the

Princess was immediately met by the palace staff, who promptly applied artificial respiration and then carefully lifted the recumbent Alyie Starstriker to an air-powered stretcher that whisked her to the palace's infirmary.

CHAPTER 17.

For three Earth-simulated days and nights, Alyie Starstriker hovered between this world and the next. During that interval, she had a vague sense of reality, drifting in and out of consciousness. There were machines attached to her, and she could perceive dimly that human figures were hovering about her. Throughout it all, she felt there was a familiar presence. At times, she called out "Jaynis", but the voice that always responded was feminine.

Finally, she opened her eyes and clearly saw the room and the bed she was lying in. Feeling her right hand being held firmly, she turned to see Revita smiling broadly by her side.

"Hello, sweet dreamer. Welcome back."

"It's good to be back," was Alyie's barely audible response.

Then Revita leaned forward and kissed Alyie softly on the lips. "I am sorry, but I vowed that if you woke up, I would kiss you. You can't imagine how long I have wanted to do this."

"Me too," Alyie whispered as she reached to stroke Revi's black hair. Coming together, their lips joined again in a longingly heartfelt embrace.

CHAPTER 18.

By the next day, Alyie was able to sit up in bed and take liquid foods. While two nurses were attending to her, Princess Revita entered her room accompanied by a gentleman in a laboratory coat. The nurses curtseyed to the Princess, and she dismissed them.

"This is Dr. Botsama," Revi announced. "He has treated you from the beginning."

"Thank you so much, Doctor. I owe my life to you."

"Oh, young lady. You had us worried a bit," said Dr. Fraja Botsama, a dark-skinned middle-aged man with gray and black hair. What I believed saved you were things beyond my control. First, you had the presence of mind to extract the arrow, which prevented the poison from reaching its full potency. Second, you are an incredible physical specimen with remarkable recuperative powers. You did lose a great deal of blood, but we were able to replace it with our synthetic blood generator. The deep puncture in your chest needed extensive surgery. It looks like you have suffered a previous wound in that area. Am I correct?"

"Yes, Doctor," said Alyie, recalling a stab wound on planet Nespar. "My left chest has become a pin cushion."

"Fortunately, through the offices of the Sidereal Federation, we were able to contact, Dr. Abel Ettiger, a human space renowned surgeon, who was given control of our robotic surgical system to remotely repair your puncture. The damaged tissue has been replaced by grafts from our human tissue generation device. In time, you will be completely healed and should regain full range of motion on your left side."

"That is good to hear. When can I get out of bed?"

"We will have you walking today, and I have given permission to have you transferred to the palace proper."

"You will be staying with me," Revita said, "for the time being."

The doctor bowed as Revita cordially asked him to leave. When alone with Alyie, the Princess did something with her implants that Alyie took as sealing off the room from outside communication.

Alyie had a question. "When can I speak to Jaynis? How much does he know about what has happened?"

"Don't worry, I have kept him up to date on your condition and all your treatments. I have also been in contact with your parents, and they would like do a hyperlink video chat with you when you are feeling up to it."

"Is Jaynis still angry with me?"

"Oh, silly. He is desperately in love with you. One of the reasons I have put a security shield on in this room is that Jaynis is currently on his way here. He will arrive in eight E-d."

"He is?"

"Yes, but the reason, I am being secretive is that he is not traveling alone."

"I don't understand."

"Alyie, there have been developments since the attack on us and at the stable. I received the confidential report that you sanctioned on the investigation of the deaths of my family members, and it concludes it was not an accident. The software that would have switched the navigation system into emergency mode was tampered with, and my father was left without the ability on the boat to counteract the effect of the storm."

"That is horrible. Do you assume that the attack on us is related?"

"I am not sure. The investigation on Ismar has identified that the poison arrows are type of curare made from tree bark popularized by an outlawed group calling themselves Neoliths who want Kanva to be a tribal society without a centralized government and a monarchy. Colonel Brockton is leading the search for the maker of the weapons and his scouring the planet. I have not seen him recently, but he assures me, he is tracking down all leads."

"Who is coming with Jaynis to Kanva?"

"Ah, that's were my discretion is centered. I have been in contact with the Sidereal Federation High Council, and they believe that an expert in criminal forensics is needed. Traveling with Jaynis is Dr. Laslow Topak, who will present himself as an academic colleague, but upon arrival he will take over the investigation of my family's murder and the attack on Ismar."

"All right. I will be ready to assist Dr. Topak in any way I can," Alyie declared.

"No you won't; you need to recover," insisted Revita. "I will be taking charge. Too long I have wallowed in my self-pity. It is time for me to live up to my heritage."

"Are you ready for this? It could get very painful."

"No more painful then losing my family and almost losing my dearest friend. If you had died, I don't know what I would have done. But you didn't, and I swear by all that I view holy that I will use all my strength and will to bring those who have done these crimes to justice."

CHAPTER 19.

Alyie improved rapidly under Revi's care at the palace. She took over the nursing duties from the staff and only left Alyie's company to do governmental business such as a Jade Council meeting. Alyie was impressed at the change in her friend's behavior. This was the strong-willed, confident young woman Alyie had known, and it brought joy to her heart. The day before Jaynis and Dr. Topak were to arrive, Revi made arrangements to transfer all of Alyie's belongings back to the latter's room. Notably, absence from Alyie's wardrobe was her uniform. Alyie protested, but Revi was insistent that the First Consul was off duty until she fully recovered. The Princess did, however, have strong opinions on what Alyie should wear when Jaynis first arrived.

"These short shorts with this charming buckle will remind him of your beautiful long legs. This silk blouse with a plunging décolleté will get his heart racing, and this transparent nightgown will seal the deal in the boudoir."

"You are really something," said Alyie laughing.

"I am trying to atone for making a fool of myself. The most important thing in my life right now is your happiness. And you and I both know for that to occur you need to be with Jaynis."

"Thank you," Alyie replied, trying to suppress some tears.

CHAPTER 20.

Upon arrival in Inmar, Jaynis and Dr. Topak, under the Princess' orders, were whisked without any fanfare to a side entrance at the palace and brought immediately to a chamber room where Revi and Alyie were waiting. Jaynis, on seeing Alyie, immediately came up and hugged her, being careful not to squeeze too tight. "I am so sorry for being such a 'you-know-what'. I missed you so much."

"You had the right to be a 'you-know-what'. I was not fulfilling my wifely duties. That will change I promise."

Jaynis shook his head, smiling. "I thought we agreed no more risky assignments."

"I think this one nearly permanently cured me of living a life of danger."

As they were about to get more intimate to continue this happy reunion, Jaynis and Alyie became aware there were two others in the room. Breaking free from Alyie's embrace, Jaynis cleared his throat to introduce Dr. Topak to Alyie and Revita. Laslow Topak was a mustached man in his late 30 E-yr., with dark unruly hair, white complexion, of middle height and build. He was dressed formally in a late 21st-century brown suit, white shirt, blue tie and well-worn brown shoes.

Bowing ceremoniously to Princess Revita, the doctor expressed his relief at her well-being. Then addressing Alyie, he said, "I am so glad Admiral, or should I say, First Consul, that you are up and about. I was expecting you to be in a much weaker condition as the result of the injury."

"I have been under great care. Her Royal Highness has missed her calling as a Healer."

"Although it is wonderful that both of you have adverted disaster, please do not be complaisant. Whoever committed this attack on you both and your staff will undoubtedly try again. You both are in great peril. I hope Your Highness has increased the security personnel on you and First Consul Starstriker. You must make sure that they are the most trustworthy and beyond suspicion."

"Dr. Topak, my most loyal palace staff are now guarding both myself and the First Consul. These individuals are from families that have served the House of Jade for generations. From your concern, do I take it you suspect someone at the palace is involved in the assassination attempt?"

"At this stage of my investigation, it is best to limit those who have access to you. I also would recommend the less you say about what I am doing the better. We need to keep those responsible for these acts in the dark about what we are uncovering."

"But I have been pestered by the Parliamentary Leader, Dev Gotsan, for approval moving forward on an investigation into the deaths of my parents as result of the report he provided. Also, Colonel Aston Brockton is currently searching for the members of a reactionary group who may behind the attack on the island Ismar and awaits further direction."

"I am not sure these should be independent investigations," said Dr. Topak.

"Are you proposing that the tampering with the Princess' family ship and the arrow attack on Alyie, Revita and her stable help were done by the same group?" questioned Jaynis.

"On a superficial level," Dr. Topak began, "they seem quite different. The sabotage of the boat's software system required sophistication and access to the Royal Family's security system. On the other hand, the attackers on the island used arrows presumably launched from Earth-like 12th E-c (CE) crossbows that would suggest a throwback insurgent group. But the more I delve into the evidence and the statements made by Your Highness and the First Consul, I see a hideous general plan at work."

"And what might that be, Dr. Topak?" asked Revita.

"It is with some difficulty I have to say, Your Highness, but the common denominator in these murders is the House of Jade. I see the goal of this campaign to be the extinction of your family."

"Doctor, excuse me," said a stunned Princess, "but I have to say what you have just told me is devastating to take in at once. I know there is unhappiness in parts of the kingdom with the monarchy, both at the local level and in the legislature, but to think some group is trying to eliminate me and my family is hard to comprehend."

"With your help, I hope to prevent them from completing their vile plan. What I would like to do is travel to the island where the arrow attacks took place. There are some inconsistencies that I would like to clear up, and I would also like to take some readings with my sensor equipment for in situ analysis. I don't want to appear abrupt, but we need to act as soon as possible. I need a small team of your most trusted aids to assist me."

"Yes, I will provide you with all the support you need. You can start out early next simulated E-d."

"I know this is asking a great deal, but I would want both Your Highness and the First Consul to accompany me. You are both the only living witnesses on that awful day. Admiral Starstriker, your memory would be invaluable in re-creating what happened when you were attacked."

Revita voiced an objection, "My dear doctor, the First Consul has suffered a grave injury. I do not want to risk her recovery. Surely, you can find all you want to know by just questioning her at the palace."

"No, Revi, I understand the importance of my presence. I am going. With you and Jaynis at my side, I am sure I will be fine."

CHAPTER 21.

That "evening", Jaynis and Alyie bundled together in her suite. Jaynis was considerate in that he thought Alyie's injuries were such that intimacy between them could be deferred until she was more completely healed. However, Alyie took advantage of their closeness to provide Jaynis with some pleasure that he had been missing for the past four E-m.

As soon as the filters at the palace let in the daylight, a small party consisting of Revita, Alyie, Jaynis, Dr. Topak, and four members of the Royal Honor Guard left the palace and took an airbus on the short trip to Ismar. Still, sans uniform, Alyie dressed in a white shell blouse covering her wound. She wore a dark green sports coat draped over her shoulders. Jaynis had helped her get into her dark breeches and the black boots she insisted on wearing to walk over the island's uneven terrain. To keep her steady, Revita presented Alyie with a handsome carved wooden walking stick with a jade handle and a sharp retractable blade at the other end to use, as Revi said was, "Just in case."

The investigative party's first stop was at the stable. Silhouettes of the murdered staff were placed on the ground where their bodies were found. The memory of that awful day came back to Alyie, reminding her of the agony she was in and recalling the image of that poor young woman convulsing in her death throes from the poisoning. Dr. Topak, who dressed in a hound's tooth wool sports jacket, oblivious to the planet's hot climate, corduroy pants, and what used to be called knickers, prowled around the stable area and in the barns dictating to his implant as he made observations. Stating he was ready to move on, the party boarded two horse-drawn coaches (mechanized vehicles being prohibited on the island) to go to the location where the Princess and Alyie were attacked.

Hailing the drivers to stop the coaches where the body of the Princess' mare, Gayatri, was found, Laslow asked Alyie to come out of the coach and stand in the exact position in which she defended Revita before she was struck by the arrow. Given assistance by Jaynis, Alyie planted her feet where Dr. Topak indicated that some blood was detected (presumably hers) and pointed her walking stick in the direction in which she had fired her laser pistol. Following the line of the stick, Dr. Topak, along with two of the guards, went into the forest searching for evidence. Alyie, who, even with Jaynis' help, could not stand upright for long, climbed back inside the coach to rest. After some time interval, the doctor and his assistants emerged with Topak saying triumphantly, "Eureka! I have found what I need. We have been fortunate, Princess, that your planet has refrained from precipitation since the attack, and we have been able to find blood spots at the edge of the forest."

"Do you think it is from the group that attacked us and my stable help?" asked Princess Revita.

"That group, Your Highness," declared Dr. Topak, "consists of a single individual."

"Laslow, what makes you conclude that?" asked Jaynis. "Five people were killed at the stable yard. That must be the result of several assailants."

"The fact that the attack on the Princess and the First Consul ceased after Admiral Starstriker fired back leads me to two conclusions. One, is that she wounded the assailant, and second, there were no others or else they would have continued shooting at her and the Princess."

"But what about the massacre at the stable?" asked Revita.

"Again, the result of a single individual. Instead of using a primitive crossbow, I suggest the criminal used a modern rapid firing bow that enabled him to kill the poor victims one after another. That also rules out the neo-primitive group Neoliths who pride themselves on using ancient tools."

"But what I don't understand," Alyie questioned, "if the attack was aimed at the Princess and myself, why did the folks at the stable have to die? Surely, they are not directly connected to the Royal Family."

"Ah. That's was my question before I came here. There has to be only one explanation: The killer was known to all in the stable. They had to die or they would be witnesses to the assassination attempt."

"But why did the killer come to the stable before stalking Alyie and me?" asked Revita.

"I know the answer from the DNA evidence I have just collected from the forest. The blood samples found were both human and equine. The killer went to the barn and mounted a horse. That's when the massacre occurred. I even know the horse he rode."

"Who is it?" asked the Princess.

"Checking the barn, I found two empty stalls, your fine mare Gayatri, G_d rest her soul, and one that had the name plate 'Charlatan'. I am also happy to report that the First Consul's stallion, Shera, is doing fine."

"Charlatan is Colonel Brockton's riding horse," said a perplexed Princess Revita. "I don't recall Aston reporting this horse missing."

"We need to find him. I suspect this horse is still somewhere on the island. Am I not correct, it would be difficult to remove an injured animal without attracting attention, Princess?"

"There is a holding shedrow for horses near the water's edge. We keep them stabled there until a barge comes to take them across the narrow bay to Inmar for events."

"Then I suggest we go there at once," declared Dr. Topak.

All returned to their respective carriages and made the short trip back to the near side of the island. Finding the shed near the landing area, they went inside and, sure enough, found Charlatan lying in a stall in a distressed condition. The Princess, examining the chestnut colt, found his right front leg severally lacerated in what appeared to be burn wounds. She immediately called for emergency veterinary assistance for the stricken animal.

"I think we now have a clear idea of the actions of the criminal," Dr. Topak pronounced. "He took a private boat to the island on the day of the attack and arrived shortly after the Princess and the First Consul began their ride. Mounting Charlatan, he killed all the stable hands on duty because they saw him. After stalking you both, he took a position in the woods where you were riding by and made his attack. After the Admiral's return fire wounded him and his horse, he made a retreat back to the shore. Leaving the horse unattended, the injured assailant re-boarded his ship and found shelter in the capital to attend to his wounds."

"Do you think this person is also responsible for the tampering with the Princess' family's boat?" asked Jaynis.

"The fact that he was known to the stable crew indicates he was an official at the palace," Dr. Topak surmised. "Let me ask you bluntly Princess, would Colonel Brockton have access to the security system of the Royal Family?"

"Yes, Dr. Topak," said a disheartened Revita. "The Colonel as Deputy Commander of the Military is also in charge of Palace Safety and has all the security codes in case the House of Jade is unable to perform their responsibilities. What could possibly be Aston's motive for doing these horrible deeds?"

"That Princess I have not been able to discern, but there is further analysis needed on the evidence I have collected that might shine a light on this dreadful darkness."

Jaynis raised the question, "Princess, have you been in contact with Brockton recently?"

"I have had almost daily communication with him since the attack, but he has not been to my knowledge to the palace. He keeps telling me he is hunting the rogues who attacked us."

"My guess," Jaynis responded, "is that he is nursing the injury that Alyie gave him and waiting for the opportunity to come back to the island to deal with his stricken horse."

“I have, in addition, a great fear,” said Laslow Topak, “that he is waiting for another chance to complete what he failed to do on this island. Again, I cannot stress how perilous your situation is Princess.”

“Let’s concentrate on finding conclusive evidence for arresting this bastard, and I will take care of my own personal safety.”

CHAPTER 22.

As the group made the quick flight back to the mainland, Princess Revita put in a request to change all the palace security passwords so that Colonel Brockton nor anyone else could gain access. However, she was thwarted by a message that the system was down. As the airbus landed on the parade grounds, a young woman palace staffer ran towards the investigative group as they were disembarking.

"Princess, I have terrible news. The climate controls on the Royal Family's frozen eggs facility have been breached and the eggs have thawed. The heat produced has destroyed them. I am so sorry, Your Highness."

The Princess stood open-mouthed as she reeled from the impact of this latest atrocity. She appeared about to lose her balance but quickly regained her composure. "The House of Jade will end with me. Why is he so bent on my line's destruction?"

Alyie reached out to hug her friend while giving her walking stick to Jaynis. The two women brushed against each other's cheeks while suppressing tears.

"Is Brockton working with a dissident group or for certain rogue members of Parliament?" questioned Jaynis.

"I can answer those questions better when I complete the DNA analysis," said Dr. Topak. "Princess, could I gain access to your family's medical history? I have a lead I want to pursue."

"As soon as the system comes back up, doctor, I will send your implant the access links."

"When I find out what I am looking for, I will let you know immediately," said Dr. Topak. "In the interim, I cannot express more strongly how much you need to be protected. I realize now we are dealing with a malice so malignant that the criminal will stop at nothing to complete his devastation of your family."

"Rest assured, Dr. Topak, my husband and I will stay by the Princess' side constantly. As First Consul, I will dispatch the palace guard to deny Colonel Brockton access to the palace grounds. They are under the direct supervision of the Royal Family and need no governmental permission to enforce the Crown's will."

After this exchange, the group walked warily into the palace, and with her guards in front and behind providing security, the Princess was escorted into her room.

CHAPTER 23.

Jaynis and Alyie, as promised, remained with Revita as she reminisced about her parents and brothers. There was a sense of melancholy and doom as the Princess recalled growing up in a star-crossed family. Revita stressed, "We never chose this life; it was a birthright and a duty my family believed we had to honor. I am sure my father and mother would have been perfectly happy living a commoner's life as long as they could be together."

Halting the conversation, when she received a message in her implant from Dr. Topak, Revi said, "The doctor is coming here presently. He has information, and I need to provide security shields to protect our conversation."

Soon after, Laslow was admitted past the guards into the Princess' suite, and he was in such an agitated state that he neglected to bow. "Your Highness, again thanks for providing me access. I have found remarkable - no stunning information. I am almost at a loss to explain."

"Please, Dr. Topak proceed. This is no time to be tongue-tied." Alyie impatiently implored.

"When I did a DNA screen of the human blood found in the woods near where both of you were attacked, I found no match with anyone in the government, palace or the populace. Indeed, Brockton's DNA on file did not match the criminal's. However, when I screened the blood found with your family's DNA, it was a perfect match."

"What?" Revita's exclaimed. "Are you saying that the person who killed my family, the stable staff and tried to assassinate me and Alyie is a member of the House of Jade?"

"No. All I am saying," stressed Dr. Topak, "is that that criminal has the same DNA as you and the deceased members of your family."

"But my family line ends with me. How could this person possess the same genetic code?"

"Think carefully, Princess. In your family history, has there been any other kin or did any of your family participate in genetic engineering?"

"Oh my God!" Princess Revita said, nearly shouting. "My brother Regnei once was engaged in an experimental trial to produce an embryonic clone of himself. He was somewhat paranoid and thought it would be good to have some, how should I say, spare parts of himself around in case needed. Once my father found out about his scheme, he ordered Regnei to destroy the clone."

"I found in searching your family medical history that Prince Regnei was enrolled in something called Doppelgänger when he was seven E-yr. Could this be that trial?"

"Yes, Dr. Topak, that is about the age he dabbled in cloning himself."

"I think the evidence points to the fact that the clone of your brother, for some reason, was never terminated. On the contrary, he grew up and rose high in Kanva's military officer staff and now for some reason, perhaps vengeance, wants to destroy the family that he was produced from."

"But Laslow," Jaynis interjected. "Brockton does not resemble any of Revi's family. He is light skinned, blonde haired and blue-eyed."

"All of these physical features could have been altered by cosmetic engineering," answered Dr. Topak. "Note that he is of the same slender shape and stature as the Princess. Height and physical built cannot be easily altered."

"However, you said, Colonel Brockton's DNA was not a match for the blood found in the woods where Revi and I were attacked. Doesn't that mean that Brockton is not a clone of Revi's brother?"

"No, Admiral. All that indicates to me is that Colonel Brockton, to hide his identity, managed to substitute a different sample of DNA when requested."

"I think the next step is for me as head of the House of Jade to requisition Parliament to arrest Aston on the charge of murder."

"Ah, Princess that would be prudent in preventing him from making what I am sure will be another attempt on you and/or Admiral Starstriker. However, as believable as my hypothesis is, we have no direct proof. Because of the un-matching DNA, we can't place him at the scene of the stable massacres; we also don't know how he broke into your family's security system to sabotage the boat or destroy the frozen eggs. Arresting him can determine if he has suffered a recent injury, but I am sure he can make excuses for the wound."

"We can't just let him roam free, biding his time to strike at the Princess again," said a frustrated Alyie.

"No, Alyie we shouldn't let him pick the time." answered Jaynis. "Maybe we can force him to act before he is ready by choosing the time for him."

"What are you suggesting, Jaynis? Are you setting a trap with Revi up as the lure?"

"Hear me out," exclaimed Jaynis. "I think Brockton wants more than just to destroy the House of Jade. I thinks he wants to inherit it. For some time, I know through Alyie that he has been trying to woo your affections Princess. My guess is he wanted to ascend the throne as your co-ruler, at least temporarily. He ruthlessly destroyed your family so that you would be the Crown Princess. However, certain events have made it unlikely you would choose him as your consort. Thinking his chances were fading away as you drew closer to your First Consul, he tried to kill you and destroyed the heirs by thawing the eggs. With your death, I assume he will then come forward and claim the throne because of his genetic link."

"Well said, Dr. Bottombrook," Laslow Topak proclaimed, "but how does this individual's craven ambition justify putting the Princess even more at risk than she is now?"

"To force him to what I hope would be a hasty action, I propose we put forward the one thing Brockton most fears - someone else, ascending to the throne. Let's have Revita name a Successor."

"Ah, the light as they say is now turned on," Laslow pronounced. "Not just a Successor, but the person he loathes the most."

"I presume you are talking about me." Alyie sheepishly exclaimed.

"To name a Successor outside the House of Jade, I would need Parliament to grant an Extraordinary Act of Permission. I am not sure they would agree to this."

"But, Your Highness, we don't need to go through with it," Dr. Topak said. "If he is trustworthy, speak secretly to the Parliamentary Leader and tell him of our plans. Hopefully, he will go along with them until we flush Brockton out."

"Let me speak to Dev Gotsan," said Alyie. "He and I have developed a good working relationship. I will alert him of our proposal and say that if the criminal doesn't act immediately after hearing it, then Mr. Gotsan is free to use his legislative skills to delay Parliament from acting on it. I think I can convince him to play along with us."

"The beauty of naming Admiral Starstriker as Successor is that she would probably be accepted by both Parliament and the people of Kanva because of her popularity and the success she has had in her role of First Consul," said Dr. Topak

"I must say if anything good comes out of this horrible nightmare, it would be naming you and your family as the Successor to the House of Jade," said a jubilant Revita. "When should I make the announcement?"

"My suggestion would be to make it on the next simulated star rise. If you can strongly hint who that would be, so much the better," said Jaynis.

"Here's my plan," proclaimed the Princess. "I will say I will be making two announcements in the next two E-d: the date of my Coronation as Queen and the name of my Successor. I will say that this person is someone the people of Kanva in the last few E-m have come to know and love. That will make it pretty obvious who it is."

After the Princess' address, my dear comrades," Laslow cautioned, "we need to prepare for the worst."

"We'll be ready," chimed Revi, Alyie and Jaynis in unison.

CHAPTER 24.

After Princess Revita Jadeite made her address, the team waited for the expected assault. To set the trap, the prohibition of Brockton's access to the palace was rescinded; the guards were instructed to keep a respectable distance from the Princess and Alyie but have their laser rifles fully activated. All involved in the surveillance were linked by their implants to scan for Brockton's bio-signature. Once he entered the palace, his movements would be tracked, and when Brockton went to strike, all would converge to foil his attempted assassination. Even Jaynis was equipped with a laser pistol which he had only fired in practice.

On the first "day" after the address, there was an uneasy quiet over the palace as tensions were high and nerves were on edge. However, nothing transpired. On the following simulated E-d, Princess Revita and Alyie dressed together in the former's suite prior to the announcement of Successor. The Princess was in full military regalia for this event that would take place in the throne room and be transmitted over the planet-wide video band. Revita had returned Alyie's uniform to her so she could appear in her First Consul garb, and the Princess dutifully helped her friend into her clothes and boots. Jaynis, who was waiting outside as a guard, escorted the two women down the spiral staircase that led to the throne room.

Greeting Dr. Topak at the landing, they all concluded that there still was no indication that Colonel Brockton was nearby. The doctor expressed his concern. "I am getting a little uneasy because Brockton, if he wants a clear path to the throne, should strike before the Princess announces Admiral Starstriker as her Successor. My fear is that he is aware of our ruse and is waiting to see if we will carry it out."

"Don't worry, Dr. Topak I am more than happy to name Alyie as my Successor. She will be right by my side when I make the announcement."

Just then, Alyie realized she hadn't taken her daily infusion to promote tissue growth from her wound and was feeling somewhat weak.

"I am sorry, but Jaynis can you take me quickly to my room? I need to take my meds. I am afraid I might pass out from standing too long at the ceremony. That wouldn't inspire confidence in me as a worthy Successor."

After some concern by Laslow and Revita, Alyie and Jaynis walked back up the stairs and down the hall into her room. Alyie was indeed feeling woozy and sat down, grasping her walking stick as Jaynis volunteered to go into the lavatory to retrieve the medicine. Soon after, the door swung open, and Aston Brockton entered, dressed as a palace guard with a peaked hat, green-colored vest, white breeches and tall over-the-knee black boots. He had drawn his laser pistol and was pointing it directly at Alyie.

Alyie tried to appear calm and spoke in a voice loud enough that she hoped Jaynis would hear. "So Colonel Brockton, you are here to attend the announcement of the Coronation date. We didn't know you were coming."

"No you didn't because I have been able to block my bio-signature from being transmitted. It is amazing what you can purchase off the Federation non-authorized market if you are willing to pay for it."

As Brockton approached, Alyie noticed a limp in his upper left leg near his groin. "I see you have injured yourself; I hope it is nothing serious."

"This is your work and you know it. How I wish I had killed you the first time. But I am not going to let you take what should be mine."

"And what would that be, Colonel?"

"I was going to marry the Princess. After her family's demise, she and I would rule this planet. However, then you came along, and I saw how cozy you tow were. She didn't want me even around her anyone because of you. So I decided to take another tack."

"That tack was to destroy her future family and try to kill the person you were supposedly in love with? It is clear the Princess made the right decision. Your actions have forfeited any claims to the throne."

"Claims to the throne? I am of the House of Jade. Her brother created me in his image then was ordered to discard me. But, he was too soft and gave me to a commoner to raise. My guardian changed my physical appearance, and I grew up not knowing my heritage. One day the old man slipped, and I forced him to tell me the truth. Since my adolescence, I have planned this ascent carefully, and I am not about to let someone like you or Revita stand in my way."

Jaynis, who had been listening to Brockton's diatribe and had alerted Revita and Dr. Topak of his presence, felt it was now or never the time to act as he flung the lavatory door wide open. Aston, who had apparently forgotten about Jaynis's presence, turned to fire. When he did, Alyie shifted the walking stick from her left to right hand, released the catch on the blade and swung it, slashing Brockton's hand holding the pistol. As the Colonel was groping on the floor to retrieve his weapon, the suite door was flung open, and Revita burst in with her palace guards and Dr. Topak. Brandishing her family sword, the Princess struck Brockton below the chin severing his carotid artery.

As the blood gushed out, Brockton turned to the Princess, crying, "How can you do this? I am your kin."

"You are not my kin," said Revita as she stood over him, leering downward as her two booted legs flanked his head. "You're my kin's slayer, on whom I have just executed the Queen's Justice.

An Earth-minute later, Brockton was staring upward, lifeless.

EPILOGUE

It was a wonderful event, full of beauty, pageantry and joy as the people of Kanva celebrated the Coronation of Queen Revita, the First of Her Name of House Jadeite. It had been three E-m. since the murders and assassination attempts, and everyone on the planet welcomed the happy occasion. So much preparation had gone into making Revita's ascension to the throne successful that it was with a sigh of relief that it was accomplished so gloriously.

As the Queen, robed in a glittering gold gown wearing a jade encrusted crown, retired from addressing the crowd from her balcony, there were inside in attendance Parliamentary Leader Dev Gotsan, the members of the Jade Council and her "teammates" Alyie, Jaynis and Laslow Topak.

Advancing to greet Dr. Topak, who bowed conspicuously, Revita said, "I can never thank you enough for your thorough and efficient detective work. You have literally saved my life and kept my line alive."

After receiving congratulations from the others, Revita made her way to Alyie and Jaynis. Refusing to allow Alyie to bow, Revita hugged her friend as if for the last time and said with tears flowing, "Are you sure you won't become my Successor? The whole planet wants you."

"No, you need to start a new branch in the House of Jade. Be open to hybrid vigor. I am not meant to be a Queen. My future and my heart lie with the Sidereal Federation. Besides, Jaynis and I are going back to Earth to start our decidedly un-royal bloodline. But, be assured, we are friends forever.

After Jaynis bowed, Revita bade him rise and said, "Take good care of her. She is the best. You don't know how lucky you are."

"I do know how lucky I am, Your Majesty. Thank you for letting go."

As Jaynis and Alyie were riding to the spaceport for their return trip to Earth, Jaynis had a question. "If you had become Queen would I have had to call you 'Queen Starstriker' or 'Queen Alyie'?"

"Well, that's a decision you will never have to make, my sweet."

"The Chronicles will say," Jaynis opined, "that she forsook a kingdom for the love of a good man."

Alyie could only reply, "You are too much," as she turned to plant a wet kiss on his lips.

THE FOREVER DREAM

CHAPTER 1.

The twins were getting anxious for their next feeding. Tessa and Tomus were crying for their mother's nipples to provide them with milk. Regional Governor Alyie Starstriker had a fixed schedule for her babies' feedings and did not anticipate this premature yearning for her services. Nevertheless, she took their hearty appetite as a sign of the robust health of these yearlings. After getting the "feed us" signal in her implant, she suspended the conversation she was having on the video link with her associates. Removing her black sports coat, she left her office on the second floor of the chateau that Alyie and Jaynis Bottombrook had purchased when they decided to initiate the In Vitro Fertilization (IVF) procedure and crossed the hall to the twins' nursery. Finding her robotic assistant Taki 2, making a vain attempt to placate the infants, Alyie instructed her to cease and hand the children one by one to her as Alyie settled in the nursing rocking chair.

Unbuttoning her double-breasted silk blue blouse, she first had Tessa suckle her left breast as Alyie soothingly cooed, "Now, Tessa Starbrook, is this what you want?"

When Alyie felt Tessa was satiated, she instructed Taki 2 to give her Tomus, who was having a fit, having to wait his turn.

"Tomus Starbrook, I know it is considered archaic, but I want you to be a gentlemen and let ladies go first."

This intimacy with the infants gave Alyie a pleasure and a sense of happiness she had never even considered previously possible.

CHAPTER 2.

After Alyie's recovery from the nearly mortal wound she suffered on Planet Kanva, she and Jaynis decided to start a family. Two fertile eggs resulted from the IVF procedure in the birth of Tessa and Tomus. Both had light hair and fair skin, with the former having her mother's green eyes while the latter mirrored his father's blue. Realizing their townhouse in Paris was too small for four, Alyie and Jaynis sold it and purchased a chateau in Montpellier, which as the result of coastal erosion over the past five E-c is now in close proximity to the Mediterranean Sea. The house had a lovely garden and an elevated terrace from which the Carnon-Plage beach could be seen. Situated in relative proximity to Jaynis' faculty position at the Université de Paris and the seat of the Regional Governance for the Sidereal Federation in Brussels, it became a welcome retreat from their respective day-to-day professional obligations.

Alyie's election to Regional Governor of the Sol System was relatively straightforward. Her main opposition was Hector Palermo, head of the Independence Party, a group dedicated to having Earth (along with its colonies Luna and Mars) leave the Sidereal Federation. Their main problem was that Earth would fare better as an independent planet than what they deemed was its current "second class" status in the Federation. How Earth would survive both economically and militarily without the Federation's resources was not addressed in their drive to sever the Earth's ties with the rest of the colonized Human Space. Despite Palermo's emotional appeal and his followers' intensity, Alyie prevailed overwhelmingly in the election.

CHAPTER 3.

Alyie's first E-yr. as Regional Governor was going well. She scheduled meetings every Earth-fortnight with her self-appointed Advisory Council. It consisted of three representatives from Earth and two, each from Luna and Mars. Her Security Advisor, Major Reg Jones, was a comrade who had assisted her in a difficult mission to Planet Nespar to resolve a disputed election. The Major was the head of the Panthera, an extremely effective 100 strong tactical unit.

Although the headquarters for the Sol System was on Earth, Alyie made regular trips via her space cruiser to Luna and Mars to meet with representatives of those two settlements. Although all three environments were part of the same region, the respective citizens expressed different priorities. Those from Earth complained about its lack of prestige and status in the Sidereal Federation. The Luna group represented mining and manufacturing interests and was always concerned about access to selling their goods in the Federation's Common Exchange. The scientific community on Mars sent proposals to the Regional Council for new research projects that Alyie made sure to have Jaynis vet for credibility. Issues that could not be resolved at the Regional level or involved the wider Federation, Alyie would take to the Sidereal High Council by getting on their meeting calendar.

On this particular E-d, Alyie was scheduled to have a Regional Council Meeting in Brussels. Fortunately, Jaynis would be working at home and could take care of the twins. Alyie, who took an extended leave of absence from Space Fleet, still was a commissioned admiral. Not wanting her Council advisors to forget her military service, Alyie dressed in a modified uniform. Sans medals, she put on her white admiral's jacket, crisp white shirt with epaulets, brown silk cravat, light brown slacks and tall brown leather boots. Pulling her light reddish hair up, she donned her admiral's cap, and after self-inspection in a mirror, deemed herself primed for the public.

Going downstairs to the kitchen, she found Jaynis feeding Tessa and Tomus with the induced lactation breast milk Alyie had provided. Planting kisses on the foreheads of both infants, Alyie turned to Jaynis and said, "Well, dear, how do I look?"

"Let's take a vote," was Jaynis' quick reply. "Whoever doesn't like the way Mommy looks, speak up."

After a brief moment, Jaynis declared, "No voices raised, I guess you passed inspection."

"Kissing Jaynis firmly on the mouth, Alyie said, "Take care. See you tonight."

Releasing the security shield on the transparent wall in the living room, Alyie stepped out of the chateau and walked down the slate steps to the lower level where her air jet was waiting. Stepping into the cockpit, she adjusted the seat, planted her boots firmly and took the craft airborne for the short ride to Brussels.

CHAPTER 4.

It was raining hard when Alyie brought her air jet down to the landing pad at the top of the Regional Headquarters building. As soon as Alyie opened the cockpit, there was a bright-eyed young woman holding an umbrella to greet her. As the liaison held the umbrella high, she attempted to drape a double-breasted khaki trench raincoat over Alyie, who was a much taller woman.

"Greetings Madam Governor. I hope your flight was uneventful. The Council members are now assembling in the meeting room."

"You are Alison Bernewithy," Alyie declared as she secured the raincoat over her shoulders. "Thank you for providing me cover from the rain."

Alison was clearly taken that the Regional Governor remembered her name. She was in her early twenties, of mid-height, blonde-haired, pink cheeked and blue-eyed. Under her trench coat, she was dressed smartly in a dark blue jacket and skirt suit. Underneath, she wore a white blouse with a large feminine bow. Her heels were black, tall and well polished.

As the two women splashed boots and shoes through the puddles on the roof, Alison said, "I have set the meeting agenda on each member's place and provided you with the notes that you sent me yesterday. Also, there is a pot of hot tea."

"Thanks again, Alison and after the meeting is over, please remain. I want to speak with you."

Stepping into the lift, Alison announced the floor number where the meeting would take place. Exiting, Alyie and Alison walked down the hall to the conference room. Finding her seat at the oval mahogany table, Alyie greeted each of the members cordially. From Earth was Mr. Max Hebron, a veteran politician, historian Dr. Fujan Wang and Ms. Karrunya Okoro, a social activist. The representatives from Luna were Mr. Sujan Roy, an industrialist, and communication specialist Ms.

Melissa Toby. From Mars were Dr. Rafael Ruis, an ectobiologist and astronomer Dr. Hiroko Sato. Finally, seated to Alyie's right was Major Reg Jones, who gave her a sly smile. The Major was a well-built mid-forties-year-old man of dark complexion and tight curly hair. After reports on tourism, education, manufacturing and research were presented and discussed, Alyie had Reg Jones introduce the main item of the meeting.

"As you are all undoubtedly aware, there has been increased activity throughout the Sol System by the so called Separatist Movement. Not content with accepting defeat in the last Regional election, the members of this group have staged protests, strikes and in some cases outright sabotage. There has been some violence and security force members have been injured in skirmishes with the insurgents. Most of the reconnaissance I have collected indicates their activity is centered on Earth, but there are incidents on Luna in disruptions in shipping and manufacturing and in hacking into the software system of the research facilities on Mars."

"But haven't arrests been made?" wondered Max Hebron.

"Yes, but they seem a decentralized organization in which the chain of command is not clear."

"What about Hector Palermo? Isn't he the leader of the Separatists?" asked Sujan Roy.

"Palermo claims no knowledge of these acts of sedition," said Reg Jones. "He is the political leader of the Independence Party, which I have not as yet been able to connect with the more revolutionary Separatist Movement."

Alyie believed it was now her time to comment. "We need a comprehensive assessment of the Separatist Movement to ascertain its goals, objectives, members and depth of support. I am appointing a small task force consisting of myself, Major Jones and Mr. Hebron and myself. It will be staffed by Ms. Bernewithy. We will conduct this investigation immediately, and when we have a conclusion, I will bring it to the

Advisory Council for recommended action. I believe we need to act fast before this becomes a full blown revolution. I do not want to summon Federation forces to quell this insurgency as it would be catastrophic to the peace and stability of the Sol System."

After receiving affirmation from the Council members, the meeting was adjourned, with Alyie requesting Reg and Max to meet her in 15 Earth-minutes in her office suite down the hall.

CHAPTER 5.

As the Advisory Council members filed out of the meeting room, Alison, as requested, stayed behind. Seated next to each other, Alyie addressed the young subordinate, "I wanted to speak to you about upgrading your position to be my Adjunct. It means more responsibility as you and I would be working more closely together. I will expect a lot from you, and colleagues of mine will tell you I can be pretty demanding."

"Oh, Madam Governor, it would be an honor to serve next to you. You have long been my heroine as a leader. Just to work in the same Regional Office as you has been a privilege."

"When you say that, you make me feel like an old relic. I have been studying you for some time. You have a solid education, and you have exhibited strong communication and analytic skills. You also have demonstrated fluency in several languages. Besides putting to use these attributes, there are a few things I insist on. First, that we have complete trust in each other, second, we always speak frankly, and third, and most importantly, all our conversations are strictly confidential. If I find this is otherwise, you will be terminated immediately."

"I completely understand, Madam Governor."

"One other demand is that when we talk privately, please address me as Alyie."

"Yes, Ma'am."

CHAPTER 6.

After their tête-à-tête, Alyie and Alison walked down to the Regional Governor's suite.

"The office next to mine will be yours. There will be a connecting interior door so we can meet without either of us going into the corridor. You will be presented with choices of furniture, carpet and wall colors. If there is anything else you want, please let the building auto-bots know. I expect you will move in, in less than an E-w. In the interim, you can park yourself in the ante-room to my office or sit in my chair when I am not here."

"Thank you, Madam Governor, I mean Alyie."

"You're welcome Alison. Now let's get ready for the Task Force meeting."

When Reg Jones and Max Hebron joined Alyie and Alison, they sat around a small elliptical table in the office suite. Alyie had signaled her auto-bot to deliver some light refreshments and hot beverages.

After some preliminary conversation, Alyie began the meeting by saying, "We need to get a clear understanding on the Separatist Movement. I want an assessment of the level of threat they present to our system."

"My contacts say they are a rogue group bent more on mayhem than any real danger to the Sol System's membership in the Federation," answered Max.

"Still," Reg Jones commented, "they seem well financed with materials, weapons and media access. I don't think we can assume they are just a ragtag bunch of malcontents."

"I believe we need to find out first whether there is any connection between Hector Palermo's party and these insurgents," Alyie added. "Even if Hector is not involved in these terrorist acts, he may have some insight into the source of this activity."

"But Madam Governor," Max exclaimed. "Would Palermo be willing to divulge any knowledge, realizing he could be implicated in these illegal actions?"

"I think a visit from myself would be appropriate as a courtesy call from the sitting Regional Governor to her former opponent."

"It makes sense," said Reg, "if Palermo wants to have a political future, he would be wise to separate himself from this fringe group. Telling what he knows to you, Madam Governor, could deliver a blow to this group without his involvement."

"Don't visit Palermo by yourself - take a security force. If he is involved with the terrorists, it would be a prime opportunity to kidnap the Regional Governor," Max warned.

"I am not going alone. My new Adjunct Alison Bernewithy will accompany me. I think together we will be a sufficient deterrent. Won't we Alison?"

All a startled Alison could say was, "Yes, Madam Governor."

"Besides, I don't want Hector to be defensive when we talk. While Alison and I are meeting with Hector, I want you, Max, to see what you can find out about the funds these Separatist rebels are obtaining. You know the adage, 'follow the money'. If you need access codes to encrypted accounts, contact my office and I will sign off on them."

"Yes, Madam Governor."

"Reg, I am afraid I have given you the most dangerous assignment. Is there any way you can infiltrate this terrorist group to find out their next targets?"

"I hope I have not acted out of turn, Gov, but I already have one of my Panthera planted among the Separatists. He has posed as a dissident member of my force who wants to experience 'real action'."

"As usual, Major. You are one or two steps ahead of me. Good work."

"As soon as I have any intel about their future actions, I will let you know Gov."

"We all have all our assignments. Let's begin and keep in close contact."

"Yes, Madam Governor," chimed Reg and Max.

CHAPTER 7.

Afterward, Alyie and Alison made arrangements for the meeting with Hector Palermo. When Alison contacted him, he was flattered that the Regional Governor would come all the way to his home in Buenos Aries to speak with him. Since their trip would be in only two E-d, Alyie invited Alison to stay with her and her family in Montpellier until they would fly to South America. After discussing items to take on the trip, Alyie sent Alison off to pack. Meeting her near day's end, the two women took the lift to the top floor and boarded Alyie's air jet.

At the chateau, Alison was introduced to Alyie's family. As the oldest daughter of four siblings, Alison was comfortable around infants, and the twins happily responded to her sounds and gestures. Jaynis, as the self-appointed titular head of the household, gave a warm greeting saying,

"Welcome to House Starbrook or is it House Bottomstriker?"

"Don't mind him, Alison. I have still not gotten used to his word play."

For dinner to commemorate Alison's promotion, they had a French-style feast of onion soup, duck confit, asparagus, sarladaises potatoes, fresh salad from Alyie and Jaynis' garden, a baguette from a local bakery and a fine wine from Alyie and Jaynis' cellar. Desert was Mont Blanc cake and espresso coffee. The adults had a fine time sharing stories of their adventures while the twins competed for attention in their respective flotation high chairs.

The next day, after working together in Alyie's home office, Alison and Alyie joined Jaynis, who was on the promenade along the Mediterranean coast, rolling the twins in their double stroller.

"Look at this shining sea," Jaynis exclaimed. "This body of water has nurtured a culture that produced Earth's greatest thinkers and artists for 2000 E-yrs. Many of the so called Western myths have come out of the lands that bordered the Mediterranean. I think of these stories as ways these ancient people tried to impart their ideas and knowledge to future generations."

"Is this how humans achieve immortality?" Alyie wondered.

"Even in the 26 Earth-century (CE), we still have not been able to extend life indefinitely," Alison mused.

"No, and perhaps that is best," surmised Jaynis. "Thus, each generation has its turn to improve the human condition and provide some guidance to their descendants. If humanity would ever achieve some form of immortality, there would be little incentive to improve or leave a legacy to others."

As it was getting cool and dark, it was thought best to end this discussion and turn the stroller around to take the long hike back to the chateau.

CHAPTER 8.

After a hearty breakfast together with Jaynis and the twins, Alyie and Alison made the final preparations for the trip to Buenos Aries. Alyie wanted the two women to present a similar look to Hector Palermo, indicating they were a closely-knit team. Not wearing her admiral uniform to indicate this was not an official visit, Alyie dressed herself (and Alison) in civilian clothes. Alyie's outfit was already in her wardrobe, but Alison's was designed and produced by Alyie and Jaynis' 3D Fabricator and completed in the morning. They both wore a faux leather and tight-fitting legacy-styled zipper black jacket. Underneath was a short-sleeved pullover white cotton blouse tucked into narrow black pants, which in turn were fitted snugly into knee-high black leather boots. Alyie fastened a holster belt around her waist and packed her laser pistol, which she assured a wary Alison that it was, "Just in case."

Kissing Jaynis and the twins goodbye, Alyie escorted Alison back into the air jet as they made the trip to the Paris spaceport, where Alyie, through her Space Fleet connections, had secured the use of a hypersonic aircraft. Seeing that the Adjunct was securely fastened in her seat, Alyie took the plane aloft, and by traveling at Mach 5.5, they reached their destination in a little over two E-hr.

Having an airbus meet them at the Buenos Aires' spaceport, the two women were shortly after dispatched to Palermo's residence on the outskirts of the metropolis. Ushered in by an elderly gentleman who was the dwelling's caretaker, they were brought into a dining area in which a table was set for an expansive lunch of asados grilled by Palermo's kitchen staff on a parrilla accompanied by a salad and a hearty red wine.

Presently Hector Palermo made his appearance. He was a tall, distinguished grey-haired man in his early 60s. He was dressed immaculately in a starched white buttoned-down shirt, open at the collar, black dress pants and what looked like patent leather shoes. Greeting both women with a half bow, he took Alyie's hand and kissed it, saying,

"Senora, I see that the Regional Governor position has suited you. You are even more beautiful than when we competed together."

"Thank you, Mr. Palermo. Allow me to introduce my Adjunct, Ms. Alison Bernewithy."

"I am happy to make your acquaintance, Senorita. You have chosen a great role model to work under. You look like an understudy for the Governor. What an attractive pair you two make."

"I am pleased to meet you, Mr. Palermo, and thank you for being so responsive to my request for this meeting with the Governor."

"You are welcome Senorita. But let's not stand here offering each other platitudes. This meal is getting impatient. Please sit down."

During lunch, the conversation was casual and friendly, with all three contributing to the overall buena voluntad.

"I have been remiss, Senora in not offering congratulations for the birth of your two children. Starting a family is a milestone event, and one, that I fear, does not occur often enough today."

"Hector, thank you. I must admit that raising children is the most challenging thing I have ever done. This is speaking from someone who flew a fighter squadron unit, dealt with angry robots, curious aliens, arbitrated a disputed election and survived an assassination attempt. Fortunately, my husband, Dr. Jaynis Bottombrook is a wonderful partner in parenting."

"Ah, I am acquainted with the vicissitudes of raising a family. I am a father of five and now a grandfather of 12. There is much work involved but in the end, indescribable joy. Blessings on you and your family."

"Thank you again, and in the future, Hector, don't be surprised if I contact you for parenting advice. That being said, the reason we came to visit was two-fold. Now that I am more or less settled into the Regional Governorship, I want to re-examine some of the issues raised during our campaign. Obviously, the most important for you is the proposed secession of the Sol System from the Sidereal Federation. I believe strongly in the value of belonging to the Federation, but I would like to hear from you how the Regional Governor's Office can make Earth's position such that there would be no cause to separate."

"Alyie, if I may call you that, the reason I ran for Regional Governor is the disrespect the High Sidereal Council has shown the Sol System and, particularly, Earth which is the cradle of humanity. Instead, it is mainly seen as a destination for tourists. I have three proposals to offer. First, the Federation Headquarters should be on this planet; second, the High Governor should always be chosen from Earth. (With your election as Regional Governor, I have hopes that will be accomplished in the future.) Third, we need a more Earth-centered approach to the Federation with the Sol System seen as distinct and pre-eminent compared to the colonized worlds. In practical terms, I believe the Sol System should receive 50% of Federation resources with the rest distributed among the other systems. Not having any of these requests even considered, my Independence Party had no other recourse but to advocate Separation."

"At first blush, your proposals appear extreme, but I believe there is room for negotiation. Moving the Federation Headquarters from planet Teegarden to Earth presents logistical and political difficulties, but I don't think that is insurmountable. You are correct, if I can trust your discretion on this matter, in that I am thinking of in the future running for the High Governor position. Making the Federation more Earth-centric involves cultivating an appreciation for its legacy through outreach and educational efforts that as Regional Governor I can prioritize in my advocacy to the High Council. The re-distribution of funds would be challenging, but my team and I will certainly make the case to the High Council on the Sol System's needs. All I ask of you is to be patient with my efforts. Would you like to serve as an advisor to me on these issues?"

"Thank you for listening to my needs, and yes, you can contact me anytime. I want to affect change but in a constitutional way. Not with the violent actions that are occurring which I abhor."

"That brings me to my second reason for paying you a visit. Do you have any idea who is behind the activities of what is called the Separatist Movement?"

"Not really. The outbursts and attacks seem to be spontaneous without a unifying center."

"Let me ask you a personal question that is completely off the record. My Adjunct and I are going to shut our implants off. Did you receive any other resources than those allotted to official candidates during our election campaign? We are trying to find who is backing these rebels."

"No, Senora. I didn't use any outside resources. However, just prior to electioneering, my campaign office did receive an inquiry from a company that wanted to inject funds into our efforts off the record. Because of laws prohibiting outside funding, we refused their offer. I was under the illusion that I could defeat you following the rules. I forgot I was competing with a legend incarnate."

"A 'legend incarnate' is a heavy title to live up to; sometimes I would like to be considered just ordinary. Getting back to your prospective benefactor, do you remember the name of the company?"

"Let me search my implant. Yes, it was called 'The Singularity'. A strange name for a corporation."

"Great, Hector. Can you send all the information you have about this company to Ms. Bernewithy? Alison, you can turn your implant back on."

"Thank you, Mr. Palermo," was Alison's response when the information was sent to her implant.

After finishing their order of business, Hector Palermo invited the two women to relax outside on his veranda and have some liquid refreshments. After a restful few E-hr., Alyie and Alison took their leave and made their way back to the spaceport for their return flight.

CHAPTER 9.

Two E-d later, Alyie was back in her office in Brussels. She called a meeting of the Task Force members to review what had been discovered about the Separatist Movement. Instead of having a meeting via a video link, Alyie deemed it would be more secure to meet in person under the Regional Office's security shield.

Addressing Reg Jones first, Alyie asked, "Does your source indicate where the Separatists plan to strike next?"

"I don't have the name of a particular target, but my source tells me that there was a call for volunteers to travel to Luna. My guess is that rebels are planning to disrupt or destroy one of the industrial operations. Sort of a show of force to demonstrate their range."

"Not knowing the particular plant makes it difficult to thwart their attack. I will put a high alert warning to all industrial buildings on Luna and assign security patrols to each. If your source reveals the real target, we can re-deploy the forces on short notice."

"Madam Governor, if I may interject," Reg cautioned. "Even if we know the target, I would not recommend lying in wait for the rebels to attack. It would signal that we have an insider, and I don't want this person to lose their cover until he/she finds out more about the Separatists' operation."

"So, Reg you are saying that we should just sit back and let them destroy a manufacturing facility to protect your insider's identity," Max Hebron surmised. "The more havoc these terrorists create, the more their movement gains acceptance."

"Max, I understand what Reg is saying," Alyie replied. "We must be patient until we have more information about the Movement, even if it means disruption and destruction. However, I still will distribute my security forces to Luna and Mars as a general precautionary step. Max, what, if anything, have you found out about the Separatists' funding source?"

"Madam Governor, this is where things get pretty murky. The uniforms and weapons recovered from some of the fallen rebels indicate they were purchased outside the Common Exchange. I had a colleague find the dealer, and, after some persuasion, which I need to bill your office for, the dealer indicated that a company called The Singularity purchased the materiel and shipped it to a warehouse in Northern Europe owned by Kurzweil Enterprises. Presumably, this is where the Separatists picked it up."

"This is interesting, Max," Alyie said. "The Singularity came up in a discussion Alison and I had with Hector Palermo. Apparently, this company offered to help finance his election bid. He refused, but it seems they now have a more receptive recipient of their funds in the rebels. Alison, I want you to try to find out more about this company, its relation to Kurzweil and who is behind it all."

"Yes, Ma'am."

As for you two gentlemen, keep digging for information, and at the first instance, let us know."

"Yes, Madam Governor."

CHAPTER 10.

Alyie had returned to Montpellier after the meeting to take over the parenting duties. Jaynis needed to go to the Université to give a lecture and meet with his student advisees. On her second E-d back, she received an urgent video link message from Alison.

"We have just received reports of an explosion at the Arrhenius Rare Earth Mining facility on Luna. Apparently, the insurgents attacked some security forces, killing three and then dropped incendiary bombs to set the plant on fire. They have sent a message Sol System wide claiming responsibility and warning of further destruction unless the Regional Office abandons the System."

"I was afraid this would escalate. This will leave me no recourse other than to contact the Federation High Council seeking armed intervention. I am loathe to put our system under direct Federation control."

"Before you do that, I have made some discoveries in the project you charged me with," Alison declared. "Do you want me to present my findings now?"

"No. How about you join me at Montpellier? I am up to my ears in changing diapers, nursing and cleaning. I could use some experienced help and certainly will value the knowledge you have gained."

Alison, realizing Alyie's subtext, said, "Sure, I have a box of vintage baby wipes."

"Good. I will arrange all the transportation. You will be picked up in about four E-hr. Pack to stay overnight."

When Alison arrived about mid-day, Alyie was playing peek-a-boo with the twins in the kitchen after she had just finished nursing them. After handing the children over to Taki 2, the women went into Alyie's home office, where Taki 1 brought baked biscuits and hot tea.

"I have activated the security shield so we can exchange messages and talk in confidence. Please tell me what you have discovered."

"At first I could find no connection between The Singularity Corporation and Kurzweil Enterprises. They are separate business entities. However, the link is historic in that there was a late 20th E-c (CE) engineer named Ray Kurzweil who espoused a theory called "The Singularity" in which humans through a combination of genetic engineering, nano-chemicals and artificial intelligence would be able to have extended lifespans.In fact, Kurzweil claimed that once this era begins, humans would live forever, barring accidents or violent deaths."

"Ok, extended life has been a dream forever, but how does that connect with the Separatist Movement?"

"Nothing at face value," was Alison's reply. "Except there is the Apeirogon Institute on Earth funded by Malcolm Dunrock who incorporates Kurzweil's ideas in the lectures, studies and symposiums it sponsors."

"Malcolm Dunrock," Alyie wondered aloud. "Isn't he the mega-rich owner of Dunrock Pharma? What does 'apeirogon' mean?"

"I had to look that up," confessed Alison. "It is a polygon with an infinite number of sides or breaking a line into an infinite number of segments. As for Dunrock Pharma, they have been trying for a couple of E-yr. to get their wonder drug Forever approved by the Sidereal Federation's Health and Welfare Board."

"Without success," Alyie replied. "The H&W Board claims the pharmaceutical had some deleterious long term effects and without further evidence cannot allow it to be marketed across the Federation."

"But how do these licensing efforts by Dunrock's company relate to the Separatist Movement?" Alison wondered.

"They may be related," Alyie replied, "in that if the Sol System secedes from the Federation, Dunrock Pharma is free to sell Forever throughout Human Space without any restrictions. It is a drastic strategy but one a person like Malcolm Dunrock who is used to getting his way might employ. I need to confront him. How can I reach him?"

"As with most commercial operations, Dunrock Pharma is located on Luna. However, Malcolm Dunrock has several residences on Earth, with his signature place, Uraniborg, a remodeled castle in the Alps."

"Work on getting him to meet with us. Use the pretext that, as Regional Governor, I am trying to learn as much about the Sol System as possible. As one of Earth's most prominent citizens, his insight would be particularly valuable to me. Tell him we would be willing to visit him in any location he wishes."

"Yes, Ma'am, I mean Alyie."

Just then, Alyie received a call on her implant from Jaynis saying he would not be coming home this evening.

"There is a visiting scholar he is meeting for dinner and anticipating how late it would be when they finished their discussions, Jaynis has decided to stay overnight in the faculty guest room on campus. Well, it looks like it's just us two girls vs. the twins tonight. See, I wasn't being disingenuous when I said I needed your help in child care."

CHAPTER 11.

After dinner, Alison and Alyie gave their complete attention to the twins, with first Alyie focusing on Tessa and then exchanging her for Tomus. After their last feeding of the day, the children were put to bed and the two now exhausted women relaxed on the comfy sofa in front of the fireplace in the study while sipping red wine that Alyie had brought up from the stock in the cellar.

Alison asked, "You and Jaynis seem so compatible. How did you two first meet?"

"We attended the same school on Mars and were often classmates. Jaynis and I have known each for a couple of Earth-decades."

"How did you know he was the one you wanted to make an eternal commitment with?"

"For me it was a gradual process. We had been friends for a while, but I started realizing that he was the one person I continually confided in, felt relaxed around and relied on when I needed help. After that my love for him just started to bloom. I have a feeling he was inclined towards me romantically before I was, but I doubt he would admit that. It is a guy thing, you know."

"I have not found someone like Jaynis, yet."

"Is there anyone you are seeing now that is, how should I say this, 'in the running'?"

"Daiki Sato is a technologist with a communications company in Tokyo. He is very kind and gracious to me. I do like him. We have been dating for over two E-yr., but I don't meet him that often, and I am not sure if we are suited for each other."

"What makes you say that?"

"I get the feeling he thinks I am too ambitious and too work oriented. He is content to stay on Earth, whereas I am interested in the whole Sidereal Federation."

"Well, I don't think there is anything wrong with having ambition. Look at my career. The importance is to achieve some balance in your life so that your professional aspirations are not all consuming. A career that depends on repeated success can be crippling personally."

"I really appreciate you showing me your family life. It helps me see what is possible."

"Listen, Alison. If ever you need some time off for personal reasons or to just decompress, don't hesitate to ask. I see you as a valuable asset and want to keep you with me as long as you desire."

"Thanks."

CHAPTER 12.

As the air cruiser was circling above the Zurich spaceport, Alyie and Jaynis were changing into the formal wear they had brought on the short flight from Brussels. Alyie wore a bright red full-length gown with a plunging neckline. Clasped around her neck was the gold necklace her parents presented her six E-yr ago for her 26th birthday. With long black gloves, gold earrings and black high spiked heels, she made a very statuesque appearance. Jaynis, on the other hand, wore his black wedding suit and patent leather shoes. Accompanying Alyie and Jaynis to Uraniborg were Alison Bernewithy and Daiki Sato. Alison also was clad in a floor-length dress, off-white in color with gold trim, which she accessorized with long white gloves and high heels. A string of pearls and pearl earrings gave her a lustrous look. Daiki had a black tuxedo on. He was a compact young man with chiseled features, smooth skin and straight black hair.

They were all attending a ball hosted by Malcolm Dunrock. After unsuccessful attempts by Alison to contact him, she received an invitation to a party Dunrock was putting together to introduce the new Regional Governor to his friends and associates. As the invite proclaimed, "It would be a rare opportunity for Governor Starstriker to meet Sol System's most influential people and for them to interact with her." As a side note, Dunrock promised to set aside some time for himself and Alyie to speak privately. He had great news to tell her.

"Well, this is not the type of confrontation I anticipated having with Malcolm Dunrock," Alyie responded when Alison sent her the invitation, "but it gets us in the door, and we should make the most of it. Do you need to get a dress? Please bring Daiki, I would like to meet him."

Just as the air cruiser was about to touch down, Alyie received a video message from her parents. Tanita Starbright and Alex Striker had taken some time off from their work at Federation Headquarters on planet Teegarden to visit Alyie, Jaynis and the twins. Having finished feeding Tessa and Tomus, Tanita put them in front of the screen so Alyie could wave hello before they were put to bed. Alyie also had Alison come and say hi, and then she and Jaynis wished the twins sweet dreams.

At the airport, the two couples were met by a man representing Dunrock Enterprises, who had an airbus waiting to fly them up the mountain to Uraniborg. Along the way, Alyie received a message on her implant from Reg Jones. Her companions overheard Alyie saying, "Good, I am glad it was done with no loss. I am curious to see how my host reacts to this."

CHAPTER 13.

When the airbus containing Alyie, Jaynis, Alison and Daiki approached the grounds of the estate, the restored castle loomed in front, all aglow in artificial light. With a drawbridge, turrets and high towers, it resembled some of the tourist attractions scattered throughout the continent. Climbing up a long set of marble stairs, the two couples were ushered through a set of enormous double doors that opened into a gigantic ballroom. Guests in formal attire were mingling, sipping drinks and eating finger food while a five-piece orchestra was playing off to one side some late 19th E-c (CE) selections. As Alyie and Jaynis made their way across the floor, heads turned in their direction as Alyie was recognized. After exchanging whispers to confirm her identity, the guests at the ball formed an impromptu reception line introducing themselves to the Regional Governor. Many flattered Alyie by saying such as, "My goodness, the video images don't do you justice." "Madam Governor, you are absolutely stunning!" "What a pleasure to meet you."

While this adulation was taking place, the music suddenly stopped, and a voice was heard on the balcony overlooking the hall. Standing over the railing was Malcolm Dunrock. He was of middle height and modest build and appeared to be of indeterminate age, although clearly not young. His ultra-smooth skin and flaxen hair did not appear natural. He was dressed in a bright burgundy sports jacket, black bow tie, formal white shirt and black trousers with a stripe down the side. His shoes were burgundy velvet slippers. Extending his arms out, he proclaimed in a booming voice,

"Welcome to Uraniborg. I offer my palace for your pleasure and amusement. Please enjoy yourself and stay as long as you wish. Before we continue the festivities, let me introduce, if you have not already met her, my distinguished guest, Regional Governor Starstriker. She brings a remarkable record to her position as former Valkyrie Squad ommander, Fleet Admiral, High Council Member and First Consul of Kanva. Please welcome her."

With a signal from Dunrock, the orchestra struck up a musical salute which Alyie felt she had to acknowledge by forcing a smile and raising a gloved arm.

Later in the evening, after Alyie had patiently listened to the words of advice bestowed on her from the guests who appeared to be primarily from the entertainment, cultural, and tourist industries of Earth, a message was delivered to her by a member of the castle staff in a black tailcoat and white gloves while she and Jaynis were enjoying a rare opportunity to dance together. The message was delivered on top of what looked like a silver plate and was on fine white paper with Malcolm Dunrock's crest - the infinity symbol (∞). Opening the note, Alyie read,

"Madam Governor, I request the pleasure of your company in my library. Please come alone and de-activate your implant. What we say to each other should be for our ears only."

Excusing herself from the dance floor, she brought Jaynis over to Alison and Daiki. They expressed concern for her safety.

"Do you really want to meet him alone?" asked Alison.

"You may be dealing with a megalomaniac psychotic," suggested Daiki.

"This may show my grudging acceptance with my dear's lifestyle, but if there is only one megalomaniac, Alyie can handle him."

"Thanks, dear for your support, I think." Alyie then turned to the staff member who escorted her through the ballroom into the library.

CHAPTER 14.

Nestled between the dark wood shelves and paneling was a large lit fireplace in front of which Malcolm Dunrock was standing. He came forward to meet Alyie and took her hand while bending down and kissing it. "What an exquisite pleasure to finally meet you. Your exploits are the stuff of legends."

"I believe your own history has quite a number of memorable moments as well."

"Yes, but I have a much longer timeline than you. In your 32 odd E-yr. you are on a rate to surpass my records. However, I see both our futures filled with endless possibilities and that is why I have invited you here."

"Good, I am glad we can talk frankly."

"Before that happens, Madam Governor, or Alyie, if I may, have you de-activated your implant?"

"Alyie it is, Malcolm. Yes I have; now we can speak unheard and unrecorded."

"Excellent! I have been wanting to tell my news and offer you an opportunity to share in what has been discovered. For some time, Dunrock Pharma has been interested in the science of senolytics. Death is the bane of humanity, giving us a finite life span that has colored our existence with a black palate in knowing that all the joys, loves and successes an individual experiences are only transitory. Senolytics is the study of anti-ageing bio-chemical agents that destroy the human body's senescent cells that accumulate in the course of a lifetime. These cells are known to cause chronic diseases associated with old age by emitting substances that produce inflammation and turn other healthy cells senescent, ultimately leading to tissue damage throughout the body. We at Dunrock Pharma are about to release Forever+, an improved version of our miracle drug which will extend human life beyond anything previously imagined by continually destroying these senescent cells."

"Malcolm. That is exciting news. I hope your new version of Forever will win approval of the Sidereal Federation's Health and Welfare Board this time."

"I have no intention of going again to that inane board of bureaucrats. Their timidity is suffocating the most stupendous breakthrough in the history of humanity. Standing before you is a recipient of Forever+. Look at me. I am over 80 E-yr. old, yet I have the body of a man half that age. Why shouldn't the rest of Human Space share in this wonderful gift?"

"Without H&W's approval, you cannot distribute your product through the Federation's Common Exchange. I hope you are not here to tell me you propose to offer it on the black exchange. As Regional Governor, you know, I can't condone that."

"Rest assured, Alyie I will not pursue that path. That involves too much back dealing and bribery. That does not befit a product as wondrous as Forever+. No, I am advancing a much bolder and decisive avenue."

"And what might that be, Malcolm?" said Alyie, although she knew what Dunrock was implying.

"Independence, Alyie. The Earth needs to break away from the shackles of the Federation so that the creative spirit born to humans on this planet can be set free to transform humanity."

"So you support the Separatist Movement that has been terrorizing people and destroying facilities throughout the Sol System?"

"I am not a man of violence, but sometimes you need a bludgeon to get people's attention. There need not be any more disruptive activities if enough influential citizens of this system agree to Independence. I have drafted "A Declaration of Independence" akin to the historic document colonists in North America crafted in the 18th E-c (CE). It would give it so much more credibility if you were the initial signee.

As Dunrock retreated to his desk, he brought out a document written in a scroll on what looked like old parchment paper. Scanning it quickly, Alyie noted it stated the Earth's importance to human history, listed grievances against the Federation and expressed platitudes about the need for freedom for all humankind. It even reused the phrase "life, liberty and the pursuit of happiness" as its intended outcomes.

All Alyie could say in astonishment was, "And you want me to sign this?"

"Yes, your signature I am sure will convince many others to join the Movement. Your involvement will provide you with a pre-eminent place in the new Earth and much more in concert with your own ambitions. I will make you Chief Commander of the Earth Defense Force, and in the new independent system, you will serve with me as Co-President. I think that will be much more satisfying than your mundane role now as Regional Governor or any future aspirations you have to the High Governor position. We will rule the Empire of Immortals!"

"I am happy we have been able to meet and for me to hear plainly your position on the Separatist Movement. I think my answer to your request to join you can best expressed in the news I received just before attending your soiree. The Panthera commanded by Major Reg Jones has raided Kurzweil Enterprises, in doing so capturing several combatants and impounding all the materiel they found. We are committed to choking the life blood from this Movement."

"You are making a big mistake, Madam Governor," said a red-faced Malcolm Dunrock. "I am not an enemy you want to have."

"No, I am not making a mistake, Mr. Dunrock. And as for acquiring enemies, I consider it a cost of doing business in my role as Regional Governor of the Sol System. I think we are finished here. I will take my leave. Uraniborg is a splendid place. It will be a shame when you no longer can live here."

Turning abruptly, Alyie left the library and proceeded back to the ballroom. Gathering her companions, Alyie shepherded them to a hasty exit back to the airport after securing an airbus.

CHAPTER 15.

Not waiting to confer again with her Task Force, Alyie called an emergency meeting of her Advisory Council the day after she returned from the party. Assembling together at Headquarters in Brussels, Alyie addressed the members of the Council saying, "I think we have conclusive evidence that the Separatist Movement has been funded by Malcolm Dunrock, funneled through his business holdings. From my conversation with him at his estate, he admitted that he was spearheading the Earth Independence effort and wanted me to join him. Max, let us know what you have discovered about Dunrock's finances."

"It took some doing, and some how do they say it, 'arm twisting', but I have found a connecting thread that intertwines The Singularity Corporation and Kurzweil Enterprises with Dunrock's Apeirogon Institute. The bank, Earth First, which provides funds to the Institute also is a lender to the two businesses. Furthermore, Malcolm Dunrock is listed as the Chair of Earth First's Board of Directors."

"So all these entities revolve around Dunrock," concluded Advisory Council member Karrunya Okoro. "I think that is the proverbial flaming laser pistol."

"Yes, I think we now have strong evidence to implicate Dunrock with the criminal activities of the insurgents," declared Alyie.

"Wait, Madam Governor, there is more," Max Hebron interrupted. "I have also found that Malcolm Dunrock is in serious financial trouble. A recent internal audit of his assets, which I have been able to obtain, show that all of his businesses including Dunrock Pharma are on the brink of bankruptcy. His motivation for pressing for secession appears to be more than just a case of home world zeal. This is a desperate attempt for him to escape financial ruin and incarceration."

"Great work Max. Now Reg, what have we learned from your raid on Kurzweil Enterprises?"

"Other than the cache of weapons and equipment we recovered, I found out from my insider who was 'captured' in the raid that the Dunrock Pharma facility on Luna has become a staging base for a more ambitious rebel attack. Apparently, they are attempting to shut down Luna's spaceport, thereby disrupting all the commerce between Luna and the greater Federation."

"Do you have any idea when this attack is scheduled?" asked Sujan Roy.

"My contact wasn't sure, but from the pace of shipments of materiel leaving Kurzweil to Luna, it appears the assault is imminent."

"We need to treat this as an emergency," Alyie declared. "We can't have the Luna spaceport shut down. That would be an economic catastrophe for the Sol System. Major, I want you to activate your Panthera immediately. I will commission a spacecarrier to transport your troops. I will put a special request for a Federation Fighter Squadron to provide air support. I am hoping to get my old Valkyrie Squadron. You and I will be co-commanders for this pre-emptive attack on the staging facility."

"Yes, Ma'am."

"Meeting adjourned, but I will keep you in touch with events. Alison, please stay behind."

After the Council members filed out, Alyie spoke to Alison.

"It looks like my fighting days are not over. When I am in the field, I want you to run the Regional Office. This will be the Command Center for our operation, and I will rely on you to be prompt, precise and perceptive. I will send you all the secure codes to contact the Sidereal Federation staff as well as personal contacts for my parents. You already know how to reach Jaynis. I never used to worry about these things."

"Please be careful, Alyie. The confidential report you had me obtain from the Federation's H&W Board indicate that the animal trials on Forever showed side effects that included hyper-activity and a highly elevated degree of manic behavior. I have to believe Dunrock's reasoning has been affected by his use of this drug. I think we are dealing with a lunatic."

"Alison, thanks for your concern, but if Dunrock is a lunatic, what better place to deal with him than Earth's moon."

CHAPTER 16.

Three E-d later, everything was in place for the assault on Dunrock Pharma. Alyie secured the use of the spacecarrier Hercules which she would command with pilot Lieutenant Nullah Balbuk. Reg had his Panthera fighters outfitted with suits and helmets for the harsh Luna surface. The Valkyrie Squad reached Earth space just before the last of the Panthera boarded Hercules. Alyie from the ground sent a welcome message to her old teammates, Olga Fercouska, Hollie Pederson, Zarah Khoury and Wang Li, briefing them on the mission.

Olga, now Captain Fercouska, said, "Gee, Alyie, did you need to invent this pretext for us to see you again?"

"Thanks for coming so quickly after I asked Admiral Cranshaw for your services. I hope we can deal with the problem promptly and then have you all land on Earth for a real reunion.

Prior to takeoff, Alyie contacted the premiers of Earth, Luna and Mars to inform them that she was issuing an arrest order for Malcolm Dunrock. She also placed him on the no-fly list, preventing him from boarding a Sol System or a Federation spacecraft.

Once in flight, the spacecarrier and the four Valkyrie fighter craft made the quick trip to Luna. After making a single orbit, they glided over the harsh cratered surface until the target was in sight. Alyie was in her admiral uniform with cap, full medaled double-breasted white jacket, and crisp white pants tucked under her tall black leather boots. With one black gloved hand on her laser pistol handle and the other hand grasping the flight controller, she broadcasted the video message,

"I am Admiral Starstriker, Regional Governor of the Sol System. You need to cease and desist from your activities. Put down your weapons and leave the building holding your hands high. If not, you will come under attack."

The response was immediate as a laser missile was fired out of the building. It was quickly shot down by Hollie Pederson with a heat-seeking anti-missile. Realizing there would be no immediate surrender, Alyie nodded to Reg Jones, who gave the command to his unit to attach their oxygen tubes to their nostrils and begin the ejection process. Ten ultra-thin tethers made of carbon nanotubes were dropped by Nullah Balbuk out of Hercules' cargo bay. Then the Panthera soldiers grasped the tether lines and began descending below. Meanwhile, the Valkyries started firing their incendiary missiles on the plant.

Once the Panthera were all on the ground, the Valkyrie bombardment ceased as Reg Jones led them forward. The rebels escaping the burning building faced a much more professional unit than they had previously encountered. The damage done from the air prevented them from using their all-terrain vehicles, and they were quickly overwhelmed by Major Jones' unit. Taking all who surrendered prisoner, Reg awaited further orders from Alyie on Hercules before advancing into the facility.

Communicating to him through her implant, she said, "I want this plant completely destroyed, but before that we need to evacuate any insurgents that are still inside."

"We have done a thermal signature check and although it is a little difficult with the fires burning inside, we have located some infrared activity that identifies about 10 humans huddling in what looks like a storage room," Reg replied.

"Can we get them out without endangering any of our people?"

"Let me form a sub-group of my Panthera that have their suits coated with a heat resistant film. That should give them enough time to get in and out of the building."

While waiting for the extraction of the prisoners, Alyie tried to contact Alison to report on her success at Luna. However, there was no response. About an E-hr later, the Panthera group that entered the building emerged with eight insurgents in tow. With the news that no other humans were alive inside, Alyie gave the command to Lieutenant Balbuk to drop the tether lines again and elevate the Panthera and their shackled prisoners using the motorized controls. Once all personnel were safely onboard Hercules, Alyie ordered the Valkyrie to incinerate the Dunrock Pharma site.

With Reg joining her on the flight deck, Alyie expressed her concern about not reaching Alison. "It is not like her to not respond. I have a bad feeling about this."

Trying a second time to communicate, this time, Alyie received a reply but not from her Adjunct.

"So you have destroyed my plant and captured my troops. You think you have shut me down, but I am about to prove you are very mistaken."

"Who am I speaking to?" was Alyie's reply as she stared warily at Reg.

"Don't you know Alyie? It's Malcolm who with some friends have taken over your Regional Office."

"Where are the staff and my Adjunct Alison Bernewithy?"

"Oh don't worry. We are keeping them safe with us, at least until you agree to my demands."

"I am not agreeing to anything until you let me see and talk to Alison."

After a slight pause, Alison's image appeared on Alyie's implant. She appeared a little disoriented, and her eyes expressed worry.

"How are you? Have you been mistreated?"

"No harm done so far to the five of us here."

"How did Malcolm and his thugs get in?"

"Oh, Alyie, we admitted them on false pretenses. They said they were the Regional Governor's advance guard. I am sorry for letting you down."

"You have nothing to be sorry for," Alyie assured. "And I will fix this. I promise."

Suddenly, Malcolm's leering face was flooding Alyie's brain. "Well, you see she is well and to have her returned to you safe and sound, all I need is for you to rescind the arrest and no-fly orders and provide me a fully energized air jet for my use. It appears my time on Earth is ending, and I will look beyond the Sol System for my next adventure."

"I am on Luna now. Let us negotiate in person as soon as I return to Earth."

"Ah, you are stalling for time. I won't tolerate any tricks. Let's see. It should take you an E-d to return. By this time tomorrow, I will expect you to have met my demands. Bring the air jet to the roof of this building. Come alone, unarmed and don't be late."

Alyie, who was internally reeling from this unexpected turn of events, still had the presence of mind to make sure all were securely fastened on Hercules as it made its return to a troubled rendezvous on Earth.

CHAPTER 17.

With Nullah now at the helm of Hercules, Alyie retreated to the ship's captain's quarters. She contacted Jaynis, assuring him and her parents (who were still at Montpellier) of her well-being. However, Alyie was anything but well, feeling helpless and despairing over the seizure of the Regional Office. Removing her cap and tucking her gloves under her belt, she unbuttoned the left side of her jacket after putting her laser pistol holster aside. Taking her red silk cravat off her clavicles, she tied it around her neck. Not wanting to be alone, Alyie contacted Reg to join her in her cabin.

When the Major came, he stood at attention at the doorway, saluting. Dressed in his fatigues with a stylish black beret perched so that his gold earring pierced through his left ear lobe just showed, he looked the epitome of a professional soldier.

"At ease, Reg, and please sit down."

As Reg Jones sat directly opposite Alyie in her cramped quarters, she reached into a soft pouch and pulled out a flagon of a clear brownish beverage and two small glasses.

"Let me offer you a drink. It is what passes today as Scotch Whiskey."

"I didn't know you imbibed, Governor."

"I only started after my recovery from the wound I received on Kanva. It helps dull the pain."

"So you are still experiencing the effects of the injury. I thought it was completely healed."

"It has, but, perhaps psychologically, I still feel it. Sometimes I think the poison is still in my system. Most of the time, I am fine, but when I am stressed such as now, the pain comes back."

Then, Reg pronounced, "Let's drink to banish your pain. Saludo, Mi Capitana!"

After a few rounds, the conversation loosened as they each shared stories of their respective experiences on different planets and the eccentric characters they both had encountered. Eventually, talk turned to the problem at hand.

"I have a dismal track record with hostages," said a now fully lubricated Alyie. "I have lost two in the past. I don't want to have more tragedies. I hate to admit that if it means saving the lives of the staff members, I am thinking of agreeing to Dunrock's demands. Giving him freedom to go crazy somewhere else seems a fair price to pay for the lives of Alison and her co-workers."

"I don't want to contradict your judgement, Ma'am, but perhaps you can first give me the opportunity to affect their release."

"That is tempting. What bothers me about this is that I would be committing to a plan for their escape to primarily protect my reputation, rather than putting the hostages' safety first. You see, I think both Malcolm Dunrock and I are chasing the same dream – immortality. He wants to achieve it by long life through his drug Forever; I want it by fame and glory in service of the almighty Sidereal Federation. They are both false and utterly self-centered illusions."

"Madam Governor, there is no comparison between you and Dunrock. He is seeking immortality for only himself and his own personal enrichment, while your actions are for the good of humankind. Not once, have you ever done anything that is not consistent with the general welfare of the people you serve, either in the Space Fleet, the High Council, on Kanva or the Sol System. I have said this before, and I will say it again, you are the finest person I have ever served alongside."

Alyie, who was becoming light-headed, leaned in toward Reg so that the tops of her boots were rubbing against his knees. "You really know how to make someone feel good, and you are utterly charming."

They were so close that Reg could smell her sweet fragrance. Alyie's sparkling green eyes and lustrous blonde red hair framed her beautiful face. She was overwhelmingly attractive, and her present vulnerability made her so desirable. But he realized the dire consequences of what was presented in front of him. Stroking Alyie's face gently with his callused hand, he said softly,

"It's ok to show weakness, and we can't always have success. What we owe to our duty is to try."

As she drew back from him, collecting herself, Reg said, "Don't make any decisions about the hostages until you hear again from me. I am going to look at an approach that may solve our problem."

With that, he stood up and saluted, taking his leave.

Alyie was feeling groggy and unclear about what had just nearly happened. She climbed unsteadily into her bunk without undressing and fell into a deep sleep.

CHAPTER 18.

As Hercules was approaching Earth for orbital entry, Alyie was awakened from a call on her implant from Reg.

"Hello. I have been studying the building plans for the Regional Office and noticed there is a way in through the Heating, Ventilation and Air Conditioning System. There looks like enough crawl space for me and a few of my unit to climb in unnoticed. While you are distracting Dunrock on the roof, we can sneak up the vents in the rear. Once in, we will overpower his guards and free the hostages. If we fail, then you can proceed to give him what he wants."

"You have never let me down before Major, so let's try it. By the way, thanks for yesterday."

"You're welcome, Ma'am."

Washing quickly in her cabin's lavatory, Alyie put on her Admiral's uniform with medals, sash, cap, gloves and attached spurs to her boots. She wanted the "exchange" meeting with Malcolm Dunrock to look as ceremonial as possible.

When Hercules touched down on the Brussels spaceport, Alyie video messaged Jaynis to say she was not coming directly home to Montpellier because of the hostage crisis. He put Tessa and Tomus in the image so they could see and hear from their mother.

"Be good to each other and your Daddy. Mommy will be back as soon as I can. I love you all."

The Earth's media was abuzz with the takeover of the Regional Office. Alyie had made sure there was supersaturated coverage as she stepped off Hercules, announcing she would briefly make a statement. Once on the ground, Alyie asked the crush of people who surrounded her to be quiet as she spoke,

"I am flying to the Regional Office to meet Mr.Malcolm Dunrock and to negotiate a release of the hostages. The safety of the dedicated people serving the Sol System is always paramount. Once this crisis is over, I will make another statement. I thank you for your continued restraint and patience."

Ignoring the shouted questions, Alyie was ushered into a waiting air jet by members of her security force, and soon after, she took the craft aloft.

While the press corps was chasing after Alyie, Reg Jones and four of his Panthera had quietly boarded an unmarked airbus headed for the same destination.

CHAPTER 19.

Alyie took a circuitous route to the Regional Office to allow Reg and his team enough time to arrive at the building. Once she received an encrypted "ping" indicating Reg had achieved entry, Alyie messaged Dunrock that she was making her approach to the roof. As the air jet touched down, Alyie sighted Dunrock holding a laser pistol pointed at Alison's neck.

Jumping out of the air jet, Alyie stood tall and planted her boots firmly on the roof, announcing, "I have come as you requested. Here is the air jet. As soon as you release Alison and the other four hostages, I will accede to your other demands."

"Not so fast, my dear," Malcolm replied. "How do I know you won't shoot me down as soon as I leave this building?"

"You undoubtedly heard my address at the Brussels spaceport. Wouldn't that look duplicative, if I turn around and break our bargain? Let them go, and I will I rescind the arrest and no-fly orders."

"Well, just for insurance, I am taking your pretty assistant with me. Once I get to Uraniborg and board my starcruiser, she is all yours."

"Malcolm, you need help. The Forever drug you have been taking is affecting your ability to reason. If you leave the Sol System and fly out of Federation space, you will only get more irrational. Stay here and let me get the best medical care for you."

"No. You are preventing me from my destiny. I am meant to live forever and share the gift with everyone. I pity you who could have partnered in this great endeavor. Think not only for yourself but your husband and your children. Don't you want them all to be immortal?"

"We are not meant to be forever. We each have our time in this Universe to impact it and those around us. Then we need to pass on. That is the way of the world."

While Alyie was debating with Dunrock, she spied Reg Jones coming out of the stairwell onto the roof behind Malcolm and Alison.

"I know why you are resisting," Malcolm decried. "You who are 'the best of the best', don't want to concede defeat even though you know you are beaten. I have spoiled your perfect record by confounding you. You are no match for me one-on-one."

"Malcolm that is where you are mistaken. It is not 'one-on-one'; I am not alone."

Malcolm then pivoted to see who was behind him, and in that instant, Alison pressed her right high heel hard on his left foot. As he broke his hold on Alison, Reg fired his laser pistol, knocking the gun out of Dunrock's hand. Malcolm reached on the ground for the fallen weapon, but as he was doing so, Alyie strove forward and kicked him hard with her booted right leg under the chin. Reeling in pain from the blow, Malcolm was surrounded by Reg, Alyie and Alison, who hovered over him.

"Malcolm Dunrock," Alyie pronounced, "by the power invested in me as Regional Governor of the Sol System under the Sidereal Federation, I arrest you on charges of sedition, destruction of property and conspiracy to commit murder. You reserve the right to defend yourself and seek private counsel."

EPILOGUE

It was such a beautiful day with a gentle sea breeze that Alyie and Jaynis didn't need to activate the invisible shield around their back lawn to have an outdoor dining event. It was themed as a thanksgiving event for the freed Regional Office staff hostages, but Alyie also invited her Valkyrie teammates: Olga, Hollie, Zarah and Wang, to catch up with them. In addition, her parents, Tanita and Alex, had extended their stay at Montpellier to help Jaynis with child care as Alyie was heavily involved in the aftermath of the dissipation of the Separatist uprising and the prosecution of Malcolm Dunrock.

Alyie dressed uncharacteristically casually in a loose peach blouse, flowing off-white pants and open-toed shoes. She greeted each of the staff workers privately, thanking them for their patience and perseverance during the crisis. Alyie assured them that they would be rewarded for "showing grace and courage beyond the call of duty". When Alison arrived, she was accompanied by Reg Jones. On seeing them obviously together, Alyie gave Alison a clear nod of approval and returned a sly smile to Reg.

At the dinner, all gathered around the large oak table laden with food from the pasture, the garden and the sea. The twins were, naturally, the center of attention as they giggled and gurgled, holding court when people came to play with them. As the adults were drinking wine from Jaynis and Alyie's collection and nibbling cheese from a local dairy, questions were raised about the aftermath of the crisis.

"What will happen to Malcolm Dunrock?" asked Tanita Starbright.

"I hope he stays in prison forever," volunteered Olga.

"His defense team is arguing that his reasoning was impaired because of the drug he was taking," replied Jaynis. "So, he should not be held accountable for the charges Alyie laid against him."

"However, as far as the medical team examining him has discovered, there is no known treatment for reversing the effects of Forever," Alyie added. "So, even if he is not deemed liable for his criminal actions, he will have to be confined to a medical facility, perhaps interminably."

"Has the Separatist Movement been completely destroyed?" wondered Alex Striker.

"The insurgents have been either arrested or have disbanded," Alyie replied. "When it became known that Dunrock was using their movement as a prod to sell Forever on the open market, most of the rebels loss their zeal for independence realizing they were being used as pawns."

"But doesn't Hector Palermo still have his Independence Party?" asked Reg Jones.

"Yes, the political movement is still present. I have asked Hector to join my Advisory Council. He can help me bring his concerns to the Federation High Council. Perhaps through education and a little gentle persuasion, we can affect enough change to make secession unnecessary."

"Enough shop talk," Jaynis interjected. "This is a party. Let's enjoy ourselves."

"Here! Here!" was the general acclamation. People shouted, "Make a toast Jaynis."

"I propose a toast to a happy and long life."

"But," Alyie responded, "not Forever."

THE DARK CLOUD

PART I.

"Concerning brave Captains our age hath made known."

Rudyard Kipling

CHAPTER 1.

This was a propitious day in the Starbrook household. Tessa and Tomus, now just turned five E-yr old, were beginning their first in-person class experience with other children. Previously Alyie Starstriker and Jaynis Bottombrook had a service autobot provide instruction to the twins at their home in Montpellier. Ms. Brody, as the tutoring robot was called, had given Tessa and Tomus their first educational lessons and deemed them ready for in-class instruction. Alyie and Jaynis formed a cooperative educational group with nine other parents on Earth to have the children meet weekly and receive lessons from both a human and an autobot in a classroom setting in Paris. Jaynis, who was on the faculty of the Université de Paris, would be the designated parent to escort the twins to and from their weekly sessions, but since it was their first day, Alyie would be accompanying them.

After breakfast, the twins gathered the school materials their implants indicated they needed and stood for inspection by their parents. Tessa was in a checkered skirt and dark green jacket, while Tomus was clad in short blue pants and a dark blue jacket. Given words of encouragement, the twins proceeded out the security door down the garden stairs to the air jet waiting below.

Once everyone was strapped in, Alyie tucked her golden reddish hair in her helmet and took the air jet aloft. In less than 10 E-min, they were landing just outside the red brick schoolhouse. Once the Starbrook family approached the building, other parents and their children turned to see them, as none had previously met the charismatic Regional Governor in person. Alyie, who was dressed in her "business" clothes of a short-cropped forest green sport coat, white shirt, white silk cravat pinned with a gold Sidereal Federation insignia, tight black slacks and tall black leather boots, tried to disarm the starstruck parents, by introducing her family as, "This is Tessa, Tomus, Jaynis and I am Alyie. It is so good to finally meet all of you."

After everyone was acquainted with each other, the families proceeded to escort their children into the school. Alyie and Jaynis met the teacher, Ms. Jeong Kim, who showed them where Tessa and Tomus' stations were located. Realizing their presence was an impediment to the experience, Alyie and Jaynis kissed the twins goodbye while providing words of caution.

"Now, Tessa, please do not speak until you are asked," Alyie implored as Tessa nodded her head flashing her pink cheeks and freckles.

"Tomus, stay in your station until Ms. Kim allows you to roam," Jaynis advised as Tomus wrinkled his nose from side to side.

"Be well, and remember your father and I will be back later to pick you up."

Leaving the schoolhouse, Jaynis and Alyie hopped back aboard the air jet. Soon after they were aloft, Jaynis received a message on his implant.

"This is interesting. The John Mather Observatory on Mars is detecting a diffuse neutrally charged cloud of some type of matter heading in the direction of the Trappist-1 system. It is hard to tell its size, but it appears widely spread out."

"Shouldn't Revi or should I say Queen Revita Jadeite be alerted about a possible intruder near her planet, Kanva?" Alyie queried.

"I am on it dear."

After depositing her husband on the campus, Alyie flew the air jet to the top of the Regional Headquarters building in Brussels.

CHAPTER 2.

After landing on the roof, Alyie was met by her Adjunct, Alison Bernewithy. The blonde-haired, blue-eyed woman, now in her mid-twenties, was dressed in a navy blue pants suit under which she wore a white blouse fastened at the top with a large bow. Her slim pants were tucked snuggly into tall black leather boots. Alison also sported a Sidereal Federation pin on the lapel of her tailored sports jacket.

"Good morning, Alyie. How did your sendoff of the twins go?"

"As well as Jaynis and I could wish. I just hope they don't embarrass us by misbehaving. They loved to play tricks on Ms. Brody."

"Oh, I think the presence of a live teacher and the other children would help socialize them. Besides, they're great kids. I am sure they will be fine."

"I hope so Alison, but this is as difficult on Jaynis as on myself. I feel we just passed through a one way gate. But it has to be for the best. Enough about my parental anxieties, let's talk about today. Has Hector Palermo arrived?"

"Yes, he is waiting in your office. Do you want me to order any refreshments?"

"Just some water. Have you made arrangements for us all to go out to lunch? I want to make his trip to Brussels for this meeting worthwhile?"

"Yes, we have a private room in René Magritte's. I believe we are booked in The Trompe L'oeil Room. I understand the food is delicious."

"As always, thank you Alison."

As the two women took the lift down to the floor where their offices were located, Alison gave Alyie a quick preview of the Regional Council Meeting, which would proceed after her chat with Hector.

CHAPTER 3.

Alyie went directly into her office suite while Alison went next door to her own workspace. Seated on the couch was Mr. Hector Palermo, a dapper gray-haired gentleman dressed impeccably in a dark gray suit with a white shirt and silk blue and white striped tie.

"Hector, please accept my apologies for keeping you waiting. You have flown all the way from Buenos Aires, and I have come from just nearby Montpellier. As a way of an excuse, this was the first day for my children's live class experience, and my husband and I believed we both had to be there to make them feel comfortable."

"Oh, Senora, apologies are not necessary. These are important milestones in the history of your family, and there is nothing more significant than being present for your children. I applaud you for giving this your highest priority."

"You are most kind, Hector. We don't have much time before the Regional Council Meeting is scheduled to begin, but I wanted to give you advance notice of what I will say and ask you to consider an offer I am extending."

"Thank you for taking me into your confidence. I will serve you with all my soul, Senora."

"Hector, I am in the last year of my term as Regional Governor of the Sol System, and I plan to announce at the Meeting that I will not seek re-election."

"Oh, this is distressing. Alyie, you have been a magnificent Governor in administering the details of the Office and enabling Earth to play a more significant role in the Federation. You have brought vision, energy, and new vitality to the Sol System. How can we ever replace you?"

"I still can be a significant factor in advancing Earth's preeminence if I gain my next position. There is a Regional spot opening next E-yr. on the Federation High Council from this sector of Human Space. I would like to run for that seat. If I succeed, I will be an elected High Council member that can use my position to make the Earth even more the center of the Sidereal Federation."

"But you have already used your influence to move the financial and cultural ministries of the Sidereal Federation to Earth. What more do you see happening?"

"I would like the capital of the Sidereal Federation to be declared on Earth – the home planet for humanity. I think the time is right for its recognition."

"It is amazing that when we competed against each other five E-yr. ago, I ran on an Independence for Earth platform while you were for staying in the Federation. You were victorious, and yet you have done more to advance the cause of Earth than I could ever have done. Bravo, Senora!"

"Leaving the Regional Governor's Office would be easier for me if I have confidence that my successor would carry on the initiatives I have started. When I announce publicly my decision not to run for re-election, I want to endorse a candidate to take my place, and that person would be you, Hector. Are you still interested in the job?"

"Guau! I didn't expect that. You leave me speechless."

"I know I have caught you off-guard, and I do not expect an answer right now. But after the Regional Council Meeting, we are having lunch. I plan to ply you with food and drink, and I will try to be absolutely my most charming to convince you. Consider yourself forewarned."

"I see my capitulation is at hand. Just being in your presence is nearly irresistible, but having you charm me at your absolute best, boggles this old-man's mind and some other parts. You have me already."

"Good, let's get this meeting over with, and then we can have Fiesta."

CHAPTER 4.

The main business of the Regional Council Meeting concerned the allocation of additional space for Sidereal Federation facilities that were being transferred to Earth. New Hong Kong was now the primary site for the Federation's Treasury Ministry and the Sidereal Bank. However, Alyie thought it best to de-centralize the system by having secondary locations throughout the planet. London, Buenos Aires, Melbourne and New York City were selected, and thus, plans needed to be approved for the construction of offices to accommodate the burgeoning work staff.

Alyie also had an announcement that involved an action item for the Council. "It is not official, but I am in serious negotiations to have the Common Exchange moved to Earth. When the High Council gives us the go ahead, I want to have a site for this important economic institution ready for transfer. Any suggestions?"

"Since most of the economic activity in our system occurs on Luna, I would think that it is the natural place to put the Exchange," suggested Mr. Sujan Roy, who just happened to be a Council representative from Earth's only natural satellite.

"But the living conditions are pretty austere," said Dr. Rafael Ruis. "Do you think those economic ministers and their staff want to live on a surface where there is no breathable outside air? At least where I work on Mars, we have pockets of oxygen that people can work and reside around."

Max Hebron, a political confidant of Alyie, made a case for Earth. "Since the Federation has moved the banking system to Earth, one would think that the Common Exchange should be situated in proximity. Any of your secondary locations would do."

"I have three different worlds – Earth, Luna and Mars as possible sites for the Common Exchange. Alison, would you care to cast the deciding vote?"

Alison perked up at the decision-making role Alyie afforded her. "I vote for Earth. With the Federation's Arts and Cultural Ministry coming to Paris next E-yr., I think people associated with the Common Exchange would have a powerful incentive to relocate to our homeworld. I also think somewhere out west on the North American Continent would be ideal."

"There you have it," Alyie crowed. "It's Earth, and I will say we want it to be in Denver."

"Before we conclude this meeting," Alyie continued, "I want to announce that I am not seeking re-election as Regional Governor. I have enjoyed immensely working with you on this Council, and I am proud of what we have accomplished in a short time. I will continue to fulfill my duties as Regional Governor to the last E-d of my term. Once I decide on my next plans, I will be sure to let you know. I also plan to endorse a candidate as my successor and would hope you would support that individual as well. Stay tuned."

The reaction from the Council's members was one of dismay and consternation. Alyie consoled them by hugging each one and thanking them for their support.

With the meeting adjourned, Alyie and Hector went back to the former's office as Alison made arrangements for their transportation to René Magritte's.

CHAPTER 5.

Taking an aircar to the restaurant, Alison had arranged for the three of them to be discreetly escorted into The Trompe L'oeil Room so that the other diners would not be aware of the Regional Governor's presence. Once seated, they were greeted warmly by the wait staff and presented with a bottle of champagne, compliments of the restaurant's owner.

"A toast to Senora Governor," proclaimed Hector. "Here's to the bringing of prosperity and recognition back to Earth. Saludo!"

"Cheers and here's to, I hope, the next Regional Governor," countered Alyie.

Their luncheon meal consisted of a crisp roasted squab for each, petit pommes de terre, white asparagus and a freshly baked baguette. Alyie gave Hector the honor of choosing the wine, and he picked a pinot noir from a French vineyard. As they were chatting and enjoying themselves with the food, Hector asked, "Please, my dear Alyie, tell me your secret. How did you manage to convince the High Council to move those departments to Earth?"

"I used my military background by sowing seeds in some of my contacts that the Fleet Command needed to expand their operations on Planet Teegarden as the Sidereal Federation reached out farther and farther into space. As you know, Teegarden is limited in habitable land so that any increase in facilities at Headquarters for the Space Command could only be accomplished if the non-military ministries were moved elsewhere. I also argued that it was not strategic for the Federation to put all its key ministries and departments on one world. If a calamity occurred, the Federation would lose all its Command and Control structure. Once I planted these ideas, I trusted in the intelligence of the High Council members to come around to the idea of Earth as a secondary Headquarters."

"You are truly marvelous," Hector proclaimed as he raised his wine glass to toast Alyie again. "How am I going to replace you?"

"Well, first of all, you have all the integrity and wisdom you need, and second, I am bequeathing, with her permission, my better professional half, Alison, to your service if you will have her."

Hector looked toward Alison, smiling primly in her seat. "Would you serve as my Adjunct? I have seen how close you are to the Governor."

"Alyie and I have discussed this, and yes, I am linked to her. But we both feel that, at least, in the short term, I can serve as you transition to the head of the Regional Office. But the choice is yours, if there are others you prefer to interview for Adjunct, I would be happy to step aside and join Alyie as she pursues her next endeavor."

"Todo lo contrario, Senorita Alison, I would consider myself most fortunate to have you right beside me."

"Good, then it is settled. You will run for the Regional Governorship; I will throw my full support for you, and Alison will be your Adjunct. Let's celebrate this compact."

There was music playing throughout the restaurant, and Hector invited the two women, in turn, to dance with him. First, Alyie and he waltzed around the room, and then the shorter, blonde-haired Alison took her turn with the cavalier South American gentleman. When they had their fill on the dance floor, Alyie turned to Alison and said, "Could you inform the staff to serve dessert?"

Alison reached into her right boot and pulled out a clapper that signaled the wait staff that her party was ready for dessert. Soon after, a Mont Blanc with noodles of chestnut puree topped with whipped cream was brought forward. Hot coffee was served to Alyie and Alison and herbal tea for Hector. After dessert, the trio sipped a soothing barrel-aged Belgian cognac that made them all feel warm and a little tipsy.

CHAPTER 6.

After lunch, the two women, firmly holding Hector on either side, folded him into an aircar that took him back to the airport where Alyie had arranged a hypersonic aircraft to fly him back to Buenos Aires. In a little over three E-hr., he was back in his home, safe and sound, although still somewhat woozy. Alyie had Alison accompany her into her office suite, where she wanted to chat.

"Are you still sure about being Hector's Adjunct? Don't say yes, just because I want it to happen."

"Yes, Alyie I will be his Adjunct, but I want to help you in your campaign to be on the High Council."

"I would love to have your assistance. I will probably use Lydia Foxworth to run the campaign, but she can be a little overbearing. I could use your good sense and analytical skills."

"When then it is settled, I will be your Chief of Staff."

"The problem is a conflict of interest. You are the Adjunct to the Regional Governor. Any assistance you provide to my election would be considered unethical in that I would be utilizing your time and talent to advance my career while you are working for the Federation. Besides, I need you to keep the Office running well when I am campaigning. The sector I would represent on the High Council includes the Centauri System as well as Sol so I will be off planet for a while campaigning."

"Ok, then let me help you on my free time. I will not ask for compensation, and I will be careful to log in for my work in the Governor's Office. I believe in you and want to assist in any capacity."

"Thank you. You are very generous and also valuable to me. I will make you my 'Special Campaign Advisor'. But I do want you to carve out your own career. I would like you to think about a ministry or department you would like to oversee. When I am in a better position, we can make it happen."

"I have to admit the Ministry of Arts and Culture, especially coming to Paris, is very appealing."

"Well let's hold that aspiration in abeyance until the time is ripe. To change the subject, how are things with you and Reg or should I say Colonel Jones?"

"They're good, that is, whenever I get to see him."

"Yes, Alison, I see he missed another Regional Council Meeting. Is he ok?"

"He messaged me saying he was on Teegarden interviewing prospective recruits for the Panthera. This is the fourth meeting in a row he has missed in person. Although he keeps himself informed of our doings."

"Do you like him?"

"Reg is the most exciting man I have ever known. He is so comfortable with himself and has such honor and integrity. When we are together, he gives me a thrill I have never experienced before. There is just one thing."

"I hope I am not intruding if I can ask what that is?" said a concerned Alyie.

"When he is with me things are great, but I have the feeling he is holding back."

"In what way?"

"I think there is someone else."

"Is he seeing another person?"

"I don't think so. I think this may be an unrequited love."

"From his past?" Alyie wondered.

"No, I think this is ongoing. Reg reminds me of one of those medieval knights of old Earth history who has pledged himself to an unattainable high born lady."

All Alyie could say was, "Oh, I see," as a dark cloud hovered over her mind.

"Perhaps this is all in my imagination and my romanticism for all things in Earth's past. Maybe I am not used to being with a true gentleman such as Reg before."

Recovering herself, Alyie put forth, "Well, you will just have to convince him with your intelligence, charm and beauty that reality is always preferred over something beyond one's reach."

"You are such a good friend to me. Thanks for hearing me out."

"Any time, Alison. Oh, excuse me, I almost forgot. I have to pick up Jaynis so that we can collect the kids. Bye."

CHAPTER 7.

The governing structure of the Sidereal Federation was conceived as a pyramid. At the base was each human settled planet where citizens chose their own form of government, and the Act of Self-Determination forbade the Federation from interfering. The next layer up consisted of the Regional Councils in the ten different sectors of Human Space. (Alyie Starstriker was Governor of the Sol System, in Sector I, included the Centauri System). The High Governor, head of the High Council, was elected by all citizens of the Federation and served a 10 E-yr term. Other Sidereal High Council members were elected from each sector (two High Council seats per, one of which Alyie was seeking, staggered in five-year terms), and then professional staff were chosen by the High Governor from specific fields of importance to the Federation. The High Governor chose one of the elected High Council members to serve as Deputy High Governor for a one E-yr term who would replace the High Governor if, for some reason, she/he was unable to fulfill the duties of the office. There was also a Ministry of Justice adjunct to the High Council. (Overarching this entire structure was a Sidereal Federation Council that oversaw protocols, memberships and meetings.)

On a crisp autumn morning, Alyie was meeting the campaign advisory team at her chateau on a day when Alison was off from her duties at the Regional Office. Gathered together in her living room were Alyie, Alison, Max Hebron and Lydia Foxworth. Taki-1 served a breakfast of croissants, hot oatmeal, assorted berries, juice and hot beverages. Meanwhile, the twins were having their morning lessons from Ms. Brody while Taki-2 stood by to keep them from disrupting the meeting.

Alyie was dressed in a large white turtleneck pullover top and tan riding pants. She was just clad in her stockings as she sat with her legs curled on the couch. The others were similarly casually dressed.

Lydia was first to speak, "We have already surpassed the minimum number of signatures needed for you to officially enter the race and receive Federation funds for the campaign. It is now full speed ahead."

"Max," Alyie asked, "do you have any sense of who my most likely opponents will be?"

"That is a good question, and at this stage there does not appear to be any. I know you claim not to be a politician, but in political terms that was a brilliant move to endorse Hector Palermo as your successor as Regional Governor. That stratagem completely dispersed any lingering opposition in the Independence Party that opposed you five E-yr. ago. Your election to the High Council enables these party members to have their man sit in the Regional Governor seat. I am sure you will get their vote with enthusiasm."

"What about the citizens of New Cedonia and the outlying satellites such as Cardinal Richelieu surrounding the Centauri system?" Alyie inquired.

"I have done some polling," said Lydia. "Most of the people in that system are either in the Fleet, are contractors to Space Command, belong to military families or are associated with the diplomatic academy you attended. You are a hero to most, and they see you as one of them. Many recall you growing up as a young lieutenant and can recite at length your exploits with the Valkyrie Squadron. Trust me, Alyie you are golden in that system."

"Despite this good news," chimed in Alison, "I think we should still mount a full campaign for Alyie. Winning this seat by an overwhelming margin will position her strongly in what we all know but dare not speak at loud is her ultimate goal."

"You are quite the savvy strategist, Alison," proclaimed Max. "Here I am the veteran politico, but these two women make me look like an amateur."

After finishing breakfast while discussing campaign media and travel schedules, Lydia and Max took their leave, with Alison staying behind.

"As I promised, we are going riding today. Jaynis, for my last birthday, had a stable built, and we now have two horses – Thorin and Elsa. You will love Elsa; she is a sweet 10 E-yr. old mare."

"But Alyie, I don't have any riding clothes."

"Oh, you of little faith. Did you think I would not provide? Jaynis, before he left for work, used our 3D Fabricator to make you boots, britches and a rather attractive riding jacket. Remember we have your measurements. Come this way."

As Alison suited up the white britches, black boots and blue riding coat provided, Alyie got into her brown riding boots and put on a brown and orange stitched tweed riding coat on top of a bright yellow vest. When both were fully outfitted and fastened on their riding helmets, they walked down the garden path to the stable where their horses were waiting to be saddled. Thorin was a spirited black stallion, while Elsa was a gentle snow-white mare. After mounting, the two women took a walking path that led to the beach where Alyie planned their ride.

"As you could see from Lydia's plans, we are kicking off my campaign at the Fleet base on New Cedonia next week. It is the perfect venue for my launch. I am taking my whole family and flying a spacecruiser. I want you to accompany us. I have granted you vacation time."

"But I have never left the Sol System before."

"That is precisely why I want you with me. It's time to let go and expand your horizons, literally. Besides, I want everyone to know you."

"Thanks, Alyie."

"Let's see if you still thank me after your first experience with hyperspace."

Then Alyie tapped Thorin with her riding crop, who immediately thrust forward as Alison on Elsa gamely followed as the pair galloped down the windswept beach beside the blue waters of the Mediterranean.

CHAPTER 8.

Gaining use of the space cruiser Phaedra, Alyie's passenger list included Jaynis, Tessa, Tomus, Lydia, Alison and two of Lydia's staff. Alyie and her co-pilot Fedor Greysan were the only ones fully acclimated to travel through hyperspace. In an effort to reassure the twins, Alyie arranged for Jaynis to be in the seat next to Tomus, and across the aisle, Alison was with Tessa.

After liftoff, Phaedra was put on course for the nearest hyper-knot in the Sol System. Alison growing anxious about the oncoming jump, asked Jaynis, "What's it like?"

"Think of it as a tortuous exercise routine. When we go into the hyper-knot, you will feel squished beyond imagination as spacetime shrinks, and then coming out you will be stretched until you think you are being torn apart. Other than that, it is no big deal."

"Oh, that is reassuring, I think."

"Don't be surprised if you feel dizzy or nauseous. That's what the receptacle in front of you is for."

After that remark, Alison took a firm hold of Tessa's hand.

On the second E-d, Alyie announced, "We are approaching the hyper-knot. Get ready everybody, here we go."

With Jaynis holding Tomus' hand and Alison with Tessa, the jump began with the twins squealing with delight and two adults holding on as if their lives depended on it.

Once they were through the hyper-knot, Tomus yelled, "Wow! That was great; let's do it again."

Tessa added, "Ms. Alison why do you look so pale? Please don't squeeze my hand so tightly; you're hurting me."

CHAPTER 9.

Back in normal space, Alyie set the space cruiser on course for New Cedonia, the Federation's Regional Space Fleet base, where she began her military career. She hadn't realized how much she missed the exhilaration of flying through interstellar space. In the three E-d it took to reach the station, Alison and Jaynis took care of Tessa and Tomus' needs while finding time to chat.

"What are you working on at the Université?"

"I have my ongoing research on gravitational wave astronomy. But I am also currently monitoring the motion of this mysterious cloud moving slowly through Human Space."

"Oh, yes," Alison remarked, "Alyie mentioned that it may pose a danger to Kanva where her friend Revi reigns."

"Well, it is too early to say if it is something to worry about. There is some radiation emitted as it encounters particles drifting in space, but the waves are all over the electromagnetic spectrum. The fact that the cloud is so diffuse makes it unlikely to be anything dangerous. Our early thoughts are it is made up of residual elements from the supernova explosion of a super red giant star. We have found signatures of hydrogen, helium and carbon all the way up to iron in its spectrum."

With Fedor in the Captain's Chair of Phaedra, Alyie went back to join her family and Alison. But once in the proximity of New Cedonia, she returned to the flight deck to initiate the spacecraft's docking procedure into the assigned spaceport.

Announcing the approach, Alyie declared, "New Cedonia, this is Phaedra from the Sol System. We are requesting permission to dock."

"Permission granted, Admiral Starstriker and welcome back."

CHAPTER 10.

After Alyie and her entourage arrived at the space station, she was treated with the fanfare that befits a returning hero. Among the many personnel stationed at New Cedonia to greet her were her old Valkyrie Squadron teammates, Olga Fercouska, Hollie Pederson, Zarah Khoury and Wang Li. The Regional Governor of the Centauri System, Rear Admiral Erik Stringer, who served under Alyie to help foil a plot by renegade robots against the Federation, was also present to welcome Alyie back. This resounding reception was just what Lydia Foxworth wished, and she recorded the adulation given to Alyie for dissemination across Federation Sector I.

"Thank you so much for your kind greetings," Alyie proclaimed. "I am here to re-introduce myself and have you meet my family. This base is very important to me. In many ways, it instilled in me the sense of duty and honor I have tried to live up to in my service to the Federation. I come here not to tell you my plans but to listen to your needs. If I am elected to serve on the High Council, I want to be able to carry your priorities to the highest level of the Sidereal Federation. I would like to hear from as many of you as I can."

As Alyie greeted everyone, she presented Jaynis, Tessa and Tomus. The twins made a splendid appearance, eliciting remarks from the assemblage such as "darling", "precocious" and "just like their parents" which made Jaynis particularly proud. Alyie also made sure to highlight Alison's role as her able and trusted associate.

A quick stop at the Cardinal Richelieu Station orbiting planet Pyeonghwa followed where Alyie's former instructors at the Sidereal Federation's Diplomatic Academy gave glowing testimony to Alyie's worth and ability.

After returning back to Earth, Alyie and her team began campaigning in earnest. The designated four E-w election period sped by quickly. There were three other candidates for the High Council position, but since they were unable to muster the minimum number of signatures, they were not entitled to Federation campaign funds. With no real resources, they offered no tangible opposition, and Alyie won the election in a Mars slide.

After accepting congratulations from present High Council members and the High Governor, Alyie also received a nice message from Hector, who had won his election to replace Alyie as Regional Governor. Since Earth was now an important cog in the administration of the Sidereal Federation, Alyie easily negotiated that she could still reside in Montpellier but make occasional trips to Teegarden for in-person High Council meetings.

CHAPTER 11.

A few E-w into her tenure as a High Council member, Alyie received a summons from the High Governor to meet one-on-one prior to the next High Council meeting at Teegarden. So as that date grew near, Alyie packed and bid a sweet goodbye to Jaynis and the twins for the trip to the Paris spaceport. Taking a space cruiser for the four E-d journey to the Federation's primary headquarters, Alyie could not help but reflect on how her life had evolved. Now 36 E-yr of age, she had started in the Fleet at 21 and had transitioned to a full-fledged statesperson. The requisite of an elected High Council member was no active military affiliation, so Alyie, with some regret, submitted her resignation to Space Command.

After being escorted to her office suite and room on the 14th floor of the Headquarters building, Alyie changed into the clothes she would wear for her tête-à-tête with the High Governor. Alyie dressed in a pants suit of light gray with red pinstripes that consisted of a jacket that had stylishly concealed buttons that covered her silk blouse and red cravat. Her Federation insignia was pinned to the lapel of the jacket. She pulled her light red hair back in a bun. Shod with very high black heels, Alyie immediately regretted not wearing her signature sturdy boots.

The High Governor's office suite was on the floor above. As Alyie exited the lift, she noticed a change in the ambiance. The previous High Governor, Mr. Ji-hoon Park's sense of décor, was austere and functional. The message now conveyed by the hallway was of elegance and beauty. The walls were painted in soft pastel colors, and paintings from across Human Space were hung discretely. Being escorted into the High Governor's anteroom by the High Governor's long-time Adjunct, Ms. Hilda Barton, Alyie was told to proceed immediately into the inner office as the High Governor was ready to meet her.

When Alyie entered, she found the High Governor seated to one side behind a gorgeous mahogany desk. As their eyes met, bright smiles were exchanged, and Felicity Erickson stood up and came across to hug Alyie.

"I am so happy to have you with us. This is what I have been waiting for during the past five E-yr."

"Once you were elected High Governor, I knew it was time for me to try for a position on the High Council. I am so delighted to be on it with you."

Alyie as a young Valkyrie Squadron captain, had served under Felicity Erickson in a delicate mission to Planet Ergo. Ambassador Erickson was also influential in getting Alyie to attend the Federation's Diplomatic Academy that launched Alyie on her post-military career. Felicity had aged beautifully. Her silver hair had turned a snowy white, but her fine chiseled face and creamy complexion remained the same. She moved, unlike Alyie, in her off-white-colored high heels with a suppleness that belied her age. Felicity's bright blue eyes sparkled with warmth, energy and curiosity. She was dressed in an aqua-colored pants suit over a beautiful white silk blouse adorned with a silver necklace and matching earrings. On the lapel of her sports jacket was fastened the special insignia designating her status in the Federation, and on the middle finger of her left hand, she wore the High Governor's signet gold ring.

"Please, let's sit and talk on the sofa," Felicity suggested. As light refreshments and hot beverages were served by Hilda, the two women chatted amiably about issues both trivial and profound. Felicity wanted to know all about Tessa and Tomus. She had not seen them since their Name-Bestowing celebration five E-yr ago. Alyie was curious about the surprises Felicity encountered in her first five E-yr. as High Governor.

"There were problems I had anticipated and some others that caught me off guard. My dear, Alyie, the Federation needs some serious introspection and some major restructuring. We need to be more forward thinking. The status quo will not provide stability nor peace."

"What are the major problems, if I may ask?"

"For samplers, we need, on the one hand, to explore new worlds for human expansion, but on the other hand, guard against agitation of the like you encountered on Earth a few years ago. Also, we need to anticipate non-human civilizations in space that will wish to interact with us. The Omegi you encountered wanted to be left alone (with the possible exception of you and your friend Mateo), but that may not be the norm. Unfortunately, the cumbersome current High Council structure makes it difficult to implement these changes."

"Those are significant issues, indeed, Felicity."

"And I fear I will not bring them forward sufficiently in the second half of my term as High Governor. But that is precisely why I have called you for this meeting. I am asking two things of you today."

"Whatever, you ask, I will fulfill to my greatest capacity."

"The first is administrative. With the new election cycle completed, the High Governor gets to select this year's Deputy High Governor, and I have selected you to fill that position."

"But Felicity, I am newly elected; surely there are more experienced members you can choose?"

"Alyie, don't be understating yourself. It does not become you. First of all, you have had a previous term on the High Council; second you have the experience as a Regional Governor. Then there is the matter of your stellar career as an Admiral in the Fleet, and, of course, you have also for a time been in charge of planet Kanva. I doubt there is not a single person in the whole Federation who is more qualified than you."

"I accept your offer, and I hope I can live up to your expectations."

"Alyie, I am thinking beyond this one year duty. Unless you seriously object, I plan to renew your appointment for each of the remaining E-yr. in my term. My goal if you hadn't guessed is to position you to become my successor. With all this experience, I don't see how you could lose the next election."

"That is a lot to digest in one sitting. I am so fortunate having you as my superior. In serving as your Deputy, I will have no better mentor as High Governor."

"No need to thank me. I am doing this for the Federation. In the near future, it will need a person of your ability to carry it forward. The second request I have of you today is more immediate and of smaller scope. I am making a trip to Kanva on a good will mission soon, and I want you as Deputy High Governor to remain in Teegarden until my return. I think it is important symbolically to assure the citizens of the Federation that there is always someone present in the High Governor's seat. I know this will cause some family issues, but I hope it will not be too disrupting."

"Jaynis tells me a mysterious dark cloud is headed in the direction of Kanva's star system. Felicity, is it safe to make the trip?"

"That is the prime reason I am going. Your friend Queen Revita is concerned about a growing panic among her citizens. She and the Parliament have been besieged with urgent requests to initiate evacuation operations. My science advisors on the High Council have assured me that the force shields on the spacecruiser I will be traveling on can stop every type of radiation except gravitational which this cloud does not produce in any significant amount. My safe arrival will be a message to the citizens that there is no danger in space to them."

"Yes, of course I will stay on Teegarden."

After finishing their food and drink, the two women freshened themselves and proceeded to go to the meeting room where Felicity announced Alyie's appointment. Most High Council members signaled their agreement with claps and nods, but there were a few who stayed notably silent.

CHAPTER 12.

When Alyie informed Jaynis of her prolonged stay on Teegarden, he was disappointed but took the delay as part of the new rhythm of their family life. Fortunately, Jaynis' sister Bernice was visiting from Planet New Tulsa and agreed to extend her stay to help with Tessa and Tomus. Alyie promised Earth-daily video hyperlink sessions with him and the twins. Also, Alison, upon learning about Alyie's situation, volunteered to take care of the children at her flat on her off days, an offer Jaynis heartedly accepted.

The space cruiser Igraine lifted off from the Teegarden spaceport with High Governor Erickson and a cadre of Federation officials aboard. Alyie wished Felicity a safe voyage and gave her gifts to present to Revi. Alyie, in her role as Deputy High Governor, found there was little in the way of duties to perform. In a conversation with the Director of Safety and Security, Alyie learned that Reg Jones was on Teegarden. The Colonel had departed Earth when Hector Palermo became Regional Governor to the Sol System and was now stationed here training some new Panthera fighters. Alyie tried messaging him from her implants but received no response. One E-d she went to the Panthera's unit complex but was told the Colonel was unavailable. However, the security officer let slip that every 5th E-d Colonel Jones goes to the Federation's firing range just before star rise for target practice.

Picking a date when Reg was scheduled to shoot, Alyie dressed in casual clothes of a green turtleneck with a black and white silk scarf, tight black trousers, tall black boots and a raincoat draped over her shoulders. She fastened her holster belt around her waist, making sure that her laser pistol was fully charged before leaving her room for the shooting range. It felt good to be back, at least briefly, to her old military routine.

Teegarden's five E-d synchronous rotational period made a "morning" every fifth day. It was a dismal rainy day when Alyie entered the target practice facility. Surveying the shooters, she spied Reg's broad back and shoulders. He was dressed in his battle fatigues, combat boots and signature beret on top of his curly brown hair. Fortunately, there was an open place next to him for her to shoot. Taking her place after slipping off her raincoat, Alyie spread her legs, drew her laser pistol from her holster and began shooting at the distant targets. Noticing the high accuracy of the shooter next to him, Reg turned and was startled to see who it was.

"You are a hard man to find, Colonel Jones. Why haven't you returned my messages?"

"I have been busy with Panthera work and haven't had the time."

"You also were negligent in fulfilling your responsibilities to the Regional Council when I was Governor."

"I am sorry, but every time there was a meeting of the Council, I had a conflict."

"Reg, I know you to be a man of many talents, but lying is not one of them. What is going on?"

"You are making things difficult for me. The less I say the better."

"Reg, if I have offended you in any way, please accept my apologies. I know I did I terrible thing coming back from Luna, four E-yr. ago and put you in a difficult position. I am so sorry, and I beg your forgiveness."

"You have nothing to be sorry for. The problem is not with you, but it is with me. I find I can handle my emotions best if I stay away from you."

"I see, but your estrangement is affecting others. Alison, who you know has strong feelings for you, wonders why you keep her at a distance. I, who value your ability above almost all, question whether I can rely on you in the future."

"I know I have not done right to Alison and I have promised myself that I will make it up to her. As for you, Alyie, no matter how I feel, I will always serve you with all my heart and soul."

"I realize things cannot be as you may wish, but know you will always have my respect and my friendship. I hope that will be enough."

Alyie gently touched Reg's right shoulder, and he tenderly stroked her face. Suddenly, Reg became rigid as he received a distress signal from his implant. Alyie was also experiencing an urgent message.

Reg was first to respond. "Igraine has been destroyed. All aboard are lost. I am ordered to escort you back to the Headquarters building under a Code V warning, which indicates a possible attack on the Federation. Please follow me, Madame High Governor."

THE DARK CLOUD

Part II.

"And whereas all the other things, whether beast or vessel, that enter into the dreadful gulf of this monster's mouth, are immediately lost and swallowed up, the sea gudgeon retires into it in great security, and there sleeps."

Montaigne

CHAPTER 13.

Still in a state of shock over the death of her friend Felicity, Alyie was ushered back into the headquarters building by Reg, and together they took the lift to the third subterranean level. Assembled in the heavily fortified bunker were Fleet Commander Admiral Steely Cranshaw and Ground Forces Commander General Ivan Presoff. Cranshaw was a longtime colleague and former superior to Alyie, while Presoff, who Colonel Jones currently served under, had moved up the ranks of the Ground Forces to be its head.

Also present was the Sidereal Federation High Justice Omar Alabi, who was designated to administer to Alyie the Oath of Office of High Governor. "Do you, Alyie Starstriker," Justice Alabi recited, "swear to the best of your abilities to uphold the principles of the Sidereal Federation as High Governor and serve its members with fidelity, integrity and justice?"

"I do," Alyie murmured, still somewhat dazed. The High Justice then activated in Alyie's implants all the necessary codes and access privileges afforded a High Governor. He pinned on her left breast the gold insignia of the Sidereal Federation High Governor - a human figure straddling a starfield. Alyie extended her right hand, and Justice Alabi placed the signet ring engraved with the same design as the insignia around her fourth finger.

"Madam High Governor," started Admiral Cranshaw, "at this stage there is not much information. We have flight records of Igraine until she disappeared. All systems were fully operational. Her force shields were activated, and the trip out of the final hyperspace knot went without a blip. Suddenly when she began entering the Trappist-1 system, energy outbursts were recorded and a short time later nothing. A scan of the last coordinates of the spacecraft show the space is completely empty. Other than residual radiation, the area is devoid of any material objects."

Alyie turned to General Presoff, asking, "Is there any evidence that it was destroyed by an intruder's missile?"

"No, Madam High Governor, at this time we have no evidence, and frankly with the force shields activated, it is difficult to imagine what type of weapon could have been used. All electromagnetic attacks would have been repulsed, and we have no evidence there was gravitational wave penetration."

"My next question is more provocative. Is there any evidence that Igraine's destruction was caused by an internal event?"

"Again, Madam High Governor, at this stage, there is no evidence of a bomb or malfunction of the spacecraft's operational system."

"What preparations have been made in the case this was an attack?" Alyie inquired.

Admiral Cranshaw replied, "Under a Code V emergency, all Federation forces throughout Human Space have been alerted to prepare for a defense of their respective installations or to be in readiness to receive target coordinates for an assault. All they need is your order, Madam High Governor."

"I want both of you to join me in the High Council meeting I am calling that will begin in an E-hr. We need to find the cause of this catastrophe as soon as possible. I will see you in the Conference Room."

"Colonel Jones," spoke General Presoff, "I want you to personally guard the High Governor. Until we can completely rule out treason, remain with her."

"Yes, Sir."

CHAPTER 14.

As Alyie and Reg entered the lift, Alyie automatically asked for the 14th floor where her current office was located. Reg questioned, "Should we not be going to the High Governor's suite on the 15th floor?"

"No, I am not ready for that."

"Understood."

In her office suite, Alyie asked Reg to remain in the anteroom while she prepared for the imminent High Council Meeting. After doing a quick security check, Reg left her alone as he stood guard right outside. Soon after, Reg could hear sobs and moans coming from Alyie's inner office. Resisting the urge to rush in to console her, he stayed outside until she bade him to enter.

"This is so sudden. I was with her a few E-d ago. She was so full of life and hope about us working together. How can I step into the High Governor's position under these circumstances?"

"Alyie, I know this is very difficult for you. No one anticipated this course of events, but you have to trust High Governor Erickson's judgement. This was the reason she chose you to be the Deputy High Governor. She knew if anything happened to her, you would be the best person to take her place. Now is the time to fulfill that trust."

"Thank you Reg. I needed to hear that. Let me freshen up a little. Presenting myself to the High Council as a weepy High Governor would not make a good first impression."

To appear a little more formal, Alyie put on a dark blue sports jacket and transferred the Sidereal Federation insignia to its lapel. She exchanged her black and white scarf for a blue and green one. With her face washed, she and Reg took the lift one flight up to the High Council Conference Room.

CHAPTER 15.

Due to the haste at which the meeting was called, not all Council Members could be in person. Those off Teegarden were video hyperlinked in. Alyie sat in the High Governor's chair, calling the meeting to order.

"As you all know by now a terrible tragedy has occurred. All passengers and crew along with the spacecruiser Igraine on route to Kanva have disappeared. Admiral Cranshaw and General Presoff are here to inform you what we currently know about this horrible event."

After the two military men went through the same analysis they had given Alyie, questions were raised, which the Admiral and General answered to their best abilities.

After an animated discussion, Alyie tried to summarize. "As I see it, there are four possible causes of the destruction of the Igraine,

- A natural phenomenon of yet we know not of.
- A missile attack from a weapon or enemy we have no knowledge of.
- An internal event caused by either a malfunction of some system, or
- A terrorist bomb loaded into the spacecraft."

"As for the last, I think we need to ask the question, who benefited most by the death of High Governor Erickson?" proposed Ms. Frida Geranova, a middle-aged gray-haired two-term elected High Council member.

"I am not sure what your implication is Frida," wondered Mr. Kamesh Thakur, another elected High Council member.

"Well, don't we find it remarkable that soon after Ms. Starstriker is elevated to the Deputy Governor position, the High Governor is killed?"

Reg, who was standing behind Alyie's chair, would not let that stand. "Madam Council Member, be careful of what you are saying. False accusations carry punishments."

"Colonel Jones, I was expecting you to come to the defense of the Deputy Governor." Geranova, smiled sarcastically, arching her eyebrows and pointing her aquiline nose forward. "What were you and she doing this morning at the shooting range? We have your little clandestine tête-à-tête on video you know."

"She is to be addressed as High Governor, Madam," responded a now enraged Reg.

Alyie, who felt she was punched in the stomach by Geranova's insinuation, recovered herself enough to raise an arm preventing Reg from advancing forward to confront the Council Member.

"All these scenarios do not lead us to a conclusion. We need firm evidence. I propose an Investigative Task Force with broad authority to find out the cause of this calamity. If High Council Members believe I will not be objective, they can select the Task Force members whom I will approve of unconditionally. All I ask is you do it in haste because the longer we wait the more unease we cause throughout the Federation."

From a brief discussion, it was agreed that the Council would meet in private and offer four names to be on the Task Force. Alyie requested they inform her within the next E-hr of their choices. Alyie, also in her first formal action as High Governor, appointed Kamesh Thakur as Deputy. With that, she and Reg abruptly left the Conference Room.

CHAPTER 16.

Alyie and Reg walked solemnly down the hall back to her office without speaking. When they arrived at the door, Reg said, "I will stay posted till I find one of my Panthera to spell me, but I will be back soon."

He looked at Alyie, who had tears in her eyes and a woeful expression, and whispered, "Stay strong."

She answered softly, "You too."

Once in her office, Alyie contacted Jaynis immediately on her video hyperlink.

"Yes, the news is everywhere. What a tragedy!" Jaynis proclaimed as his image came into view. "How are you doing? You don't look well, or is there a problem with the reception?"

"No, I am in fact miserable. The death of Felicity and her traveling companions is horrible in its own right, but there is some bad stuff going round concerning me."

"What are you talking about, Alyie? You are now the High Governor."

"Frida Geranova has all but accused me of plotting Felicity's death to gain power."

"That is absurd. She is jealous that Felicity chose you instead of her, and this just proves how bad a High Governor she would have been."

"Jaynis, there is more. The High Council Meeting is supposed to be confidential, but I am sure Frida will find a way to publicize what else she said about me and Reg Jones."

"You and Reg? What is she talking about?"

"I met Reg earlier at the shooting range. I needed to set things right with him. About four years ago when we were returning from Luna after destroying the Separatist's staging base, I did something out of line."

"Wasn't this when you discovered that Malcolm Dunrock was holding Alison and others hostage at the Regional Office here."

"Yes, I was feeling terrible, and my wound from Kanva was throbbing. I invited Reg to join me in my cabin for a few drinks which I over indulged in. I am sorry Jaynis, but I made a pass at him which he gentlemanly rebuked."

"And?" Jaynis asked.

"That was it. Nothing else happened, but Reg has been avoiding me ever since, and today before we got word of the destruction of the Igraine, I sought him out to tell him I was sorry. I asked him to forgive my behavior just as I am asking you now."

"So, if I understand you, Alyie. You are telling me this brief encounter with Reg now because you expect that crow Frida Geranova to use it to suggest you and Reg are lovers and traitors?"

"At this moment, I am more concerned with you and how you feel than my future in the Sidereal Federation."

"Alyie, I have known you most of my life. We went to school together, became best friends, then eternal partners and now have two beautiful children. You have made my life happy beyond imagination. If your little indiscretion above the Earth with Reg is the only mark on your faithfulness, then consider it forgotten. It is just background noise in the continuum."

"Jaynis, I don't know what to say. I am so grateful to be with you."

"What are you doing about the disaster?"

"The High Council is deciding on members of an Investigative Task Force to determine the cause of the catastrophe. I agreed to stand apart from its selection to insure objectivity."

"I don't like that, Alyie. You are the duly chosen High Governor. Don't let Geranova have her way."

"I am thinking of resigning if I don't have the trust of the High Council."

"That is exactly the wrong thing to do. You need to be High Governor and not cave into this baseless attack. You have the skills and ability to find out what happened. Not some group of bureaucrats. However, from the reports I heard, you did one thing correct - name Kamesh Thakur as Deputy. That foiled Geranova's scheme to gain the High Governorship."

"Thank you Jaynis, I needed that support."

"Also, I am working on a hypothesis for the cause of the destruction. I will get back to you as soon as I am more confident in it."

"I love you, Jaynis. Why do you put up with me?"

"Because there is no one better."

CHAPTER 17.

Alyie needed to make other calls. The next was to her parents, who were traveling to Planet Horab orbiting the star HD 85512. This was a long-delayed 40th E-yr wedding anniversary trip. After updating them on the loss of the High Governor and her colleagues, Alyie warned them that a High Council member was spreading vile rumors to unseat her. Tanita Starbright and Alex Striker were veterans of Federation infighting and told their daughter to not let these insinuations distract Alyie from discharging her duties as High Governor.

"Whatever happens," Tanita declared, "you have our full support and love."

"Thanks, Mom and Dad."

After speaking to her parents, Alyie received a message on her implant from Kamesh Thakur that the High Council had chosen its members for the Investigative Task Force, one of which was Frida Geranova. Alyie was not surprised. Next, she made the call she dreaded – to Alison Bernewithy.

Reaching her, Alyie immediately felt a coldness in her friend's voice.

"Yes, I have heard all about the 'accident' as some are calling it. And I have sources that tell me that there is a suggestion that somehow you were involved."

"Well I am calling you to tell you that is untrue, spun by a person on the High Council who wants vengeance for being passed over."

"What about the reports about you and Reg. Are they fabrications as well?"

Alyie repeated to Alison the details of her meeting with Reg this morning on Teegarden and the act four years ago that precipitated it.

"I knew there was someone else, but I never guessed it was you. Why didn't you tell me?"

"I was ashamed of my behavior, Alison. But what is important is that Reg did nothing wrong, not four years ago and not today. Please believe me."

"Yes, he did nothing wrong, but he still yearns for you. Don't you realize the effect you have on people, especially men?"

"No, Alison. When Reg and I met today before we heard the terrible news, we reached an accommodation. I think Reg is now ready to move on."

"Listen, you have been my role model, inspiration and superior for the past five years. I idolized you as many have. Throughout your career, you have used the devotion others have given you to your advantage. There is more I could say to you, but I prefer to end our conversation. Good bye."

CHAPTER 18.

When the shades of her bedroom lightened to give the appearance of a new day on Teegarden, Alyie woke and promptly washed in the shower that adjoined her office suite. She decided that on her first day as High Governor, she would primarily dress in white. Putting on a white crisp buttoned-down shirt and getting into snow-white trim-fitting trousers, she draped a creamy white sports jacket over her shoulders. Offsetting all this whiteness, Alyie girdled around her waist a black leather belt and donned her tall black boots. Fastening her red cravat with the High Governor's insignia pin, she completed her wardrobe by putting her fully charged laser pistol in her right boot.

Striding through the office to the door leading to the anteroom, Alyie found Reg waiting.

"Don't tell me you remained on guard all night?"

"I took some breaks when some relief was available."

"Oh, Reg. I don't deserve you."

"I am just following General Presoff's orders."

"What you can do for me if you wish is help me move my belongings from here to the High Governor's suite; if that is not too much trouble."

"You are now the High Governor. You don't need to ask."

Ordering a cadre of service bots, Reg coordinated the transfer of goods which were mostly Alyie's clothes and accessories, to the High Governor's suite, which Alyie was able to enter with her newly activated passcode.

Standing with Reg in the beautiful ante-room that was re-designed by Felicity, Alyie thanked him for his help and then declared, "In my capacity as High Governor, I am giving you two orders."

"Yes, Madam High Governor."

"The first is to leave me. I can take care of myself."

"But I am under strict orders to stay by you. You were a witness that commission."

"Well, as High Governor, I am superseding that order. Besides," as Alyie drew the laser pistol out of her boot, "I am not unarmed, and you know how well I can shoot."

"Yes, Madam High Governor."

"The second order is to contact Alison. You need to speak to her."

"Yes, Alyie, I will."

"Now good bye."

CHAPTER 19.

After Reg had departed, Alyie walked through the anteroom to the main office. Surrounded by the beauty and taste that Felicity bestowed on the room, Alyie felt like an intruder. She circled around the mahogany desk until finally finding the courage to sit in the chair. As she took her place in the High Governor's seat with her jacket hung over her shoulders like a cape, Alyie glanced at the signet ring that was now on her hand and the brooch that adorned her jacket. She was now the High Governor, the leader of over 20 billion humans in 30 odd settled worlds that spanned a diameter of nearly 60 l-yr. Alyie reflected that this was the culmination of all that she had strived for in her professional life. But it all seemed now so unnatural and hollow. And tainted with mistrust and the whiff of scandal. Alyie kept brooding on Alison's remarks that insinuated Alyie had used the affection and loyalty of others to advance her career. Was she really that manipulative? Did she take advantage of her closest comrades and family members?

Fighting through a miasma of disgust and despair, Alyie's day turned around when she received a hyperlink call from Jaynis.

"I know how Igraine was destroyed."

"You do?"

"Yes, it had been fooling me for some time as the spectral readings were all over the scale, but I worked it out last night. However, before I come forward with my explanation, I need to provide absolute proof. Those sceptics on the High Council I am sure will not take the word of your eternal partner."

"How are you going to get the evidence?"

"That's where you come in. You are still the High Governor, are you not?"

"Yes, I am."

"I need you to grant me permission to take a spacecruiser to the Trappist-1 system in the vicinity of where Igraine disappeared."

"That whole space is a No-Fly area by Space Fleet orders."

"Well, I need to go there, and the High Governor has the power to grant me a waiver."

"It's dangerous. I have lost my friend; I do not want to lose my husband."

"You won't lose me, my dear. I have something that the crew of Igraine didn't."

"What is that, Jaynis?"

"The knowledge of what is out there."

"Jaynis, how are you going to obtain a spacecruiser?"

"I already have one. I called the Regional Office here a short time ago, and Alison requisitioned the Bellerophon."

"Alison?" Alyie exclaimed. "I wouldn't think she would wish to assist us."

"What do you mean? She is a team member."

"When I told her about the rumors about Reg and I, she grew quite cross."

"Alison did mention she said things to you she now regrets. She is afraid you are so angry with her you now have cut her off. She expressed how sorry she is."

"I am the one who needs to be forgiven."

"Well, I am sure you two will kiss and make up shortly. Now are you giving me clearance to fly?"

"Only under the condition that you have an escort. I am going to order the best I know – namely the Valkyrie Squadron. You will rendezvous on the other side of the hyper-knot that leads to the Trappist-1 system."

"I don't need them for this mission."

"Well unless they accompany you, the mission is a No-Go."

"Alright, they may come in handy. I can use one or two of their rockets to test my theory."

"Jaynis, please be careful. Are the twins being cared for?"

"No problem, my love. Bernice and Alison have made a full schedule of parenting duties while I am away. Let me know when you have arranged my escort."

"Send me your flight schedule. You are the best ever!"

"Same here."

CHAPTER 20.

The rest of the "day" Alyie remained in the High Governor's inner office, except for one time to peek in the hallway, where she found that Reg Jones, although obeying her exact order to leave, had arranged for a rotation of pairs of Panthera soldiers to be stationed continuously as guards. Alyie's first action was to re-arrange the office. She contacted the service autobots assigned to the High Governor to move furniture. The main result was now the desk was in the rear center of the room so that anyone entering from the anteroom would see the High Governor sitting behind it staring at them. Setting her own appointment schedule, Alyie was ready to begin her first full day as High Governor.

She broadcasted a hyperlink video message that was sent throughout the Federation expressing sorrow for the death of High Governor Erickson and all members of Igraine. Alyie assured everyone in Human Space that the High Council was fully functioning and had already begun an investigation to ascertain the cause of this terrible tragedy.

Her first visitor was Hilda Barton. The older woman, who had served Earth decades with Felicity, was in a distraught condition, but she believed it was her duty to report to the new High Governor. Alyie told her to take all the time off she needed to grieve. When she was ready to return, Alyie promised Hilda she could continue to serve as the High Governor's Adjunct if she so desired. The other request Alyie made was that she would like Hilda to help plan the Federation's memorial service for Felicity and the others lost in the spacecraft's destruction.

After Hilda's departure, Alyie contacted Admiral Cranshaw to waive the No-Fly order in the Trappist-1 system for the space cruiser Bellerophon and the Valkyrie Squadron, who will serve as an armed escort. That done, Alyie contacted Captain Olga Fercouska, Commander of the Valkyrie, briefing her old comrade about this mission.

"So you want us to baby sit your hubby?"

"Yes, but please follow his instructions. This mission carries the potential for extreme danger. He is going to conduct a proof of concept test. I don't want to lose him, but your safety is also paramount."

"Yes, Ma'am. Oh, excuse me. Yes, Madam High Governor."

"Consider yourself excused."

The next visitor on Alyie's agenda was Kamesh Thakur, the newly appointed Deputy Governor. She had requested an immediate meeting with him. Kamesh was a small man of dark complexion who entered the inner office sweating profusely in a state of high anxiety, no doubt flustered by the presence of the fierce Panthera guards stationed outside. Alyie bade him sit down in the chair on the other side of the desk.

"Good day, Mr. Thakur. What can you tell me about the status of the Investigative Task Force?"

"Madam Governor, they appear to be off to a slow start. There is some disagreement on the scope and focus of the investigation."

"I want you to know I have begun my own inquiry. When there is something discovered, I will call an emergency meeting of the High Council to present the evidence."

"Yes, Madam Governor."

"Also, I am meeting the Chair of the Sidereal Federation Council later to enact reform in the membership of the High Council. In the current structure with 33 members, it is unwieldy. I propose to reduce the number by first having only one representative elected from each of the 10 Sectors, and second, have the appointed group ad-hoc only to be used when there is a special need for their expertise. The new body will be called the High Governor's Board. I will keep you informed about the steps we need to make this happen."

"If your reform is successful Madam High Governor, half of the current elected members will be removed from the High Council."

"I am sure we can work together to decide an equitable arrangement of who goes and who stays. Do you not agree?"

"Yes, of course I would be happy to work with you, Madam High Governor. Thank you for including me in this needed reform, and of course, for naming me Deputy High Governor. If I may ask, do you have any plans for an Installation Ceremony for yourself as High Governor?"

"That will happen in time Mr. Thakur. First, we need to resolve this crisis. My formal installation as High Governor in any case, will not occur until there is a memorial service for all who lost their lives aboard Igraine."

"Of course, Madam High Governor."

"I think our business today is concluded. Let me escort you out."

As Alyie was ushering Kamesh Thakur out of her inner office, she offered her right hand to him. He held it, bowed his head and kissed her signet ring. Alyie found the experience odd but satisfying.

Next was Dr. Abba Niji, Chair of the Sidereal Federation Council. After hearing Alyie identify the key elements in her reform plan, Dr. Niji reviewed the process that would need to take place for approval in which the final step would be a Human Space wide referendum. Alyie insisted she wanted it to proceed as quickly as possible.

After Dr. Niji's departure, Alyie had a brief lunch brought to her by an autobot. She then set out to do what she had been dying to do all day, reach Tessa and Tomus. She contacted Jaynis, but he was at the Université procuring equipment to take on his trip.

"Call Alison, this is her day to be with them. She flew over this morning."

Using a video hyperlink to Earth, Alyie found Alison outside with the children playing a space game on the mobiles.

"We are playing Hyper-world," said an out-of-breath Alison. "The goal is to get me dizzy to re-create how I felt when we traveled to New Cedonia."

It was hard to tell whether Alyie was happier to see the children or view Alison's smiling face.

"I am so sorry I held back the truth from you. It violated what I asked you to always be."

"I am sorry for the things I said to you. You who have the burden of literally the Universe on your shoulders now."

"Well, technically it's only Human Space, but I appreciate your thoughtfulness."

"Reg contacted me, and we are scheduled to have a virtual date this Earth evening. I have a feeling you had something to do with this."

"No mind. All I want is for you both to be happy. Please let me speak to Tessa and Tomus if you can pull them away from their adventure."

"Hi, Mommy. We are trying to make Aunt Alison puke but so far no luck."

CHAPTER 21.

In the 10 E-d journey it took Jaynis aboard Bellerophon to rendezvous with the Valkyrie Squadron, relations among members of the High Council grew increasingly tense. The majority supported Alyie and scoffed at the suggestion she had anything to do with the disaster. A minority headed by Frida Geranova kept pressing on about Alyie's supposed involvement. Geranova forced the Investigative Task Force to secure and examine all Alyie's comings and goings since she arrived on Teegarden to assume her seat on the High Council. The continued service of the Panthera as bodyguards to Alyie and news of the High Governor's structural reforms also heightened the sense of alienation.

Alyie let the bi-polarity exist around her, going about her official duties mindful of the importance of Jaynis' mission. She was in frequent contact with her friend Queen Revita Jadeite of planet Kanva, apprising her of the situation. The Queen was concerned about the fate of her planet and its citizens. All space traffic in and out of Kanva was prohibited until the cause of Igraine's disappearance was ascertained.

"But Alyie," Revita admonished. "Our planet depends on imports of goods to survive. We cannot go much longer without supplies. In addition, our economy depends on exports and tourists. With this lockdown, there is growing unrest among my people. I'm not sure how much more they can take."

"I know Revi this must be difficult, and my heart goes out to you and your people. Jaynis assures me he knows what happened, but he wants to supply proof to quell the unrest here in Teegarden."

"I abhor those politicians. How dare they impugn your integrity? I never liked the idea of a pure republic. A monarchy, absolute or constitutional, such as here is best. Maybe you can change that."

"I have enough problems with the High Council as it is now constructed. I am trying to make reforms, but I doubt they are ready to do away with elections."

"I think Empress Alyie Starstriker, First of Her Name has a nice ring to it, don't you?"

"You are impossible. Listen, once Jaynis delivers the proof he is seeking, I will personally address your people."

"Great. You still have a lot of good will here from that time you served as my First Consul."

CHAPTER 22.

Finally, Alyie received hyperlink messages from both Jaynis and Olga. Because of the Trappist-1 system's distance and paucity of nearby micro hyper-knots, the transmission was time delayed. Jaynis was first to be imaged, saying, "Commander Fedor Greysan has made contact with the Valkyrie, and we are all proceeding to the area where the destruction took place. Get your High Council together so they can witness this test."

Olga then broke in, "Madam High Governor we are shadowing Bellerophon and waiting instructions from Dr. Bottombrook."

Alyie replied to both, "I have received your transmissions and will inform you when the High Council has convened. Please take care."

Alyie sent a signal for an emergency High Council Meeting to take place in an E-hr. Again dressing in white and black, she was accompanied by Hilda Barton and her ever-present Panthera guards to the Conference Room. With most of the High Council members present, Alyie sent the signal to Jaynis and Olga to begin their transmission.

Frida Geranova, visibly upset, complained, "Why have we been brought here? You are interfering with the investigation which, if you recall, you authorized. Is this some theatrics to throw us off course?"

"Ms. Geranova, I am interested in truth, not fancy. Do we not want to find out the cause of the tragedy by all means available?"

While Alyie was speaking, Jaynis' image came on the large video screen in the room. All conversation stopped as he began to speak.

"Members of the High Council, greetings from space. We are approaching the area where the Igraine was destroyed. I want you all to witness how it happened. Captain Olga Fercouska, once receiving permission, will fire an incendiary missile at the dark nebulous cloud that has been drifting in this space. Visuals aboard my spacecraft and the other Valkyrie starfighters will record the event."

Some 10 E-minutes later, Olga chimed in, saying, "Madam High Governor requesting permission to fire."

"Permission granted, Captain Fercouska," Alyie replied.

Again there was an agonizing (especially for Alyie) 10-minute delay, but eventually, all in the Conference Room could see the missile launch, reach the periphery of the cloud and suddenly be destroyed amid a hail of radiation.

After the buzz of comments from the members of the High Council had quelled, Jaynis' face once again appeared on the screen.

"To prove this destruction was not associated with the explosive nature of that missile, Commander Greysan has agreed to jettison the escape pod aboard Bellerophon. We will observe the pod suffer the same fate even though its force field will be turned on."

Alyie grew alarmed. "Jaynis, without that pod you have no emergency escape vehicle should Bellerophon be incapacitated."

"Don't worry, your girls will keep us safe," came Jaynis' delayed response.

Once the escape pod was ejected, it was aimed directly at the nebula, and when reaching the cloud, it again was quickly decimated.

Dr. Fitzhugh Thornberry, a planetary scientist on the High Council, spoke, "Dr. Bottombrook do you know the cause of what we have witnessed?"

"Yes, I do," came Jaynis' delayed reply. "It is matter-antimatter annihilation collisions. I did not recognize it sooner because the pair photons always produced in these type of events are usually of a particular frequency. From Earth we had analyzed the radiation spectrum of the interaction of particles interacting with this cloud and found it to be a wide range of frequencies. I have spectroscopes on board that have recorded the emissions you just observed which everyone is free to examine."

"What could cause this cloud to drift through space, Dr. Bottombrook?" Fitzhugh Thornberry inquired.

"This nebula must be the remains of an antimatter star. It has elements of antihydrogen, antihelium, anticarbon, antioxygen, etc. up to, I believe, antiiron. As it drifts through space, any conventional matter that comes in contact with it will be destroyed in these annihilation events. A ship like Igraine with all the diverse elements in its construction was easy prey for this antimatter monster."

"I didn't think antimatter stars could exist," puzzled Dr. Thornberry.

"Well, they do now. My guess," said Jaynis, "is that this cloud is part of what remains of an antimatter star that went supernova some time ago. The material may have originated in the beginning of the Universe when matter and antimatter were created. Who knows how long this cloud has been drifting in interstellar space."

"Well done, Dr. Bottombrook, Commander Greysan and Valkyrie," Alyie expressed. "Your mission is accomplished. Return home safely."

"Alyie," Jaynis responded, "our mission is over, but the problem very much remains. The course the dark cloud is taking is on a trajectory towards Kanva. We are looking at an unmitigated catastrophe in the making."

CHAPTER 23.

As the result of Jaynis' proof, all talk about Alyie's involvement in the death of High Governor Erickson ceased. The Investigative Task Force was dissolved, and Frida Geranova and her associates found themselves increasingly isolated on Teegarden.

In the intervening time for Jaynis to return to Earth, Alyie put the Sidereal Federation in crisis mode, trying to devise a way to prevent the antimatter cloud from entering Kanva space. Scientists on Mars at Chandrasekhar University had determined that the nebula was about 70 million km wide along its major axis (about ½ the distance from Earth to Sol). At the speed it was traveling, it would reach the outskirts of Kanva in about 5 E-m. Even if the nebula just grazed the upper atmosphere, it would destroy enough particles to make the surface air on Kanva unbreathable.

Alyie, as promised, addressed the populace of Kanva, telling them truthfully the danger before them and promising that the Federation was doing everything in its power to avert a disaster. Of course, this did little to stop a general panic, as many could find flights to escape the planet, taking routes directed away from the oncoming dark cloud. Revi was very worried, but as titular head of the planet vowed to stay to the end, trusting her good friend to find a solution.

In meetings with the heads of Space Fleet, Ground Forces, Transportation and Commerce, Alyie examined possible crisis-averting scenarios. The first was a missile attack on the cloud, triggering annihilation events that would destroy most of the antimatter contained within. However, the size of the nebula, Admiral Cranshaw determined, would require an arsenal beyond the Federation's resources. Consideration was given to a systematic evacuation of Kanva. The Transportation Minister, Ms. Sonja Dubois, and General Presoff calculated that Kanva, with a population of about 100 million, would require approximately 20,000 spacecarrier trips to take all citizens off the planet even if each ship could hold a maximum of 5000 passengers.

Faced with daunting challenges with both these proposals, Alyie pressed her team to seek other solutions.

CHAPTER 24.

Through all this crisis planning, Alyie made time for administrative actions. She messaged Alison, who was at the Regional Governor's Headquarters in Brussels. After catching up on personal matters, Alyie turned the conversation to the reason for the call.

"I am now initiating the protocol to have you named Minister of Arts and Culture. I want to make sure you still want the position."

"That is terrific, Alyie. Yes, I do, but what about my role here in Brussels?"

You won't start until the present Minister's term is over six E-m from now. I also want your appointment to commence with the opening of the new center in Paris. We'll have a joyous celebration of both."

"Thanks so much, Alyie."

"Give my best to Hector, and thank you for the help you've given me and Jaynis with the twins."

A short time later, Reg Jones came into the office as requested by Alyie, standing erect and saluting her.

"Reg, you don't have to do that anymore, I am no longer commissioned."

"Ok. Greetings, Most High Madam Governor," he replied, trying to repress a smile.

"Colonel Jones your stubborn insistence on providing me with bodyguards has had an addictive effect."

"How so?"

"I have become so enamored of them that I want to make their presence permanent. I have ordered General Presoff to transfer command of the Panthera from Ground Forces to the High Governorship."

"Great, Alyie. You have my full endorsement. It is high time in coming."

"I know you have been on a recruiting initiative to increase the Panthera' numbers. I want the Force grown to 2000 strong without sacrificing quality. Half this number will be stationed at Headquarters to provide security."

"They will be called the High Governor's Elite Guard. I will select only the best to serve you."

"Thanks Reg."

After Colonel Jones took his leave, Alyie felt it was time to determine the fate of Frida Geranova. Alyie sent two of her Panthera guards to summon the woman to the High Governor's Office. With the security force field on to block transmission of any recordings or messages, Frida entered into a state of some distress at this abruptly called meeting.

"Am I under arrest?" Geranova nervously asked.

"No, not yet," was Alyie's curt reply.

"I know I may have spoken rashly, but I was just looking for an explanation for the disaster."

"You spoke and then spread heinous lies about me. You impugned my integrity. You tried to implicate me in a scandal that could have destroyed my family."

"Well I am sorry if things got out of hand."

"You will no longer serve in a government in which I am the High Governor. I have two documents on my desk, one of which I will seal with my ring. The first is to the Sidereal Federation Council seeking your impeachment from the High Council on grounds of 'Conduct Not Befitting a High Council Member'. If you are impeached, which I assure you will happen, charges of libel and slander will be brought on you by the High Justice. The second document is your letter of resignation from the High Council which if you sign, I will accept. Decide now which one I will affix my seal to."

"You leave me little choice High Governor. Hand me the resignation letter."

After Frida signed the document and returned it, Alyie removed the force field, messaging her guards to enter.

"Take Ms. Geranova back to her room. You have one E-hr. to vacate your quarters. If you are not on a flight heading out of Teegarden by next Earth-morning, I am going ahead with the impeachment proceedings. Good bye."

CHAPTER 25.

When Bellerophon emerged from the hyper-knot that put it into Sol System space, Jaynis hyperlinked Alyie, knowing there was now almost no time delay in the transmission.

"Have you and your Headquarters group worked out a plan to stop the nebula from destroying Kanva?"

Oh, Jaynis. We have looked at missile attacks and a general evacuation, but both don't look promising."

"Well, I have been consulting while in transit with my old colleague Seo-jun Gwan on Mars and that High Council Member Fitzhugh Thornberry, who is a pretty good fellow, and we think we found a viable, although ambitious alternative."

"Please tell. Things are getting pretty desperate here."

"We are going to build a cage to trap the beast."

"It must be a pretty big trap for the beast is nearly ½ AU across."

"Yes, dear, it will need to completely encircle the monster."

"What material, Jaynis will this trap be made of?"

"Not material, Alyie, but magnetic fields will hold the beast at bay."

"Magnetic fields only act on moving charged particles. Didn't you say the cloud is neutrally charged?"

"Yes, it is mon-capitaine, but charged particles are seething inside each element in the cloud that we can trap magnetically."

"I think I need a primer on antimatter and how you propose to trap it before the cloud destroys Kanva."

“Alyie, let’s start with the basics. Antimatter is identical to ordinary matter except that the atoms that comprise it have oppositely charged elementary particles.”

“Yes, Jaynis I am aware of this. The antiparticle of the negatively charged electron is the positively charged positron, and the antiparticle of the positively charged proton is the negatively charged antiproton.”

“Good, my dear. Now, antihydrogen, the simplest anti-element is comprised of a negatively charged nucleus consisting of an antiproton that is surrounded by a positively charged positron. The others, antihelium, antilithium, etc. are built up the same way with the positrons on the outside and the antiprotons in the nucleus.”

“But aren’t these antimatter elements neutrally charged with the positive positrons balanced by an equal number of negative antiprotons?”

“Yes, but they have magnetic moments due to their quantum spins that can be affected by certain types of magnetic fields. We can use this property to create an equilibrium effect that will keep them away from the walls of the trap indefinitely, thereby preventing annihilation.”

“This sounds too good to be true, Jaynis.”

“Well, before you declare victory, know that to build and deploy these magnetic coils in space will be a project way beyond what the Federation has ever attempted.”

“Give me the details.”

“I am forwarding the proposal my team and I have developed. Let whoever you wish review it, but remember we are fighting an unforgiving time line. So production of this trap needs to begin immediately if not sooner.”

“Ok, Jaynis. Plan to see me when you arrive back on Earth.”

CHAPTER 26.

Alyie arrived at her home in Montpellier shortly after Jaynis' return. She dressed in a copper-colored pants suit, beige blouse and cream-colored heels, an outfit she hoped would please Jaynis. She was so happy to see him and the twins after such a long absence. However, she did not come alone. Reg Jones assigned a squad of four Panthera to accompany her. The chateau was not equipped for these types of guests, but Jaynis devised makeshift bunks in the stable barn for two while the other guards were housed in the guest rooms. Jaynis rolled his eyes upon their arrival, which Alyie countered by saying, "I think, dear, we need to re-assess our living conditions." However, the greatest beneficiaries to these non-invitees were Tessa and Tomus, who relished playing adventure games with real-life soldiers.

Despite the Panthera's ubiquitous presence, Alyie and Jaynis still had the privacy of their bedroom, which they utilized to get re-acquainted in the most intimate ways.

The next morning, Alyie convened a video hyperlink meeting with the High Council, Admiral Cranshaw, General Presoff, Jaynis' group and several engineers. The plans to construct two gigantic coils of super-thin conducting wire to generate the requisite magnetic fields were presented.

"You are asking to produce not one but two coils of length about 100 million km, if I am not mistaken, Dr. Bottombrook?" asked a flabbergasted General Presoff.

"Yes, General," Jaynis replied. "They will be deployed in parallel around the minor axis of the antimatter cloud and serve as a helical coil producing the necessary magnetic field to trap the antimatter. We need two coils to provide optimal magnetic field configuration."

"How are we going to get these coils in space to surround the cloud?" wondered Admiral Cranshaw.

"I spoke to Dr. Alex Striker at Space Command, and he recommends a constellation of spacecraft. We can splice each coil, into, say, eight segments and have a separate spacecarrier transport a tightly rolled up segment. When in formation, the 16 carriers will unravel the wire in two loops around the cloud at opposite ends and then join adjacent segments to form two continuous coils. Synchronizing the operation, the required electric current to produce the magnetic field can be supplied by radioactive piezoelectric generators inserted at the junctions of each segment. Once the trap is set, the spacecarriers acting in consort will tug the antimatter cloud in a direction away from Kanva. Far enough out in empty space, the carriers will release their contact with the trap and allow the caged cloud to drift harmlessly."

"You make it sound plausible, but the scale of operation is tremendous. Where do we find the facilities to build such coils?" said Mr. Martin Agnew, a High Council Member who was also an economist.

"As High Governor, I have declared a State of Emergency and have acquired for use in manufacturing the material five facilities on Luna which will be using computer-aided-designs sent by the engineering team to retrofit their operations for immediate production of the necessary components. We need to act in extreme haste, so I want the High Council's endorsement of this proposal now."

"Madam High Governor," Admiral Cranshaw interjected. "The fate of Kanva depends on the success of this trapping mechanism. As you know Alyie, mission design in Space Command also includes a backup plan. If Dr. Bottombrook and his associates' plan fails or does not work as anticipated, what is our recourse?"

"Admiral Cranshaw, the only alternative I see is an emergency evacuation of the planet, trying to get as many citizens out as the time allows. Let's plan as best we can on this contingency."

"Yes, Madam High Governor."

CHAPTER 27.

With the plan for the magnetic trap set in motion, Alyie contacted Queen Revita. "We have faith in this mission, but I think it would be best to proceed with a measured evacuation of your planet. The more of the citizens we can get off Kanva, the less we will have to if the plan fails. I want you to come visit us in Montpellier. Tessa and Tomus will be thrilled to live in the same house with a real Queen."

"Thanks, Alyie for your invitation, but as I told you before, I am remaining with my people. Besides if you and Jaynis believe in this mission, then what is there to worry about?"

After disconnecting from Revi, Alyie thought to herself there was plenty to be concerned about. A sequence of procedures had to work precisely in order for mission success. In her mind, Alyie outlined the needed steps in chronological order.

1. The coils need to be manufactured to specifications in time for launch. (With five processing plants, there was redundancy in that if there was a failure at one, the slack in production could be picked up by the other four.)

2. Once fabricated, the coils needed to be cut into segments, rolled up and loaded on Luna into the spacecarriers.

3. The spacecarriers needed to successfully navigate the two hyper knots to enter Trappist-1 space. (On advice from Admiral Crenshaw, it was decided that each coil would be broken into seven segments, and two of the16 carriers would serve as a backup if any of the other 14 had a mishap on transit or a malfunction in deploying the coils or activating the generators.)

4. Once in the vicinity of the cloud, the carriers would need to circle around it and carefully unroll the segments.

5. Autonomous devices would need to insert the piezoelectric generators at the junctions of each segment of the coils.

6. The generators would all have to generate electricity in phase to produce the enormous magnetic field to trap the antimatter.

7. If the trap is produced and holds the antimatter, then the spacecarriers would need to work in tandem to tug the cloud away from Kanva.

8. Once at a safe distance, they can release their hold and return to base.

After going through this mental exercise, Alyie felt a pulsating pain in her left breast from her old wound. Her first thought was to have an alcoholic drink, but then she had a much more comforting idea.

CHAPTER 28.

Bellerophon had just come out of the hyper-knot that put it into Teagarden space. The twins were so happy to experience hyperspace again that they asked if the cruiser could be turned around for another loop. Alyie, Jaynis, Tessa and Tomus were heading for Federation Headquarters. Alyie thought it best she stayed in her seat as High Governor to supervise and coordinate the final steps in preparing Operation Grendel. Prior to taking off from Earth, Alyie and Federation engineers toured the facilities on Luna that were manufacturing the coils. Everything seemed to be proceeding in order despite the hectic work schedule that necessitated the plants operate almost continuously. Fleet Command was also in the process of sending the 16 spacecarriers to Luna to begin the loading process as soon as the coils were fabricated. Alyie had considered commanding the constellation, but Admiral Cranshaw convinced her that her place once the mission began was at HQ.

On Teegarden, the Starbrook family settled in at the High Governor's mansion within a short distance from the Headquarters building. It was a roomy but austere environment. The children were mainly cared for by Taki-2 as both Alyie and Jaynis were regularly in meetings. An updated version of Ms. Brody continued providing them with their lessons.

As the launch date drew near, there was great anticipation for Operation Grendel. If the schedule of the mission followed as prescribed, the constellation named Bewoulf would rendezvous with the antimatter nebula about an E-m before it would enter Kanva's upper atmosphere. Alyie realized that much of her reputation as High Governor depended on the mission's success. She found herself in her quieter moments in prayer for the people of Kanva, trying to minimize her own self-interest.

On the appointed date, Alyie, seated in the High Governor's chair, sent a Federation-wide video hyperlink message thanking everyone involved in the mission for their dedication, expertise and cooperation. Alyie then signaled Mission Control on the Luna spaceport to begin the countdown. When it reached zero, Alyie gave the command to launch, and, one after another, the 16 spacecarriers took off from the Luna spaceport with their conducting coil segments tucked unimaginably tightly in the respective ship's cargo hold. Operation Grendel to save Kanva had begun.

CHAPTER 29.

Eight E-d later, Bewoulf made it through the two hyper-knots successfully with all 16 spacecraft intact. As they approached the location of the antimatter cloud, Alyie believed it was time for her to take her seat in the Command Center at Headquarters. (Jaynis would remain at the mansion to mind the twins, but he would stay patched into the Control Room if his expertise were needed.)

Treating the crisis as a military mission, Alyie dressed in her Admiral uniform (sans medals) of a white double-breasted jacket, white buttoned down shirt and black tie. She wore white pants with a black strip down each side tucked into her tall black boots. Underneath her jacket, she held her laser pistol secure in the belt hostler. Only the insignia in her jacket's lapel and the signet ring identified her as High Governor. After pulling her hair up and putting on her white cap, Alyie gave Tessa and Tomus warm kisses and hugs. Jaynis and Alyie looked longingly at each other before embracing tightly and wishing good fortune.

Going outside the mansion, Alyie was met by Reg Jones, who would be her escort and primary guard through the completion of the mission. The Colonel was dressed in one of the new uniforms that Alyie had helped design for her Elite Guards. Contoured closer to the body than the more loose-fitting Panthera fatigues, the dull black uniform was made of special polymers that could withstand the blasts of all but the most powerful lasers.

Seeing Alyie come down the steps in uniform, Reg stood at attention and saluted.

"At ease, Colonel, I am no longer commissioned."

"Then I salute your High Governorship."

"I may not be that much longer either, Reg. If Operation Grendel doesn't succeed, I plan to turn in my resignation."

"Didn't we speak once before about accepting failure?"

"I remember Reg, but it is difficult for me."

"I have always been buoyed by Rudyard Kipling,"

> 'If you can meet with Triumph and Disaster
> and treat those two impostors just the same.'

"Thanks. Just your presence near me through this mission is enough. You have such strength."

"I am always here to serve you."

CHAPTER 30.

Co-Commanders Homare Suzuki and Francois Benoit of Bewoulf messaged that they were now in a position to encircle the dark cloud's minor axis, and all systems were going to unfurl each group's set of coils. Alyie gave the command to proceed. Due to the length of segments that needed to unravel and then join together, the process would take approximately 4 E-d to be completed. As each segment was unrolled, it took about 10 Earth-minutes for the message indicating success to be transmitted. The co-commanders in their communications revealed they were close enough to the nebula to observe the crackling of annihilation events as the cloud's antimatter contents interacted with conventional particles in the surrounding space. The beast was snarling at them.

Everything was going well until it was time to test the piezoelectric generators that were connected to adjacent coil segments. In Ring A, as one of the completed loops was labeled, there was a red signal at one junction indicating that the generator at this site was not functioning. Commander Suzuki ordered one of the two "spare" spacecarriers to execute a maneuver that would allow its autobots to extract the bad generator and replace it with its own. Time was of the essence as the antimatter cloud was getting dangerously close to the as yet un-electrified coils. If the nebula's material came in contact with Ring A, it would destroy it, and the mission would cease. How Alyie wished she could be there to directly supervise this mission. Admiral Cranshaw, General Presoff, Deputy Governor Kamesh Thakur and several staff members present in the Command Center all joined Alyie in deep concern that the mission now hung in the balance. Only Reg Jones remained in a state of calm readiness.

Finally, after what seemed an excruciatingly long interval, the message came from Commander Suzuki that all piezoelectric generators were now operational. With sighs of relief from those assembled in the Center, Alyie promptly gave the command to activate all generators.

After another 10 Earth-minute delay, Co-commander Benoit announced that the magnetic field was now turned on. Doppler Imaging from the commanders' spacecarriers reflecting off the cloud's outer layer indicated no motion relative to Bewoulf. The trap was set!

Amid fist pumps and hugs by Cranshaw, Presoff and company, Alyie calmly ordered the commanders to activate the tractor beams on their constellation and pull the trap with its prey away from Kanva and toward empty space. When the change in trajectory was confirmed by Suzuki, some eight E-hr later, Alyie issued the order to release the tractor beams and head back.

"Congratulations Commanders Suzuki, Benoit, and Bewoulf pilots. Operation Grendel has been accomplished."

Accepting congratulations from all in the Command Center, Alyie turned to Reg, who gave her a firm thumbs up. She returned the gesture with a silent thank you.

Alyie first messaged Revita with the good news.

"I knew you wouldn't let anything happen to my planet. Alyie, you and Jaynis are the best."

Next came a call to Jaynis, who, of course, knew about the success.

"Does this mean that Tessa and Tomus get to see their Mommy soon? You have been gone almost two E-w."

"Not only will I be able to see my kids, but I can soon give my special personal thanks to the greatest physicist of our age."

"I am assuming you mean me, but I don't want to seem conceited."

"Oh, silly man."

EPILOGUE

Two E-m after a solemn memorial service to honor High Governor Felicity Erickson and the others who perished in the loss of Igraine, Teegarden was transformed as the site of a thunderous celebration for the Installment of Alyie Starstriker as High Governor. At the parade grounds outside the Memory Garden, there was a raised stage where Alyie would be seen throughout the Sidereal Federation taking (once again) the Oath of Office. In attendance were Alyie's family: Jaynis, the twins, Tanita Starbright, Alex Striker, Talia Silverfoot (Jaynis' mother), Chadwick Bottombrook (Jaynis' father) and Bernice Bottombrook. Among Alyie's friends and colleagues were Queen Revita Jadeite, Alison Bernewithy, Hector Palermo and Mateo Santiago.

Officiating at the Installment was High Justice Alabi, with Admiral Cranshaw, General Presoff and members of the High Governor's Board all serving as witnesses.

In the tent behind the rostrum where she would emerge, Alyie was chatting with Revi and Alison as they assisted her in getting dressed. She wore a cream-colored gown with gold sparkles designed by Revita that was full length and contoured close to her body with a train that followed behind. It had a plunging neckline that displayed the dazzling gold necklace Revi had presented Alyie in grateful thanks for her success in saving Kanva from destruction. Revi had also given Alyie a diamond tiara to wear, but Alyie refused it, saying it was out of place. The autobot hairdresser had Alyie's reddish locks flowing freely with gold highlights. On her feet, Alyie wore ivory-colored high heels.

The whole series of events surrounding the Installment was orchestrated by Lydia Foxworth, who brought in a 100 strong children's choir, 200 musicians, light shows and holographic animations to celebrate Alyie's ascension.

Just before she was about to go on stage, Alyie spoke to both Tessa and Tomus. "Now Mommy is going to go outside while Daddy, and Aunt Alison will take you to sit in front and watch. Please be good."

Tomus was first to exclaim, "You don't look like Mommy."

"Have you become a fairy princess?" Tessa wondered.

"No, I am still Mommy, and I will come down and join you as soon as I finish speaking. I love you both."

When it was time, Reg Jones came inside the tent with four other Elite Guards to escort Alyie onto the stage. He was dressed in formal military attire and looked quite the gentleman in his double-breasted black jacket, trim pants and highly polished boots. The ceremonial sword he carried had been a gift from Alyie. It was her grandfather's.

After taking the oath before the assemblage and the billions of viewers across Human Space, Alyie spoke.

"Citizens of the Sidereal Federation, I accept the High Governorship with full humility. I realize the honor and responsibility this position entails. I will serve you with all my strength, will and heart. Today marks the dawn of a new Federation. I have constructed a High overnor's Board that will enable me to rule more effectively and respond ore quickly to the challenges ahead. I see this new Federation as xpanding its horizons, increasing its enterprises and forging new pathways in human history. Please join me as we begin this next chapter human history."

After finishing her acceptance speech, Alyie received loud applause from the attendees on Teegarden. As she was projected on the enormous viewing screen for all of Human Space to see, Max Hebron, who was sitting in the third row with Kamesh Thakur, exclaimed a little too loudly, "Thus, begins the reign of Alyie Regina."

"Regina?" Kamesh turned to Max. "That means Queen doesn't?"

"Yes, it does," Max replied.

"She is not Queen, but High Governor."

"Queen and High Governor are just titles, but no doubt Alyie's reign has just begun."

"You seem to forget Mr. Hebron that Alyie Starstriker is just serving the remainder of what would be Felicity Erickson's term as High Governor. To me that does not constitute a reign."

"It is you who are forgetting, Mr. Thakur. Because she assumed the High Governor position instead of running for it, she is eligible in five E-yr. to be elected High Governor for a full 10 E-yr. term. Things can change, but as of now, who will oppose her? In my counting 15 E-yr. is a reign. That's unless she changes the Federation Constitution to extend her rule even further."

"Oh, Max. I see what you mean."

"That's why we should all hail Alyie."

"Yes. Hail Alyie," Kamesh replied, "and G_d protect the Federation."

CHARACTER LIST IN TALES OF ALYIE STARSTRIKER STORIES:

• Valkyrie Commander (VC) • The Dark Cloud (DC) • The Invictus (I) • House of Jade (HJ)	• ET Daemonium in Machina (EDM) • The Omegi (O) • Forever Dream (FD)

Alyie Starstriker and immediate family

- Alyie Starstriker: Original Commander of the Valkyrie Flight Squadron in the Sidereal Federation (VC, EDM, O, I, HJ, FD, DC).
- Jaynis Bottombrook: Astrophysicist and close confidant of Alyie Starstriker (VC, EDM, O, I, HJ, FD, DC).
- Tessa Starbrook: daughter of Alyie and Jaynis and twin of Tomus (FD, DC).
- Tomus Starbrook: son of Alyie and Jaynis and twin of Tessa (FD, DC).
- Tanita Starbright: Alyie Starstriker's mother and former Sidereal Federation Space Commander (EDM, O, I, FD, DC).
- Alex Striker: Alyie's Starstriker's father and tactician for Space Command (EDM, O, I, FD, DC).
- Talia Silverfoot: Mother of Jaynis Bottombrook (I, DC).
- Chadwick Bottombrook: Father of Jaynis Bottombrook (I, DC).
- Bernice Bottombrook: Sister to Jaynis Bottombrook (I, DC).

Valkyrie Squadron Members

Ginetta Jiang (VC, EDM), Olga Fercouska (VC, EDM, O, I, FD, DC), Hollie Pederson (VC, EDM, O, I, FD, DC), Zarah Khoury (EDM, O, I, FD, DC) and Wang Li (EDM, O, I, FD, DC).

Sidereal Federation Officials

- Ji-hoon-Park: High Governor (EDM, O, I, HJ).
- Alastair Cromwell: Deputy High Governor (O).
- Raphael Rodriquez: General in Army Command and High Council Member (O).
- Steely Cranshaw: Admiral in Space Command and High Council Member (VC, EDM, O, I, DC).
- Felicity Erickson: Ambassador (VC, O, I, DC).
- Mateo Santiago: Ambassador (O, I, DC).
- Peter Bukanti: Ambassador (I).
- Daiyu Lee: Planetary Scientist and High Council Member (O).
- Singh Khan: Communications specialist on High Council (O).
- Johnathan Eubanks: Trade representative on High Council (O).
- Rosa LoPresti: Communications specialist on High Council (I).
- Frida Geranova: High Council Member (DC).
- Komesh Thakur: High Council Member (DC).
- Fitzhugh Thornberry: Planetary Scientist and High Council Member (DC).
- Martin Agnew: Economist and High Council Member (DC).
- Hilda Barton: Adjunct to High Governor (DC).
- Omar Alabi: High Justice (DC).
- Abba Niji: Chair of Sidereal Federation Council (DC).
- Sonja Dubois: Transportation Minister (DC).
- Ivan Presoff: General and Head of Ground Forces (DC).

On New Stanford

- Philbin De Witt: Robotic engineer on New Stanford (EDM).

- Achaeans (Intelligent Machines): Odysseus (Leader), Diomedes, Ajax, Nestor and Teucrus (EDM).

On Planet Ergo

- Enrico Vincenti: Co-head of Trade Guild (VC).
- Destano Vincenti: Co-head of Trade Guild (VC).
- Gianni Vincenti: son of Enrico Vincenti (VC).
- Nicoletta Vincenti: daughter of Enrico Vincenti (VC).
- Albus Silberstein: Tachyon scientist (VC).

On Omega X

- The Omegi (O).

On Nespar

- Adeola Igwe: King and leader of Amhara Tribe (I).
- Ziyad Maher: First Minister (I).
- Abdu Mukasa: Second Minister (I).
- Talib Masu: Leader of Kunari Tribe (I).
- Seth Bullwark: Former Star Fleet Commander (I).

On Earth

- Maxim Hebron: Former Regional Governor (HJ, FD, DC).
- Lydia Foxworth: Marketing and Campaign Manager (HJ, DC).
- Fujan Wang: Historian (HJ, FD).
- Hector Palermo: Independence Party Leader (FD, DC).
- Malcolm Dunrock: Owner of Dunrock Pharma (FD).
- Karrunya Okoro: Social Activist and member of Advisory Council (FD).
- Sujan Roy: Industrialist and member of Advisory Council (FD, DC).
- Melissa Toby: Communication Specialist and member of Advisory Council (FD).

- Rafael Ruis: Ectobiologist and member of Advisory Council (FD, DC).
- Hiroko Sato: Astronomer and member of Advisory Council (FD).
- Daiki Sato: Technologist and boyfriend of Alison (FD).
- Nullah Balbuk: Pilot of spacecarrier Hercules (FD).

On Kanva

- Revita Jadeite: Crown Princess (HJ, DC).
- Anan Jadeite: Deceased King (HJ).
- Isthar Jadeite: Deceased Queen (HJ).
- Tasmar Jadeite: Deceased Prince (HJ).
- Regnei Jadeite: Deceased Prince (HJ).
- Aston Brockton: Colonel and Deputy Military Commander (HJ).
- Dev Gostan: Parliamentary Leader (HJ).
- Fraja Botsama: Medical Doctor (HJ).
- Lisel: Young girl in the city of Kandy (HJ).

Other Characters

- Reg Jones: Major and Commander of Panthera (I, FD, DC).
- Laslow Topak: Criminal forensic specialist (HJ).
- Martin Shushauser: Cybersecurity specialist (I).
- Erik Stringer: Commander of starbomber Deliverance (EDM, DC).
- Ruth Beyer: Planetary specialist (O).
- Matthew Klingson: Security Officer (O).
- Xi Meng: Security Officer (O).
- Sanford Mason: Technology specialist (O).
- Daphne Fugo: Linguist (O).
- Arjuna Choudhury: Space Fleet pilot (EDM).
- Abel Ettiger: Surgeon (HJ).
- Seo-jun Gwan: Colleague of Jaynis Bottombrook (I, DC).
- Igor Melkova: Fleet Academy colleague of Alyie Starstriker (I).

- Alison Bernewithy: Adjunct to Alyie Starstriker (FD, DC).
- Fedor Greysan: Pilot of Phaedra and Bellerophon (DC).
- Homare Suzuki: Co-commander of Beowulf (DC).
- Francois Benoit: Co-commander of Beowulf (DC).
- Jeong Kim: Teacher at a cooperative school in Paris (DC).